THE RUG UNFOLDED

and Cleopatra twisted out of it, rolling to her feet to stand
before Caesar—not jewelled and richly dressed as a queen,
but completely naked, her young body damp with sweat and
glinting in the candlelight.

Caesar was motionless as he looked his fill of this nude Venus
who had suddenly appeared before him. He knew her—the
young queen of Egypt. But she had come to him as a woman,
not a queen, he knew. He gestured and the guards left the
room.

Caesar was hers, now—hers to use as she must if she were to
live . . . and as the quick hunger of her body demanded. . . .

CLEOPATRA

a novel by

JEFFREY K. GARDNER

WILDSIDE PRESS

CLEOPATRA

ONE

The Lochias Palace, 58 B. C.

1.

The little girl was shivering in fear.

She stood naked in the waters that filled the great porphyry pool where it was her habit to bathe and swim twice a day, especially in this summertime heat that was the curse of Alexandria. Her eyes were constantly moving, though no other muscle in her body stirred except when she quivered to the inward terror that held her in its grip.

The Lochias palace was still, as silent as one of the great marble mausoleums that studded the Sema where her ancestors, the Ptolemies, lay buried beside the golden sarcophagus of Alexander the Great. At this hour, just before Ptolemy Auletes reclined to the usual banquet that was his evening meal where he regaled his guests with his expert fingers on the flute, the palace should be filled with the faint hum which told of slaves coming and going, of the changing of the guard, of the sound of the chariot wheels and the sandalled feet of slaves with gilded sedan chairs bearing guests.

There was only utter stillness.

And so Cleopatra was afraid.

She was eleven years old and a princess. She told herself there was nothing to fear. Her father was king in Egypt— Ptolemy XII Auletes, direct descendant of that first Ptolemy who was general to the fabled Alexander and founder of this magnificent city on the Inland Sea—and the most powerful man in this corner of the world. Her royal parent would let no harm come to her. At his word, men lived or died, men laughed or wept. He was god, as the people of Egypt believed their Pharaohs were gods in the old days.

Surely, nothing can threaten a god!

The little girl had lost her taste for water. She ran up the steps between two rows of golden posts which suspended handrails between them and scampered for her fallen pelisse.

5

The night was hot, sultry, but her ivory skin knew only an ominous chill.

Her hands wrapped the woolen robe about her nakedness. Bundled to the crown of her thick black hair in that fluffy stuff, she folded her arms about herself and went on shivering. Her nurse should be here, to rub her down with unguents and oils from Punt. Teenut was never away from her for so long a time. Auletes would be very angry if she were to tell him that Teenut had left her by herself this way. True, she was not as important a princess as her older sister Berenice, who had a husband already, but she was a member of the royal family, and whoever might harm her risked an agonizing death by torture.

Oh, why was she thinking such gloomy, morbid thoughts?

Usually she was a laughing, bouncing creature, running swiftly to play with the leather ball which the gatekeeper at the Paneum had made for her, or teasing the big black panthers safe in their golden manacles. She had her quiet moments too, for all her few years of life, her dark head bent above some scroll in the Museion, which was the great library where was stored the knowledge of her world. Yet even then, while her mouth pouted in the concentration of her thoughts, she was happy. Was she not learning all about the land in which she lived? True, she would never rule it; Berenice would be queen with her brother Ptolemy as king when their father died; but knowledge was power of a sort.

She desperately wanted to be powerful.

"Teenut," she called. "Teenut?"

Her voice rang in the quiet air with a quaver unusual for little Cleopatra, who was always so sure of herself, so certain. Auletes said she was the one child of his loins who was most a Ptolemy. Perhaps because her skin was white as ivory is white, rather than the dusky reddish hue of Berenice who had her coloring from her mother.

Cleopatra wondered often about her own mother. She had never seen her, to her knowledge. It was whispered that she was a Greek from Athens, somebody important whose husband had been an ambassador to Alexandria a decade ago. The babe who had been born to her stayed on in Alexandria; she herself was hustled homeward by a husband who bore shipping contracts signed by Ptolemy Auletes that would make him a rich man in a few years.

This was only rumor, however, whispered into her ears by Teenut in a moment of unusual confidence when the old nurse had imbibed a little too freely of the wines of Meroe. Cleopatra scowled and stamped her bare foot. Teenut! By the horns of Merwer, she would have her flogged. What kept her? It was almost the dinner hour, and—

What was that?

The clank of a scabbard hitting against a metal lappet. She would know it anywhere, that sound. There was enough of the tomboy in Cleopatra to make war and warriors glamorous in her mind. For hours it was her habit to sit under a silken canopy in the court exercise yard and watch the Macedonian Household troops at their sword and shield play, casting their spears, or at just plain drill.

Ah, and now she heard the tramp of sandalled feet, many feet marching as one. Soldiers, trained soldiers armed and moving purposefully. In Lochias palace and at the Hour of the Discomfiture of the Enemies of Ra, which was the time of banqueting? The fear that had been in her and which had ebbed a little came back into her veins in full flow. Gathering the pelisse about her thighs, she ran lightly, easily beside the pool and to the far end of the chamber where a door led into a narrow backroom corridor.

A glowing torch cast yellow radiance on the paintings that decorated the corridor as she ran along it. How many times had she stood in admiration of these brilliantly colored walls which showed Alexander and his mother Olympia with the snake that had supposedly fathered him? Alexander burning the royal palace at Perseopolis, Alexander cleaving the Gordian knot with his blade, Alexander defeating Darius, all were here. It was a part of her heritage as a Ptolemy, as a distant daughter of that Greek general who had named this city after him. She did not look at the paintings now. She could think only of her safety.

There was a blue door ahead of her.

The blue door gave entrance to her own apartments, where she could clap her hands and summon slavegirls. Charmion, who was only a little older, or Mnefert, who was practically ancient, being close to twenty. And Teenut. Oh, Teenut, most of all!

She slid around the jamb and came to a sudden stop. Anger flushed her cheeks. She stamped her bare foot.

"Teenut! Teenut, wake up. I'm going to tell father about your neglect of me. I waited and waited and you never came."

She ran across the room to the woman who lay so quietly on her side amid the cushions scattered before the gold and ebony bedstead, and went down on her knees. Her hand reached out, caught the woolen stuff of her palla and tugged.

7

Languidly, the old nurse rolled over onto her back.

Cleopatra screamed.

A dagger had been driven to the hilt between her withered paps. The wool of her palla was red and wet with blood; her face was ashen in death. The girl whimpered, sitting back on her heels and staring at the braid hilt of the dagger. It was a curved klepesh of the type carried by the Royal Guards. Her numbed mind told her that no guardsman would dare kill Teenut, knowing how much she was beloved of Cleopatra. Not unless—not unless more than just an old nursemaid were dying this night.

Now she understood why she had been afraid. While she had been in the pool she had heard a voice cry out. Some instinct must have recognized the voice as that of Teenut, realized the terror in it. Whoever had come killing Teenut might be hunting for Cleopatra as well. First kill the maid, then the child. An eleven year old girl could not escape from a palace steeped with blood; an older woman might know people who could be bribed to look the other way.

The little girl mewled her terror, rocking back and forth.

"Father, father—help me," she moaned.

Teenut had known this was coming. Had she not told her only the day before yesterday while they were walking in the garden that flanked the Eleusinian Sea, of the many marvels that were happening all across the world? The great statue of Diana at Ephesus, already covered with so many breasts, had been seen to sprout ten or more! The earth had shaken in Crete and a hidden vault had opened to the sky to reveal a golden statue of a massive bull. A woman had given birth to a monkey and a lion cub—Teenut admitted that she did not believe this last, it being against nature—and the great helmet that had been Alexander's own and was kept always in the royal museum had leaped from its shelf and fallen with a mighty clangor.

"Terrible days are ahead, little one," Teenut had whispered. "Three Vestal Virgins in Rome were buried alive for consorting with men. The sword of Hannibal on exhibit in the Temple of Serapis began to sing in words no one could understand. It's bad, little one. Bad, bad."

Isis forgive her, she had laughed at the old woman.

"These are happenstances with a natural explanation," she'd hooted. "I learned about these things in the Museion. It was an earthquake in Crete that uncovered the golden bull, no more. Somebody whose duty it was to clean and polish Alexander's helmet didn't put it back firmly enough, or more

8

probably, simply dropped it. As for the statue of Diana in Ephesus, maybe the priests did it themselves with painted bladders. Who knows?"

Ah, Teenut had been right, however. Terrible things were happening in Alexandria tonight. Her right hand clenched into a fist and beat up and down on her knee. She had to get away, somehow she must escape.

She froze rigid. Feet were moving along the main corridor beyond the painted pillars of the foyer. A soldier was coming back to search the room. If he found her here, he would stick a klepesh between her ribs.

There was no place to hide.

Her knees shook so much, she could not stand up.

Achillas was commander of the Macedonian Household guards.

A big man, he walked with an arrogant swing to his wide shoulders that betrayed the ambition which beat so strongly behind the ribcase of his huge, hairy chest. Heavily muscled, he wore the metal and leather caligulae on his calves in the Roman fashion, and a cuirass of iron overlaid with silver from which were suspended silver lappets which clanged musically at his every stride. A baldric held the long spatha in its silver scabbard that had been a gift from Pompey himself when he visited Alexandria some years before.

In his way, Achillas was a handsome man. A short black beard was trimmed close to his heavy jaw. His lips were wide, full, betraying the animality of the man. His forehead was low, his black hair cropped to the skull. His eyes were wide apart and flecked with streaks of gold that gave them the appearance of a tawny tiger's yellow orbs. He was popular with the rich Alexandrines, with the men because of his power over a weak king, with their wives because of his bull strength.

He came to a halt in the doorway of the princess' apartment, studying it through narrowed eyes. Short minutes ago he had stood in this same spot while his men cut down the old nurse and searched the rooms for Cleopatra. The girl should have been dressing for dinner. Too late, he remembered the pool. She had not been there, either.

He moved forward lightly for all his great bulk, kicking the cushions in vexation. His eyes glared with the feral hunger of a wild beast. The girl had to be somewhere. Set send he find her, and quickly. Set was the god of the underworld; Achillas held to the old Egyptian gods, despite the fact that there was

Grecian blood in his veins. He vowed a lamb to Set if that dark god would help him in his search.

He opened the blue door and stared down the corridor, seeing one of his men on guard, lancebutt grounded. The guard assured him no one had come through the blue door since he had moved through the royal bath to assume his post.

Achillas grunted and turned back into the room.

She had to be somewhere!

Growling in his teeth, he rummaged through the entire apartment. Once, in a paroxysm of rage, he lifted an ebony and gold stool and brought it down across a brass lamp. The resultant clangor drowned out his oaths. Where could she be? There was no place here to hide. He had searched the rooms thoroughly. And—the little one had to die; it was Berenice who ordered it and Berenice was now queen in Egypt.

His hand half drew his long sword, then thrust it back into its scabbard. Could the girl have fled the palace? But no, it was not to be thought of; the coup had been planned too well, had been executed too swiftly, too quietly.

He was wasting time here. Achillas swung about toward the open doorway, moved between the pillars. A last glance he flung about the room, angry, oddly disturbed at his failure.

Cleopatra was close to stifling, pressed against the dead body of old Teenut and shrouded by the folds of the woolen tunic. Blood was tickling onto her throat. She could feel it wet and still warm, and its touch almost made her faint. Trembling, she pressed closer to the dead body. Teenut had sheltered her in life, let her go on protecting her even in death.

Achillas was searching for her. She recognized his voice.

The Guard commander had always been friendly to her, ready with a smile or a comfit dipped in honey. Cleopatra wondered if she ought to make herself known to him but something about his voice, the angry movements he made, kept her frozen where she lay under old Teenut and her shawl.

In one sense, she was not afraid of Achillas.

He was a man, and Teenut had told her enough about men to let her understand that even the best of them were animals where a pretty woman was concerned. If only she were a little older, with more flesh on her hips and with real breasts instead of these nubbins she bore, maybe she could cajole Achillas into letting her go.

Men were made with a little fire in their loins, Teenut had said. The fire was always there but sometimes it was no more than a mere spark or perhaps a red coal smouldering in sullen waiting. It needed a woman to fan that spark to a blaze, to the burning fury which stirred manhood to quivering life. There were men to whom a pair of breasts was tinder to their lechery. Others found delight in plump buttocks or in long, slim legs, in the curve of a gently rounded belly. Right now, she had none of these attributes and so she must shiver and hide away from big, hairy Achillas.

The room was silent. Cleopatra stirred, wanting to lift a fold of the tunic and look about her. She drew a deep breath and held it, the better to hear. Still there was no sound.

Her black head peeped from under the tunic which she lifted in a little hand. The room was empty. Quickly she wriggled out from under Teenut, trying to disturb her as little as possible, still clad in the woolen wraparound in which she had fled from the bath.

She was alive, but what good would life be to her unless she could find some way to flee from the palace which was so likely to prove her tomb? Breathing hurriedly, she clasped her temples with her palms and bent her head the better to think. She was staring with wide eyes at the tiled floor. For a moment she did not believe what she saw, there on that mosaic surface.

It was a shadow, the shadow of a man.

Cleopatra whirled, choking back a cry of fear.

Achillas stood grinning down at her, a floor lamp at his back. He had taken off his caligulae, his baldric, even his cuirass with its metal lappets which might clank and so betray his movements. In his right hand, so big and so hairy, he held a naked sword.

"Ho, little one. Tell me, where did you hide? My men and I looked everywhere."

Her hand gestured at the dead body of Teenut. "Under her," Cleopatra whispered, and read grudging admiration in his eyes.

"You're a sly thing, I give you that. Imagine hiding under a dead woman. Weren't you afraid?"

Her black hair swirled as she nodded. Achillas was talkative, which might be a good sign. Not yet had the sharp spatha been lifted to drive into her tender flesh. If she could use her wits, perhaps she might yet find a way out of this predicament.

"I was afraid," she went on. "I'm not afraid any more."

He chuckled. "You're not?" He lifted the long sword and let her see its glittering blade where the red flames of the oil boat made it shine as if with red fire. "Even when you know I've come to kill you?"

"You aren't a fool like the others," she said calmly.

11

Achillas gaped at her, scowled, then lifted his left hand to rub it back and forth across his thick black beard. He was an Egyptian but there was Greek blood in his veins from a Thracian grandfather, an adventurer who had come to Alexandria to sell his sword to royalty and who had remained to open a wineshop and marry a woman of Memphis. His skin was reddish, but his eyes were blue. He still owned the wineshop but because of his stature as Commander of the Royal Guard, he now owned two taverns which made him reasonably wealthy for a soldier and fostered ambition in his blood.

"Not a fool, you say?"

"Only a fool would fail to let me live because if anything should happen to Berenice, I would rule all Egypt."

"That's just the reason I'm going to kill you, pretty one. Berenice herself gave me the order. She wants no younger sister threatening her queenship."

"And who will protect you, Achillas—when she gives the order for your death some day? She may well do so, you know. As commander of the guard you possess power here in Alexandria. Perhaps too much power—to please Berenice for very long."

He frowned down at her. She was putting ideas in his head with her glib little tongue. He had no especial love for Berenice who was a haughty piece like all the Ptolemies, but she was his queen now that their palace revolt had succeeded and it was good policy for him to obey her. His grip tightened on his sword.

Cleopatra read his intention in his eyes.

"Wait," she cried breathlessly. "My father. What about my father?"

"He got away from us to the harbor. Somebody must have blabbed. That's the trouble with these family intrigues. You never know who to trust."

"He'll go to Rome. He's been in Rome before, paying out monies to the Senators to have himself confirmed as king of Egypt."

"Stop talking, child. I've come to kill you."

"Listen to me!" she snapped, and stamped her foot. Before her blazing eyes, he drew a deep breath. By the paps of Hathor, this one had royal blood in her veins. You'd think she was queen in Egypt the way she acted, instead of being marked for slaughter. Achillas had to grin at her admiringly.

"My father has escaped to Rome. If I know him, he'll have treasure hidden somewhere which he'll offer to Pompey or to

12

Cicero for their favor. If they send a Roman legion to Alexandria, will Egypt stand against it?"

Achillas shook the sword before her eyes. "Little idiot, why do you keep talking?"

"You're afraid, Achillas," she accused soberly. "I don't blame you. Can you imagine what my father will do to the man who killed his younger daughter? Can you, Achillas? He would take a month to kill you, slowly and in agony."

"Shut up!" he cried.

"He might reward the man who saved her life."

"I dare not," he breathed.

Cleopatra wondered about Achillas. She remembered the things Teenut had told her about men and their lusts. From all palace gossip, Achillas was a man. It was too bad she was not a little older and of marriageable age. She could offer her body to him with a promise to make him her consort if he would overthrow Berenice and seat her instead on the throne.

As it was, she was a child.

And yet, he had called her 'pretty one.'

Cleopatra let her wrapper slide from her shoulders. It fell slowly to pool about her bare feet. She stood proudly naked, letting him stare at her. As was the fashion with highborn Egyptian women, there was no hair on her body, only on her head where it tumbled in a thick black mass to cover her shoulders and halfway down her back.

Achillas licked his dry lips with a furtive tongue.

"Kill me, then," she told him.

The man stood bemused before her body, Cleopatra saw. His eyes lifted and fell, almost caressingly. Truly, Teenut had spoken with a straight tongue. There was something about a man which could be turned as though to water by sight of female flesh. She was only a child, no woman yet, and still Achillas breathed faster and his eyes bulged.

"Have you a place to hide me, where you and only you can come to see me?" she whispered. "If you let me live I would be very grateful to you. I would do anything you wanted. My father would be grateful, too."

She gave him no time to think, to remember Berenice and her commands. Still naked she came and pressed against him, felt him lift his hand and run it down her back to cup both buttocks. She was warm and fragrant from her bath, and her skin was soft and smooth as rich cream. The man quivered.

"Hide me, Achillas. Wrap me in a robe and carry me to one of your taverns. You must have private rooms there where I

13

would be safe. Who would think of looking in a wineshop for a princess of Egypt?"

He nodded, his face flushed red as any Aswan brick, his lungs laboring like a bellows before a forgefire. His hands fell away from her flesh but he continued to stare at her as if she were a krater of water and he a thirsty traveler. It seemed that his muscles refused to act so that it was the girl who must cross the room, snatch up a robe of white wool and wrap herself in its folds.

"I've left a hood so you can cover my face with it," she told him, smiling strangely. The touch of his palms upon her skin had lighted a queer tingling in her loins. Teenut had not said that she might enjoy the caresses of a man. It was a pleasant feeling and one concerning which she must take thought.

Cleopatra was learning a lesson this night she knew she would never forget. A man and a woman held a mighty force within their bodies, a force that could turn the knees to water and the blood to molten metal. It was exciting, it took the breath away, it made a joy of living. She had only to steal a glance at Achillas' face to know that he had responded to the lure of her nakedness just as she had to the strokings of his palm.

Isis! If she could do this as a mere child, how marvelous this attraction would be when she was a grown woman! Her tiny red tonguetip came out to touch her lips. She was tempted to let the general lift her, carry her off to some room above his stinking wineshop, just to sample this new pleasure with him.

She was too clever for that, however. Alone with him in his tavern, she would be helpless to deny him whatever he might want. If he were brutal, cruel as some lovers were cruel, she would be helpless before his strength. No one among the common people who came to his inn would believe the girl who screamed for assistance was a princess of Egypt. They would think the shock of defilement had deranged her mind.

Berenice would not care. Dead or alive and being defiled, it was all the same to her older sister, as long as Cleopatra never returned to the palace to cause her embarrassment or to threaten her throne. No one would care about little Cleopatra Thea Philopater one way or the other except Achillas, and when he was done with her he would strangle her and throw her body on a dungheap.

She shivered. All this would happen to her unless she could prevent it. But how could a mere girl escape from a man used to fighting hardened warriors? And assuming she could

14

escape, where in Alexandria could she hide from him? Or from Berenice? Cleopatra bit her lip.

Achillas was advancing upon her. His big, hairy hands came out, swung her up and across his shoulder. She hung like a dead thing, head and arms down his back, her legs along his chest. He patted her rear.

"Good girl. Just lie like that, bonelessly, so no one can tell I have anything alive in this robe. I'll get my cloak, throw it around you. That way you'll be hidden even more."

Cleopatra had seen Achillas walk like that, with his red mantle thrown over his left shoulder. She'd always thought that habit of his with his military cloak an affectation. She wondered now if he had ever carried anyone—or perhaps some priceless treasure—out of the Lochias palace before.

He went into the hall, put her down while he donned his cuirass and baldric, slipped the caligulae up his calves. His cloak he threw over her carelessly so that she and her robe would be hidden from anyone who might come walking along these corridors.

The halls were empty. The slaves would be cowering in their quarters, wanting neither to see nor be seen on this night of deposed kings and young queens newly come to power. Only soldiers were about and they were too used to the sight of Achillas and his red cloak to pay him any heed.

Under the robe and shrouding mantle she tried to follow his movements. She could see nothing of the corridors along which he strode, for the cloth folds were so tight about her head she had all she could do to keep from smothering. She had a vague idea where his Head of Horus tavern was located, along an off-street of the Street of Canopus. Cleopatra tried to remember what she knew of the city as glimpsed from a sedan chair or a chariot-floor on those rare times when she traveled through it. The Street of Canopus bisected the city proper from the Canopic Gate in the east to the west, where it entered the Necropolis. South of it was the Rhakotis, which was the Egyptian quarter, and the wide shoreline of Lake Mareotis. This street was one hundred feet wide and lined with great marble columns. It touched the Jewish section of the city, it fronted the Temple of Pan and the gymnaseum with its shadowed porticoes, it gave entrance to the Hippodrome outside the city and the Grove of Nemesis.

None of this was any help to her. She knew no one who would dare shelter the younger sister of queen Berenice. Her lower lip trembled. She might have wept had not she felt the heavily muscled body of Achillas suddenly tense.

"What news, Habu?" he called out.

"None, general. The Fluteplayer got away like a greased pig from children. We couldn't find his ship in the dark. As luck would have it, he slipped past the shoals at the harbor mouth while we were searching the Diabratha."

"It won't do him any good."

"To make sure it won't, Berenice is sending some of her counsellors to Rome, too—either to bribe the Senators or get rid of the Piper. I hope they do one or the other. If Ptolemy Auletes comes back with a Roman legion, we'll all of us pay for tonight."

"You worry too much, Habu," grumbled Achillas.

The other man grunted. Achillas moved on and now Cleopatra detected an urgency in his stride that showed he was perturbed. Cleopatra could understand that. If he were found with the princess under his cloak Berenice might not believe he was carrying her off to enjoy her for a while before he tightened a rope around her little neck. Berenice would suspect him of treachery, of planning a counterrevolution and setting Cleopatra up in her place.

Berenice would have Achillas flayed alive.

There was fresh air around her and a sound of voices. The barracks would be to her left here, the gardens off to the right where they overlooked the great breakwater. And still no one challenged Achillas.

Cleopatra realized she was holding her breath in excitement. She let it out slowly. She must make her move now. Soon it would be too late. They were out of the palace grounds, entering that section of the city between the Regia and the Rhakotis quarter, a labyrinth of narrow alleys and cobbled streets where the stone houses leaned into one another with an air of drunken gaiety.

She wriggled. Instantly his hand lifted to hold her motionless. He growled, "Be still, girl!"

"I want to breathe. I'm suffocating," she protested.

"All right, let me take a look about. Street's empty. By the rays of Ra, all Alexandria must've heard about the trouble at the palace. Nobody's showing their face. Go ahead, then."

Her hands came up to disarrange the folds. Gratefully she breathed in the fresh, sultry air of summertime Alexandria even as her eyes ranged down the street and across a distant square.

"Where are we?" she wondered.

"Close to the Canopian Way, near the Temple of Isis."

"All right. I'll lie quietly."

16

She lulled his suspicions with the limpness of her body but her mind was alive with nervousness. It was now or not at all that she had to make her run for it. Just a few steps more. There. She could see the marble blocks of the Street of Canopus below them.

Her body writhed, twisted. Like an eel she slipped down from the robe and the military cloak. Naked she landed on her feet even as she heard him grunt in surprise and turn to her, a big hand reaching out.

"Are you mad?" he breathed.

She ran, lightly, easily, a silver nymphet in the moonlight. Achillas grated a curse, spun about and came after her. She fled on bare feet, he pounded along with armor clanking, scabbard in his hand for easier running.

The Temple of Isis rose before her, all white marble and gold statuary in the Alexandrine night. Towering columns shadowed a portico in which were set twin bronze doors. Behind those massive doors was the open sanctuary of the temple where worshippers gathered to give gifts and make sacrifice to the goddess. Ah, if they were bolted as they often were at night, she would be lost! Achillas was right on her heels, almost ready to reach out and seize the flying black hair which bobbed on her white shoulders.

She ran into the door, hit it with her body.

For one frightened instant she thought it was locked against her. Then slowly it opened inward and she realized, as she slipped inside, that its weight was so heavy her tiny body had had difficulty in moving it on its hinges. She was inside now and racing across the tile floor.

Achillas was right behind her. She could hear him close the door, hear also the snick of the bolt as he drew it between its flanges.

Her heart was slamming in her ribs in mingled fright and excitement. Isis, mother goddess! Save me, save me! I am a woman like yourself. This man behind us is an enemy, being male. Her bare toes barely touched the floor as she raced forward.

The great statue of the goddess rose upward toward the groined ceiling. Of ivory and solid gold, she sat a throne of silver and ebony, holding her son Horus on her knee. One hand was under her left breast, lifting it toward the child. A fixed smile touched her full mouth above which her eyes—strangely lifelike in the light of the torches below—glistened as if alive. A giant headdress rested on her plaited black hair. Naked to the waist, she wore a linen tunic below it and a

17

jeweled pectoral just above the jutting ivory bosom that was tipped with giant rubies.

Cleopatra slid to the floor between the rows of flickering floor oil lamps resting on golden tripods. On her face she fell, her arms stretched out.

"Mother Isis," she cried. "Help me—"

Subdued laughter grated at her ears. Achillas had come up behind her, stood on straddled legs grinning at her helplessness. Cleopatra turned, resting on a thigh and a propped arm as she looked up at him.

"Foolish child," he grinned, his eyes moving along her bared legs and belly. "Isis is only a name, a statue if you will. She has no reality so how can she protect you?"

"Isis is our mother," she whispered.

"Come. Enough of this nonsense," he growled.

She could see the lust in his eyes and thick, smiling lips. He would become her lover this night above his tavern. Brutally he would take her, ravish her virginity, probably even relish her screams of agony. Not every Egyptian soldier got a chance to enjoy the body of a royal princess. Safe from harm, from retaliation.

He might keep her for a day or a week or even months, if she proved exciting enough. Sooner or later she would pall on him as women seemed always to pall on their lovers after a time.

"No," she whimpered, sliding along the floor, "no, no."

His hand went out to clasp her ankle.

She was staring at him in horror when she saw the change come over him. His eyes that had been on her body lifted toward the goddess. Emotion—fear, excitement, disbelief—leaped into his eyes at what he saw. He was opening his lips to cry out when something flew past her and took him in the middle of his forehead.

He fell facedown and lay unmoving.

Gasping in relief, she whirled toward the statue. It was unchanged, motionless. Isis held the same maternal pose with Horus. Her ivory flesh gleamed in the torchlight, her full mouth smiled.

Movement in the shadows near the headdress of the gigantic statue took her eye. A man with a striped claft half hiding his features came along the ledge formed by the uplifted *suti* feathers and disc of her headdress. About his middle he wore a cotton kilt. His hands were folding over a thin length of supple leather. Cleopatra recognized it as a sling.

The man stood a moment staring down at her. He was

18

white of skin and his feet were bare, the better to give him a grip on the smooth gold and ebony of the hawk diadem. He made a little movement of his hand and Cleopatra turned her head.

A priest of Isis stood facing her, his face grave.

"We heard you cry for help, Cleopatra. As you can see, your goddess answered your call." His hand directed her eyes to the motionless figure of Achillas.

"Is he—is he dead?"

"Merely unconscious, though I've no doubt that when he wakes he'll wish for death. His head will ache as if filled with stinging bees." The priest permitted himself a tiny smile that moved only the corner of his lips. "Sathales is from the Balearic islands which are noted for the uncanny marksmanship of their slingers. I bought him years ago in the slave market. He comes in handy every once in a while. Now then, what are you doing here?"

She gasped out her story before the impassive face and motionless body of the priest. He stood as though carved from red sandstone like the titanic figures of the gods at Karnak, his pleated linen tunic belted by an apron of gold beads. Only his eyes were alive, and his ears.

He nodded slowly. "You shall have sanctuary here. We shall send a message to our sister temple in Rome, and from it get word to your father the Pharaoh that you are safe."

The priests of Isis held to the old ways, she realized, and the old terms. There had been no Pharaoh in Egypt for centuries, except among the Temple hierarchy. King or Pharaoh, Ptolemy Auletes would learn that his younger daughter was alive. It was enough.

Cleopatra came to her feet. The priest bowed.

His obeisance restored some of her lost confidence. Here at least she was royalty. Her little chin lifted and she moved forward as if garbed in the long linen kalasiris and regal khat, rather than just her own skin. The priest bowed lower as she moved past him.

His hand indicated a small doorway in the throne of the statued goddess. Its joining with the decorations of the throne was so perfect that she suspected it would remain undetected even in strong sunlight, which never reached this corner of the temple.

Satheles was waiting with a lighted torch in a hand. His eyes were lowered so that he would not look upon her body. Cleopatra smiled faintly, wondering if he had been made into

19

a eunuch. The priest came after her, touched a stud in the corridor wall; the door swung shut behind them.

"Achillas will recover his senses in a little while. We do not want him to find us here."

"He saw something before—before Satheles hit him with a slingstone. I saw his eyes widen."

The slave chuckled. "A shadow, highness—no more."

"We were working in the temple when we heard him running across the square," said the priest. "We hid in the statue as we often do on feast days to observe the worshippers. When you ran in and we recognized you, we prepared for trouble."

"What will he do now?"

The priest smiled. "Stagger out into the night and wonder if Isis is really as mighty a goddess as she appeared to be this night. Oh, he'll keep a still tongue in his head, if that's what's worrying you. He wouldn't dare admit that he smuggled Cleopatra out of the palace—then let her escape."

"I was so frightened," she murmured, shuddering.

"Naturally. You're still a little girl."

She wondered about that, as she walked in the priest's footsteps along the secret passageway which led from the statue to a section of stone wall which opened to a touch of the priest's hand. She would never be the same after this night of fear and horror. A man had stroked her, awakened strange instincts in her flesh. She told herself that when the opportunity came, she must learn more about this attraction between a man and a woman.

As the stone wall swung back, Cleopatra saw that she was in the chamber below the main altar. Only a few lamps burned here, casting grotesque black shadows that hid and then revealed, as they danced to the flickering flames, the painted form of her own grandmother, Cleopatra IV, being led into the Underworld by Isis, then a golden boat of the dead where Cleopatra Berenice lay in state, and still another representation of her as she had been when alive, enthroned beside her husband, Ptolemy Lathyros.

She supposed she would be a painted image some day, too, after she had died, and wondered if she would be that important to the world. Her little fists clenched as she walked and her chin lifted stubbornly. If she had anything to do with it, she'd be important.

Power! That was the key to greatness.

She must learn how to achieve power, in one way or the other. If she were powerful enough, the world would notice her. She wanted very desperately to be noticed. It was a back-handed compliment, she guessed, that Berenice thought her important enough to be killed this night. At least, it was a beginning.

2.

Egypt divided its year into three seasons.

There was the spring, the *ahkit*, for this was the time when the rains came and the rivers were in flood, due to the tears wept by the goddess Isis when the dog star rose in the sky. Winter, the *perit*, was a time of growing things, when the flood waters ran off into the ground and nourished the budding corn and grain. *Shemou* was the harvest time, when the corn ears and the grain kernels stood high and straight for the scythes of the reapers.

It had been a summer night when Ptolemy Auletes fled away from Alexandria, warm and sultry. The lotus and the papyri had been in full bloom, the waters of the Nile at lowest level.

Now the flowers lay dead in their beds and even the waters of Lake Mareotis, that Cleopatra could see through a round opening in the wall of the Isis temple gardens, were sadly shrunken. Summer was gone, and winter, and now it was almost spring, and in a day or two the rains would come and with them the Nile would burst its banks. Even now the priests were arranging the many thousands of those tiny images of the god Hapi and his escort Repit, to be sold to the people who thronged the temples to pray and sacrifice for good crops in the coming year.

This was the time of the Sôpdit festival of the goddess Isis, for the new year was upon them. As she walked between the rows of dead asphodel stalks and dry marble fountains, she knew that she would have to buy a tiny statue of Hapi, the river god, and hang it in the temple. It would have to be of gold, naturally; anything less would debase her in the eyes of Ranefer, the priest who had saved her life half a year before. Lesser mortals would buy lead or clay Hapis; or if they were well to do, images of lapis-lazuli or faience or even silver; but her Hapi must be gold.

She would borrow money as she had so often in the past, from Ranefer. He gave freely, generously and with a laugh, but Cleopatra understood that he totalled up her debt in some reckoning of his own. His eyes glinted at times with the same light she had seen in the gaze of greedy merchants when they came to the Lochias to offer merchandise for sale.

Ah, let him be a greedyguts. She was alive and that was what counted most, these days. Her other sister—Cleopatra VI—was dead, she knew from word brought her by Ranefer. At least Berenice had succeeded in killing one of them. The boys—both of them called Ptolemy—were still alive. Berenice did not fear them. They could never take her throne away, only sit beside her as royal consort. Berenice was already married, however, to Archelaus of Komana.

It was Archelaus' lookout to protect himself.

She lived in the Temple compound as might a little mouse, eating whatever food was left out for her, walking in the gardens during the sunny days and reading in the scroll chamber when it gloomed, by the light of half a dozen oil dips, then scurrying off at night to the little room that held her bed, a chair, and a teakwood chest. The teakwood chest was empty save for the few tunics that Ranefer had bought for her, giving it out that it was for a niece of his sister in Thebes. There was also a copper bracelet he had purchased from a visitor from Memphis. This was all her worldly wealth.

Footsteps swung her around toward the huge wooden doorway which led into the Chamber of the Lotus. The door was being closed by a slave as Ranefer walked toward her in his short, choppy stride. He was smiling broadly.

"Good news, princess. We've had word from your father, the great Ptolemy. He is in Rome, quite safe and sound, a visitor at the summer villa of Pompey the Great."

She was rigid in delight, arms straight at her sides, her hands clenched into fists, raised a little on her toes. She could feel the thumping of her heart as if it were an inner voice assuring her that all was well in her world, and would grow even better.

"Tell me," she breathed.

"His voyage across the Great Green which the Romans call the Mare Internum, was made without incident. First he stopped off at Rhodes to speak with Cato, asking his help—without success, I may add—then resumed his journey. In Rome he was welcomed by Pompey, and set up residence in quarters furnished for him by the banker Rabirius Porthumus who loaned him money once before when he visited Rome. It was later he moved to Pompey's villa.

"Auletes has been lavish with Rabirius's money, lining the purses of the Senators with gold. When you told us that

Berenice was sending a number of her counsellors to Rome to buy friendship for her reign, we alerted Ptolemy to his danger."

A thin smile touched the lips of the priest. "The king has good friends among the Roman people. One by one, these counsellors have died. Of poisoning, of strangling, of stab wounds. Your father alone remains to plead his case, to pay over as many talents as the Senate and others in power decide it's worth."

Ranefer made a little bow. "He sent a small purse of gold denarii along with his news. He says to tell you that he loves you and that you will soon be a princess again in the Lochias palace."

Cleopatra said calmly, "You shall be rewarded, Ranefer. When Oser-reph dies, you shall be named high priest."

Ranefer checked a smile of satisfaction and inclined his head even lower. It had been a lucky night for him when this girl came seeking sanctuary in the Temple. The few silver pieces her visit was costing him would be repaid a million times over when Ptolemy Auletes came back to power.

She said imperiously, "I shall need a golden image of Hapi to hang in the Temple at the time of the Sôpdit feast, and—and one of his consort, Repit." She might as well be generous to Isis, for it was Isis who had saved her life. Besides, she was a Ptolemy. And so she forgot thrift as she added, "You must make them twice the normal size, Ranefer. Both of them. You understand?"

Ranefer winced. The purse of denarii would scarcely be enough to cover one such statue, let alone two; he himself must advance the monies; Ranefer consoled himself with the knowledge that once he was named high priest of Isis here in Alexandria, he would become a wealthy man.

"It shall be done, princess."

Her hand dismissed him. Cleopatra wanted to be alone, to hug her slim young body in delight, to sing a little out of sheer exultation. Her rope sandals carried her along the flagstones of the garden paths. Father was coming home. With the backing of Rome, perhaps even with a legion detailed to his command. Oh, it was exciting. It was so good to be alive. So good. She drew a deep breath of the cool air and—

Her eyes widened in surprise.

She was looking out the round moon window of the garden wall. A face was staring in at her, the face of a boy only a little older than herself, his eyes just as wide as her own.

"Who are you?" she asked coolly.

He swallowed hard. "M-my name's Conon."

"What are you doing spying on me?"

"I'm not spying," he protested. "I help my father take away the food scraps and the leavings from the priests' tables. We're late today. Our donkey died."

She let her gaze go over him. He was a mixture of races, she saw. His skin was the color of bronze, but that could be from constant exposure to the hot Mediterranean sun, for he wore only a cotton kilt at his lean hips. There was Greek blood in him, and Egyptian, of that she was sure. His shoulders were reasonably broad for a boy his age, and his arms were thick with muscle. Cleopatra thought suddenly of Achillas, and smiled.

"Talk to me," she commanded.

"What shall I talk about?"

"Yourself. Where do you live?"

"In the Rhakotis quarter, on a street called Kebenet. We aren't rich, but we aren't poor, either. We have five slaves."

"If you have so many slaves, why do you work?"

"To build up my body, to make my muscles big. Some day I'm going to be a gladiator and fight in the Stadium out beyond the Serapeum. A man can get rich by being a good gladiator."

"He can also get himself killed."

"Not me. I know how to use a sword. My uncle taught me. He used to be a soldier. He got a wound at Pelusium that crippled one leg, but his arms aren't crippled and he can show me how to handle a sword."

"You could make more money in The Macedonians, if you had someone in the palace who liked you."

Conon hooted. "As a Royal Guard? No chance of that. Who do I know in the Lochias? Once I stood outside its walls and tried to see one of the princesses. The only person I got even a glimpse of was some sentry in silver armor walking his post."

"Just the same, you might," she added mysteriously.

"Sure. And maybe some day I'll talk to a queen."

Cleopatra smiled and nodded. Conon gave her an amused look but it was mixed with admiration; she saw that he was plainly taken with her. She came closer, leaned against the edge of the recessed opening. Conon brought the fresh air of the outer world to the stuffy Temple. It was fun seeing him, talking to him. Perhaps he could give her gossip that the priests of the Temple never heard.

They spoke together for over an hour, there on opposite

24

sides of the moon window. Later, Cleopatra was to realize the symbolism of the stone and masonry that separated them; it was a tangible indication of the fact that they came from two different worlds.

TWO

The Temple Of Isis, 55 B. C. ·

1.

In Alexandria, Cleopatra was fourteen years old.

She was bored to tears with the Temple and its gardens. The fragrance of its flowers, the stately beauty of its palms, were as nothing before the depression of her spirits. She drooped her head when she walked, she ate listlessly, she took little interest in the rumors and the tidbits of news furnished her by Ranefer.

For three years she had been a prisoner in the Temple. There was no other word for it, she told herself as she paced the garden paths. She had lived here in such high hopes during that long first year, believing that her father would soon return from Rome, soon take his place as king where now her sister ruled. But there had been so many disappointments.

Everything had been ready then for Ptolemy Auletes to claim his throne. The legions would come with their golden eagles raised high and Berenice and Archelaus would run for their lives. Ah, and then—the Sibylline books had been consulted in Rome and an old prophecy found which stated that when Royal Egypt came pleading for help he must be treated well but not given military assistance.

Her father left Rome and went to live in Ephesus.

For two years he dwelt there while Cleopatra remained a prisoner, growing up. The Temple priests treated her with respect, even awe, but they did not help overcome her boredom. The scrolls she memorized in the Temple library were only lengths of papyrus. The languages she learned from the many priests who came here to visit were only words she mouthed, without meaning. Even the air she breathed was tinted with the smell of incense as if to remind her always that freedom was not for such as Cleopatra Thea Philopater.

Conon was her one contact with excitement.

She had followed his daily life with bated breath, seeing in her mind the bowls of spelt porridge he ate for breakfast, the rope bedstead in the little room just beneath the roof where he slept, the sword and the shield he used while practicing swordplay with his uncle Telecles. How often had she wished she could accompany him to the shops when he was sent to purchase lentils or bread for the family meals. Or to the streetstalls where he promised to buy her a berry tart.

A little over three months ago he had applied to the gladitorial school attached to the Stadium. He was big for his sixteen years, heavily muscled and quick of movement. Handsome, too, in a rugged sort of way. His thick brown hair he wore close to his skull—so no opponent could tangle his fingers in it and hold him helpless—and his lips were full and firm. Cleopatra thought often of kissing them just to see how they would feel against her own ripening mouth.

He was to come visit her at the moon window today, only he was late. One more disappointment, she thought, and felt her chin tremble. It was hard to be a princess, especially a princess without a kingdom who must remain secluded in a cold, quiet Temple.

"Sssst!"

She whirled toward the moon window, eyes wide with pleasure. "Conon! You came."

"Of course I came. I have news. That's why I was late. Zoser—he's the *lanista* at the gladitorial school—told me I was to fight today. Isn't that good news?"

"I'm happy for you, Conon," she smiled.

"You could come if you want. I've arranged to get a free pass for any friend who wants to see me."

She gasped at the thought. Gods! Just once to get out of these garden walls, to walk with Conon through the crowds on their way past the Temple of Serapis to the Stadium. It would be worth even capture. Though of late, Cleopatra had wondered about that; Ranefer kept telling her of the risks she would run if she let herself be seen in the streets of the city, but she doubted that anyone who had known her as a child would recognize her now.

"I can't," she said wistfully, and shook her head.

"Oh." He looked disappointed. "I was going to buy you a berry tart, too."

She frowned. She was three years older than she'd been

26

when Achillas chased her into the Temple, taller and more rounded. Her breasts were those of a grown woman, full and heavy to her palms when she cupped them sometimes before a polished silver mirror Ranefer had bought her with monies sent from Ephesus. Her hips were wider, her legs shapelier.

There would be no one who might recognize her if she left the Temple. No one had any reason to suspect that Cleopatra Thea Philopater was alive. Even if Berenice herself were to come face to face with her, she would not know her. At least, she didn't think she would. No, Ranefer kept her here because he had a lot of sesterces invested in her; he didn't want his security to go off and leave him holding a deflated purse.

She looked down at herself. She was wearing the traditional white tunic of an Egyptian girl with its crossed straps that bared the breasts; over it she had thrown a plain cloak. She was modest enough for street wear. Her plain sandals would not give away her identity.

"Why not?" she asked suddenly.

Conon brightened. "You mean you will?"

Cleopatra held out a slim arm to him, felt his big hand clutch her fingers, draw her upward to the sill then through the moon window. She landed on her feet lightly, laughing up into his face. Never had she been so excited, so filled with delight and anticipation.

She still held his fingers. "Run, Conon! Run with me."

They raced across the grass plats that bordered this corner of the Temple down as far as Lake Mareotis. The breeze was laden with the smell of salt water and newly cut grass; Cleopatra drew it into her lungs, standing on tiptoe with her eyes closed. Her lips were widely smiling. This was why she had been born, for this happiness, this sense of exhilaration.

"Thea?"

Cleopatra looked at him. Long ago she'd told him her name was Thea, which it was, but nobody ever called her that, since it was only a way to distinguish her from her sister Cleopatra who had died in girlhood. Conon knew her as Thea, the only daughter of a rich merchant who'd gone overseas to do business with the Gauls and Britons.

"We don't have too much time," Conon went on. "I have to get into my *manica*—that's the chain sleeve I'll wear on my sword-arm—and my greaves. I thought we could go to a shop along the edge of the Forum and buy some tarts."

Glee shone in her eyes. "Berry tarts?"

He nodded, laughing. She was quicksilver in her moods, this girl. Conon had fallen in love with her a long time ago. Seeing

27

her now, with the wind pressing her thin cloak and linen tunic to her body, he realized she was the most beautiful girl he had ever seen. Such a girl was not for Conon the son of Kalikos, who collected garbage from the temples and the mansions of Alexandria; his hope was based on the fact that sometimes—very seldom, but sometimes—a gladiator became so successful he grew rich and famous. Even the daughter of a rich merchant might not hesitate to marry a wealthy gladiator.

It was his one hope.

They ran together across the grass toward the Gate of the Sun. The Forum was not near; they would have to cross the Street of Canopis and pass the Theatre to reach it, but they were young, the blood ran easily in their veins and Conon, for one, was in love.

For Cleopatra, just being free was enough.

They mingled with the crowds, rubbing elbows with the riff-raff of the Eleusian quarter, with harlots and with soldiers in bronze cuirasses and helmets, with merchants in Greek himations and Egyptian tunics or in the ornate talliths which the wealthier Jews affected. Here were swarthy men from distant Parthia, slim sailors off the fat trading ships or the slim military biremes anchored in the roadstead, grave scholars taking a stroll to free their heads of the stuffy air in the Museion.

"They don't know me now," Conon told her once, staring around him, "but they will some day. They'll look at me and nudge one another with their elbows and ask me how I feel, whether I'm going to beat the Nubian or the Lydian or whoever it is I'll be fighting that day."

Cleopatra stifled a giggle and nodded, eyes wide and innocent. She wondered what the people around them would do if they recognized her. It would be more than nudging one another with elbows, she'd bet. "You'll be famous, Conon. I know it," she said out loud.

His arm hugged her. Almost instantly it fell away. She could guess why, and turned her face to hide a smile. She wore nothing but the thin linen tunic and the only slightly thicker mantle. Her own hip burned where it had brushed him; she supposed his male flesh felt the same. When she glanced at him sideways, she saw the remnants of a flush staining his face.

She felt tender toward him. He was so obviously in love with her, she almost felt sorry for him. To her, he was no more than a good friend with a strong attractive male body. Was

28

this enough for a woman to think she was in love? She did not know. All her readings, all her study, could not help her answer such a question.

They had to make way for chariots half a dozen times as their drivers lashed the horses and shouted warnings to the people in front of them. The bumping, thumping wheels, the pounding of the horses' hooves scratching sparks· from the cobblestones, all were an integral part of this great metropolis which by rights belonged to her father, not her sister.

If Ptolemy Auletes should come back and be king again in Egypt, Berenice would die, she supposed. If that were to happen, she herself would be queen, when her father died. She glanced around her imperiously. These people shoving and pushing against her, would a day come when they might understand they had so treated their queen?

"Here we are," announced Conon.

She caught the smell of baking bread, of cakes and tarts. Conon was holding out two copper obols to the baker, selecting two tarts on a wooden tray and handing one to her. Clutching it with her fingertips, Cleopatra bit deep into its honeyed chewiness. She munched, her eyes mere slits of pleasure. Never had anything tasted quite so good.

When the tart was gone, she opened her eyes. Conon was grinning, holding out another. "Go on, take it," he urged. "You enjoyed it so much I had to get you one more."

"What about you? You have no money to waste on me."

"I can't eat much before the events. Remember, I'm fighting this afternoon." He said it proudly, hoping that the people around them would listen and look.

"Who?" she asked as her teeth sank into the tart.

"I don't know. When you're a beginner like me, they don't tell you ahead of time. Maybe they think you'd be frightened, otherwise. I wouldn't be frightened."

He did not tell her that he would be fighting for her, that this was his first step in the career which was to bring him money and fame. Someday he would tell her, but not now.

When she was done with the second tart, he caught her elbow, drawing her away from the stall into the middle of the crowded Forum. They had to hurry, he said. It was noon already. In two hours the contests would begin. She must be in her seat at the start in case he was one of the first to fight.

They walked to the Street of Canopus and moved with the crowd thronging to the Stadium. From the chatter about them, Cleopatra gathered that the most exciting event on the program this afternoon was to be a battle between a net and

29

trident man and a swordsman from Illyria who had something of a reputation. A close runner-up to this in popularity would be two black spearmen from the African jungles pitted against a starving lion. Blood would run on the arena sands today and half of Alexandria wanted to be there to see it.

She let herself be guided by Conon. At the entrance gate someone thrust a bronze disc into her hand. She was told to walk at once to the eighth section, where she would be seated by the wall that sheered up from the stadium floor. It was one of the best seats in the great Hippodrome.

Conon found his way to the *carcere,* the tiny room assigned him in which to don the sleeve of steel links, the cotton loincloth, the heavy bronze greave for his left leg and the cothurns that formed the costume of the *secutor,* the sword and shield man. A huge flanged helmet, fitted with a steel mask for his face, together with his sword, completed his dressing.

He felt like a man for the first time.

He wished that he had one of the little copper mirrors that his mother and his older sister, the married one, used when they applied malachite to their eyelids and did up their hair into the coronas which were so popular now, since it was a favorite hairstyle of Queen Berenice herself. He wanted very much to see how he looked. He had never been permitted to wear the *manica* and the *ocrea* before.

Conon walked out into the hall, joined a black Nubian in a leopardskin who was a *retarius,* a net and trident man. Other men were lounging against the walls of the long corridor; some stood casually, unconcerned about their fate, others whispered prayers to whatever gods they believed in, lips moving slightly, gently. Some of these men were slaves, the property of rich Alexandrians who trained and fought them like animals, wagering on their performances, flogging them for failure—if they lived—or freeing them after they had won a lot of money. There were others who, like himself, were freemen, commoners who were big and strong, whose musculature guaranteed them a fairly easy life if they were talented with weapons.

He was the youngest man here. He caught pity in the eyes of the veterans, the jealousy on the faces of the older men; he wondered which of them he would be facing shortly in a battle to the death. He had no nerves; long ago he'd threshed this out in his mind; he knew the risks that attended the life of a gladiator and he accepted them willingly if by accepting them he might better his lot in life.

30

He was sick to death of the stink of garbage, of decaying meats and rotting vegetables. Anything was better than that kind of life. Some nights he could hear his mother berating his father, turning him out of their bedroom until he washed himself down with herbs and water and applied a mixture of incense and perfume to his body.

None of that sort of thing for Conon.

He would rise a step above—

"You there, boy!"

The *lanista* was looking at him, crooking a finger. Hard hands pushed at his shoulders, moving him forward so swiftly that he stumbled. Coarse laughter rang along the corridor.

"Go to it, boy."

"Show them how a youngster does it."

"Maybe some rich widow will take a fancy to you."

Rich widow? Hah! They should have seen the young beauty he'd brought to watch his first combat, then they wouldn't be laughing at him. He needed no rich widow when Thea was waiting to walk home in the dusk with him.

The manager of the arena was talking swiftly, in jerky sentences. "Matching you with a rope and dagger man from Pamphylia. I know, I know. You've never practiced against anything like him. I had no choice. It was that or nothing."

The *lanista* shoved him under the lifted iron grille and through the stone arch that fronted the arena sands. Conon heard the crowd roar at sight of him. He was a local boy; maybe they were cheering for him. He hoped so. He would not admit it to anyone except himself, but he had lied to Thea in the Forum. He was frightened, all right. He was almost too terrified to walk forward toward a man in a black loincloth twirling a rope who waited for him to come within range.

Conon lifted his chin.

If he intended becoming a gladiator, he must begin now.

Cleopatra stared down at Conon as he came walking across the arena sands, her eyes wide, her fitful breathing lifting her bosom upward into the suddenly tight linen of her tunic. Oh, what a fine figure he made, with the mail *manica* glinting in the sunlight, his helmet shining as if it were on fire. Sunlight danced from the bright blade of his Thracian sword.

The ropeman had been twirling his lariat. It sailed outward now so swiftly it blurred in her eyes. Its wide loop fell over Conon—but no! At the last moment he darted sideways,

31

cutting at the rope. He caught it full with the edge of his blade but failed to pierce it.

"There's wire in it," a man said to her wondering expression. "Takes more'n a sharp blade to slice through that thing. Otherwise, there'd be no contest."

The roper was circling Conon, moving inward on bare feet. His deft hands had gathered the rope, held it ready, loop out. Conon ran forward, sword held high. The rope flashed.

"Ohhh!" Cleopatra screamed, rising to her feet.

The noose had slipped along the blade, moved past the hilt onto Conon's wrist. It tightened suddenly as the man yanked on it. Caught by the taut rope, the young gladiator was jerked off his feet. His sword flew from his hand and he went down hard on his knees.

The ropeman hurled himself forward, dagger bared.

A great shout rose from the people in the seats. This was not to be a long affair, this match between sword and rope. Sometimes they went on for hours so that other events had to be run off while they still fought, the swordsman trying to get in cutting range, the ropeman seeking to stay away from his blade and trip him or strangle him in the always ready noose.

But this fight—

Cleopatra could not close her eyes to blot out the sight of Conon kneeling helpless and the dagger falling to meet his naked chest. There was a flurry of sand as the Pamphylian dove.

Conon was diving too, sideways and away from that flashing knife, both hands going out like the paws of a cat, so swiftly they could scarcely be seen. His big hands tightened on the dagger-wrist of the ropeman and then both men went down into the loose sand.

The crowd screamed its delight.

The ropeman arched his back, trying to wriggle out from under the weight of the boy who held him so desperately. Conon was big and strong, and burdened by the heavy greave and helmet, was a considerable weight to be tossed loose. Slowly Conon was turning the wrist he held, burying his face against the shoulder of the ropeman to protect his eyes from the free hand that came clawing for his face.

They fought silently, grimly, while the throng screeched.

Slowly the right hand of the Pamphylian was being turned to drive the dagger inward toward his ribs. Cleopatra stood with the others, hands balled so tightly her fingernails dug into her palms. Her breasts and belly were wet with the sweat of excitement.

32

"Conon, Conon, Conon," she kept crying.

The ropeman opened his fingers, let go of the knife. It fell even as the Pamphylian scratched with his right hand at the face of Conon. Cleopatra held her breath. Was he blind? Had that flailing hand sliced its nails across Conon's eyeballs? Isis help him! she prayed.

No! He was moving crabwise on his knees away from that hand, diving facedown onto the sands. What was the matter with him? Had he gone mad from pain? Now he reached out and caught hold of the dagger, springing upward with a wrench of muscles.

Only a young man could have twisted himself in such contortions. The dagger glinted in the sunlight as it drove upward. Then its blade slammed to the hilt in the unprotected belly of the ropeman.

The Pamphylian screamed with the agony of his insides spilling out of slit flesh. He dropped both hands to clutch at himself, bending far over. He went to his knees on the sand.

Conon was on his feet at last, staring down at the dying man.

The crowd was shaking *mappae,* those white napkins with which the onlookers showed their approval of a gladiator. Here and there a coin flashed, to fall into the arena. Men with rakes were racing across the sand to cover up the spilled blood, to drag the wounded man away to the *carcere* where he could die in peace. Not that they were influenced by pity or sympathy; the contests must go on. There would be other dying or dead men to look at, very shortly.

Conon tried to find Cleopatra with his eyes but failed. Once he thought he saw her. A young girl with long black hair done up in a ponytail was leaning over the wall blowing kisses, but the sweat was running down into his eyes and stinging so that tears sprang up to blur his vision.

Wearily he picked up his shield, his fallen sword.

He walked after the body of his opponent.

2.

Cleopatra was waiting under the arches that formed a portico south of the great Hippodrome. When Conon came out she ran to him, arms held wide, let herself be caught up and hugged. She could feel the hard flesh of his body all along her own and she found it exciting. It may have been the sight of blood in the arena, the remembrance of men stumbling to their deaths, screaming in agony as cold steel ripped their

33

bodies that excited her so much; a love of cruelty was part of her heritage from her Ptolemaic ancestors. Her blood was molten, feverish.

His hands held her hips as he stared into her eyes. Tiny fires lurked in his bright eyes. She could sense the challenge in them, the heat of his young manhood, the love he had for her. And she delighted in it.

"You don't have to hurry back yet, do you?" he panted.

"I should. You know Ranefer will be wild."

"I thought we could stop at a tavern I know not far from here—on the way to the Temple, really—where we could drink a cup of wine."

As well be killed for a wolf as for a lamb. "All right, Conon. We'll stop at your tavern."

He kissed her, bending her softness in his arms, his mouth hard and fierce on her soft lips, suddenly and with surprising strength. She had no time to stop him and she realized as she felt his tongue questing at her lips, that she did not want to fight him off. Her mouth opened slowly, admitting his tongue. Gently, she bit it.

He was breathing like the bellows of a forge when she writhed away, carolling laughter. "You don't get out of treating me to a cup of wine by kissing me like that, Conon."

"It just came over me, Thea. I didn't mean to offend you."

"You didn't offend me," she smiled slyly.

On the contrary, Conon was ripping veils from her eyes and from this narrow prison of her flesh in which she had walked all her life. Her body sang a lilting tune, a paean of delight. The pleasure which Achillas had roused in her sleeping quarters at the palace was almost certainty, now. The throbbing tumult of her blood was making her dizzy, so that she staggered a few steps until Conon put his arm about her slender waist and pulled her against him.

She felt his hard hip brush against her, felt the taut muscles in his thick right arm, the arm that had killed a man short hours ago. Her head felt so heavy she rested it against his chest.

Their sandals made slapping sounds on the cobblestones but she heard them only faintly. A metalworker carrying his tongs, hammers and awls brushed her elbow but she did not feel him. Two carpenters working on a table before a house door, a young girl slave carrying two red Samian water jars, a man with a wicker basket filled with olives passed her by, but she saw none of them.

She walked as in a dream.

34

The arm at her waist hooked her around and through a white limestone doorway. Above her head a sign carved like a ram's horn creaked on rusting chains. She went into cool dimness, down three stone steps and into a great common room where men and a few women sat at wooden tables clutching leather wine jacks. There was a smell of spilled wine and stale beer and cooking onions in the air.

"Over here," someone said.

A wooden stool was under her rump and Conon sat beside her, pressing close, lifting a leather cup and pushing it into her hands.

"Thea? You all right?" he wondered.

"All right. Oh, yes," she breathed. "Yes, yes."

The wine was tart but cool, nothing like the Meroe or Falernian she had sipped at the palace but heady stuff nonetheless. It dulled the sweet lassitude of her body, roused her to an interest of the room about her.

She had never been inside a street tavern. She found it fascinating. Near the door was a raised level of sundried bricks, wide and spacious, where three men sat eating onions, bread and cheese. A railing separated this corner of the tavern from the lower level, where a dozen great wooden tuns were propped on a long counter set with a number of leather cups. Heavy draperies hanging on poles made a backdrop against which a slavegirl stood turning a spigot so the wine could flow more freely.

Her ears came alive so that she could understand the conversations of their companions at the nearer tables. Cleopatra smiled faintly as one of them held forth on the gods. He was a bearded man, a Greek possibly, or an Illyrian.

"This cult of Osiris is what makes me laugh. Imagine cutting a god into bits and scattering his pieces around the ground to make it fertile. Rain! Rain or Nile water, that's what makes things grow, with the sun. Even more ridiculous is the idea of his wife gathering the pieces and putting them back together again. Rubbish, the lot of it."

"The Jews think there's only one god. Yahweh, they call him. They claim he made the sun and the moon and the stars. They think a savior will come one of these days."

A pert serving maid was passing. An Egyptian caught her by the wrist, drew her in against him. "What do you think, pretty one? What kind of god do you worship?"

She giggled. "As far as I'm concerned, the customer is god." When the lean man pinched her buttock she yelped and fled, laughing.

"There you have it," nodded the Egyptian, his striped claft fluttering. "We make our gods to please ourselves. To the girl, a man who orders from her and leaves a coin on the table is her god, for he clothes and feeds her. All religion may be as simple as that."

A loud voice was saying at the next table, "I tell you he'll be back—yes, and with the eagles at his heels."'

"Pah, the Romans are too superstitious to stir a finger. Didn't you hear about the Sibylline books and—"

"Pah yourself! What's a prophecy to a thousand talents when a man needs money? Somewhere the Piper will find a man who's bankrupt enough to do what he wants. Rome owns the world, any part of it she wants. She hasn't reached out for Egypt yet because the time isn't ripe. And maybe because the Piper still has a few brains in his head."

The Piper! Ptolemy Auletes, the fluteplayer! It was his nickname. Cleopatra sat up straighter, her sensual excitement forgotten before this news. Her father—about to land in Egypt? To take his rightful place on the throne? She turned toward the table where the men sat talking.

"I don't believe it. Pompey is Auletes' friend, and Caesar is enemy to Pompey. Do you think Julius Caesar will let Pompeius Magnus get his hands on Alexandria and the cornbin of Egypt?"

"Caesar would only take it away from him."

"Don't be too sure of that. Pompey's a great general."

"Sure, but so is Caesar."

The heavier man paused to take a long swallow of his beer, then thumped the table for a refill. He drew the sleeve of his dirty white kalisiris across his lips and leered.

"It won't be to Pompey or Caesar, or Lentulus either, that Ptolemy will turn, take my word for it. Each of them is too afraid of the other to make such a bold move. It'll be one of the lesser lords—somebody like Aulus Gabinius who's proconsul of Syria—someone who owes no allegiance to any of the big three, desperate enough for gold to order out his legions. Oh, he'll have a reason, never fear for that. But any excuse will do in Rome when you can bribe Senators."

The third man who had remained silent but interested in the discussion moved his jack about the table in little wet circles. "Berenice the Fourth or Ptolemy the Twelfth—what in hell's the difference to the man in the street, anyhow?"

The other two nodded, scowling blackly.

No difference to them, no! But to Cleopatra Thea Philopater, princess of Egypt and a prisoner in the Temple of

36

Isis—gods, how much it meant! Her father coming home. With the legions ready to put him back on the throne with their pilums. She wriggled in excitement.

Conon saw her movement but did not understand its cause. He put his hand on her thigh and stroked it through the thin linen of her tunic. Never had his palm felt anything so soft and smooth, like cream firmed by a magical enchantment.

"My palm hand's too rough, Thea," he said softly. "I ought to use my lips. Maybe it would show you how much I adore you."

She turned back to him, smiling proudly. Adore! Yes. This big hulking Conon who had killed his first man this afternoon did not know it but he sat beside a royal princess, someone as far above him as Isis herself! He should not be permitted to make love to his goddess but—certainly he could adore her!

She lifted her winecup and sipped, smiling at him with her long-lashed eyes above its rim. She would love to be adored by Conon. The mere idea of it sent a dart of exquisite yearning through her young loins. Her hand went out, caught his fingers, turned them so his palm lay upward to her stare. Her fingertips touched the calluses a moment, then moved to his firm, wide mouth.

"Your lips *are* softer, Conon. Very soft and smooth."

His hand quivered, so great was the emotion that stirred in him. Hastily he swallowed what was left of the cheap Cretan wine.

"We'd better go, Thea. They may—may miss you at the Temple."

"Liar," she whispered sweetly. "You just want to get me alone out there in the dusk, don't you?"

His mute eyes were all the answer she needed.

He paid the fee and clutching her arm tightly, led her out of the tavern onto the cobbled street. It was almost dark. The moon hung low in the night sky, a pale crescent of silver. Quickly he hurried her along until she was almost running.

Where the shadows were darkest beneath a building overhang he turned her, pushed her back against the wall. The bricks were cool through the linen of her garments and made her realize how flushed must be her body, how alive with animal heat.

His head bent to touch her soft throat. Cleopatra let her eyes close, sank deep into this drugged torpor of the senses, her breasts full and hard as Parian marble. His hands were against her hips, stroking her flesh through the linens she wore.

37

Their roughness felt good for they inflicted a tiny thought of pain.

"Conon, Conon," she breathed.

His mouth was at her breasts, kissing them.

A rumble of chariot wheels sounded to one side. The drumming beat of the four horses that pulled it at such a reckless pace made a thunder in the dusk. Men cried out as they fought to get out of its way. Their voices rang loud in the hum of city life.

"Romans. Romans beyond the Canopic Gate—cavalry!"

The shout was like the bellow of a bull.

Romans! Romans! Romans!

The cry was taken up in full flood by a thousand roaring throats. Cleopatra heard that outcry, tensed to its meaning. Her palms caught Conon by his cheeks, lifted his mouth away from her rigid nipples. His heavy breathing was an orchestration to her own sobs.

"Listen, listen," she whimpered.

"Auletes at the gates. Auletes!"

"With Romans, with the legions."

Isis! This was an end to her waiting. No longer would she be a prisoner in the Temple, no longer afraid to travel the streets under her own name. Now she would once again be a princess.

His hands caught her wrists, drew them away from his face. His mouth went down to her breasts but the mood was gone for Cleopatra. She stood straight, upright, smiling proudly at the night.

"Did you hear, Conon? My father's coming home."

Something in her voice drove the passion from his blood. His face lifted and he stared at her. "Your father? The merchant?"

"My father—king Ptolemy Auletes."

"The *king?*" His voice was tinged with awe.

She glanced at him, nodding. "I am Cleopatra. My full name is Cleopatra Thea Philopater."

His features seemed to crumple as his eyes filled with incredulity, with awe and then with terror. He dropped to his knees as if he had been poleaxed.

"Egypt," he breathed, "—forgive me."

His lips kissed the bare flesh of her sandaled foot.

As might a worshipper bent in adoration of his goddess.

3.

The Temple was in a ferment of excitement.

Ranefer was beside himself with despair. Only now had the news come that a detachment of Roman cavalry on scout detail was skirmishing in the Grove of Nemesis. A thousand armed riders, forerunners of the dreaded legions, were just beyond the Gate of Canopus.

They would not stay long. They were only the eyes of the army, sent ahead to spy out the land. Their orders had no doubt been to search and learn what troops Berenice IV might have to stand against the legions. Their commander—a young man with a bull neck and shoulders a yard wide—had no doubt taken it on his own authority to appear before the gates of the city like dread *larvae,* those dead, wicked spirits who appeared to people only when calamity threatened.

This alone was enough to make Ranefer weep with joy. It was the fact that Cleopatra had disappeared which made him want to cry in quite another way. For three years she had been so docile, so obedient. Of course she cost him money—paps of Hathor, what money she cost his sadly shrunken purse!—but at least she was hostage for repayment. She had been his bond for fortune, either from her sister Berenice to whom he would not scruple to sell her if he must, or from her father.

For the dozenth time he ran into the gardens, searching every bush, every tree, with eyes that blurred with tears of self-pity. The bushes were empty. No one sat on the marble benches. Head bowed, he turned back toward the wall gate.

"Ranefer!"

Disbelieving, he raised his head. He swung about. There on the flagstoned path where she had not been a moment before, Cleopatra stood facing him with her head held high, her eyes glittering brightly.

"Where've you been?" he croaked.

"What does it matter? I'm here—as are the Romans."

"You've heard?"

"Enough to let me know I won't have to stay here any longer. Oh, to be free again. Free to go where I want, do what I want."

"Yes, yes. I know. It's been hard. But if—"

"Yes, yes, I know," she mocked him, laughing. "If you hadn't saved my life, I wouldn't be here now to enjoy this moment of my triumph. And your money wouldn't be quite so valuable as it is now. How much will you charge for the princess of Egypt, Ranefer? Ten Talents? Twenty?"

"Not so much, royal princess," he murmured, head bowed low.

She regarded him. After all, he had saved her life. "Be advised, Ranefer. Don't go to Auletes with news that you have his daughter in return for the payment of money. Seek him out, turn me over to him—-and run away."

"Eh? What's that? All the sesterces I spent—"

"Leave the king to me, Ranefer. After all, I am your friend. When I tell Ptolemy how you saved me, fed me, clothed me out of your own pocket—while he's in his cups, to be sure—his generosity will know no bonds."

"Princess, it shall be as you say," he breathed.

"And, Ranefer—take me to the city gate. Now."

"Are you out of your mind?"

"I won't be recognized. I walked the streets all day. I went to the Stadium. I sat in a Rhakotis tavern and drank crude wine." Her sandalled foot—the same foot which Conon had covered with kisses short minutes before—stamped imperiously. "Fetch slaves! A sedan chair!"

Ranefer drew a deep breath. The coming of the Romans had made a difference in their relations. He must understand that fact; no longer was she an exile. She was a princess, heir to the throne of Egypt. When the Piper became king and died, she would hold his golden sceptre.

"It shall be done as you say, highness."

He went with her himself, pacing before the sedan chair, using the long staff that was an emblem of his office to scatter the people crowding the streets. For all Alexandria to see, he was escorting a noblewoman in a sedan chair so heavily hung with curtains no one could look inside. Six brawny slaves were at its handles, making it a light burden. Ranefer walked swiftly while the Nubians followed at his heels.

When they came to the Gate of Canopus, Ranefer approached the litter, extending his hand and assisting Cleopatra to the marble flagstones of the great avenue. She was veiled and hooded; only her gleaming eyes could be seen above the length of byssus which covered the lower corner of her features. With a hand resting lightly on his arm, she permitted the priest to bring her to the steep stair which was a part of the high wall.

On the wallwalk she went away from Ranefer to a space between two merlons and looked out over the Grove of Nemesis to the Eleusian quarter. Against a distant hillside she could see the red dots of Roman campfires. Her palm stroked the cool stone of the wall top. Out there was her redemption, her fulfillment.

A clatter of hooves along the gravelled road caught her attention. A number of cavalry troopers were approaching, led by a heavyset young officer with a bull neck whose helmet was crested with a fan of red. He looked regal, commanding, and she felt drawn to his sheer animality.

He held a torch high in his hand. She could see his proud, fleshy face. It seemed he looked right at her, though of course he could not see more than the himation in which she was shrouded.

"Tell your queen we're coming soon," he shouted. "Within a week or two, maybe a month. Tell her to run unless she wants to have her head lopped off."

Laughter from the riders on either side of him made him grin. His horse danced between his bared thighs, hairy below the lappets of his cuirass, above the heavy bronze greaves.

Cleopatra felt herself respond to his bold stare. She leaned over and called down, "Who are you, Roman? What's your name?"

"You wouldn't know it, lady! So what's the difference?"

His hand sawed at the reins, turned his big black horse as his toes nudged it to a gallop. Ringbits jingling, scabbards clanking against their lappets, his riders followed him in an eruption of hoofbeats.

Cleopatra had spoken for the first time with Mark Antony.

THREE

The Lochias Palace

1.

The supply train moved like a lazy snake along the river road that twisted past the beds of alluvial mud stretching westward, and headed straight across the limestone plain toward the clay-brick fortress of Pelusium. At its point rode fifty mounted swordsmen in the red cloaks affected by the Macedonian Household troops. Their leopard-hide shields, reinforced by bronze strips, made a sparkle of color ahead of the plodding asses covered by wicker panniers holding food and armor.

From the high walls of the fort, hungry men watched the supply train move toward them. For close to a month these men had been besieged by the cavalry arm of the Third Legion under the command of young Mark Antony. Rumor said the Third was moving now through the wilderness of Shur and what had been the ancient land of Goshen on its way into Egypt under the leadership of Aulus Gabinius. If the cavalry could capture Pelusium, it would open a doorway to the land of the lotus and the papyrus through which the proconsul of Syria could enter.

Cavalry was no attacking force to use against a fortress, however. Military strategists in Alexandria said Marcus Antoninus was a madman. Only the men trapped inside those high, mud brick walls understood the method behind that alleged madness. Though they had no siege engines, the Roman cavalry had one weapon which was even more effective than catapults and ballistas. They could starve their enemies to death or into surrender. Their swift Syrian mounts were everywhere, cutting off food and water and weapons from the defenders.

Where were those Roman cavalrymen now?

True, it was almost dawn. Perhaps they slept. Maybe for once Berenice and Archelaus could out-think Antony. There were no Roman cavalrymen anywhere visible.

Ah, and then—

Up from the ditches bordering the river road they came, a swarm of helmeted men with the curved shields of the Third Legion, the short stabbing swords in their hands. The men on the brick walls could hear their yelps of triumph, their deep-voiced shouts of anticipated victory.

The defenders of Pelusium moaned in despair.

Their moans changed suddenly to cries of delight. From the big wagons forming a major part of the supply train, tarpaulins were thrown back as men with the leopard-hide shields and long lances of Old Egypt sprang into view. Horus! Surprise had been countered by surprise.

The fifty attacking Roman cavalrymen were now outnumbered. Swords flashed and shields were lifted all along the roadbed. The high Macedonian helmets of the Royal guard flashed about the shorter Roman helmets. The attack dissolved into individual duels.

The men in Pelusium roared with delight. The Romans

42

were breaking off the attack and galloping away. Almost at a run, the supply train was coming toward the Fort. Orders snapped out. Men ran for the great bolts which locked the wooden gates against entrance by an enemy. The bolts were lifted down. The gates swung open.

At a gallop, the supply train came into Pelusium.

The first man through the gates hurled his spear. It transfixed an Egyptian who came running with a big grin on his swarthy face. Impaled by that six foot length of steel and wood, he stood a moment, staring in agonized surprise at his bleeding belly. He toppled forward limply, understanding coming to him that they had been tricked.

On every side the Macedonian riders were sending their spears flying through the air, unsheathing their swords, dismounting and running to the attack. The men in the wagons were joining them, leaping from tailgate after tailgate, shouting—Horus of the crocodiles!—shouting Roman words. Swords clanged and drew sparks. The shields appeared to lock together, forming a semi-circle before the open wooden gates.

The defenders hurled themselves against that wall of shields seeking to break it, to close the gates. For now men on the wallwalks were yelling that the entire force of Roman cavalry was racing along the river road from where they had been in hiding. Once those riders came swarming through the open gateway, Pelusium was lost to Egypt.

The fight was bitter, savage. Men fell on every side to be replaced within the time it takes a man to move two steps forward. Half the shield ring about the gate was down. The ring had grown smaller, yet still it protected that vital entrance.

The Egyptian commander screamed at his men. They answered that cry by surging forward, using sheer weight of numbers to force the few attackers backward. A few more moments now and the last Roman would be cut down—

A javelin sailed through the air, over the heads of the men behind the shield wall. Another came, and then another. Now the Roman cavalrymen were at the gates, breaking through their own men, stabbing, thrusting, cutting.

Despair seemed to grip the Egyptian soldiers. They were being asked to face now, not merely a handful of daring men but the entire mounted troops of the Third Legion. It was a task beyond their abilities. Cursing, swearing, dying, they fell back into the inner court.

Sunlight glinted on a golden standard where an aquilifer shook it high above his head. At sight of it, the Romans roared and surged forward, bursting the thinning ranks of the Egyptians, pressing on to make the attack a number of individual duels. At swordplay the Romans were almost invincible, due to their strict military discipline and training.

Within an hour after the supply train had trotted into Pelusium, the fortress had fallen. The Egyptian commander was turning over his sword to Mark Antony. The thunderbolt standard of the Ptolemies was coming down, to be replaced by the Roman eagle.

2.

Cleopatra sat with her knees pressed tight together, staring up at Conon who stood so diffidently before her. He wore a kaunake spattered with dust, for his ride from the battlefield where Archelaus had tried to stem the Roman advance had been a long, hard one on a horse loaned him by Ranefer. There was a dried swordcut on his arm where a soldier had taken a swipe at him, and his deep chest rose and fell as he gulped down air.

Ranefer stood slightly to one side and behind the high-backed chair which young Cleopatra sat as if it were a throne. Her cheeks were flushed, her eyes feverish.

"Go on, Conon," she urged. "Go on."

"They met a few miles south and east of Pelusium," Conon told her. "The palace soldiers had already deserted to the Romans but the main body of troops were under the command of Archelaus. Your father—King Ptolemy—had his own standards raised beside the eagles. I could see them from the top of the hill where I watched."

He was trembling a little, still in the spell of the battle, still seeing the solid bulk of the legions moving forward, shields held rim to rim, giving room only for the throwing of the pilum, then the quick play of the short legionary sword, the *gladius*. Dust lifted all around the level plain so that it made a yellow haze, but he had caught glimpses of the battle from time to time, when a breeze off the desert blew away the yellowish motes.

The legion was like a solid wall moving slowly forward, something like the phalanx of Alexander the Great. It was irresistible, its swords and javelins cutting down in death the men who flung themselves against it in their desperate attempts to rip gaps between the shields. The braying of the curved trumpets, the rallying horns, the screams of wounded horses as the cavalry units sought to turn the flanks, the screams of dying men, the clash of swords, made a symphony which still lingered in his ears.

"The battle didn't last very long, I guess," he grinned. "Not really, that is. The Egyptians fought well but they were outmatched. I saw Archelaus on a white horse fighting with two Romans, then the flat of a blade took him behind his head. He fell forward over his mount's withers. He bounced when he hit the ground.

"One of the Romans went after him, lifting off his helmet, grabbing his head and holding bare his throat while he put the edge of his sword to it and slit his throat."

Cleopatra nodded, pressing her soft thighs together against the wildness in her veins, squirming on the cane seat of the chair. Archelaus was dead! Berenice herself would die soon. But not quickly, in the heat of battle as her husband had died. No, it must be a slower death for this sister who had ordered her own dying three years before.

"Take me to the palace," she commanded, rising.

"Princess," protested Ranefer in honest shock. "You'd be playing right into their hands. If Berenice were to lay hands on you—hold you as hostage—she might compel your father to make terms favorable to her. Stay here, unknown to all but a very few, where you're safe."

Cleopatra bit her full lower lip. Excitement raged in her blood. Impatience was a flood river in spate sweeping away the dam of her reason. She slapped her palms together as she moved back and forth, lifting hands to her hair as if to make certain it was properly coiffed, smoothing down the skirt of her linen tunic about her hips.

"I can't stay here," she wailed. "I *can't.*"

Conon looked at the frowning Ranefer. "Maybe we could go to the Forum and mingle with the mob. The city is flooded with people waiting to get a look at Gabinius and the king. By now the news of his victory will be everywhere."

"The Forum," she breathed, nodding. "Then when Ptolemy rides in—"

"I forbid it," shouted Ranefer.

"No one forbids Cleopatra, priest," she reminded him and stretched out a hand to the brawny youth. "My old cloak, Conon. It's in the hall on a bench. I intended using it to disguise myself to get to the palace. It'll serve to keep me unknown until the legions arrive. Have you money?"

"A few copper obols, no more."

Her palm turned upward before Ranefer. "Give me silver

pieces. Enough so that Conon and I may pose as lovers—buy some sweets—or perhaps a small wineskin."

Ranefer rolled his eyes in dismay, but he nodded, setting his lips firmly. "All right, highness. But I'm going along."

"Of course you may," she answered him. "After all, I can understand your wanting to protect your investment. Come, Conon!"

A chariot waited in the courtyard, driver lounging on the rail. As Ranefer approached he sprang down and grasped the reins. Cleopatra sat on the little seat, face turned away from the horses. Ranefer stepped to the right and grasped the hand-rail. Conon mounted the Syrian stallion which had been furnished him by the Temple priests.

"I'm more at home on a horse," he said to Cleopatra, gesturing at the chariot. "I'd fall off one of those things if it went at any speed."

The driver cracked his whip. The four horses lurched against the breast-straps. With a rumble of ironshod wheels over the flagstones, the chariot gathered speed. It went out the courtyard gate at the gallop with Conon in its dust.

The streets of Alexandria were thick with people crying out to one another, demanding news, passing on rumors, pushing, scuffling. They scattered before the big chariot painted with the doves of Isis, shouting to Ranefer, asking who the woman was who rode with him.

"A concubine for the Piper," someone guessed.

"To make his first night in Alexandria a happy one."

"Too bad you aren't taking a boy to Berenice—"

"—to make her last night happy, too!"

Laughter almost drowned out the rumble of the wheels, the pounding of the horses' hoofs. Cleopatra sat quietly, face hidden under the robe, hands clasped on her thighs, a tiny smile curving the corners of her lips. At last she was going home, back to the palace where she belonged. No more would she have to breathe the close, stuffy air of the Temple or walk its gardens that had been so much like a scented prison.

Her eyes touched Conon, saw him big and husky, heavily muscled. Isis, what a fine lover he'd make her! Perhaps tonight, in her old room that looked out over the Diabratha and the harbor waters, that brightened every so often when the great lantern atop the five hundred foot tower of the Pharos lighthouse made daylight of her bedchamber, she would take him between her thighs.

As they approached the Gymnaseum, the throng was so great that not even a Temple chariot could make headway.

46

Cleopatra rose, beckoning to Conon, indicating that she wanted to-ride before him on the big bay.

His arm hooked her slim waist, lifted her across the horse's back. She sat pressed into him, breathing quickly, her eyes darting over the heads of the crowd. She paid no more attention to him than if he were a chair or the floor on which she might stand. Conon sensed this, but was pleased by it rather than dejected.

This was Cleopatra in his arms, the princess of Egypt.

At her nod, he would have rushed to his death. The fact that he loved her was of no moment to him. She was unattainable to Conon, son of Kalikos. She might as well have been the goddess Isis herself; sometimes in his dreams, indeed, this was how Conon thought of her. And so he used his senses, his quick eyes and strong hands and loud tongue, to break a passage for the bay and its two riders.

"The Forum, Conon. They'll have to cross the Forum."

The bay sidled forward, but it met with opposition. Shoulders and bodies pressed into it, thrusting it back and sideways. The bull voice bellowing over their heads made little impression on the Alexandrians. They shouted right back. No young gladiator and his doxy were going to seeing Ptolemy before their betters.

Someone threw a stone. Luckily, Conon saw it coming, lifted his arm and took it so that Cleopatra would be safe. Fury blazed in her eyes as she saw him wince against the pain.

"Someone will die for that, Conon! I promise it."

"I'm glad they threw it, Thea. It means no one knows you. You're safe. Don't you understand?"

She smiled tenderly. "Does my safety mean so much to you?"

"Your safety is my life," he answered soberly.

She caught his hand and squeezed his fingers tightly.

The movement of the crowd forced the horse against the stone wall of a building nor could Conon do anything to change their position. Pressed into the building wall and under an overhanging balcony, they could not move. The mood of the mob when they sought to go forward changed to sullen anger.

Wisely, Conon shrugged his shoulders and desisted.

"They'll pull us to pieces if we rouse their anger any more," he growled, and Cleopatra nodded. "We can see the Forum from here, anyhow. When the—your—fa—when the Romans come, we can yell."

It was hot under the spring sun of Alexandria. Sweat ran down her back and side where she was pressed into him and his arm was like hot metal at her hips. The bay shook its ring-bits and snorted, stamping its hooves. It did not like to be hemmed in this way. Its lips drew back, showing big white teeth as it whinnied in anger.

Cleopatra patted its neck, bending to hush it with her melodious voice. As the horse quieted, she caught another sound in the air, a rhythmic, swinging sound. There was the faint clank of distant metal striking metal.

"The legions," someone yelled.

"They come, they come!"

"Conon—you hear them?"

"I hear, prin— Thea."

Her eyes were amused as they flashed at him. Trust Conon to maintain the disguise even now, while the eagles sparkled in the sunlight and the pilums made a small forest where the legions walked. She craned her neck, trying to see above the crowd.

The first century was moving through the Forum, closely followed by rank on rank of veterans swinging steadily along at their ground-eating pace. Their eagles shone for all to see and after them the captured standards of those tribes and nations over which they had won victories. This is the Third Gallica, those banners said, and these are the symbols of our victories. There was pride in every set of rigid shoulders, every pair of marching feet.

A rider on a white horse trotted through the crowd.

"Antony," whispered Conon. "The man who took Pelusium."

Cleopatra caught her breath. "He's the one I spoke to from the wall. He told me his name wouldn't interest me. Well—it doesn't!"

"Ptolemy," whispered a voice and the whisper spread.

"Ptolemy, Ptolemy!" other throats shouted.

Cleopatra quivered in her impatience. "Oh, Conon—he'll be gone before I see him!"

"Stand, then!" he advised.

Her hand on his shoulder, his fingers at her middle, she was lifted upward to her sandalled feet on the bay's broad withers. Conon had his hands beneath her tunic to clutch her naked legs with widespread fingers. The backs of her scented thighs pressed his face. Above him, Cleopatra was shrieking with joy, waving her hand that held a scarf, crying out. She must be seeing her father, Conon thought, and knowing he was losing this girl he loved, touched his lips to the thigh where it pressed so close against his face.

"Father, father! Here!"

Her hood fallen back, her black hair glistening in the sun, Cleopatra went up and down on her toes. Her right arm waved. Below her, Conon was adding his deep voice.

"The princess," he bellowed. "Cleopatra! The princess Cleopatra!"

The crowd turned, saw her and thought it recognized her. The crowd took up the cry so that at last it reached the ears of Ptolemy XII Auletes where he stood clinging to a chariot handrail. Aulus Gabinius in a chariot preceding the royal chariot, looked interested. He shouted an order to a tribune.

A score of twenty legionaries advanced into the crowd, buttends first, stabbing out with them, jabbing, hitting, making an opening to the accompaniment of oaths and jeers. They moved slowly between the cursing, peering thousands while Cleopatra stood proudly, awaiting their arrival.

The interlocked shields held above their heads made a canopy that hid them from sight of the youth and the girl waiting on the bay horse. All they could see was the score and more of rectangular targes as they moved, like some fabled monster, toward them.

Conon felt Cleopatra stir.

"They'll open to let you through," he said.

"No," she called down at him. "I'm going—"

Her muscles tensed. She stepped forward, a sandalled foot reaching for the first of the shields with the thunderbolt insignia raised on its metal surface. A roar went up from the crowd as she ran daintily on top of the shields toward the waiting chariots, black ponytail dancing behind her.

Aulus Gabinius waved an arm and more legionaries ran to add their shields to the upraised road over which the princess of Egypt sped so lightly. Now she was a dozen feet away, still running. She leaped. A centurion stepped forward to catch her in his arm, to swing her upward and into the chariot where Ptolemy Auletes waited to embrace her.

The throng bellowed its approval of her showmanship.

Her father clasped her tight, kissing both her cheeks, smiling down at her with wet eyes. She could smell the Falernian on his breath, realized he was not quite drunk. Then she turned and waved to the Alexandrines and blew kisses with her fingertips to her lips.

Ptolemy Auletes was a big man with a huge paunch but there was a kingliness about him that touched the hearts

49

and throats of his people. They roared in approval as he hugged Cleopatra and waved at them. He was a fop and a drunkard, but he was their king and his ancestors before him had ruled in this city for three centuries. Egypt would not be Egypt without a Ptolemy on its throne. They forgot his custom of playing the flute and his wild parties. They saw only their rightful ruler come back to them.

Beside him, Cleopatra shared his triumph.

Cupping hands to her mouth, she called to Conon.

"The palace. As soon as you can, come!"

He nodded and waved an arm.

The curving trumpets blew again, a loud and rousing note that went between the marble buildings of the Forum as far as the Brucheion, which was the royal compound. Somewhere in the Lochias palace Berenice would hear that blast and know her doom was coming to meet her. The Macedonian Household troops still loyal to her reign would be tightening their shield straps for the final battle with the Roman legionaries who would soon be hitting the palace gates in a wave of flashing swords.

To Cleopatra, those Roman horns were announcing her return to royalty. With one hand on the rail of the chariot, the other on her father's wrist, she stood with chin uptilted, a tiny smile curving the corners of her full red mouth.

As the first detail of the Third Legion went into the palace yard, she turned a flushed face to her parent. "Follow them in, father! Be there when they drag Berenice out."

He caught the excited triumph in her voice. "If you want, Cleopatra. I must admit I'm not unmoved at the thought of sleeping in the Lochias myself, this night." His lips pursed thoughtfully. "That young man on the horse, the one you were with. Is he a noble?"

Her laughter rang out. "A commoner, but he adores me. A young gladiator. I mean to make him my personal bodyguard." Her plucked black brows drew together. "Never again will I cower in my bedchamber while a man with a sword in his hand hunts me—so he can kill me!"

"Poor dear," he murmured, squeezing her with an arm. "You've been through so much, so much."

"I haven't suffered any more than you, dear one."

"No," he agreed heavily. "It hasn't been easy."

Their voices were drowned out by the sound of swords meeting, clanging together. A man cried out in pain. A detachment of the Household troops were making a stand at the great gateway flanked by mighty pylons of red sandstone

50

and carven images of the first Ptolemy in a high-crested Grecian helmet.

Cleopatra held her lower lip between her small white teeth, standing on tiptoe with her hands clenched into fists by her sides. Ah, this was life, seeing men fighting and dying that she might sit her throne some day. She wondered, casting a glance at him, if her father were so affected. It was almost aphrodisiacal in its delight, she thought, and remembered Conon.

The battle did not last very long, so that she was almost disappointed. Within scant minutes the Romans smashed the thin line of Royal Guards, left them lying on the ground in pools of their own blood, pushed through their remnants and into the palace proper. Half a dozen centuries followed them inside at the run.

The breeze grew stronger off the Harbor as they waited, standing in the chariot. Aulus Gabinius paced the flagstones. red military cloak swirling at his heels, sending an occasional glance at the girl where she stood slimly curved in her revealing tunic. Cleopatra knew he was eying her and wondered if he could see that her nipples had erected in the excitement of seeing men die.

A woman screamed inside the marble bulk of the Lochias. Berenice? Or one of her serving women?

Cleopatra squeezed the chariot rail, aware that her palm was damp, that nervousness was a quiver in her soft thighs and in her belly. This waiting, this sense of not knowing what might be taking place in the palace, was close to being painful.

Gabinius lifted his helmeted head, turned it toward the pyloned gate. His hard face was rapt with attention. It was as if he listened to sounds inaudible to other ears.

Then Cleopatra heard the sounds, too, the tramp of military sandals, the clank of scabbards, the metallic rustle of lappets meeting. A detail of the Third was moving along the palace corridors toward the gate.

Two centurions emerged into the sunlight, dragging a woman between them. Cleopatra stiffened. It was Berenice, her older sister. Clasped by her wrists, her arms held wide apart, she was being drawn like a balky donkey down the marble steps onto the flaggings and toward the chariot where Ptolemy Auletes stood.

A part of her linen garment had been torn in the struggle she had put up before she had been taken prisoner. Through its rents Cleopatra could see her dusky flesh, the heavy

51

reddish breasts swinging as she writhed. There were scratch marks on them.

Berenice was sobbing softly, almost to herself, in her terror. Tearstains on her face and the disarrangement of her thick black hair could not hide her fleshy beauty. Some years older than Cleopatra, she had taken many lovers. Archelaus alone was not sufficient to her sensual appetites. She had revelled in cruel pastimes, amused herself with the lives and fortunes of both men and women.

Now she was face to face with judgment.

To her father she was dragged, held there while the Fluteplayer stared down at her. For a crazy instant, Cleopatra thought to read pity and forgiveness in his eyes. She wanted to scream out that this woman had almost been her death.

Wisely, she held her tongue. Ptolemy shook his head and made a clucking sound with his tongue, "Unnatural daughter," he said suddenly. "What am I to do with you?"

"Let me live," she moaned, eyes sunken in the still lovely face lifted to him. "Only let me live." As if aware that a girl was beside her father, she turned her head. Her eyes grew wide. "You! I thought you dead!"

Cleopatra leaned across the handrail and let the anger she had bottled up inside her these past three years come into her voice. "I fled away, Berenice. I've been living under the protection of the gods! No thanks to you. If it were up to you, I'd be rotting in the ground right now."

"Father," whimpered Berenice, "don't kill me. I don't want to die."

Ptolemy lifted a corner of the toga he affected—its edges were tinted in royal purple—and with it hid his face. Understanding the finality of that gesture, Berenice screamed, lunging forward so fiercely that she came close to breaking the handholds which restrained her.

"No," she screamed. "Not that—not death! Put me away."

Gabinius made a motion with his hand. "Take her to the dungeons. Put her in chains so she cannot hurt herself."

Screaming, wailing, her throat raw with terror, Berenice IV was pulled away from the chariot that held her father and her sister. Her dark hair hung limp about her shoulders, its once splendid coiffure damp and matted. Once she slipped as a sandal came loose on her foot, and went to a knee. Her handsome leg was exposed by the up-pulled hem of her torn tunic.

Cleopatra permitted herself a tiny smile. Her eyes were narrowed so that it seemed she almost squinted against the

52

redness of the setting sun. In her mind she told herself, This is what happens when a queen loses her power. This shall never happen to me. I shall not permit it! She drew a sigh that was accompanied by a tiny shudder.

The chariot rolled forward, into the Brucheion.

3.

Conon stood rigid outside the wooden doorway that was painted with the thunderbolt and eagle design of the Ptolemies. He wore the silver armor and tall, crested Macedonian helmet of the Household Guard. Tall caligulae of fur and silver adorned his feet and calves. A sword hung from a silver scabbard in a baldric of red leather set with silver studs. Never in all his life had he been so clad; he was sensible of a distinct uneasiness, as if he might be accused of having stolen all this finery.

The armorer who outfitted him had been talkative. "She's taken a fancy to you, the princess has. Ordered your armor herself. All red and silver and set with her own thunderbolt design. I've been working on it the past three hours."

Conon nodded mutely. It was the day after the legions had entered Alexandria. Yesterday evening he had come to the palace and been told to return next day at noon, that the princess was closeted with the proconsul of Syria and with her father and had no time to spare for commoners. For himself, Conon would have turned his back on the Lochias and walked off into oblivion but he remembered the warm ivory and ebony beauty of Cleopatra Thea Philopater and his knees grew weak; besides, he had the faint suspicion that if he did not return, she would send for him.

Now he understood why she had not seen him yesterday. The armor was her gift. It fitted him perfectly as he knew from the glances he'd sneaked at himself in the polished copper oval hanging on the wall in the armorer's shop. He looked older, bigger, in the silver cuirass and he walked more confidently.

The door opened and a girl came out. She was a pretty thing, an Egyptian with thick black hair caught up in a caul of gold wires. She wore the traditional tunic with its cross straps that left her breasts bare.

"Conon?" she asked.

When he nodded, she stood aside, smiling at him in friendly fashion. Later he was to discover that her name was Charmion, that she was a confidant of the princess and, with Iras who set her hair, went everywhere with her. She had been in hiding in Alexandria; with the coming of the Romans, she had returned to the palace.

Conon walked with an unconsciously heavy stride across the black and white tiles of the apartment floor. Tall tripods held flaming oil lamps and the stone walls were fitted with iron torcheres so that the room was alive with light. Charmion ran ahead on silent feet. She moved with such fluid grace and ease, so quietly and unobtrusively, that Conon momentarily forgot her presence.

His eyes were so taken with these palace rooms that he felt he was in an entirely different world. Great draperies which could be lowered to shut out the sea breezes, hung from tall poles. A diorite statue of Neith, the war goddess, of a deep wine color tasseled with gold, was fronted by a low brass bowl holding incense; at an opposite angle stood a small statuette of Isis; between them were three teakwood chests which held garments and jewelry. Low benches stood against the walls, heavily cushioned. Fans of tinted ostrich feathers made splashes of color against the stone.

It was a world of wealth and opulence. This much he sensed as he strode along behind Charmion, and it awed him. Used only to bare brick walls in which were hammered wooden pegs from which to hang his few garments, to wooden bowls that served as plates, to crudely made tables and chairs, Conon stumbled and he almost fell when a satin pillow hit his ankle.

"Oaf," laughed Cleopatra.

Conon swallowed hard. She stood between two floor lamps, garbed in transparent byssus which revealed the flesh tints of her body. A narrow jeweled apron hid her loins; a great golden collar inset with rubies rested on the upper slopes of her protruding breasts; golden sandals made her feet look even tinier than they were. Upon her carefully coiled black hair, a great gold and enamelled Amen-Ra cap was placed. She looked not unlike the statued representation of the long-dead Queen Nefert-iti he had seen on the walls of the Museion.

Conon fell to his knees with a clash of metal.

Cleopatra looked impishly pleased but she said, "Oh, get up, Conon. There's to be none of that between you and me."

"Highness, I—"

His mouth felt dry, his tongue swollen. Only his eyes could speak and the dumb worship she saw in their depths made Cleopatra know that this man belonged to her far

54

more than anyone she might purchase in the great slave market.

"You are to be my bodyguard, Conon. You will also be a prefect in charge of a cohort of The Macedonians. I think you may become even more important, here in the Lochias. Now stand up and let me look at you."

She nodded her approval after a brief glance. "You will cease to fight in the gladitorial games. You may visit the *ludi* to keep in shape, however. I want a fighting man to guard me, not a fop encased in silver." She turned away. "Charmion, are we ready for the banquet?"

"Yes, highness."

Cleopatra made a little sign and Conon came to stand two feet behind her right elbow. He knew his assignment, to guard her against possible injury or assassination. He would have given his life to save hers, and he vaguely understood that in some manner, Cleopatra was aware of it.

They moved into the banqueting room in a fanfare of long golden trumpets and guests rising to their feet and bowing low. Everywhere Conon looked he saw lowered heads and bending backs. These were the noblemen and women of Alexandria; they counted their wealth in Roman sesterces; they were the intimates of the Ptolemies, and almost as powerful. He had seen their great marble mansions along the Street of Canopis and in the Via Serapia, dodged their galloping chariots, carried away their castoff clothes and the remnants of their feasts. Until this night, he had held them in awe.

The hall was set in the Roman manner, with low couches and small tables close at hand so that even in a reclining position a guest could reach out for a wine goblet or a bowl of fruit. On a raised dais a golden divan held King Ptolemy. To his right sat Aulus Gabinius, proconsul of Syria. To his left an ivory and gold couch awaited Cleopatra.

She took her place with a little smile for the Roman. She understood well enough by this time that to remain powerful in Alexandria, one must court favor with the men who commanded the legions. Gabinius bowed and smiled in answer.

Charmion brought her a gold cup of Mareotic wine.

For Conon, the banquet was a time of marvel. His eyes were never still, drinking their fill of the Nubian acrobats who performed feats of agility in the great square between the couches, the belly dancers from Syria, the dagger throwers who formed a line of knives around a living girl in a great wooden board. He watched as the Alexandrines ate themselves to nausea, then went outside to the gardens and emptied out their stomachs by tickling the backs of their throats with feathers.

Cleopatra ate sparingly and drank only a little wine.

After a time it came to him that this was no orgy but a simple meal according to royal standards. The food and wine would have done the quarter where he lived for a month. And so he understood that whatever a king or a queen did, it must be done in lavish style or not at all.

Ptolemy Auletes ordered his golden flute brought to him and with it, entertained his guests. Their applause was loud, tumultuous. They were approving not so much the quality of his playing as the fact that he had come back to play at all. Everywhere there were smiles, joyous nods, much handbeating.

Conon was surprised when he saw Cleopatra yawn. Everything had been so new to him, so different, that he still retained a fine edge of interest. His attention was caught by a number of noblemen supported by their slaves as they approached the dais to pay their respects to Ptolemy. Household slaves were waiting in the shadows beyond the painted columns to clear the tables, to clean the couches stained by spilled food and wine.

It was the seventh hour of the night. Normally Conon would have been asleep long ago, for as a gladiator he needed rest. One of his duties, apparently, was to remain awake until the princess herself was asleep. He settled himself to a long vigil, but within minutes Cleopatra beckoned Charmion who came from the shadows with a wrap, for the night had grown cool, and threw it about her shoulders.

Cleopatra glanced back at Conon. He stood rigid, unmoving, taking his role of bodyguard seriously. She was glad to see that; it showed he was sensible of the honor she had bestowed on him. From him her eyes moved to a young Parthian slave, a youth with curly black hair, an almost hairless torso and fine muscular legs. He wore the traditional cotton apron of the household serving man, no more. Cleopatra touched her full lips with her tonguetip.

In a way she felt sorry for Conon. She could not summon him to her bedchamber as she intended doing with the young slave. All during the night, while she pleasured herself with the Parthian, he would stand guard beyond the huge doors. She sighed and drew her wrapper closer about her body, knowing how much Conon wanted her; but it could not be. She had come to realize that to become too familiar with her own bodyguard might make her dependent on him sometime in the future, and dependency was a sign of weakness.

56

She walked with stately steps away from the banqueting hall. Charmion was at her left elbow, Conon at her right. There was a heaviness in her middle, a sense of need, of hunger, that was no stranger to her flesh. Often she had felt this sensual fury in the Temple. There she had been helpless to relieve it. Here in the Lochias palace, her slightest whim was a royal command.

"The boy?" she whispered to Charmion.

"—will be waiting in the bedchamber, highness."

Cleopatra wondered if Conon heard. At her doorway she glanced at him but his face was impassive. Wrinkling her nose at him she slipped through the opening; listened while Charmion gave him his orders. Then she kicked off her slippers of gold brocade and ran on bare feet past the fluted columns.

The boy was waiting, obviously nervous. He was young, only a year or two older than herself, but handsome. She walked up to him, letting her wrap slide from her shoulders. She put her palms on his hairless chest and stroked him down to his navel while he trembled. Tiny fires glowed in his eyes.

"You know why you're here?" she asked.

He nodded, then closed his eyes convulsively as she removed the cotton apron and fondled him. His chest lifted and fell to the heaviness of his breathing. He would have put a hand on her but she struck it away imperiously.

"Not yet," she ordered. "Not until I give permission."

After a few moments Charmion came in and closed the heavy curtains behind her, pulling them across the archway into the atrium. When she saw the boy, she giggled and flushed. Then she ran to Cleopatra, unhooked her gold collar and let it slide down, catching it and placing it on top of a chest. The jewelled apron was next and then her fingers busied themselves with the fastenings of the byssus tunic.

The tunic fell in a froth of white tissue.

Except for the Amen-Ra cap on her head and the gold slippers on her feet, Cleopatra was naked. She stood before the youth proudly as his eyes went from her slim ankles up her full white thighs to her loins, to her gently mounded belly and the thrusting heaviness of her breasts. The pulse in her middle was throbbing strongly now. Within the hour she would be a virgin no longer.

There was no fear in her, no dread of pain. This was a moment which she must live that a lifetime of pleasure could begin. Instinctively she understood that if the youth could rouse her sufficiently, she would scarcely feel the instant of his penetration. She turned and walked toward her bed, sat on its edge and beckoned the Parthian to approach.

When he stood before her, she pointed at the floor.

"Kneel," she said and let her thighs fall open.

Dawn was a pink radiance on the floortiles of the outer corridor when the atrium doors opened and the Parthian youth came out. There were dark rings under his eyes and exhaustion in the lines of his face. Charmion was with him, her garments rumpled from the periods of sleep into which she had fallen on her own small couch. Her lips were tight with distaste for she had no stomach for this sort of thing.

"Take him to Hardedef," she told Conon, "but send a relief detail to take your place, first."

Conon scarcely heard her. He was staring at the Parthian youth with hate in his eyes. Now he understood the faint cries and screams which he had heard during the night. In his innocence, he told himself, he'd believed the princess was having a nightmare after the rich food she had eaten. Fool, fool! All he needed was one glance at this handsome face, the marks of tiny teeth on his flesh, to realize what sort of nightmare it had been.

To Charmion he nodded. "The princess will be all right?"

"She sleeps. I'll stand behind the doors after I bolt them, until your relief appears. To Hardedef, now."

The youth walked at a stumbling pace. His every nerve was crying out for sleep, for rest. Beside him, Conon wondered if Cleopatra intended summoning him back tonight. His right hand balled into a fist and he found himself surprised at the destructive tide of fury sweeping through his veins.

Hardedef was the palace chief of slaves. A big man grown to flab, he ruled the section of the palace where the slaves were kept with an iron hand. The Nubians, the Pannonians, the Asiatics who served the household walked in perpetual fear of him. Too well they knew that their royal masters and mistresses paid them little heed; they were scarcely more than animals; if anything happened to them, no search would be made. Since Hardedef possessed the power of life or death deep in these stone recesses of the Lochias, a wise slave walked quietly and spoke silently and agreeably when he was near.

The fat man glanced up from his first breakfast of barley cakes and wine as Conon appeared. His tiny eyes, almost lost in the rolls of fat that were his cheeks, slid sideways to the Parthian. He grinned lewdly.

"Had herself a time, did she? Wore the boy out."

"Hold your tongue, fat one!"

Hardedef blinked. He was used even to the sight of free-men attached to the palace fawning before him. He knew everything that transpired in the Lochias, for his slaves made a most efficient spy system. Nothing was left unsaid or undone before them, since they were looked upon as little more than necessary furniture. Such information made him valuable to everyone.

He put his big hands on the tabletop and came to his feet, face flushed with fury. "Fat or not, no man talks to—"

Conon lifted out his sword, touched its sharp point to Hardedef's groin. His grin was cold, hard. "Dog, if you enjoy life keep a still tongue in your head when I'm about. I won't kill you—only make a eunuch out of you—and tell anyone who wants to know that my swordblade slipped while I was demonstrating a stroke to use in the arena."

Hardedef paled. He knew as well as Conon that nobody abovestairs would care whether or not he was sexless. What difference did it make to Ptolemy Auletes or to his sons and daughters that the chief of slaves could no longer enjoy the prettier of the slavewomen who were at his mercy? No, no. He would still be alive; it would be looked on as a happen-stance of fate, no more.

He sat down, his forehead wet with sweat.

Conon put his sword away, nodding at the Parthian whose eyelids were almost closing in sleep. "Charmion said I was to turn him over to you. What do you intend doing with him?"

"Let him sleep, of course," Hardedef grumbled.

Conon was disappointed, but he went with the chief of slaves to the little cubicle where there was a small bedstead covered with a woolen blanket. Hardedef led the Parthian to it, watched while he stretched out on his back. Before the chief slave was at the door, the youth was asleep.

Hardedef said sullenly, "I'll come back in an hour and strangle him." As Conon raised his eyebrows, he added. "I do this to all the slaves when they've spent a night with the princesses. First Berenice, now Cleopatra. Someday when she gets older, it'll be for Arsinoe."

"Berenice, too, eh?"

"All the Ptolemy women have a fever in their blood for men. I remember the king's mother—I was only a boy then —and the expense she put the palace to, buying Nubians. She had a compulsion for them. Oh, well—royalty must have its pleasures."

Conon looked at the sleeping Parthian. His face was hard. "Let me take the cord, Hardedef. And count me your friend."

"After your threatening to—not likely!"

Conon grinned and slapped the fat man on his big paunch. "Oh, come—no need for bad blood between us. A few words spoken in heat—forgive them."

Hardedef looked the big youth over from his caligulae to his crested silver helmet. No idiot, he knew this one was a favorite of Cleopatra, just how much of a favorite he realized when he understood that she had chosen a slave instead of him to cool the heat of her royal blood. Wise in the ways of palace politics, he knew she was afraid to put her emotions in his hands.

And so Hardedef grinned and nodded. He reached into a leather pouch hanging from his belt-rope and tossed it.

"Give him an hour. He'll be so helpless with slumber he won't feel the cord. Come back to the other room with me. Share a cup of Mareotic."

Conon whistled softly. "Mareotic! We live high, here in the Lochias."

"We do when our masters trust us. What the king eats, I eat. What he drinks, I drink. If you're wise, you'll do the same."

"As long as it doesn't interfere with my job."

"Which is to protect the princess," Hardedef grinned.

Conon nodded soberly, wondering at the amusement of the fat man. He went with him into the antechamber of the slave quarters, sat and ate barley cakes and drank wine until the bronze water clock in a wall recess showed him that an hour was gone. Then he took the knotted cord and walked down the hall to the little room where the Parthian slept.

The chief of slaves was right. The youth did not feel the cord until it began to tighten around his throat. His eyes bulged, his fingers came up to grip and then fall away from the powerful hands that held him helpless. The muscles of his body stood out in the torment of his writhing and his mouth was wide open for the air that never came. After a few minutes his body was limp, lifeless.

Conon whispered. "For you, Thea."

There were tears in his eyes for a lost dream.

Two weeks later when he had occasion to visit Hardedef again, he found Cleopatra, in an overly tight tunic that strained to hold her hips and big breasts, standing beside the chief slave's table. Conon stared a moment, then went to a knee.

"Highness," he said. "I thought you and your father were on Lake Mareotis in the royal barge. I—"

A burst of laughter from Hardedef interrupted him as the fat man slapped his flabby thigh. The girl stared from Conon to the slavemaster, then back at the big youth. When he could control his mirth, Hardedef gasped, "This isn't the—the princess. It's only a slavegirl who looks like her. Her name's Ione. She's a Thracian. We had her off the slave blocks only this morning."

Conon got to his feet, marveling at the resemblance.

Hardedef went on, "We keep slave doubles—or as near doubles as we can find—for all the royal family. For Ptolemy, for Cleopatra, for the two boys and Arsinoe. Sometimes when a public appearance has to be made—the temper of the Alexandrine crowd is uncertain—better a slave gets hit with a flying stone than royalty."

"She fooled me completely," Conon breathed.

"You want her?"

Conon flashed a glance at the fat man. "What's her price?"

"Nothing—now. I've been asking around the palace about you, Conon. I've decided we must be friends, you and I. It won't be long before you command the palace guard. I have control over the slaves. Between us, we can rule the Lochias."

Conon considered, head a little bent. Hardedef was correct, as he almost always was in his evaluation of a situation. A gift for intrigue had been born into him. He could be handy to a man who was only a prefect in the palace guards but who aspired to command them.

His eyes touched the white legs of the slave girl. Isis! If he didn't know better, he would swear this was Thea before him. The girl wore a simple tunic, bleached white, the crosstraps of which formed an X on her chest on either side of which heavy white breasts protruded firmly. Her nipples were dark brown, and he could see the faint blue of veins just beneath the taut, plump skin. Her hair was black and long, falling down her back to her waist.

There was a flame in his groin and a fire in his lungs. It was hard to breathe. His eyes ate at the girl until she gasped suddenly, went red, then gave a little smile. Conon chuckled. She even smiled like the princess, with a dimpling curve to the corners of her lips.

"A partnership, then," Conon nodded. "What security do you ask?"

Hardedef grinned at him. "Only your word."

"You have it," the youth said and held out his hand to the

61

girl. With a brief glance at the chief of slaves, who gestured impatiently, she stepped forward and took his fingers with her own.

They went down the corridor and turned into the cubicle where he had strangled the Parthian. Here on the same bed where he had avenged his lost love, he would seek to regain his personal freedom. Men said that once you enjoyed a woman you were no longer caught by the fleshly chains of her body. It was a theory he meant to test.

When he took her breasts in his hands gently, he felt her quiver. He asked, "Are you virgin?" At her nod, he was pleased. Perhaps Ione could be Thea for him in more ways than one.

"To me, your name is Thea," he said softly, drawing her against him, kissing her soft, moist mouth. "Do you understand? Thea. No longer Ione."

"Thea," she whispered, and felt him lifting her tunic.

His palms were beneath the white cotton, caressing her thighs, the firm flesh of her buttocks. The girl trembled, not from fright but from a new sensation. Her skin was ripe with excitement, her very pores tingled in delight. Never had her breasts been so hard, her large nipples so stiff.

Deep in her throat, she moaned.

Swung into his arms, she was placed on the thick woolen blanket covering the rope springs of the bedstead. Frantically she twisted, lifting off the tunic over her head, baring herself to his stare. Then she was stretching out her hands to him, helping remove his cuirass by undoing its leather straps, raising it off, then kneeling before him to unfasten the caligulae that came almost to his knees. He removed his cotton subligaculum and stood naked before her.

"Come, Conon—come to your Thea."

With a hoarse cry that was mixed with a sob in his throat, he clasped her to him, rained kisses on her upturned face, her lips, her smooth warm shoulders. Her fingers were spread wide as she clung to him, holding herself against his nakedness, trembling violently in this wildfire of excitement. Her shoulders moved from side to side, her bared hips slipped this way and that in a steady rhythm.

She fell backward onto the cot, drawing him with her. She cried out once in pain, then many times in pleasure.

FOUR

The Stadium

1.

Berenice IV, who had so recently been queen in Egypt,
hung spreadeagled in chains inside a dungeon cell below the
arena sands of the great Heptastadium which crowned the
westerly slopes of Alexandria. She could neither sit nor kneel
without pain, for the manacles bit too tightly into the soft
flesh of her wrists to permit such freedom of movement. All
she could do was stand and listen to the screams of men
dying in agony.

Tears lay on her dusky cheeks. Her eyes were sunken in
horror. Arms widespread, held by massive chains bolted into
the walls on either side of her, she quivered and shook,
whimpered and made mewling sounds as those men who
had helped her palace revolution four years ago now paid the
penalty before all the world to see.

All except Achillas!

Sly dog that he was, Achillas stood high in favor with the
newly restored king. Yet it had been Achillas who first had
tempted her to play the role of rebel with his lies and
counsels. A swift coup in the night, a bold stroke, and she
would rule from the gold and ivory throne of the Ptolemies.
Such had been his advice. Now Berenice hated Achillas with
a deadly venom. First to rebel, first to play the fawning
traitor, he stood among the small group in the royal box
where Ptolemy Auletes watched men die in agony.

Berenice groaned as a great roar shook the walls about her,
drowning out the cries of a man being flayed alive with sharp
skinning knives until his body hung in taut ropes, a raw red
thing with nerves and tendons exposed to the hot Alexandrine sunlight. Could this be the death in store for her, alone
and friendless on the arena sands? With fifty thousand people
leaning forward on the stone benches, breathless and avid for

her suffering? She writhed and twisted, the chains clanking to her convulsive movements.

After a little while, she quieted.

At least, the deaths she had decreed had been painless. Quick stabs with klepesh or dagger or sword, to be rid of undesirables in her kingdom. At first, of course. Later with her husband Archelaus she had taken pleasure in seeing men tortured to death, here in this same stadium.

Ah, and what a different sensation it was, knowing she was to be among those who were to die today. What was it the gladiators said, aping the secutors of Rome? *Morituri te salutamus!* We who are about to die, salute you. Not for her, that motto. She hated her father, hated her sisters and her brothers almost as much as she hated Achillas.

They were clever in their cruelty. A hairdresser and a masseuse had attended her early in the morning, the ornatrix to coiffure her thick black hair and set it with the golden uraeus that now crowned her head, the other slave to massage her body into some semblance of its normal loveliness. She was beautiful, except for the fear and horror etched on her face. Never had she seemed so queenly, so attractive. It was a refinement of cruelty worthy of a Ptolemy. She wondered whose idea it had been to dress her so. Her father might have thought of it; more likely it was Cleopatra. It would please her younger sister to parade her before Alexandria in her queenly garments, then watch her killed.

Footsteps sounded in the outer corridor.

Ah, Isis! Not so soon. Not so soon.

Two Nubians in leopard aprons came into the room, unbolted her chains where they fastened to the wall and wrapping those big links around their hands, dragged her, sliding and slipping across the stone floor, out into the runway.

She tried to hold back but it was impossible. The manacles bit into her wrists, the chains were like arms themselves, holding her upright, so taut the Nubians held them. She was borne along suspended between those chains as if she were no more than a feather.

Up the ramp she was pulled and onto the arena sands.

The sunlight was hot, blinding.

The chains yanked her forward, stumbling.

The great stadium of Alexandria was built on a westerly slope of the hill that ran from Lake Mareotis northward to the city of Alexandria. It rose tier on stone tier in the form of a mighty oval whose outer facades were faced with Carrian

64

marble and ornamented at regular intervals with towering statues of the gods. Around it was a low portico and a continuous arcade of arches bisected by slim columns. Grass plats and rows of flowers, marble benches, fountains and sun-dials made a garden in which it was set like a precious stone.

The immense wealth of this city of many races was reflected in its arena. As famous in its way as the Circus Maximus in Rome, it attracted famous gladiators to its games. Here were staged races and battles to the death, simple duels and bloodlettings. Here came the flower of the Alexandrine nobility to be entertained and amused, to shout and roar its pleasure.

For once, the spectators in the Stadium were silent.

All eyes were turned toward the far end of the arena where a woman hung on chains between two giant Nubians. Men and women left their stone seats, crowded the narrow railings or stood on tiptoe, simply staring. This woman—so lovely, so beautiful, so regal in the golden uraeus on her head —had been their queen short days ago. Now she was marked for a degrading death.

Ptolemy Auletes was drunk. His head lolled against the high back of the alabaster cathedral which had been fashioned in imitation of his throne. His eyes stared over the white sands without blinking, thick lips downdrawn and heavy brows furrowed above his mottled cheeks.

Cleopatra wanted desperately to spring to her feet, to stare as did the others who had no dignity to maintain, at the sobbing, terrified woman being drawn through the sands toward the royal box. She could hear the low hum of conversation on all sides, however; to this she listened, trying to picture in her mind how her sister might look when brought to a stop below her.

At her elbow and a pace to the rear stood Conon, shield on his arm, hand on his swordhilt. She wondered if he was watching Berenice and had to bite her lip to keep from asking. Her hands were fists on her rigid thighs; for the first time she felt the weight of the golden pshent which rested so gracefully on her head. The thin linen of her tunic seemed suddenly intolerable. She wished she could be anywhere but here. Suppose she and not Berenice stood on those sands?

Before the coming of the legions, Berenice had been the most powerful person in Alexandria. Her whim was a royal command. Somewhere along the line, Berenice had made a mistake, a grievous mistake. What had it been? Cleopatra thought she knew. Berenice believed in her own infallibility.

So far from Rome, she had ignored it. Now she was paying for that mistake with her life.

I must never make that same mistake! Never!

The roaring of the crowd grew deafening.

Cleopatra dropped her eyes. Now she could see her sister between the chains sliding forward as the Nubians dragged her, her feet leaving tiny furrows in the sand. Her legs were stiff, her mouth open and her eyes wide in fright, in utter horror.

The Nubians stood still, looking upward. Berenice hung between them, unable to fall down. Ptolemy Auletes stirred and leaned forward.

"False daughter," he said heavily. "For setting yourself up against the father who has always loved you, you must die."

A tremor went through the girl on the sands. She lifted her head, looked upward. Her eyes went this way and that. After a moment, they grew fixed.

"I see a man behind you, father, who deserves death far more than I," she said clearly, deriving strength from her hatred. "I see Achillas. It was his tongue that whispered temptation into my ears, promises and lies. Yet he stands with you on the podium as an honored guest."

"Achillas tells a different story. Achillas came to us before the battle joined, bringing troops and Household guards to support our cause."

"Twice a traitor," she sobbed.

Cleopatra let her head turn very slightly. She was looking straight at Achillas now, and the man knew it. He was unchanged from that night—was it only three short years ago?—when he had carried her from the Lochias into the streets of Alexandria. She was older herself, fourteen and a woman as the East reckoned women.

She understood the hatred in Berenice. Ah, how she understood it! For hours she had argued with her father and with Aulus Gabinius, seeking to convince them that Achillas must die. Neither of them would listen to her. They agreed the man was a scoundrel and deserved death, none more so; but he was powerful and popular here in Alexandria and the time was not yet ripe when he could be killed without serious consequences from the fickle populace. Ptolemy Auletes was not so secure on his throne, even with the help of the Third Legion, that he could risk mob action against his rule. The corn shipments to Rome might be disturbed and Gabinius would not permit this possibility.

And so Achillas lived. Cleopatra glared at him and told

herself that she must wait, wait with patience. There would come a day—

The king was speaking. "Unnatural offspring of our loins, you have raised your hand against me, against your sisters, to gratify your insane ambitions. For this you must pay the supreme penalty."

His hand, set with half a dozen ruby and emerald rings, flashed in the sunlight. Two women sprang forward from below the overhang of the royal box, running toward Berenice. Their hands lifted off the uraeus and catching hold of the linen tunic, shredded it to her toes.

Berenice cried out against such violation. She stood naked, clad only in her jewels, the pectoral on her throat and bracelets on her wrists and upper arms, and her golden slippers. The uraeus still gleamed on her head. The crowd bellowed. It was a subtle refinement that their sophisticated minds enjoyed. Berenice, who had risked everything for the trappings of power, still wore them, yet she was no more than a common woman, an Eleusinian quarter harlot whose flesh was available for all to see.

The chains tightened, turning her, beginning to parade her around the oval arena. She screamed against this degradation but her scream was drowned out by the thunderous approval of the throng. Let all Alexandria see the nudity of this woman who had lorded it over them, let them see what only her husband and her lovers were accustomed to behold. As she threw back her head, the uraeus fell off, symbolically.

She could not cover herself. Her arms were stretched to the limit, almost pulled from their sockets by the taut chains. She had to walk along upright, for she could not fall down and if she drew up her knees the manacles bit into her wrists so tightly that she screamed from the pain.

Around the arena, slowly. Then back to the podium.

Now a wooden block was brought forward. Beside it walked a huge man with a great axe in his hands. Berenice turned her head and stared at its sharp, curving blade. A shudder ran down her back.

The block was set before the weeping girl. She was forced to her knees directly in front of the royal box. Her head was pushed onto the wooden block so that her long black hair, disarranged by her struggles, fell loose to the ground. She knelt naked and the shivers running down her body made her flesh ripple.

The axe lifted high. It poised.

67

The blade made a flash of color in the sun.
A head rolled on the bloody sands.

2.

Cleopatra unwrapped the scroll and read its painted words. It had been smuggled to her in the hold of a corn ship bringing pottery and leather goods from the Tiber to the shops of Alexandria. It bore the words of a priest of the Temple of Isis which stood in the Campus Martius, and it advised the princess Cleopatra of events which were taking place in Rome and in the world about it.

Julius Caesar and Pómpey the Great were quarreling again. Men said that even the Roman world was not big enough to hold them both; they were heading toward a showdown fight. The battle might come next year or ten years from now, but it was inevitable. Pompeius Magnus, who had begun his career as an officer under Sulla, was a vain man, cautious in all things—some said he was actually timid—but for a score of years, until the rise of Julius Caesar, he had been the most powerful man in Rome.

Fifteen years before, Pompey had overcome all resistance in the province of Spain, and returned to a military Triumph along the streets of Rome. When Spartacus and the slaves had rebelled it was Pompey who had brought his legions to fight beside his fellow Consul, rich Crassus, claiming equal credit for the victory. From rebellious slaves he turned his eagles against the pirates swarming over the Mediterranean. In a three month campaign, waged brilliantly and ruthlessly, he had broken their power.

Given command over the entire Mediterranean Sea and its coasts for fifty miles inland, he now moved his legions against Mithridates of Pontus in Asia Minor. For five years he lived in the East fighting pitched battles, conducting audiences with representatives of the many kingdoms which stretched from the islands of the Aegean Sea as far inland into continental Asia as Media and Parthia. He conquered Pontus and Armenia and planted the Roman eagles on the shore of the Euphrates river. He created cities where none had been before, brought down kingly dynasties in ruins, and established new reigning houses.

In his greatest Triumph, more than three hundred former kings walked in chains behind his chariot. The crown of emperor was offered him, but he spurned it even while secretly hoping that the people would brush aside his refusals and demand that he accept it.

While Pompey played at warlord, the star of Julius Caesar was rising even more spectacularly. A prisoner of Sulla at seventeen, his name was on a list of those proscribed either for political treachery or because their great wealth tempted the newly made Dictator and his followers. His life spared, Caesar acted as praetor while Pompey was conquering Asia Minor and Cappadocia. He became governor of Spain when Pompey came back in person to take over the reins of power.

Elected consul with Pompey and Crassus to form the first Triumvirate, he pushed many of the laws promulgated by Pompey through the Senate, not hesitating to use strongarm tactics when these seemed called for. Within a few years he was admittedly the most talked-of man in Rome. He used this fame as a stepping stone to secure the governorship of Cisalpine Gaul.

He conquered Gaul in eight years.

Cleopatra sighed and lifted her eyes from the painted words. A wind was blowing off the Eleusinian Sea. It rippled the skirt of her linen kalasiris about her knees and filled her lungs with fresh salt air.

"Caesar has renewed the triumvirate," she said to the tall, lean man who stood with hands clasped together before him, head bent a little sideways as if to catch even the sound of her breath. "He and Pompey and Crassus are still the powers in Rome."

The tall man with the grave face, which was old beyond its years, nodded slowly. "Power is a jealous goddess. She will not have three lovers at once."

A brief smile touched her lips. "One only. But—which one?"

"Only the gods can answer that," Appollodorus said.

Impatiently she shook her head. "The gods know nothing. But—I must. I must know which of them will come to rule. It is to him I will pay my money for his protection and his friendship." She turned back to the scroll.

"Imhotep goes on to say that rumors in Rome have Crassus dead in battle with the Parthians. There is nothing to confirm this, but if it's true, it would leave only Caesar and Pompey, Apollodorus. My choice narrows to them, it seems."

"Pompey is in his fifties, Caesar in his late forties."

She flashed a scornful glance at him. "I don't mean to take them for lovers—merely as friends. I have plenty of young slaves to please my body. It's my throne that worries me."

Apollodorus indicated the parchment. "What else does it

say? Anything which may give us a clue as to which way the wind will blow?"

She shook her head dispiritedly but lowered her glance. "Very little. Julia is dead. She was Caesar's daughter by Cornelia and Pompey's wife. She was a bond between them, I suppose. If she's dead and this rumor about Crassus is true —things will happen fast. I must be prepared for them."

Cleopatra rolled up the scroll and handed it to her counsellor as an indication that their audience was at an end. Apollodorus bowed low.

It was time for her to closet herself with the new slave, the young boy from Pontus who was tutoring her in his language. Gossip said that Cleopatra in turn was tutoring him in certain illicit pleasures, but there was no proof of this, while all the palace had heard her conversing with the boy when he served her wine at the palace banquets.

In Alexandria proper, the Third Gallica legion had been left behind by Aulus Gabinius to form a backbone for the throne where Ptolemy Auletes sat half the time in a drunken stupor. As time went on, its members married with the women of the Rhakotis and the Jewish quarters. Some of them even set up shops. But they paraded weekly along the Street of Canopus, usually under the eye of Ptolemy himself, as a constant reminder to his people that where the Fluteplayer stood, there also stood the eagles.

Cleopatra took her place beside him on these occasions in a chariot of ivory and ebony, all black and white, with Conon in his silver armor at her elbow. She wanted the people to see Conon, to recognize him as a familiar, so that when he spoke it would be known that he carried commands she herself had issued.

Rabirius Porthumus, who had financed his return to power, was made his Minister of Finance by Ptolemy Auletes. All taxes were collected by this Roman official with the help of the legionaries based in Alexandria. Rabirius also held the purse strings for such men as Caesar and Pompey. As a result, he found himself particularly popular with young Cleopatra who often invited him to sip wine and eat honey cakes in her apartments.

Since she always wore transparent garments under which her ivory body was no mystery, Rabirius found himself answering her questions about his two most famous clients in something of a bemused state. Never once did he sense the wit and wisdom behind those searching inquiries. He considered her a lovely thing, somewhat shameless and libidinous as were all Ptolemaic women, but completely mindless. He answered absentmindedly, believing her babble to be harmless and amusing, being more taken with the curvature of her haunches and the size of her breasts than with her words.

Cleopatra indulged his eyes. She would pull up her tunic to inspect a shapely leg almost to the curve of her buttock while he would stare and lick his thick lips wth a heavy tongue. The leg would be turned this way and that before him, freely and without shame or reticence.

"Is it completely hairless, are you sure? I'm testing a new depilatory, you know. I'm told Caesar is bald. Is he? It doesn't interfere with his military brains, though, does it? Is he as good as or a better general than Pompey? Better? Why?"

She pretended to be taken with the hairlessness of her armpits—casually exposing the slope of a breast as she lifted her arm while holding a mirror to it—but she listened while he explained about the conquest of Gaul and—more recently —Caesar's invasion of an island called Britain.

Rabirius told her that Pompey was in line to be made sole consul in Rome, now that Crassus was dead, but he didn't believe Caesar would stand for that, Senate or no Senate. Caesar with his legions would cross the Rubicon and force civil war on Rome if he had to. Caesar was too ambitious to be second man in his world.

"And between them? Which would you choose?"

She was standing before a large window open to the Eleusinian Sea and the sunlight streaming through it made a nothingness of her gauze garment. Rabirius Porthumus drew a deep breath. It seemed that she was nude in silver sandals before him. She turned a little so that he could stare his fill in comfort, away from her calm hazel eyes.

"Hmmm?" she wondered.

"Eh? What? Oh! Caesar and Pompey, yes. I have a financial stake in both of them. I'm no prophet, mind—but I would never bet against Caesar. The man is far too clever for poor Pompey. Talk as you will about legions and generalship, it all comes down to the mind of a man. And where it comes to brains, there simply isn't any contest."

"Tell me about this Julius Caesar. Is he married?"

Rabirius Porthumus talked until his tongue wearied, though his eyes did not. Cleopatra even invited him into the great hypocaust while she swam naked in the pool and let herself be massaged by slave-girls.

71

"I know you won't go blabbing about it," she teased him, wrinkling her nose. "You're a sensible man."

The Roman banker kept his luck to himself, for he wanted no news of what he did with Cleopatra to reach his wife. He contented himself with establishing a small household on the outskirts of the Eleusinian quarter and filling it with pretty slavegirls with whom he could do the things he could not do with the princess of Egypt. But he looked all he wanted and his tongue kept merry accompaniment to his rolling eyeballs.

3.

The following spring an Alexandrine mob rose up in protest against the high taxes by which Rabirius Porthumus sought to recoup the fortune he had spent to put Auletes back on the throne. The rebellion was put down by the legion, but it left a bad after effect.

Rabirius was unpopular in Alexandria.

Cleopatra said to him, "Why not go back to Rome? Leave your affairs in my hands? I'm your friend. You know that."

The Roman realized he could not stay on in Alexandria. Sight of him always roused the mob to boos and catcalls. As easily excitable as a newly captured panther, these Alexandrines might not stop at vocal assaults, one day; Rabirius shuddered. Cleopatra was right. The city had become dangerous.

And yet to leave this Ptolemaic princess as his proxy was unthinkable. His scratched signature commanded many thousands of talents; he was one of Rome's richest men, he had a fortune tied up in Egyptian corn, in hides from Germania and Grecian marble. To give Cleopatra access to those riches might beggar him.

The girl was smiling as if in sympathy with his dilemma. He had no friends in this Egyptian city, no one to whom he could turn, no one he could trust. Of them all, this little witchwoman was the most intimate with him.

"You will want security, naturally," she dimpled.

He stared at her, nonplussed. What could she offer as security? Her father was Pharaoh only because of Rabirius' money; she was a penniless heiress to his throne. Her laughter was soft, disturbing, as if she could read his mind. Cleopatra turned from an ivory statuette she had been fondling and moved toward him. She raised her arms and put them around his neck.

Under her thin linen tunic she was naked. He could feel the

72

warmth of her belly, the firmness of her thighs. "I shall give you a memory, Rabirius Porthumus. A memory of a day and a night which you shall never forget. This shall be our guarantee that I am your friend, your partner in business."

When he would have spoken, she placed her fingers across his lips. They were scented and their touch made his flesh grow feverish. Between her thumb and forefinger she pressed the corners of his mouth, parting his lips. As his head came down, she moved her mouth on those open lips; he felt the touch of her tongue. Energy ran in him. He was no longer a middle-aged man but a youth.

There was an electricity, a force, in Cleopatra Thea Philopater that enthralled any man who came within touching distance of her. Even while his arms went about her slim middle, while he savored the pressure of her loins to his own, he thought that all his fortune was as nothing to this magical moment. For months he had been forced merely to look at this body he now held. Today and this night—all night long —he would indulge himself with it, to satiation and exhaustion.

Money was dull, dead gold.

Cleopatra was the wine of Venus.

An hour after dawn, Conon was in the royal apartment.

Cleopatra was sitting on a curule chair, legs crossed, wrapped in a thick woolen robe. There were dark rings under her eyes and her lips were swollen as if she had gorged on kisses and sterile caresses. She held a scroll in her hands that she kept tapping against her knuckles. Her eyes glanced at him sharply as he came to a stop and saluted.

"This is an authority given me by Rabirius Porthumus. Under my signature I can command any act that will work to the safety of his monies here in Alexandria."

Conon waited. She drew a deep breath. "He leaves on the noonday tide for Rome. When his ship is hulldown on the horizon, I want you to go to his bank, seize his gold bars and jewels, his coin coffers. You will take them secretly to a hiding place only you shall know, and bury them."

"If I am seen? Followed?"

"What would you advise?"

"I can't take soldiers with me. They'd draw too much attention. I still have many friends among the gladiators, however. I think a bodyguard of fifty should do the trick. I'll hide their armor on the packasses, the same ones that will carry the gold. We will throw off pursuit—or kill it."

She nodded, smiling faintly.

73

"You understand I merely guard against emergencies, Conon? I want no undisciplined mob getting its bad hands on all that wealth."

"I understand, princess."

She said musingly, "I have been so long dependent on Rome—I would like for once to make Rome dependent on me."

4.

The world moved while Conon was away from Alexandria.

Ptolemy Auletes died in a drunken sleep, cradled in the plump arms of his Phrygian mistress. A maidservant ran to tell Cleopatra the news. For once she was caught by surprise. Conon was away so that she had no one who could carry out the orders that seethed in her mind. The Household Troops would obey Conon. They would not obey her, not while Achillas was still in the Palace.

And Achillas had become friendly with her brother, Ptolemy.

They came together into her apartment, Achillas with his scabbard clanking against the lappets of his silvered cuirass, big and heavyset like some tame white bear, the slender Ptolemy still with the marks of his last night's debauch on his young face.

"Greetings, queen of Egypt," he called out.

Cleopatra glared at him but she moved her hand to dismiss her servants. Summoning what dignity she could, and confident that her inner turmoil must reflect itself in her features, she crossed to her ebony and ivory curule chair.

"Greetings, brother," she replied when she was seated.

"Egypt belongs to us both," Ptolemy stated. "We shall be married and rule as the Pharaohs ruled a thousand years ago."

She knew well enough that it was the custom of the ancient rulers of her land to wed with one another, brother and sister, and so to perpetuate the royal family. In those years Egypt had been alone in its might; there were no other sovereigns considered fit to wear the royal uraeus. Her lips curved tightly. These were different days, she thought grimly.

She inclined her head, thinking furiously. No need to upset Ptolemy or Achillas now. In a way, she was glad she was being offered part of the throne; the memory of the night when Berenice had seized power was still strong in her mind. By sheer will power she made herself smile in a friendly manner.

74

"It will be a pleasure to wed with my brother Ptolemy."
*Liar! Liar! He is a scrawny little chicken! Mean and petty
and vicious!* "It will be an honor to rule Egypt by his side." *If
he thinks I mean to bed with him, the more fool, he!* "I leave
everything to you, to prepare the wedding, to arrange the
details."

Pleased surprise registered in her brother's face. Obviously,
he had anticipated difficulty. Achillas scowled honestly, instantly suspicious. He was the cleverer of the two, and would
bear the closest watching. She did not trust Achillas.

She rose and permitted Ptolemy to kiss her cheek.

Over his shoulder, she watched the general. He was biting
his lip and looking vexed. Cleopatra felt the urge to laugh. At
least she was keeping them off balance, which was the best
she could do with Conon off somewhere with the treasure of
Rabirius Porthumus.

The world beyond Egypt was in upheaval, too.

The growing bitterness between Julius Caesar and Gnaeus
Pompeius was aggravated by the overwhelming defeat of Pompey and his seven legions in Parthia. Nobody loves a loser,
least of all the Roman people. Caesar became more popular
than ever. Informants told Cleopatra that these two men
were moving fast toward a final showdown.

Cleopatra had her own troubles.

Wedded to her brother, she found she had to contend not
only with the boy but also with his three guardians. Achillas
was the one she feared most, for he commanded the Egyptian
armies. The eunuch Pothinus was placed in charge of the
Royal Treasure. The savant Theodotus, who tutored young
Ptolemy, was a sly man with a devious, unprincipled code
of conduct, whose advice always looked one way and struck
another.

Slowly, Cleopatra discovered that power was being taken
from her hands. Though she sat beside her brother, it was his
voice that condemned men to die, his hand that waved them
to life, his the signature which was of paramount importance
on any state document.

Conon had come home from the rocky wastes of Arabea
Petraea, where he had hidden the treasure of Rabirius in a
pit covered with broken boulders and stone rubble. The slaves
who had performed the service Conon himself had slain, lest
they be tortured to make them speak of its hiding place. The
gladiators he had left at Memphis.

"At least we're rich," she told Conon while complaining to
him of her brother and his three advisers.

He offered to kill Ptolemy but she shook her head. "It would solve nothing. Achillas would turn to Rome, holding me captive, offering Egypt as a Roman province with himself as governor."

There were times in the months that followed, when she almost wished she had let Conon commit murder for her, because inexorably, Pothinus and Achillas were drawing a noose about her throat. Little by little she became merely the shadow of a queen, her words melodious but meaningless, her presence only ornamental.

The priests of Egypt alone were her supporters. When the white bull Buchis—holy sanctuary of the sun-god Amen-Ra —breathed its last at Hermonthis, it was Cleopatra who carried its successor in the royal barge from Thebes to the temple at Hermonthis. It was she who performed the rites so perfectly that there was mention made of it in the sacred scrolls. She gave what she could to the priests, supporting them in all matters; and perhaps because Achillas scorned the priesthood, and as a sop to her queenship, he permitted her these small favors.

The end came on a warm June night when her brother, now fifteen, presented himself to Cleopatra in her bedchamber. As her husband, he had come at last to claim his marital rights.

Because of the sultry night, which the salt air from the Mediterranean Sea could not dispel, Cleopatra slept naked on her bed. The fitful breezes off the water dried the perspiration on her hot, flushed body. At first she thought his hand only another zephyr.

When she opened her eyes, she found his lips pressed to her breast. In revulsion, she doubled up her legs and kicked out at him, driving him onto his rump on the floor tiles. He landed and sprawled there, staring up at her.

"You pig," she snarled. "Get out of here!"

"Not until we lie together as man and wife should."

Her scornful laughter scratched his pride. "Lie with you? Rather with an ape out of the African jungles." She saw Charmion watching from the shadows of a pillar and made that secret signal which would cause her to fetch Conon.

Young Ptolemy bit his lip in vexation. He remembered the words by which both Pothinus and Theodotus had told him how to behave toward this sister of his. He was king in Egypt. She was his queen. She owed him not only the duty of bearing his children but the added obligation of comforting his flesh.

When he stuttered something of this to her, Cleopatra

76

threw an incense bowl at him. It caught him on the temple, breaking the skin and making it bleed. She did not bother to draw anything around her nudity. It may have been sheer perversity that made her want him to see the body he could never possess.

While he held a cloth to his cut head, he reviled her with words. "Any slave who catches your fancy, you take to your mattress. I'm surprised I didn't find someone here with you tonight. Slaves. Roman soldiers who are big and handsome enough to please you. Egptians. Nubians. Cilicians. Syrians. They parade in here as though this were a room in a Rhakotian brothel."

"Anyone but you, brother mine. Anyone!"

"By Isis! It shall be as you say!" His fist beat up and down on the floor of the bedchamber. "It shall be anyone. Anyone at all! Sailors just off their ships. Camel drivers. Condemned criminals. I'll set up a room where I can watch you being—"

A hand caught him by the neck, lifted him upward. He was held with his feet an inch from the floor as a cat might grip a mouse. Like that he was shaken back and forth.

"You're speaking to the queen of Egypt," Conon rasped.

The boy opened his lips, gagging. His eyes protruded from a red face. He waved his arms and kicked, but he was helpless in that iron hand. Conon looked at Cleopatra who put her fingers over her lips to smother laughter. At her gesture, he loosed his fingers. Ptolemy fell to the floor and sobbed.

When the boy-king had his breath, he said, "You'll pay for this, the two of you. I'll have you chained to a spit and roasted alive, you—you animal! And as for you, dear sister—"

He told her in vivid detail what she would be forced to do with the human dregs he would bring to service her in the quarters which would be both her prison and a royal brothel. Until his lips foamed with spittle he talked while Conon and Cleopatra stared at one another over his head, sober and alarmed. When he was done, and lay there weeping softly with shame and frustration, Conon bent and yanked him to his feet.

His arms he forced behind him; when Ptolemy protested, he clapped a big, callus-palmed hand over his mouth. In his ear, Conon hissed, "If you want to stay alive, silence your tongue!" His thumb and a forefinger caught the boy's nose and pinched it shut. The thin body began to flop back and forth, denied air for its lungs.

"Will you be quiet?" Conon rasped.

The boy nodded. He stood shaking, quivering, as the Guards

prefect tied his wrists with a leather thong. After a time he asked what they intended doing with him.

Cleopatra said pleasantly, "I ought to let Conon run a dagger between your ribs. However, you're more valuable to me alive. You will come with us, brother dear, as far as Pelusium. Then we will release you."

"You won't," the boy shrilled. "You'll kill me."

"I'll kill you if you make trouble before then," Conon stated grimly. Staring into his hard face, young Ptolemy whimpered, seeing his death in those terrible eyes. He began to weep again, almost to himself.

They went in two chariots by way of the Sun Gate. Conon handled the reins of one, with Ptolemy crouched at his feet, Cleopatra the other, with Iras and Charmion wrapped in woolen stolas against recognition. They drove swiftly, displaying the royal seal—which Conon had twisted off Ptolemy's finger—when they had to pass a gate inspection.

Ten miles from the city, Conon lifted the trembling Ptolemy and dropped him in the dust behind his chariot. They left him sobbing there, clawing at the dirt with his fingers in a frenzy of despairing fury. They left him his throne but not his honor; they took with them their freedom and the bitter knowledge that once again Cleopatra was fleeing for her life.

FIVE

The Harbor of the Happy Return, 48 B. C.

1.

The hot wind of the Levant fanned her moist temples as Cleopatra stared seaward. She was standing on tiptoe, straining her eyes to watch the big Roman trireme which was easing slowly shoreward from the open water. Her arms were rigid by her sides, her hands clenched into fists.

"I don't like it," Conon growled.

"I have no other choice. You know that."

The city of Pelusium was to their right, Alexandria to their left. They stood on a stretch of rocky beach facing northward. Behind them were a score of armed horsemen, an escort detail with which they had ridden fast since sunup to reach the shores of the Mare Internum. Far behind them was the little army that Cleopatra had managed, by drawing on the Nile cities, to surround herself with as a bulwark against the military forces of her brother.

"You may be recognized and captured," Conon went on. "You know what will happen if you are."

"Ptolemy will do what he promised to me."

"Not if my sword can—"

Her hand touched his wrist. "I must follow my destiny, Conon. It draws me back to Alexandria. I was rotting in our camp by the Red Sea."

"At least you were alive. And safe."

She threw back her head so that the samiel wind blew her black hair like a flying veil behind her. She breathed deeply, lifting her breasts upward into the thin robe she wore. "Life? Safety? A vegetable has these, Conon. Something in me demands more than that." She pressed her hand between her jutting breasts. "A fever beats in me. A fever for power, for the knowledge that I am of some importance to the world."

He grunted. To Conon it was enough that he had Cleopatra at his side, that her safety depended on him and the little army he commanded; he could not fathom the driving need to sit a throne which infected this woman he loved.

As though she understood the turmoil in him, she moved closer and let her head rest against his deep chest. "Poor faithful Conon. Am I such an enigma to you? Can't you understand what the news of Caesar's victory over Pompey can mean to me?"

Word of the battle of Pharsalus had come to their encampment on the edge of the Red Sea four days ago. Roman fought with Roman, Julius Caesar against Gnaeus Pompeius, the legions against one another. Pompey had gone down to bloody defeat, and had fled in a trireme to seek asylum in Egypt with his wife, Cornelia.

Cleopatra had been electrified. This was the opportunity for which she waited! Not for her the dusty sands and the salt waters of the Red Sea, the small tents and rock-ringed cooking fires. She hungered to pace the marble halls of the Lochias Palace, to sit at table and devour the honeyed tongues of flamingoes, the brains of peacocks, charfish livers, the thousand and one delectable dishes invented by the Court cooks.

Where the gods fought, men might sip of ambrosia.

To Cleopatra and her world, Romans were as gods. Their legions were unbeatable, their citizens sophisticated, their laws famous. Rome was a city where all the world came to marvel. It was filled with masterpieces in marble—looted, it is true, from Greece, but nevertheless used now to decorate the city on the Tiber—and the chests of its bankers and rich Senators were heavy with raw red gold.

All she needed in the world was coming to her grasp. Pompey! Caesar! Yet questions burned in her mind. Had the defeat of Pompey been as bad as rumor said? Or was his retreat from Greece merely a strategic withdrawal? If she cast her lot for Caesar, would Pompey triumph in the end? And what would Julius Caesar—if he were to emerge ruler of the world—want with a dethroned queen? Her mind went around and around as fatigue and uncertainty added to her dizziness.

Conon held her with an arm that was heavy with muscle. His body yearned for her, yet always she denied herself to him; not because she did not love him, for she did. Sometimes she tried to imagine what life with him as her husband might be like. She would be happy, she understood that; but something inside her demanded more than happiness from life.

He said, "Even if this Caesar proves to be the conqueror gossip says he is, what good will it do you?"

"I don't know, I don't know. He's an old man—well, he's fifty years old, anyhow—and he's used to all the best things in life. He may laugh in my face when I go to him and ask his help."

"No man could laugh at you," he growled.

She rubbed her hip against him, giggling softly. "You're prejudiced, Conon. Caesar's had two wives. And innumerable mistresses. Even young boys, I've heard my father say. He's probably jaded and bored."

"Then make him come alive."

She considered that, leaning her weight on him, clinging to his hairy forearm where it banded her waist. Give Caesar a new zest for life. Teach him what Cleopatra Thea Philopater might mean to him. Ahhh, this was easily said. It was the accomplishment that would be difficult.

The sound of a cymbal came to them across the water. The trireme was swinging about, ready to drop anchor. The scrape of anchor chains running through a capstan came clearly to their ears. At the same time they saw half a dozen chariots racing across the stone quay to the edge of the water.

Cleopatra pushed away from Conon.

"Achillas," she breathed. "And Pothinus. They've come to meet Pompey. Isis! Have I guessed wrong? Can Caesar's victory be so final if Ptolemy and Achillas are willing to give sanctuary to Pompey?"

Risking discovery, she moved across the rocks to a stair leading upward to the quay. Conon rasped curses and flung a corner of her robe over her head. The touch of his hand recalled her to her senses. She draped the hood about her face folding it so that only her eyes were seen. Conon beside her was swathed as effectively in his military cloak.

Side by side they moved along the quay wall until there was only water ahead of them. With this uninterrupted view of the harbor they saw that a boat was being lowered from the trireme, that a man in a white toga was being helped down a rope ladder and into the longboat.

"Pompey," she whispered and stared, knowing disappointment. He looked fat and heavy, his shoulders rounded as though despair worked in his middle. No conqueror, this one, she understood intuitively from a single glance at him. What then were Achillas and Pothinus doing here to meet him? Surely their spies must have reported his defeat?

The boat came across the water like a beetle with oars for legs. Pompey sat in the stern, elbows on his knees, his head hanging just a little, not heeding where he went or the direction from which he came. Cleopatra wondered at the thoughts that roiled in his head, and felt a touch of pity for him.

Her eyes went to the quay, where stone steps sloped down into the harbor waters. Achillas was standing on one of those treads, watching the boat come closer. The knot of men around the chariots were staring coldly; Cleopatra became aware of tenseness in the air.

The oars lifted and dipped, rose and fell.

The longboat bumped a submerged step. Pompey who had risen to his feet, swayed as he lost his balance. Achillas stepped closer, reached out a hand to catch hold of him. He held him carefully, assisted him to step onto the stone tread beside him. The boat veered off, moved back toward the ship.

Cleopatra cried out.

Sunlight flashed on a dagger in Achillas' hand. The long blade drove down at the unprotected back of Pompey who was in the act of turning to ascend the wharf stair. The blade sank deep.

Pompey stiffened and cried out hoarsely. As if his voice were a command, men leaped from the waiting chariots, knives in their fists. They ran down the steps and plunged them into Pompey's chest and belly. The Roman stiffened. His arms came up as if to ward them off, to do battle as he had fought all his life.

A woman screamed across the waters. "Cornelia," whispered Cleopatra, pushing Conon ahead of her as she turned to run. "His wife. Hurry, hurry. We mustn't be seen to be spectators of the murder. Observe how empty the rest of the quay is. Run, Conon."

They raced for their horses.

Behind them Pompey was slipping downward into the reddened waters, blood streaming from his chest and belly, from back and neck. He was dead before the waters closed around him, bearing up his body as if for all the world to see that Great Pompey was no more. He lay facedown in the harbor and the waves lapped at him, bumping him back and forth against the stone steps.

2.

"Achillas is a fool!"

Cleopatra sat at a tavern table with Conon and Appolodorus, her adviser. She spoke softly, but her voice carried a strong conviction. Appolodorus looked about nervously but the sailors who frequented this dockside inn were too busy with their hired harlots to notice anyone else. They might as well have been in the middle of the Nubian desert for all the attention paid them.

"I mind two years ago when the Roman soldiers left behind in Alexandria by Aulus Gabinius staged a series of riots. You remember, Conon. I sent word to the Syrian proconsul who ordered his two sons to take command and bring them back to Syria. The Romans murdered them both.

"I arrested the leaders of the assassination group and shipped them to Gabinius to do what he willed with them. And what did he do?"

"He freed them," nodded Conon.

"And returned them to me, saying that no Egyptian had the right to arrest Romans. These men had murdered his sons. I ask you, how much self-control can a man have?" She drew a deep breath. "What do you think Julius Caesar will say about Achillas, who did more than arrest a Roman, who killed one of their great men?"

"A man who was the enemy of Caesar," reminded Appolodorus.

"Is Caesar less a Roman than Gabinius?"

It was a question that troubled all three of them, for on it might depend their fate. Cleopatra turned her winecup slowly between her hands. Conon gripped his cup so powerfully it bent in his fingers. Appolodorus finished the Taenotic wine in his mug and filled it from a nearby pitcher.

All Alexandria was astir with the news.

Julius Caesar, the man who had smashed Pompey on the plain of Pharsalus, was in the Lochias Palace. His heavily armed legionaries paced the wallwalks that looked out over the Eleusinian Sea, or marched in maniples of ten across the Brucheion, the steady tramp of their sandaled feet echoing in the wind. Rome was in Egypt, Rome with her military might, with her warships, with her greatest man to guide her destinies.

Ptolemy was as quiet as a mouse that cowers in a corner as the cat hunts it. Achillas and the others, the eunuch and the tutor, shivered in his shadow. Which way would Caesar jump? No man knew and every guess was no more than the dust blowing across the cobblestones of the Via Serapia. His ships swung at anchor in the great harbor and his men made camp near the Grove of Nemesis outside the city gates. His was the power, his the authority.

One word from Caesar and blood would run in Alexandria.

Night lay across the flat rooftops and the stars were a blanket of distant campfires high above their heads as a small galley holding Cleopatra, Conon and Appolodorus came past the stone quay that jutted from the great mole. Its oars made only muffled sounds as they lifted and fell to the cadence of Conon's chanted words. The waters of the harbor ran in little gurgles under the sharp prow.

Cleopatra clasped her arms and shivered. She wore a thin cloak over her nakedness, and her eyes turned often to the long, thick roll which was placed lengthwise of the boat and wedged between Appolodorus's feet. Was she being a fool? To come like a temple harlot to Julius Caesar like this, without clothes and lacking adornment, in the early hours of the Alexandrine night? Twice her tongue moistened her lips to say the words that would send them veering about and back the way they had come. Caesar would laugh at her. He would summon her brother and Achillas and throw her at their feet, naked and defenceless.

Isis! Anything but that! She could stand up to torture but not to the shame of being handed over to Ptolemy to do as he would with her. Her white teeth bit hard on her lips, making them swell from the pain.

Her hand stretched out, then was jerked back. No! By all the gods, no! She had made her decision after long thought, and she must hold true to it. These last few moments of doubt must be put aside, buried under the cold reasoning which had induced her to make this move.

The prow bumped the quay. Conon stood up and stepped forward lightly, lifting the heavy carpet, carrying it to the wharf. Here he unrolled it, let it run its length on the cold stone.

Cleopatra put her hand up to Appolodorus, allowed him to assist her from the thwart where she had been sitting to the moldboard, then onto the dock. One glance told her the Roman watch had made its rounds and would not be back for an hour.

The robe slipped to her ankles. Naked she stood in the pale moonlight, all silvered flesh and slim elegance, proud and regal in her unclad beauty. What need have I for gauds? she thought. Daintily she stepped forward and lay down on the rug.

Conon and Appolodorus rolled up the carpet, encasing Cleopatra in its length. She could breathe quite easily, she assured Conon when he worried. Appolodorus told him the carpet with Cleopatra in it did not make too heavy a burden for his muscles.

"If harm befalls you, Caesar dies!"

Dear faithful Conon, she thought as Appolodorus set off along the quay to a door leading to the palace proper. *Always my safety is uppermost in his mind. Without him I would be nothing. He is my strength, the strong hands I would have possessed had I been born a man.* In an instant of understanding she realized why she would never admit him to her bedchamber; it would be like wasting her own strength. *The little slaves he enjoys*—her lips curled wistfully—*and who look so much like me, do no more than draw the tensions from his muscles.* Only with Cleopatra would he grow weak, unsure of himself.

The steady sway of the carpet as Appolodorus walked with it made her faintly drowsy, letting her remember that other night so long ago when her beast of burden had been Achillas. Life has a way of being repetitious, she decided. It was warm inside the rolled carpet and her skin began to perspire.

Oh, mother goddess of the Nile! Don't let me go to him rumpled and wet, with my hair at loose ends and sweat running off my nose. She tried to wriggle, to tell Appolodorus to stop. This was a mistake! She ought to have gone to Caesar as a queen outraged by the betrayal of her brother and his cronies, in jewels and silken garments, with her flesh perfumed and her hair coiled high and piled with pearl ropes. Not like this, naked, unadorned. Queen? Say rather, stupid streetwalker!

She began to jiggle. Appolodorus was running. Her ears caught the movement of pacing feet, the grounding of a lance-butt. Appolodorus paused.

She heard a latch click as he opened a door.

A guard shouted, came running. More voices echoed the alarm.

Appolodorus cried, "A gift, noble Caesar! A gift for the greatest man in the world!"

"Let be, let be," a deep voice said.

Cleopatra visualized the Roman guards standing with their pilums raised to hurl at her, and shivered. If one of them should penetrate the rug, ah! There would be an end of everything! She felt herself lifted, the rug turned around.

She was being dropped slowly as the rug unfolded. Light came to her eyes as a blurring movement of color. She went out of the rug still rolling—Isis, let my rise be dignified!—and then she was tumbling as might a trained circus performer, rolling to her feet and standing with her chin up and her arms at her side.

She stared down at a tall, thin man with great, dark eyes blazing in a sunburned face. A bald man, with greying hair at the temples and the top of his head. His cheeks were faintly sunken and his neck was corded. He looked older than her father who had been a fleshy man and not one to wrinkle easily, but there was something about him—an air, an attitude —that gleamed up at her from the marvelous eyes, where amusement swam and the dawning of something akin to worship.

Cleopatra could not know that she was damp with sweat and flushed, that her black hair had come loose during her ride and hung down in ringlets about her dusky shoulders. Her lips where she had bitten them were swollen, but seemed to pout with elfin charm, and the mounds of her breasts from being too long crushed by the carpeting, thrust outward. Her legs were slim but ripely curved and her little globe of belly was a promise of her womanhood.

Caesar had been writing on a wax tablet with a stylus. The stylus stood suspended above the ivory leaves while he looked his fill of this nude Venus risen from the carpeting as might Aurora from the sea. He knew her instantly; he had seen too many coins with her profile stamped on them to be mistaken. But the reality was so different from the graven image.

She looked not so much a queen as she did a woman. Alive. Throbbing. Filled with a vitality that matched the loveliness of her face and figure. Had she come before him as the cold silver statue she planned, with not a hair out of place, with not so much as a spot of color to her cheeks, she would have been no more than one of a thousand statues he had admired on the Palatine Hill, where stood the Temple of Ceres. Ah, but this way!

She was a woman, not royalty. And as a woman, she won his heart. The stylus in his hand flashed where it caught the light when he gestured. The Roman centurian gave a short nod and barked a command. Appolodorus drew a deep breath, understanding instinctively that Caesar had no desire for onlookers. He bowed and went out into the hall with the Romans.

The door closed softly. The latch clicked.

"I bring you Egypt, royal Caesar!" Cleopatra breathed.

The bushy eyebrows quirked. "Royal?"

She dimpled a smile. "A man such as you needs no crown or Etruscan gold wreath on his head to proclaim what he is."

He leaned back so the round of the chair could support him. "Are you brilliant as well as beautiful?".

"As you are clever as well as conquering."

His palm slapped the desktop as he chuckled. "Well said. Ah, but Rome sits while Egypt stands. It isn't fitting." He rose to his feet, walked around the desk and came to stand before her. "Egypt is a sister nation. A companion to Rome. I shall hope in time to come—a beloved companion."

There was a magnetism about the man, Cleopatra admitted as she lifted her hands and cupped them at his jaw. She had male slaves who were far handsomer, years younger, and more heavily muscled than this aging general, but they lacked this awesome inner force, an energy which shone from his dark eyes like a blinding ray of sunlight. If she closed her eyes to his outer form, if she permitted only that force to get through to her—

The touch of hands underneath her breasts made her shiver. That same power was in his fingers. She had heard priests of Isis argue that the same force that was in the lightning was also in human bodies, to a lesser degree. If this were so, then Caesar had it in a greater quantity than any other man. It burned through his flesh to her own, made her understand that never had she bedded with a man like Caius Julius Caesar.

Her breasts were large but he held them easily as he brushed his thumbs back and forth over the rigidly standing nipples. His head bent while his lips kissed. To her surprise, she saw that he was trembling. From old age? From weakness? Now he was kneeling, clinging to her thighs, her buttocks while his mouth moved here and there on her flesh.

"You are no woman, no queen," he whispered.

"What am I, Rome?"

"A goddess. Astarte. Aphrodite. Venus. Isis."

"I am your goddess, Caesar."

His caresses made her ripple with hunger for his love. She stood on quaking legs, head thrown back so that her long black hair, now completely disarranged, brushed her quivering buttocks. Never had she been so filled with the sweet liquors of passion. They seemed to flow in her very veins, flooding to overflowing. A moan was forming in her throat. She tried to fight it but her lips parted and it welled free, low and desperate, the keening of a woman for her mate.

Against her skin she felt his lips smile.

Happy laughter trickled from her lips. "So! You tease your goddess, do you? Knowingly! To excite her. But what about you, my darling?" As she babbled softly her hands touched

87

him, threw back his toga, tore off the thin garment he wore beneath it.

He was not so old. Gods, no! For all the leching he had done, he was almost like a young man. His face was wrinkled but his body was smooth, almost hairless. And he was so obviously enjoying the attention she was paying him.

She came against him, moving gently. His arms were tight about her, holding her so close that she felt she must be branding him with her nipples, her shaven loins. His kisses roamed her soft throat, her shoulders, crushed her swollen lips.

He lifted her, carrying her as though she weighed no more than a feather to a cot that had been set up for him in an alcove overlooking the harbor waters. A cooling breeze was blowing from the sea, as if to calm their fevered bodies. They felt it only as an added caress as they tumbled across the bed.

Their bodies moved together as one. The moan in her throat erupted into a scream of pleasure minutes later as the maelstrom of their desire seized and caught them both, whirling them higher and higher, in a spate of sensation where consciousness faded and only emotion remained.

A fist pounded the latched door. A voice screamed shrill commands. The voice was drowned out by a deeper voice that snapped orders as if accustomed to instant obedience. The shrill voice was borne away, receding along the corridor seemingly blown by a high wind.

Cleopatra lifted her head from the hairless chest of her lover. "My brother. He fancies himself being disgraced."

"Your brother? Oh, Ptolemy." Caesar was silent as he stroked the smooth back of this young woman who was like no other woman in his life. Her long black hair was scented and heavy as it trickled across his shoulders when she raised herself on her hands to look down into his face.

"Ptolemy—who sits the throne of Egypt," she whispered.

"Ptolemy the pretender, you mean to say," he answered.

She laughed and bent to his lips, kissing them softly. Her hands slid down his chest, caressingly, to his hips and beyond. Against his mouth she murmured, "If you rule in Rome and I rule in Egypt and we unite as—as now we are uniting—then —ah, gods! The world belongs to us. To us alone."

"To us," Caesar agreed and shuddered in his pleasure.

3.

Ptolemy Philopater was weeping.

He lay across an ebony couch and sought to muffle his screams in the heavy brocade pillows with which it was covered. From time to time his clenched fist hammered at his hip.

"She was sitting right beside him, smiling at me as though she pitied me. Me, the Ptolemy! I reign in Alexandria, which is to say in Egypt. Don't I? Don't I?"

"You do, lord," agreed the eunuch Pothinus.

"Then how can he flaunt this woman in my face? This wife of mine he takes to bed with him in adultery? He insults me by being with her so much. Cleopatra! Cleopatra! Oh, how I hate her!"

Pothinus was worried. He and Achillas and Theodotus leaned on a weak reed in this son of the Fluteplayer. For all his vices, Ptolemy Auletes had been a man, no milksop like this sobbing, shuddering thing on the couch. He had gone to Rome when Berenice threw him out and had come back in triumph. There was nowhere for his son to flee, of course. Rome was here in the city, in this very palace, in the form of Caius Julius Caesar.

If Ptolemy had been a girl, all might not be lost. There was nothing anyone could do about that, however. Pothinus drew a deep breath. He ought to gather what riches he'd been able to amass in the past few months and flee for his life to some outland like Parthia or Pontus. Time was running out for him, but there might be that much time left.

He was turning on a heel when Theodotus entered the room, covered with dust and sweat, having ridden the two hundred miles from Pelusium at a hard gallop. He was breathing heavily but his lips smiled, so Pothinus took heart. He watched as the scholar went to the table where stood an ewer of wine and filled his goblet with it.

Ptolemy had given over his weeping. He sat transfixed, staring at his tutor. "What news? Is there any hope?" he asked plaintively.

"Hope? What need of hope, here in Egypt?" Theodotus declared, smacking his lips, wiping them with a cloth kerchief. "Achillas has twenty thousand men under arms, with any number of chariots. Caesar has less than one legion, no more. He is outnumbered twenty to four. How can he possibly snatch a victory from us?"

"He's holding a reception now, him and that harlot sister

89

of mine. He's introducing his legates and his tribunes to her, telling them she's queen of Egypt." The youthful voice broke. "He ignores me. He leaves me here all by myself as if—as if I were no more than a slopsboy at a banquet."

Theodotus grinned at the eunuch. "He's going to do more than that. He's going to speak to the Alexandrines, telling them he's here to restore order, to establish peace. Cleopatra will reign beside her brother, he will say."

Ptolemy straightened and a curious expression crossed his features. "Will he, Theodotus? Why, that isn't so bad. He won't stay here very long, then—maybe a week, no more than two weeks, certainly. He'll want to go to Rome to accept his reward for having crushed Pompey, to consolidate his gains."

"When he goes, you'll rule again. Is that what you're thinking?"

"Won't I?"

"Idiot!" snapped Theodotus. "You'll rule as Cleopatra ruled before she ran away. In name only. It will be *her* name on the documents, *her* words that are obeyed, *her* decisions that will count."

Ptolemy stamped his foot. "I won't endure that!"

"You'll have no alternative. Cleopatra will be Rome's choice. Her every command will be backed by the legions. You'll walk a tightrope or die."

Ptolemy went white and began to shake.

The eunuch scowled. "I can see why Caesar will command that Cleopatra rule with her brother, to avoid rebellion, an internal war which will cost Rome money to put down. Rome wants peace in Egypt because she depends so heavily on our corn shipments.

"But this other thing—these veiled threats to Ptolemy—saying his life will be as nothing once Cleopatra sits beside him, I don't agree with that. If you rise up against Caesar, you'll pull Rome down around our ears."

"Has Caesar only friends in Rome? What of Pompey's sons? Surely they'll prove friendly to us. Grateful. With Caesar dead, they will take power. We'll make alliances with them, perhaps give them concessions where it comes to the corn shipments."

"I don't know," Pothinus muttered gloomily.

"Achillas and I have decided. He's on the march right now."

Pothinus went to the recessed window and stared out over the city rooftops. He was secretly afraid of the turn events were taking. When there had been only Cleopatra to put aside, he had been confident. But—Rome! Caesar! These were opponents against whom he had no stomach.

His palm rubbed the rough stone back and forth.

As if the sensation might drive away his fear.

SIX

In the Brucheion

1.

The Egyptian army made a dust cloud to the east.

From a balcony of the Lochias palace, Cleopatra studied it beneath an upheld palm. She frowned slightly, remembering her hatred for Achillas, who was its commander, and realizing the fact that the Egyptians outnumbered the Romans four to one. The balance of power lay with Achillas once again. It might be a long-ago night repeated when the Egyptians broke through and took the Lochias.

She shivered, wondering how the might of Rome could help her now. In time, the legions would come, of that she was positive, their eagles and their *signas* held before them. They would come too late to save the life of Cleopatra Thea Philopater, however.

The dust cloud grew larger. Soon it would be moving past the Hippodrome, then battering the Canopic Gate for admittance. They might not have to batter at all; Caesar had withdrawn his men from the city proper and was holed up in the palace compound, the Brucheion.

Caesar had one advantage.

Ptolemy was still living in the Lochias. Cleopatra knitted her brows, putting her mind to this new problem. Achillas was oddly confident as he marched on Alexandria, with the person of the king he served in the hands of the enemy. It was as if he knew the future, could predict what was about to happen.

What was it that made him so confident?

For one thing, Julius Caesar might die, leaving the legionaries leaderless. And Ptolemy might succeed in fleeing from

91

the palace to his army. Should both those events take place, then Cleopatra might as well commit suicide.

Ah, she fought with phantoms! It would be better if she were to examine her reflection in a polished copper mirror, to make certain she was garbed in a manner befitting the queen of Egypt and mistress of the Great Caesar.

She clapped her hands, summoning Charmion.

It was time to bathe, to don the scented linens of Byssus, the priceless pectoral of emeralds and rubies that had belonged to her great-grandmother, Cleopatra III. The ornate uraeus must be readied for her head, her black hair properly coiled so that it would make a good fit.

She gave herself to the warm water and to the oils and unguents with which her flesh was massaged by slavegirls. Appearances must be maintained, at all costs. Not once could she show her fears to Caesar or his officers. She must be the embodiment of Royal Egypt. Now was the time to go before Caesar in the robes and trappings of her queenhood, as it had been the time to go naked before him when Appolodorus had unrolled the carpet.

When Iras lifted the mirror which reflected back her perfect beauty, Cleopatra was satisfied. She nodded at Iras and smiled at Charmion. As she moved past the row of pillars to the outer hall, she lifted a sweetmeat from a platter resting on the table and tossed it to her pet dog, a big, shaggy saluki hound.

Its jaws opened as it leaped and caught the tidbit.

Cleopatra froze to the thought in her mind.

Iras, who was carrying the heavy head-dress, almost bumped into her. "Is there anything wrong, highness?" she wondered.

Cleopatra shook her head impatiently. What she imagined was too ghastly to contemplate. And yet—ah, it was just possible! She glanced at the dog and gestured with her hand. "Bring the leather," she commanded, and a young boy ran to fetch a leash.

Roman spear-butts thumped the floor as she approached the banquet hall. One thing about these disciplined soldiers, Cleopatra thought, they don't know when to be afraid. Four times their number were coming to give them battle, yet they acted as though they were on barracks duty somewhere along the peaceful Tiber.

Her chin went up. She could be no less brave than they.

Caesar rose from the couch where he was reclining as he talked strategy with his officers. The Romans—all in armor with only their helmets missing—stood and made her little bows. She thought they bent their heads more to honor Caesar than Cleopatra Thea Philopater, but this was as she would have it. Men fought best for a commander they loved.

Then she was lying back on her own couch, smaller and far daintier than the golden sofa where Caesar would dine; it was a subtle form of flattery, she realized, but she knew Caesar was pleased by it. It was symbolic of his strength, of his authority over her.

"Now I know why Venus never shows herself on earth any more," he whispered in her ear. "It's because she knows that were Paris alive today, he would award the golden apple to you and not to her."

The Roman had a way about him, she thought, smiling faintly. She pressed his hand with the fingers of her right hand while she used the left to summon the slaves who would serve the banquet. As they came from the arches, she sat upright in shocked surprise. Wooden plates? Wooden bowls? Where was the gold plate with which the royal banquets were served? Angrily, Cleopatra glanced around her.

"Pothinus! To my side."

The eunuch financier of young Ptolemy bobbed his head apologetically. "The golden plate has been taken by the Romans, highness. They need it to bribe the mob to help them fight Achillas."

Cleopatra did not glance at Caesar though she knew intuitively he was stiffening in resentment. She said sweetly, "Now this I do not believe, Pothinus. What I do believe is this, that you yourself have taken the plate and hidden it away for a reason."

"What reason might that be, highness?"

Cleopatra bit her lip, only vaguely aware that a slavegirl was heaping her wooden platter with slices of roast grouse and pheasant. The eunuch would never be so daring unless he were positive there was no personal danger in this to him. She turned to Caesar and cried out sharply, half rising.

The Roman was lifting a lamb collop to his lips. Startled, he looked up. Cleopatra reached between their couches, took the meat from him and tossed it through the air. The saluki hound bounded forward, leaped. The great jaws closed and it began to chew.

Cleopatra signalled with her hand. "Wait!"

Within seconds the big dog was on the ground, convulsing, a bloody froth at its tightening jaws, its eyes glazing over in the swiftness of its death. The Romans were leaving their seats, drawing their swords.

Cleopatra said to Pothinus, who was slowly turning green, "Now I can give you my reason for the missing plate, man who is no man. You poisoned Caesar's food. Soon he would be dead, the Romans left leaderless. Perhaps you even planned to accuse me of the deed, hoping his officers would kill me in revenge.

"The gold dishes and goblets you took away and hid, planning to tell Achillas that the Romans took them with them. Thieves, you would name them. But you would be the thief, Pothinus. You alone."

The eunuch turned to run. The flat of a sword caught him across his face, pitched him sideways into a small serving table. Strong hands raised him out of the mass of overturned platters and scattered food into which he had fallen. Half dazed, he was held erect by the hands of the thickly thewed soldiers.

All during this, Julius Caesar had sat quietly. Only by his glistening eyes and the red flush on his cheeks did he betray the excitement working in him. It seemed he enjoyed sitting back and being protected by this young Egyptian queen. It was a new experience for him. He wondered what Cleopatra would do now.

She was biting her lip, considering the eunuch.

"Was my brother in on the plot?" she asked abruptly.

"No," screamed Ptolemy. "I knew nothing. Nothing!"

On the ivory and gold couch beyond that of Caesar the boy was a trembling, quivering picture of livid fear. The winecup he was holding shook so much that he seemed drenched in blood where the Setinian spilled across the white toga that he wore in imitation of Roman custom.

"It's all your fault, Pothinus," babbled the hysterical youth. "If you'd gone along with Achillas and Theodotus—but no. You had to disagree with them, do things your own way. You said yourself the gold would tarnish—show where the poison in the food had leaked out and—"

He broke off, horrified. His hand went to his lips like a claw, as if he would tear them from his body lest he be punished for their treachery. He huddled back into the cushions, drawing his legs up to his chest in a foetal position.

"I didn't know. I didn't! I didn't!" he kept repeating.

Caesar waited. Cleopatra was smiling coolly, looking down at this youth who would have ruled Egypt in her place. The snivelling milksop couldn't even keep a still tongue in his head. All she had for him was contempt.

"Take Pothinus below, to the dungeons. He must be ques-

94

tioned under torture, since the reputation of a Ptolemy is at stake."

The eunuch screeched, "No! You heard him yourself. He knew about the plan. The gold platters—we had to replace them with wood so the poison wouldn't show. You heard him say it. No. Not the torture. Ah, gods. . . ."

He was screaming as the soldiers carried him across the room. Ptolemy was crying aloud now, racking sobs that shook his body. Cleopatra felt her lips curl as she glanced at him.

"Finish your meal, brother mine. You are in no danger."

Ptolemy stared at her, eyes wide. His cheeks were wet with tears and an occasional sob racked his thin body. "In—in no danger?"

"Not if you can obey orders."

"I can. Oh, I can. Yes, indeed. Look—see me eat. Watch me, Cleopatra. I'll do anything you say. Only I—I don't want to die."

Caesar was silent, waiting.

Cleopatra came to sit beside him, ordering more food to be brought both to Caesar and to herself. Slaves were to be fetched to test them for more poison.

Caesar said mildly, "The boy is as guilty as the others. I should imagine this would be a heaven-sent opportunity to you."

"It is, but not in the way you think."

He was a patient man. He could let this young Egyptian beauty tell a story in her own way. He reached for a goblet of wine which had been tested by a young Syrian and sipped the Falernian slowly and with relish.

Cleopatra said, "Achillas advances on Alexandria filled with the courage of a lion about to leap on a defenceless gazelle. Yet before him is the man—and some of the soldiers—who smashed great Pompey."

"Admitted. The fact puzzled me."

"As it did me, until I realized that Pothinus might have you poisoned. It's why I brought my hound with me to the feast. To test your food—and mine as well. The plot failed, we know.

"I say we know, because Achillas—as he advances and finds the city undefended and the palace abandoned—will think that it succeeded."

"The palace abandoned?"

"Only as far as Achillas is concerned. You will pretend to ferry your men on board your thirty-four warships—by having them lie down in the bottom of the boats on the return journey. Actually they will remain here in the palace. When Achillas enters it, you will hit him hip and thigh, take him completely by surprise."

Caesar stared at her with his big eyes. He chuckled first, then roared with laughter. Cleopatra watched him, an uncertain smile on her mouth. Did he laugh in appreciation of her grim jest? Or in mockery at her simplicity? Then his arm was about her and hugging her against him.

"A Minerva come to life!" he shouted, and summoned his officers to gather close about him.

As the eager faces formed a circle, Cleopatra preened herself. Always the presence of men acted as a stimulant to her. Her fingertips brushed her black hair that was perfectly coiffed under its weight of seed pearls, and touched the pleated linen of her costly tunic, of the type known as *mafortes*.

"Achillas must be informed that his plot succeeded," she went on. "We must leave nothing to chance. My brother must send someone to him—a trusted messenger who knows nothing of what happened here. He will say that mighty Caesar is dead, that the Romans are in a panic, evacuating the palace, taking to their ships."

Caesar laughed softly, nodding his bald head.

"Have you a place to hide me, where I won't be suspect?" he wondered.

"The best place of all—your coffin." When he made a wry face, she clapped her hands in delight. "Not inside it, silly. Your coffin will be carried to a boat, to take you to your trireme. You will be one of the pallbearers, covered by a white cloak for mourning, as will your other officers. No one will be close enough to recognize you. The servants and the slaves of the palace will be dismissed or sequestered so that no spying eyes may see. The servants who have waited on table must be imprisoned in the dungeons until after Achillas enters the palace."

Caesar made a motion of his hand and wrist. Two young officers nodded and turned to issue orders. Within minutes, with trained discipline, this section of the Lochias would be cleared of all but Romans. It would be time then for the little drama to begin its run.

2.

Achillas came with a blare of curving trumpets and the steady tread of marching feet along the Via Canopia. He rode a white stallion before his chariot corps, clad in armor so heavily silvered that where the sunlight touched it, it seemed sheathed in yellow fire. He made a martial figure. A handsome man with grey at his temples amid the black hairs, his shoulders broad and muscular, he rode with a hand on the hilt of his sword, arrogant and overbearing.

Spies had told him enough to confirm what he had learned from messengers sent by young Ptolemy. Julius Caesar was dead. His body had been taken aboard one of the triremes in the harbor. Cleopatra—in fear of her life now that her protector had been poisoned—was also on board a Roman ship.

Little good it would do her, Achillas thought. He had laid his plans well. No fool, he knew what it meant to fight against Rome. He must leave no survivors to carry the truth to the city on the Tiber. All must be slain, so that when Rome sent for an accounting, it could be told that Caesar had intended setting himself up as king in the delta lands, as a first step toward becoming king in Rome. It would be a story well calculated to rouse the anger of the two sons of Pompey, now in Greece and awaiting an opportunity to drag down the man who defeated their father and drove him to flee to his death on an Alexandrian quay.

Even while his army marched into the city, Achillas' navy was slipping around behind the Roman fleet. With fire and sword they would hit those ships, prevent them from raising sail, hold them helpless in the harbor while they were destroyed.

Not a single Roman would live through the holocaust.

On the deck of the trireme that lifted to the gentle swell of the harbor waters, Cleopatra stood rigid in fear. High overhead a blazing red fireball hurtled through the night sky like an avenging meteor. It hissed, burning brightly—then plunged deep in the water fifty yards from the deck where she dug her fingernails so tightly into the arm of the man beside her.

"Isis," she hissed. "That was close!"

"Achillas is a smarter man than I gave him credit for being. He's sent ships around behind Pharos island. There—you can see them now." Caesar pointed.

"He's cut us off from the sea."

The Roman smiled tightly. "Neither of us ever intended fleeing, did we? So in one respect it makes no difference. On the other hand, I need my little fleet, such as it is. Believing us all to be on shipboard, Achillas thinks he has us just where it will do him the most good."

97

Two more fireballs flew high into the sky from great wooden onagers, curving red against the stars and plunging downward —faster, faster!—until the breath of the onlookers caught in their throats before they fell amid eruptions of steam and geysers of water into the harbor.

Now the Roman catapults were returning that fire. Red globes of burning pitch shot upward from the big triremes until the sky was pocked with flames. A sodden thump on the foredeck of their own vessel swung Caesar and Cleopatra around. A half-ton ball had splattered on the plankings, had showered the wales and overseer's walk with globules of red fury. The foresails were streaked with flames.

Half a dozen legionaries were screaming in agony where the pitch had seared them. In full battle armor they were running to the rails, leaping, chancing death by drowning rather than stand the agony of those flames.

His strong arms swung Cleopatra off her feet while Caesar bawled orders. Ropes hummed as a low, fast dinghy was lowered.

"Get about that boat," the Roman rasped. "It will take you to the palace. Be quick about it, girl."

"But you? What about you?"

"I'll follow. My word on it. My soldiers fight better on land. I'll evacuate everyone but the ships' crews needed to fight off those Egyptian biremes. Most cf my men are in the Lochias, waiting for Achillas to ride in. I never expected an attack from the sea."

As his brawny arms swung the lithe Egyptian queen over the high moldboard, Caesar smiled ruefully. "You may think me remiss as a commander not to have foreseen the possibility. I did—but there was nothing I could do about it except hope the opportunity would not occur to Achillas."

His hand caressed her shoulder before he released his hold on her. Bending over the rail he called down, "So that you may hope for victory, be advised I've sent riders and a fast ship to Syria, asking for reinforcements. Pray to your Egyptian gods that they get here in time to rescue rather than revenge us."

Cleopatra sat up straight in the stern of the long tender, trying to keep her wits about her. As her eyes turned across the waters, everything seemed to be a nightmare of red flame and harsh voices. Pandemonium was everywhere, with soldiers bawling orders, sliding down ropes into longboats, running on the blazing decks with leather buckets of seawater to fight the flames. Two of the nearer Roman vessels were spraying the oncoming Egyptian ships with flights of javelins fired from huge ballistas. Soon now they would meet in combat.

The harbor entrance was on fire; by its red flames she could make out the bobbing heads of men swimming for their lives in the cold water. More than that! A few missplaced fireballs had landed on the great library. And that vast building was burning, fanned by the westerly winds. Cold dread ran into her middle. This was the pride of Alexandria, this library! It contained over four hundred thousand scrolls, the knowledge of a world written down on papyrus and on parchment!

Tears filmed her eyes as her fists clenched. "Oh, no. No!" she whispered, drumming her fists up and down on her knees. "This must not be. It must not!" In a moment of stark insight, she understood the terrible loss to the world if the library burned and everything in it were destroyed.

"Hurry," she cried to the rowers. "Perhaps we can still save it."

The oarsmen bent their heavily thewed backs, but the steersman was compelled to negotiate a path between falling fireballs, which slowed their forward progress. Turning, putting a hand to the tiller shaft, Cleopatra stared back at the trireme from which she had come. It was on fire, its sails and shrouds alive with flames. Between the trireme and the tender she saw another longboat with Caesar in it.

Even as she stared, the tender overturned. Men were flung into the cold waters. Cleopatra leaped to her feet. "Caesar!" she screamed.

Her cry alerted the man at the tiller. With a muffled oath he swung the tender about, sent it speeding back the way it had come. Both hands on the moldboard, Cleopatra stared down at those red-flecked waters. Somewhere here was Caesar. He must not die, not like this! Her hammering heart told her that with Julius Caesar dead, she also must die. There would be no escape then from Achillas and from Ptolemy.

Leaning out over the water, she saw two white scrolls clenched in a hand. The fool! The loveable fool! Even in this moment of his life's danger, with enemies hemming him in before and behind, Caesar could still think about books and knowledge!

"There," she called, pointing. "There he is!"

He swam with a fold of his purple toga clenched between his teeth, left hand lifted from the water to preserve his precious scrolls, swimming only with his right arm and his kicking feet. His head bobbed. His greying hairs plastered wetly about his balding pate.

Cleopatra stretched out her arms.

She seized his left hand, took the scrolls from him and placed them in her lap. Then she was bending outward, trying to lift him; the steersman abandoned his tiller to aid her with his more powerful muscles. Together they brought Caesar from the water into the boat.

"My men," he gasped. "The others. We must save them."

He looked like a young man, standing so proud and tall amid the red fires on all sides of them. Impatiently he pushed back his wet hair, wrung out a fold of his toga. His eyes blazed. The lines of age in his face faded out. It was as if this personal danger, this threat of disaster to himself and to his ambitions, touched secret wellsprings deep within his body.

His voice cracked like a whiplash over the tossing harbor waters. "Men of Rome, we fight together this night. Side by side as if we were together in the legion shield-wall! This way, this way. Those of you who can swim—help him who cannot. In this way you'll all be saved. Easy, now. Remember you are Romans."

He talked on, not shouting but making his voice heard above the clamor and the tumult. He saw everything, did this man, pointing out a struggling soldier to two others, staring at the blazing library and making a comment that Cleopatra was never afterward to forget. "For this tragedy, history shall always blame me!" His fist slapped into his palm while he watched the battle between Roman and Egyptian triremes and biremes so close to the great lighthouse, impatient, vaguely angry that he could not be there also to aid by his encouragement.

Cleopatra turned to assist a man drowning close by the tender. Her strength was not enough to raise him; Caesar came to help her. In the process, her thin tunic was torn, stained with cold sea water. Her pearl caul broke and her thick black hair came tumbling down. Wet with spray, feverish with excitement, she laughed exultantly.

When Caesar looked at her in surprise, she cried, "No one can beat you. You're no man, you're a god!"

"My men think so. It is what makes them invincible. I hadn't credited you with so much discernment." He was laughing at her with his eyes, she saw, teasing her.

As gaily she cried, "It takes a goddess to recognize a god at a time like this. I am Cleopatra!"

He nodded and touched the top of her head with a palm. There was a tenderness in him that surprised her, for she knew how ruthless he could be. The boat surged under them

100

as the oars bit water. The quay loomed up in the redness of the burning ships.

"I will be busy this night, Cleopatra. I can spare no men to guard you. You must hide somewhere so as to be safe."

"I have Conon," Cleopatra said simply.

Ah, and where was Conon? she thought, as Caesar handed her up onto the wharfstones. He had remained behind in the palace with the soldiers, telling her that his place was where he could fight. Certainly he would have seen the battle of the fireballs; the building roofs above were lined with silent Roman legionaries, staring seaward; Conon might be among them.

Cleopatra gathered what was left of her thin linen garment about her hips, stepping along the stone wharf past little puddles of water. Caesar was surrounded by his centurions and legates; he had no time now to bother about the young queen of Egypt. She felt curiously alone, almost deserted.

Then metal clanked in the shadows and Conon was beside her, bulking big and solid in armor and a red cloak. He held a white hooded robe in his hands that he threw about her shoulders.

"Come along with me. I've made arrangements."

She asked no questions, moving beside him lightly and gracefully, letting him talk. "Achillas is outside the royal quarter now, the Brucheion. His men are bringing up battering rams. They'll attack any moment. I want you out of harm's way."

Pride flared in her at that. "I'll take every risk that must be taken, Conon. What sort of queen do you think me?"

"Cleopatra will show herself on the battlements," he promised grimly.

She stared at him, lips a little open. In the white cowl her oval face was warm with color, her hazel eyes brilliant between long black lashes. "You speak in riddles, Conon!" There was anger in her soft voice but he only grinned at her.

They were moving along a narrow corridor that led down by way of a sloping ramp into the slave quarters. When they came out into the large room where Hardedef was accustomed to sit—he had been dismissed to the Temple of Isis along with most of the other slaves—there was a woman waiting for them.

She stood proud and regal in hawk headdress and jewelled collar, a thin linen robe and plaited girdle. In her hands she held the systrum and the ankh. She was Cleopatra to the flesh.

The young queen stood gasping. It was as if she stared into

101

a silvered mirror at her own reflection. Then she swung on Conon, laughing softly.

"Is this your plan? To put her on the battlements in my place? While I stand safe in the shadows?"

His face was grim. "It is. I have Caesar's consent."

"But not mine!"

"Cleopatra, be reasonable! Your life is worth more than hers and mine. I'll be beside her, to make it look good. Achillas knows you wouldn't stand in any danger unless I were by your side to protect you with my shield."

Cleopatra smiled gently. "You are so right, Conon! Achillas would know I wouldn't stand there for his men to see unless you were beside me. Therefore, I shall stand there. And without you. You shall be with this girl."

"Ione," Conon growled.

"Ione, then. She shall wear rags of mine, I'll wear the hawk headdress and her baubles. I shall stand on the battlements while you and she lurk in the shadows."

"I won't do it," he said slowly. "Ah, Thea—don't make me."

"Thea," she breathed. "You haven't called me that in a long time."

"You're the queen."

"And as queen, I ought to be obeyed."

The sound of shredding wood came to them, drowned out by the victorious roar of attacking soldiers. The battle was beginning. Achillas and his army were inside the palace walls.

Cleopatra shrugged out of her woolen robe. Ione met her imperious stare, flushed and dropped her head, began undoing the fastenings of her jeweled pectoral. Conon only groaned, making fists of his hands and moving them helplessly through the air as though he sought something against which to use them. He seemed indifferent to the fact that two beautiful women were stripping themselves naked to his eyes in the room.

Then her torn, stained tunic fell at her ankles and Cleopatra stood with the torchlight shining on her ivory skin. Casually, as if unaware that the movements of her arms made her breasts jump faintly, making her less the queen and more the woman, she drew out the broken caul of seed pearls from her hair. She heard the hissed breath in Conon's throat and smiled gently, almost wistfully.

Ione slid down her own byssus garment, stood straight. There was a touch of pride in her eyes as she glanced at her queen. She too was naked. No man by looking at either of them could tell the slave from the queen, Conon thought, and then amended it.

There was a way, of course. Their bearing was not the same. Ione was a slave, and lacked the imperious dignity of royalty. Her chin did not tilt so high, her eyes were not quite so calm, her gracefulness a little too studied. Conon sighed.

He loved Cleopatra. He always would. And yet there was an air about her, perhaps because of her very royalty—he was only a gladiator, the son of a man who labored with his hands for his livelihood—which he could not match. Caesar could do it. He could not. Nor could Ione.

Cleopatra said, "I'm flattered."

She walked around Ione, studying her shapely body. She laughed softly, pleased.

"Your little friend is almost my double, Conon."

Ione flushed as her eyes begged Conon for help. He grumbled, "Cleopatra, we have no time to—"

Her hand waved him to silence. She was quite obviously enjoying herself. "Hardedef bought her to imitate me, didn't he? To take my place at public functions which might bore me? I've never laid eyes on her before. You have, of course—and more than your eyes, I'll wager." She squealed in delight as Conon went red. "Until tonight, she's never really earned her keep."

Her hands clapped. "Tonight she shall! While I stand on the battlements, you and Ione shall play at lovers in the shadows, hidden securely from Achillas and his soldiers. It's an idea that intrigues me. It shall help me to laugh when the arrows come flying at me."

"By Hathor, I won't—"

"Conon!" Her sandalled foot stamped. "It is my command!"

More gently she turned to Ione, signalled her to help her dress. The slavegirl made an obeisance, came with the transparent *mafortes,* the jeweled pectoral, the bracelets and golden slippers, and last the great hawk crown for her thick black hair. When she was done, with the ankh and the systrum in her hands, she was incarnate Egypt.

Cleopatra touched the girl with her hand, then smiled at Conon. "Remember, you must pretend she is Cleopatra this night, Conon. Fight for her with your life if she's attacked."

"And you? What of you?"

She only shook her head as the corners of her mouth dimpled. She turned on a heel and moved down the corridor into darkness. Conon stood watching the corridor until the last

103

faint footfall came to him. Then he sighed and turned back to Ione.

"Get her things on," he said gently. "We have a job to do this night, you and I." There was a cold, terrible look in his grey eyes that made the girl shudder. She bent and lifted the ripped tunic, raising it over her head, shaking it down about her nakedness. It was like a mist before her body, hiding nothing.

Conon stared at her, the breath catching in his lungs. Gods! She was Cleopatra to the red henna on her soles! Not Cleopatra the queen, but Cleopatra the woman. Thea, grown a little older and without the regal bearing, with nothing of her royal haughtiness about her.

He waited until she put on the fallen rings and bracelets Cleopatra had shed before he moved to her and put his hands on her curving sides to the deep mounds of her breasts. She gave a low cry and came to him, lifting her heavy mouth to his kiss.

They clung together for long moments, Conon with his blood on fire because of what he had seen this night in this subterranean chamber, Ione because this man loved her in his own peculiar way. Her arms tightened about his neck and she let her loins caress him.

It was Conon who first pushed away, head jerking upward.

"We have to be on the battlements, pretending to hide in the shadows yet letting ourselves be seen. Otherwise—"

His muscular shoulders shrugged. The lover was gone from him before the necessity to be a soldier whose duty must come first. He lifted the white woolen robe, flung it about her. With an arm like an iron bar at her back he brought her with him up ramps and staircases, past empty rooms where rich drapes and gold and ivory furniture made a mockery of the lusts and greed of the men and women who fought to possess it.

They came out into the night air under a sky alive with redness from the fires that burned from the Library to the very walls of the Brucheion. The air was thick with the screams of men in agony, with the clang of sword on sword and shields, the heavy thud of a battering ram slamming into a bolted door. Below them the palace compound was filled with fighting, cursing, struggling men.

Ione shrank back against him, crying out softly.

Conon grinned mirthlessly. "It isn't a pretty sight, for sure. But when men battle over thrones, it's a common one. Come along."

104

He brought her with him through the shadows and the pools of light cast by the wall torches, finally halting her in a well of blackness made by an angled wall abutment. This was as good a place as any to watch the fight—and Cleopatra.

Royal Egypt stood on a tower walk not two hundred paces from them, head held high, glittering in the jewels and ornaments with which she was adorned. It was as if she watched a sunset rather than the struggle far below where men fought and died that she might wear the uraeus.

No one saw her, at first. The Egyptians were too concerned with winning the palace, too busy watching Roman shields and short swords—those deadly *gladii*—to turn their eyes elsewhere. Life and death hung for them on those sharp points and keen edges and every man of them wanted most to stay alive this night.

The Romans were fighting with their backs to the palace proper. Their shields formed a gently moving wall that shifted and bent and surged forward in response to the wavering tide of fortune. Egyptian bowmen in chariots moving through the open compound gates dared not fire for fear of hitting their own men in the forefront of the battle.

Conon forgot Cleopatra long enough to study the fight. The Egyptians had the weight of men on their side, but the Romans fought with a cool dispassion and an expert knowledge of their weapons that made a mockery of numbers. Discipline! This was the Romans' secret! As it was the secret of the successful gladiator who must practice and practice with his weapons until they became a part of him. The Romans were being forced back, with here and there a body in its armor rolling where sandalled feet used it as a stepping stone; but they were giving way slowly, slowly.

The deep whisper in the air that made Conon lift his head and stare around was the sound of fireflames eating at wood and scorching stone. The Library was a sheet of red, the harbor installations were blazing brightly, framing the Roman triremes and the Egyptian ships like toys against them as they fought. Even a few parts of the Jewish quarter were beginning to burn.

Alexandria would remember this night!

A voice carried to his ears. "There. Look there!"

It was an Egyptian officer in a fur kalisiris over his armor, pointing with his sword. Eyes turned upward along that blade —beheld Cleopatra!

"The royal bitch! Cleopatra herself! Kill her!"

As one voice, the answer came. "Kill!"

Bowstrings twanged. Slim shafts flew upward. Conon groaned and beat his fist against a wall merlon. If one of those points should find her flesh—*Osiris, god of death and the underworld, seek not your victim there!*

Whether due to the tricks of the flames or the shifting currents of the wind, the arrows broke against the walls before and in back of Cleopatra. She stood proudly, chin uplifted, a tiny smile on her mouth. Was she thinking of him and Ione? Conon wondered. He would not put it past her.

Rasping a curse, he reached into the black well of shadow and caught Ione by a wrist. "Come on, girl. We'll let them get a look at us!"

She ran lightly beside him, shrouded in the woolen robe. As the torchlight caught its whiteness, made it stand out stark against the darker walls, men howled from far below.

"It's Conon, the watchdog!"

"Who's that with him?"

"Cleopatra!"

"Aie! She wouldn't be far from him this night."

"The other is a fraud!"

The bowmen swung away from the woman on the tower walk. Now their shafts came thickly, heavily, like drops of rain in a cloudburst. Conon smiled a cold grin which bared the teeth, and lifted his shield. He gripped a sword in his right hand for his eyes were those of an animal and his reflexes almost so; he could swipe at an arrow as it ran through the air and catch enough of its shaft or fletching on his blade to deflect it from its target.

It was close, hot work. Only vaguely was he aware that Ione had sunk to her knees behind him and was clinging to his thick legs with her bare young arms. The thought touched him that Cleopatra would never do this; she was too much the queen. And yet, oddly, it made him all the more determined to keep Ione from harm.

She was no queen but a girl caught up in the power fight of princes. All she wanted was a man to call her own and his child or children, to fulfill her function as a female. Well, by Neith who was the war goddess of old Egypt! He would see to it that she did.

His shield lifted, caught half a dozen points. His blade flicked away another, a second and a third. More were coming, now. His shield must ever be before his eyes. Something hot and fiery drove into his lower thigh. He heard Ione cry out. One shaft had slipped past his defence, had dug into him. It weakened his leg but he was no milksop to complain of

106

handicaps. He put more weight on his left leg and moved the swordblade even faster.

He wondered vaguely what kept Julius Caesar.

Certainly the man could not delay much longer. His line of legionaries was thin to the point of non-existence. Even now, Achillas was gathering his men for a last final assault that would sweep away those shields and stabbing swords.

The flights of arrows slackened as bowmen were called to reinforce that final assault. Achillas marshalled his men well, Conon saw when he could snatch a look. First the spearmen with their javelins, then the swordsmen with their shields, ready to spring forward when the spears had done their work. Behind them all were the bowmen, firing over their heads until contact should be made.

A trumpet sent its notes into the air.

Egyptian javelins flew like hail.

Doors opened in the compound walls. From them streamed a steady flow of heavily armed legionaries, veterans of the Third and Tenth legions, men who had fought with Julius Caesar in Gaul and against the Helvetians, who had wet their sandals in the cold waters off the coast of Britain.

A yelp of dismay went up from the Egyptians. They had thought these men penned securely on the burning triremes! To see them now, calm and confident behind their curving shields, was like taking a sword against the throat of their own bravery.

The battle joined, if it could be called a battle.

Mostly, it was a slaughter.

The soldiers who had driven back the few legionaries opposing them in the compound for so long were no match for many times the number of their fellows, hungry for the killing. Roman *gladii* flashed and stabbed. Egyptian mercenaries fell to flood the compound cobbles with their blood, twitching and writing in pain and the fear of coming death.

Achillas was a madman, bellowing at his troops.

He was military strategist enough to understand that this was checkmate for his hopes of capturing the Lochias. The best he could do now was withdraw with as many of his men that he could save.

It was over, all but the killings and the flight of a beaten army through the streets of Alexandria. Conon gave a deep sigh and pushed away from the wall merlon where he leaned. His eyes went to the tower walk.

Cleopatra stood there, still proud, still regal.

Still—alive!

His heart leaped at sight of her. He turned to Ione with words on his lips. "Knew you ever such a woman, Ione? She was born to be a queen, to rule—girl! What's wrong?"

Ione lay in a puddle of her blood, motionless.

Gently he turned her over. An arrow stood out between her breasts, deep-driven with the savage strength of some hired soldier. The shaft that had sliced his thigh had taken her in the chest. There was a tiny smile on her lips and her eyes were wide apart in death. The fear was gone from her, now.

Conon put his arms about her body and cradled her, rocking back and forth. And for the first time since his early boyhood he wept bitter tears. Osiris had granted his prayer. The god had spared the life of Cleopatra.

But he had come for Ione in her place.

SEVEN

In the Swamps Along the Delta

1.

One battle rarely makes a war.

Achillas withdrew what was left of his forces from Alexandria, sullenly and slowly as if daring Caesar to come to grips with him. The Romans remained within the Brucheion, content with their holding tactics. Achillas set up camp on the edge of the desert and waited.

Within the palace, Julius Caesar fretted.

He was well aware that he risked his entire future, here in this Egyptian city. Across the Mediterranean, Pompey's two sons would be making their own bid for power. Every minute he spent here, strengthened them. Yet he could not tear himself away, either from Egypt or its young queen.

Egypt meant corn to Rome. The man who held those corn ships in his hands owned Rome, for he alone could feed it. Even more powerful than a man's purse was his stomach. Where there was no food, money meant little. It was a calculated risk he took, and he accepted it.

Ah, if only his reserves from Syria and Asia Minor would arrive! Then he could go on the offensive, not remain holed up here in these stone walls. His strategy of war depended on swift, offensive movements. Hit the enemy fast and hard. Shift position. Hit again! Cooped up in the Lochias, he was forced to fight an alien strategy, one which appealed neither to him nor to his troops.

Only one thing made this sort of life worthwhile.

Cleopatra!

The young Egyptian queen was the very breath of life to him in these days. She presided over banquets that he would have believed impossible, knowing conditions to be what they were. Fleet little boats sliced through the blockade thrown up by Achillas, bringing meat and fruit, rare wines and fresh vegetables. There are men who will take any risk for enough money, and Cleopatra—how, Caesar did not know—had the gold with which to pay them.

She kept his men amused, too. Girls came from the Rhakotian quarter, veils around their faces, by two and threes, dancers all of them, harlots all of them, eager for a fistful of the golden coins with which Royal Egypt paid their fees. They cost the Roman legionaries not so much as a thin copper obol.

As a Cilician youth arranged his hair by fitting over it a wreath, Caesar considered his features in a silver mirror, letting these thoughts run through his head. He marveled at Cleopatra. He was well aware that while she struggled for her queenhood and her royal inheritance, she must also struggle with the restless people of Alexandria, keeping them in a good mood. Moreover, she must cope with the spies that Achillas employed, and also with her brother Ptolemy in his fits of pique and anger.

She was like a Pamphylian juggler, one of those entertainers he would see tonight at the feast. A dozen balls would fly through the air, deftly caught and thrown back only to be caught again, all at the same instant. He himself could perform such a feat with men and their ambitions; until Cleopatra had tumbled out of that carpet at his feet, he had met no other person so capable.

The ornatror stepped back, bowing.

The wreath was placed to perfection. He looked almost as regal as he thought himself, Caesar conceded. His purple toga hung without a wrinkle and the rings on his fingers flashed fire where the torchlight caught them. In all, he made an imposing figure.

It was time for the feasting. He walked toward the door, the golden hem of his garment swinging easily to his stride. The slaveboy bowed low.

Cleopatra was not hungry. She toyed with the rich fare which her slaves brought to the serving tables, tossing aside a date and a juicy orange. Her mouth, however, was very dry —from nervousness? because of excitement?—and she reached often for the golden goblet that held the chilled white Mareotic wine.

Her eyes looked sideways at Caesar who also played with his food. She had begun to worry about Caius Julius Caesar. Was the man regretting the fact that he had permitted himself to become so closely allied with the young queen of Egypt? While he sat penned up in the palace at Alexandria trying to win Egypt, he stood to lose the world. He knew it. Cleopatra knew it. They rotted here in the Lochias. All Achillas need do was wait. Time would master Caesar, if nothing else could.

Ah, Time! It was a harsh taskmaster. It neither asked nor gave mercy. It rolled on and on, gathering one and all in its grip. Every living thing paid obeisance to Time. Time gave nothing but accepted all.

And yet—

There was a way to master Time, to hurry it a bit. The trouble was, would Time prove her ally or her enemy because of what she intended doing? She did not know, could not know until Time itself gave the answer.

Her ringed hand replaced the goblet on the table. Even the Mareotic seemed to have lost its flavor. Her eyes moved around the great banquet hall, studying the faces of the Roman officers. They all seemed sullen, angry; the waiting was jarring on their nerves, too. Perhaps after tonight the waiting would end.

Iras moved from the shadows, making a motion with her hand. Cleopatra felt her blood beat faster. She slipped from the couch where she had been sipping wine, smiling at Caesar, telling him she would soon return.

She followed Iras along a palace corridor, walking swiftly. At every stride her hand opened and closed into a fist, betraying the worry that ate in her. She could be making a mistake, a mistake that would not only cost her this struggle for the throne of Egypt but her life as well. But she had reasoned out the move so carefully, it seemed the only thing to do.

Iras slowed where two corridors converged and stood waiting. Under her breath, Cleopatra asked. "He is inside with her? You are positive?"

"I saw him enter myself, highness. Ten minutes ago."

"Ten minutes ought to be a long enough time."

They went on. This corner of the palace was quiet, unguarded, and sounds traveled quite easily. They walked silently, slowly now, and when they heard a low moan, Cleopatra smiled. Everything was proceeding as she had planned. Iras stepped to a doorway, lifted a heavy black drape, invited the young queen to step inside.

Framed in the doorway, Cleopatra saw a thick standing candle illuminating a huge round bed, and on the bed, two bodies writhing lazily. One of these naked bodies was that of her young sister, Arsinoe—a true Ptolemy, she thought, always a slave to bodily passion—and the other was that of her Greek lover, Ganymede. Cleopatra moved into the room on noiseless sandals.

Arsinoe was crying out now, her head rolling back and forth on the bedcovering. Her slim white legs kicked convulsively in answer to the ecstasy in which her body shuddered. Cleopatra frowned. She had always considered Arsinoe a child; she was only—how old was it?—fifteen years. Yet she acted like a dockside harlot. She was absolutely shameless!

Against her will, Cleopatra felt her blood stirring to the sight of what these lovers were doing with one another. Their eyes were closed, their mouths open. They trembled as Isis, goddess of earthly love, caught them in her erotic grip and would not let them go until each had paid her tribute.

Cleopatra waited, aware that her young loins hungered as she stared at the man and the child-woman on the bed. She had forsaken other lovers since Caesar had come to Alexandria, and of late Caesar had been a worried, fretful man, given more to the problems of Mars than of Venus. Ganymede had a young body, tireless in its devotions.

Arsinoe screamed and her eyes came open.

Wide apart, those black eyes stared unseeingly up at Cleopatra. Her mouth was twisted grotesquely as she went on clawing at the shoulder of the dark-skinned youth bent above her. Cleopatra stepped forward, put a hand on the back of the Greek. His flesh was damp with sweat but firm and smooth. Her tongue came out to moisten her lips. She fought against the urge to caress the youth herself.

"Arsinoe," Cleopatra whispered.

They did not hear her. She had to speak again. Closing her eyes, she said more firmly, "Arsinoe! It's Cleopatra."

Ganymede gave a harsh cry, rolled free of the girl and sat on his rump on the bed, too overcome by surprise to hide himself from the royal eyes. He began to tremble as he saw his queen studying his body.

"I should have you gelded," Cleopatra said softly.

Arsinoe cried out and crawled across the covers to shield her lover from the royal eyes. Her thick black hair was damp, matted to her shapely little head and wet shoulders. Her breasts quivered and leaped to the fury of her breathing. The candlelight on her moist ivory flanks made them glisten. There was no fear in her, only anger at her interrupted assignation.

Cleopatra smiled down at her. "Little fool. If Caesar had found you this way, nothing on Earth could save your Ganymede."

For the first time, now that her blood was cooling, Arsinoe understood the danger in which she had placed her lover. Had she accepted the embraces of some handsome boy, then had him slain as was the custom, nothing would be said. Dead tongues cannot whisper royal secrets. It was the fact that she wanted to keep Ganymede alive, to pleasure her again and again, that was her crime. Ganymede deserved to die for having made love to a princess.

"Wha—what are you going to do?" Arsinoe panted.

"Should I betray the man who trusts me?"

"Please, Cleopatra—say nothing!"

Wisely, Cleopatra understood that her sister would do anything to save the life of this youth she loved so much, but she shrugged, pretending helplessness.

"How many others know of your secret meetings? Probably every slave in the palace. Word will reach Caesar, sooner or later."

Ganymede was shivering fitfully. He was young, handsome, dark of skin and with curling black hair that clung close to his skull. There was a matting of thick hair on his chest and on his upper legs. He was like a stallion, Cleopatra thought, and for the moment, envy of her sister touched her. Arsinoe had nothing to worry her pretty little head about but the satisfaction of the desires that gnawed in her belly.

Well, she would give her a few worries!

"Ganymede must run away," Cleopatra said at last.

"No! I won't let you take him from me!"

Arsinoe got to her feet, stood between her sister and her lover, head thrown back defiantly. Stark naked like this, she seemed more than her fifteen years. Her breasts were large and heavy, her hips wider than Cleopatra had thought. She wondered idly how long Ganymede had been coming to this bedchamber.

Cleopatra asked mildly, "Are you defying me, Arsinoe? Don't you realize that if I wanted, I could whisper a few words in Caesar's ear and accuse you of plotting to let Achillas into the palace with a band of soldiers in an assassination attempt against the Roman? How long do you think you'd live, then?"

Arsinoe whimpered, all her bravado gone. She knew well enough the hold this older sister of hers held on Caius Julius Caesar. She whirled and flung herself at her lover, trembling, quivering, clinging so tightly to him her nails drew blood from his skin.

Over her shoulder, Ganymede felt Royal Egypt touch him with her gaze, saw her tonguetip come out to moisten her mouth. He knew this young queen liked his strong body. He toyed with the idea of hurling Arsinoe from him, of falling to his knees and begging forgiveness. A moment later, he was glad he hesitated.

"There may be a way by which you and your lover can have each other without anyone caring," Cleopatra said conversationally.

Arsinoe turned her head, looking up at Cleopatra. "How?" she whispered through her sobs.

"You and Ganymede could escape. You could go to Achillas and join forces with him. He would protect you."

Arsinoe lifted an arm, pushed damp hair away from her eyes. Her mind worked swiftly. She was suspicious of Cleopatra. This was much too good an offer she was making. She would have an ulterior motive. But what could it be? Certainly she had nothing to fear from Ganymede and herself.

Cleopatra smiled her understanding. "Am I so much the ogress? Caesar has our entire family in his hands. You. Ptolemy. Me. At one word, he could wipe us out of existence. There would be no royal family in Egypt, only an empty throne begging a taker."

Arsinoe nodded slowly.

Cleopatra went on, "At least with you out of the Lochias there would be one of us still free, perhaps able to make terms with Rome later on—if Ptolemy and I should be slain."

Arsinoe tried to hide her sudden elation but it shone in her black eyes like a radiance. Once away from Cleopatra and from Caesar, it would be Arsinoe who could make a bid for power! Achillas raised his standards for Ptolemy Philopater, but he would surely listen to reason and raise them just as high for Arsinoe! Poor foolish Cleopatra! She would be playing right into her hands by setting her free. And with Ganymede as well. Not even bothering to keep him by her side as a hostage.

"You look ahead, sister," she said aloud. "You're very wise."

Wiser than you give me credit for being, sister mine, the young queen thought to herself. I know the way your mind works, being a Ptolemy myself. You won't be in Achillas' camp one hour before you begin plotting to take my place as queen of Egypt. And this is as I want it to be.

Cleopatra murmured, "You'll need money and a passport signed by Caesar. I have both in my rooms. I'll send Iras back with them. Pack only what you need. I'll have a chariot waiting outside the harbor gate."

Arsinoe watched her sister turn and walk away. Excitement was a heady wine bubbling in her veins. Isis! To get the chance to make a try at the throne. This was to believe in miracles. As the black drape fell behind Cleopatra, Arsinoe whirled and ran to Ganymede.

She flung herself into his arms with a low laugh. "Do you understand what this means, darling? You and I together—away from the Lochias—with Achillas and his army?"

"I don't trust her," Ganymede protested, still fearful.

"What's to trust? If she wanted us killed, she wouldn't go through all this rigamarole. No, no. Cleopatra means to let us get away, all right. The only thing that troubles me is—why? I don't quite believe her when she says she's so concerned about a Ptolemy ruling Egypt. Or maybe I do her an injustice."

Ganymede was lying on his back with Arsinoe soft and warm above him. "Shouldn't we begin getting ready? Iras will be back with the passport and a moneysack. We ought to—"

Arsinoe laughed down at him. "Cleopatra has been away from the feast for some time. She'll have to return there, to keep Caesar from being suspicious. It will be almost midnight before she's free to send Iras to us."

"Oh," the Greek youth said.

"She liked you, my sister did. Her eyes were crawling all over you when you were sitting there without so much as a napkin to cover you. I think she would have enjoyed being in my skin tonight." Arsinoe shuddered. "Pah! Imagine bedding down with an old man like Caesar."

Her smooth palms slid lazily over her lover's flesh. She whispered as she bent her head to kiss him, "A young man is ever so much more fun to be with. So smooth your skin, so hard your muscles." She turned her head and looked at him.

"Ganymede, I might well be queen in Egypt before all this is settled."

"Yes your highness," he laughed.

She wriggled her hips at him. "Be serious. I want to pretend I am queen. Right now. Have you ever made love to a queen, Ganymede? No? Then begin to do so. Pretend I am Royal Egypt."

As her lover caressed her with hands and lips, Arsinoe told herself, even as she began trembling, that it was even nicer than she had thought to be a queen in Egypt. It was so exciting it made her want to scream out loud.

Caesar was angry. He stood before a standing statue of the god Osiris, mummified with the flail and the crook in his hands, and scowled. He made a fist and beat it against the polished obsidian.

"You gave Achillas a weapon," he said coldly to Cleopatra who was sitting on an ebony chair and toying with her pleated skirt. "With Arsinoe at his side, he can raise an even larger army."

Cleopatra smiled to herself. At her silence, he whirled, face red with fury at what he considered her insolence. "Almost I believe myself to be betrayed," he snapped.

Without looking up from her skirt, she said softly, "Arsinoe loves Ganymede very much."

"Oh? What's that supposed to mean?"

"Achillas will see in Arsinoe a queen, true enough, but not Ptolemy's queen. His own."

Caesar frowned thoughtfully, then sighed. He could not quite follow the thought processes of this girl. Sometimes she went at matters with so oblique a viewpoint that it escaped his wits entirely.

He was not a stupid man. He realized that Cleopatra would never willingly give Achillas the chance to oust her from the throne. He had hurled his accusation at her out of pique at not being admitted into her confidence. With the black obsidian Osiris at his back he moved across the room to sit beside Cleopatra.

"Tell me," he requested simply.

Cleopatra laughed delightedly and lifted her eyes to him. "You're such a stern, grumpy man! You've been so successful for so long a time that you think all you need do to gain your ends is charge in like a wounded water buffalo. Not in Alexandria. Here you must be sly."

Caesar smiled indulgently. "Go on, please."

"Arsinoe and Ganymede will go to Achillas' camp. Achillas will be overwhelmed at his good fortune in getting his hands on such a pretty pretender to the throne. He will arrange to enlarge his army, declare Arsinoe queen and march on the palace."

"Exactly what I said."

She wrinkled her nose at him, leaned closer and nibbled at his earlobe. "Exactly what I said," she mimicked. "And that is why I said—Arsinoe loves Ganymede. It makes a difference."

"How so?"

"Arsinoe will never agree to accept Achillas as her husband, to sit the throne beside her. This will be Achillas' plan—but not Arsinoe's! She will want Ganymede. And so they will quarrel. No matter which of them wins out—we will have divided their forces. Some of the army will declare for Arsinoe, some for Achillas. There will be two camps. It lessens the odds against us, for one will not fight beside the other."

Caesar said wryly, "I'm glad you aren't a Roman. I would be very much afraid of you, I think."

2.

The winter winds held a touch of coming spring in their caress as they moved along the streets and squares of Alexandria, bringing with them rumors and strange gossip. Achillas was dead, slain by Ganymede himself before the eyes of Arsinoe. Now Arsinoe and her Greek lover commanded the Egyptian army which was preparing to hit Caesar and Cleopatra by sea and land in their fortress palace. All Egypt waited for that final battle to decide which woman would sit as mistress of this world which was watered by the Nile. Men wagered small sums and vast fortunes on its outcome. There were few who backed the Romans; on short rations for the past month, there was talk of dissension among the legionaries. It was generally agreed that Arsinoe would win her gamble with destiny by the time the season of *ahkit* was fully upon the land.

No one outside the Lochias knew of the lean ships that had come flying down the coast from Syria in recent nights, bringing messages to Caius Julius Caesar. Those waxed tablets and rolled scrolls told Caesar that the Roman legions were on the move. From Syria was coming the famous Larks legion, his favorite; from Persia, the Twelfth Fulminata and two others, twenty thousand trained veterans eager to smell battledust, rusty from inactivity on the borders of their world.

Arsinoe and Ganymede saw only Cleopatra and an old man as their opponents. In their drunkenness at this opportunity afforded them, they were blind to the fact that where a man like Caesar went, there also went the eagles. They were prepared to fight only a young queen and a fifty-odd year old man, not Rome itself.

Cleopatra stood proudly in her lightweight battle armor as Conon lifted a silver helmet and placed it over her tightly coiled black hair. He smiled grimly when he saw how eagerly she quivered, how she must part her lips to breathe. A part of him, remembering Ione, paused to feel a sudden sorrow.

"Soon now," he told her. "Very soon."

Dawn was in the sky. All night long, here along the many mouths of the Nile delta, mighty triremes had been unloading their human cargo. Men had splashed from gangplanks into morasses, guided by peasants hand-chosen by Cleopatra herself for their intimate knowledge of this strange swampland. They had begun their march so as to surround, in the darkness of a moonless night, the army commanded by Arsinoe and her young lover.

At any moment the blare of horns would summon the legions to another battle. Caesar himself was off somewhere with his officers, taking personal command of these reinforcements from Judah and Israel and Persia. Cleopatra had been left to her own devices; Caesar could spare no thought to her on this day of days. And so she had summoned Conon and a light, fast chariot.

"Do I look all right?" she wanted to know.

"You are Minerva," Conon grunted.

Her plucked black brows arched. "Oh? Minerva? And what of Neith, who is Egypt's war goddess?"

"From today on, you shall be a Roman." .

"Do you think so? Why?"

"It is your fate. You and Caesar will rule the world. How else can you explain the things that have happened? Achillas is dead. Your brother Ptolemy is still a child for all the golden armor he wears today. Arsinoe will die or be captured, her army melt away. You and you alone shall be Egypt, just as Caesar is or shall be Rome."

"You grow philosophical, Conon. I didn't realize you entertained such thoughts." She frowned at him worriedly and he grinned back at her.

117

"A man has to do something with his time in the Lochias. Ione is dead—"

"I'm sorry about that. I've told you so, often enough."

"—and without her, I've lost interest in women. There's swordplay to keep in shape, but even an ex-gladiator gets tired of that. So I've found a new friend, a Greek tutor. He teaches me whatever Aristotle taught Alexander."

She nibbled at her lip, studying him. "You're too young to put aside women, Conon. We shall have to do something about that."

"I can never have the only woman I ever really loved. The others—to be brutal, they're merely a way of enjoying myself."

"Conon."

"Mmmm?"

"Today as we ride in the chariot—call me Thea."

The air around them was bright with growing sunlight. The last legionary had moved off the horizon, tramping steadily through the muddy ooze. Only the crews remained on the triremes, standing ready in case of need. Conon squinted past the Samson post on the foredeck. It was time.

Conon dropped overside onto a rope ladder and reached up to steady Cleopatra as she came down the rungs after him, her slim white legs seeming more shapely than ever in short military kilt and golden caligulae. She laughed when she saw his eyes staring up under the kilt.

"You're to keep your mind on fighting," she told him when he swung her off the rope and into the chariot. When he flushed her laughter rang out delightedly. "I begin to think you spend entirely too much time with that Greek tutor of yours, Conon. I'll have to look about for a Greek girl for you. Someone who's more obsessed with lechery than she is with learning."

He growled in his throat as he grasped the reins and chirped to the four matched bays fastened to the traces. These were chosen horses from the Stadium stables where they held the races in Alexandria, selected by Conon with an eye to speed and endurance. If he had to run from danger with Cleopatra, he wanted only the finest horseflesh in the harness.

Cleopatra came and leaned against him, resting her cheek on his upper arm. "Did you ever think, those years ago when we used to chatter so senselessly at that moon window in the wall of the temple gardens, that you would be driving a chariot for me as your queen some day?"

"Never," he exclaimed fervently.

118

She turned her head to look up into his bronzed face. "Why do you say it like that?"

"Because if I'd known I would have run away."

"Run away? You? But why?"

"Because I would have realized then as I do now, that some day you may be my death."

She cried out angrily at him. "What makes you say that?"

"A feeling I have. Call it an intuition."

"You could still run away," she snapped acidly.

He barked laughter at her and when she understood his mood, she flushed and moved back to him. He loved her very much, this simple youth. Knowing she might mean his death, he remained beside her, ready to give his life to protect her. The notion made her feel sad, but she was most aware of pride that she could inspire such emotion.

Conon reined up on a ridge that overlooked the battlefield. No matter how much Cleopatra entreated and begged, no matter how furious she grew and stamped her foot, he would go no closer. It was near enough to see the slow, inexorable advance of the legions, the charge of the gallant but outmanned Egyptian army.

"It allows you to play at being god," he told her.

"Oh? How so?"

"You can watch the whole battle, like a true Minerva. See there! The Egyptian cavalry charges—falters as the Roman bowmen let fly their shafts. Ah, and beyond them—where Caesar sends the shield-wall forward, look how the Egyptians fling themselves upon it and—are cut down! Nothing can stand against those short swords, Thea. Always remember it."

"I wish I had a sword in my hand now," she pouted.

"You'd run it between my ribs."

"I would! I would! Oh, Conon—be reasonable! You know how much this day means to me. If—"

"If I let anything happen to you, what would Caesar do to me? No, never mind Caesar. If anything happened to you, do you think I could stay alive? I would fall on my own sword, Thea. This I swear to you."

She slapped the rail of the chariot with her palm. "Nothing will happen, nothing will happen! I want to go closer. Closer!"

"To join in the fighting?" he asked queerly.

"Yes. Yes."

His big hands reached for the reins. "You may get your wish sooner than you think. See yonder."

A group of close to ten soldiers clad in the traditional spotted leopard of the Egyptian infantryman, with crossbands

119

of iron at their chests and metal lappets jangling at their kilts, came trotting along the narrow dirt road leading to the ridge. Each of them bore the figure-8 shield and a throwing javelin. Longswords hung over their shoulders on leather baldrics.

Trotting ahead of them was a slim figure clad in gold.

"Ptolemy," Cleopatra breathed.

"Aye, your brother," muttered Conon grimly. "We've got to get out of here."

There was only one way out for them, along the road where Ptolemy and his bodyguard came at the trot. Conon smiled grimly as he loosed his longsword in its scabbard and lifted one of the half dozen throwing spears from the quiver fastened to the chariot rail. If he could lessen the odds only a little, they might have some sort of chance.

Cleopatra caught his wrist as he lifted one of the javelins. "What are you going to do?"

"Kill men," he said simply.

"But those men are on our side. My brother—" She gasped and turned, crying out imperiously, "Ptolemy! Stand where you are, if you come in friendship."

"It's too late for friendship between us, Cleopatra. You made your choice when you played the whore with Caesar. This day settles things between us."

Conon waited for no more. He threw back his arm, then stepped forward. The light spear flew through the sunlight and buried itself in the chest of a man two steps to the rear of young Ptolemy. The man dropped without a sound. Conon hurled another javelin and a third.

"What I wouldn't give for a bow," he grumbled.

Cleopatra held fast to the chariot rail with numb fingers. To be so near to victory, yet now to stand face to face with death! Conon had opened her eyes to the truth. Young Ptolemy had come to find his old enemy, his older sister who had taken him in token marriage then refused him her bed and the throne she meant to keep for herself. Even knowing the truth, she found it hard to believe.

That he should dare!

Conon threw a fourth time, but now he missed.

Cleopatra reached for the reins. "Stand steady!" she hissed, and shouted to the horses, flipping the reins along their backs. The chariot lurched forward. Conon cried out hoarsely but the sudden wind of their running took away his words.

The bays were trained to sudden starts. They hit the traces with their full weight and their hooves dug into the soft

120

loam of the ridgetop. In moments they were flying along the road straight for the oncoming soldiers.

The men with Ptolemy were hired mercenaries. In their blood beat no loyalty for this stripling who led them. At sight of the four big stallions coming down the narrow road at them, they turned to scatter. Two of them left their feet, went floundering up to their knees in shallow water. Two others dropped flat and rolled to the very edge of the road, toes and fingers scrabbling for holds. The rest of them raced back the way they had come.

Cleopatra shrilled laughter and reached for the last remaining javelin. She caught it up, flung it at her brother. The slim barb passed over his head, missing him by inches.

Conon hurled his own light spear, butt foremost, not wanting to spill royal blood. The butt took Ptolemy in the belly, doubled him up for all his golden armor and hurled him backward off firm ground. Water geysered as he fell into the river swamp, screaming shrilly.

Cleopatra cursed vividly and yanked back on the reins. "Conon, you fool! You should have killed him. Get down. Use your sword. Finish him off."

His hand closed on her wrist. "There may be no need to shed blood, Thea. Wait and watch!"

Ptolemy had fallen into a pocket of deep water that rippled and washed the road in tiny wavelets as the youth struggled, waving his arms and crying out. His hands slapped the water as he flailed them. His voice grew shriller in terrible fear an instant before he sank under those disturbed waters.

"His armor is gold," Conon said. "It's very heavy."

Ptolemy did not reappear. The waters smoothed over, grew placid. Conon could picture the boy trying desperately to strain upward, to leap toward the air that would give him life. He would be weighted down by his cuirass so that his sandalled feet would sink deeper and deeper into the mire and the mud on the morass bottom.

Cleopatra sighed, shook the reins.

Her brother and husband was dead. She alone would rule in Egypt if Caesar should prove victorious this day. She rode with a curiously light heart, as if the Delphine sybil had whispered in her ear.

EIGHT

The Nile River

1.

The Temple of Isis was filled with the noblemen and women of Alexandria. They stood in twin ranks on either side of a broad carpet up which their queen, Cleopatra Thea Philopater, and her consort, Caius Julius Caesar, soon would walk. There was a breathlessness in the very air about them that held them all in thrall. Rumors had been flying fast and thick along the Canopic Way of late. Ptolemy was dead, drowned in the Nile morasses. Arsinoe was a prisoner in the Lochias palace. Ganymede had been beheaded on the field of battle, screaming out for mercy as Caesar and Cleopatra looked on.

The victory of the legions was complete.

The Egyptian army no longer existed. Cleopatra had stated publicly that from now on her army was the Roman legion. Let all the world know this for a fact. Whosoever attacked Cleopatra and Egypt—attacked Rome as well.

Peace had come to Alexandria.

Trumpets blared beyond the bronze temple doors. The steady tramp of Roman caligulae sounded on the tiled floors. The doors swung open. Cleopatra stood on the threshold, radiant in a tunic of golden tissue through which her ivory body might be glimpsed. She wore the golden pectoral blazing with emeralds and rubies, the great Khat headdress on her ebony locks, the traditional uraeus projecting outward above her forehead, golden wings clasping the six crowned uraei at its sides. From the collar resting on her shoulders and upper bosom two metal hawks depended, to match those on the plaques hanging from her apron girdle. At sight of her magnificence, men and women gasped. Never had she looked so royal!

And at her side, in special armor created by the palace goldsmiths, was Caesar himself, the man who would be

122

known as master of the world. In a golden cuirass decorated with the Roman eagles and with the lotus and the papyrus buds of Egypt, he walked solemnly beside the woman who was his formally proclaimed wife.

Two thrones waited them on a stepped dais. One, a little larger than the other, was ornate with the fasces of Rome. The smaller throne held Egyptian symbols, the flail, the ankh, the suti feather. Slowly the man and the woman paced the scarlet carpet, savoring this moment of their triumph, this instant when they were to weld together their two lands, their destinies.

Caesar turned, held out his hand. Cleopatra inclined her head, accepted his fingers as they guided her into her gilded ivory and ebony chair. Caesar seated himself beside her. There was a smell of incense in the air, the sound of voices faintly chanting. Caesar and Cleopatra looked out over the heads of their people toward the sunlight in the Temple square.

Advancing toward them came the priests of Isis, preceded by acolytes and temple dancers. Ranefer the high priest held a scroll in his hands. His face was flushed with pride, with the knowledge that he and he alone held this newly granted power contained in the papyrus parchment gripped between his fingers. When the little group reached the stepped dais, acolytes and dancers and priests prostrated themselves.

Only Ranefer remained standing. Proudly he unrolled the scroll, held it up that he might read the words inked in black incense-carbon mixed with gum arabic and water. His voice was sonorous. The words rolled from his lips with a grandeur that gave them something of the ring of truth.

"Know, people of Alexandria and of Egypt, know also people of Rome and its provinces, know all men and all women by these sacred writings the truth of which is attested by the words of the gods themselves—by Isis and Hathor, Osiris, Khem, Horus, Neith, Nut, Pasht, Maut and Set—by holy sacrifices and sacred divination! Understand therefor, that this woman—Cleopatra Thea Philopater—and this man— Caius Julius Caesar—are this day forward to be known not merely as woman and man but as—goddess and god!"

Ranefer heard the indrawn gasps rising up from the men and women of Alexandria. He smiled secretly to his thoughts. Ah, it had been a fine night those years back when Isis had directed him to enter the temple and find little Cleopatra crouched naked and afraid at the feet of the goddess herself! How much had happened since then! By royal proclamation he was high priest in the very temple where he had saved her

123

from Achillas. Achillas himself was dead. Cleopatra ruled in Egypt as Caesar ruled in Rome, as he himself ruled this temple and all other temples of Isis everywhere in the world.

"Cleopatra *Dea* shall be her name. Caesar *Deus* shall be his name. Golden statues of them as gods are to be placed in all the temples of the land where they shall be adored and sacrificed to as is fitting to their godhood. . . . "

In the dusk of evening Cleopatra *Dea* and Caesar *Deus* sat on ebony lounges on the deck of the royal barge Thalameyos as its hundred silver sweeps touched the waters of the Nile, propelling the great vessel southward away from Alexandria toward Memphis and distant Thebes. Massive and imposing, the great yacht gleamed in the setting sun like an apparition from the Land of the Two Truths, that holy country where live the gods and goddesses.

Now that their godhood had been publicly proclaimed, they could travel among their worshippers. Already on the foredeck two priests were readying a fowl and a lamb for the sacrificial knife that would drain their life blood to the honor and glory of the new gods. Slavegirls crouched over silver lyres, fingertips gently vibrating the taut strings, filling the gathering night with melody. The scent of incense and perfume moved the length and breadth of the galley, wafted by the evening breezes.

"You are not mistaken?" wondered Caesar breathlessly.

Cleopatra smiled. "There is no mistake. I am pregnant. Before you leave for Pontus as you mean to do despite all I say—I will bear your child."

"Let it be a son," the Roman whispered.

"As Caesar *Deus* wishes, so shall it be."

They dreamed in the darkening twilight of the child who should be born to them. He would be no ordinary man, surely! With Cleopatra as his mother and Caesar as his father, he would be a god himself. Strong, tall, brave, intelligent, handsome. He must be all these things or else there was no truth in all their world.

The silver oars moved gently. The Nile moon lifted into the sky. Slavegirls came with platters of cybium slices, a sea food delicacy, oysters and pork sausages, the roasted livers of geese, the wings of plump fowl. They ate and listened to the music of the lyres and knew a great contentment. The night was warm and pleasant. With the stars high overhead, it seemed they drifted through a veritable Nirvana here on earth.

And later, when Caesar divested himself of his purple robes that were sprinkled so heavily with gold dust, he found a pretty slavegirl waiting for him on his couch. In surprise, he stared down at her dusky red skin revealed in all its nakedness.

"Girl, Cleopatra will have your skin flayed off for this."

"It was Royal Egypt who sent me, lord."

"What's that you say?"

"She carries your child, great one. Her body has become sacred. It is to be the temple of Caesarion himself."

"Caesarion?"

"It is the name the queen selected for her son."

Julius Caesar hid a smile with his hand. How much like this young Egyptian woman to consider his male desires even while she held herself aloof from him because of their child growing in her womb. She never ceased to surprise and delight him.

He had no intention of bedding down with this young female, however. He would go to Cleopatra and rest beside her without touching her. If she as his mother could remain continent, he as the father of Caesarion—he chuckled at the name—could do no less.

"Get up, girl. I have no need of you." To take the sting from his words he twisted a gold ring from his finger and gave it to her.

The girl stared from the ring on her palm to this man who had been named a god. She began suddenly to be afraid. The queen had told her to amuse and entertain great Caesar. If she failed in her task, she might be beaten. Trembling, she threw herself from the couch onto the carpet where he stood. Her arms went about his legs as she pressed her hard young breasts against his thighs.

"Master, love me," she breathed. "As my name is Athys, it is her command."

He looked down at her black hair, tumbled about her smooth shoulders. His gaze ran down her curving back to the rounded moons of her plump buttocks. He was not as insensitive to her nudity as he would have liked to be. The caresses of her breasts as she rubbed them this way and that on his upper thighs made him gasp. In all these long months he had known only the body of Cleopatra. She was so perfect, so wise in the erotic arts that he had felt no need for any other woman.

"Master, I will be beaten," the girl panted.

He put down his hands to grasp her shoulders and lift her upward but she writhed so that his fingers missed their grip and tightened instead over the bowls of her heavy breasts. Gently he caressed them, felt them extend their red nipples

125

against his palms. Caesar felt his blood beat faster. Surely it would do no harm to dally a little with this girl named Athys. It would enable him to rest more comfortably beside Cleopatra when he went to her cabin.

His hands drew the girl to her feet. His palms went to her hard buttocks, stroking them until the girl cried out softly. Then he pushed her toward the bed and lifted off his undertunic, never taking his eyes from the girl kneeling on the edge of the bed and waiting for him. A hard smile touched his lips as he walked toward her.

Cleopatra knew him better than he knew himself.

The journey down the Nile occupied almost a full month.

It was a time for relaxation and entertainment. In Memphis they attended the rites of Apis and feasted in temple gardens hung with candle lanterns. During the long travel down the stretch of river waters from Memphis to Thebes they studied the ancient scrolls loaned to them by the priests from secret vaults in the Serapion.

Caesar swam daily in the Nile while archers and slaves guarded him from possible attack by crocodiles. Cleopatra dabbled her bare feet in the river waters and munched on pomegranates, considered by the physicians of her time to be excellent for expectant mothers, laughing and jesting with him.

It was a leisurely progress southward. They were in no hurry. Cleopatra became more beautiful, for the hollows of her face filled with flesh and her breasts grew larger, swollen with milk. Even Caesar put on weight while the Egyptian sun tanned his body until he became akin to a bronze statue. Their laughter might ring out over the morning meal or in those hours of the night when only the guttering candles seemed awake. Guards could hear them discussing the writings of Thucydides, of Xenophon, the *Antiquities* of Herodotus. Cleopatra insisted on seeing a play of Sophocles in the flesh and drafted Romans, Egyptians and slaves to the roles in *Oedipus the King*.

During the early hours of the afternoon, Caesar always worked on the writing of his Alexandrine War, and caught up on certain notes of his Commentaries for which he had never yet had the time and inclination. He found in Cleopatra an apt student, eager to learn and understand the military tactics which had always won him victory, the various political factions that turned Rome this way and that, out of which Caesar had risen like the fabled phoenix from the ashes.

Theirs was a communion, not only of the body but of the

mind. Only once did Caesar broach the subject of the slave-girl Athys to her, asking was she not jealous of those hours he spent with her in his bed.

She smiled lazily. "Athys does only what I cannot do, during your nights with her. I make her tell me everything that happens, naturally. What she says, what you say, the things you do with one another."

Caesar made a wry face, then laughed, shaking his head. "And if she conceives as you did?"

"She will be allowed to have the child, but it will be strangled an instant after it is born."

"Can you be so jealous?"

"Jealous? Certainly not! I do it only to protect Caesarion. One son of Caesar in Egypt is enough."

Even in this she was wise, he decided.

All Egypt as far as he could see was grist to his hungry mind. He had vials of kiki oil brought aboard that he might study it, seeking to determine whether this product of the castor bean might be useful to him in his wars. When he saw the long pole of the shaduf with its dangling bucket dipped for water, he must be rowed ashore to inspect it. From this he turned to the water wheel with attached buckets.

"I mean to war in Africa where the heat is very great and the water supply not overly plentiful," he explained to Cleopatra. "Any method of getting water accordingly interests me."

He stood entranced by the starboard rail, studying the bird life of the river. Pelicans, ibises, herons, all drew his sharp eyes and questing mind. He watched as a clap-net was unfolded and used to snare a few ducks for dinner, marveling at the skill of these fishers for winged creatures.

The river boats built from bundles of papyrus sheaves also caught his attention. They were light craft, easily manageable. They could even put to sea if necessary. A dozen of them, filled with oil lamps so as to be set on fire, might wreak havoc with an enemy fleet, he decided.

They went ashore at the city of Abydos to visit its grove sacred to Osiris. Legend stated that the great sepulcher in the middle of the grove was that of the god, that here he lay forever in a stone tomb. Caesar removed a ring and Cleopatra a thin gold bracelet and left them behind as offerings to the god. Within walking distance of the tomb was another grove, sacred to the goddess of fertility, Min. Cleopatra walked there accompanied only by Iras and Charmion, for she wanted to be alone with the goddess and whisper prayers to her.

Caesar spent the time while she was gone discussing the

Wepawet festival with the high priest. Tolerant of religion as were most Romans, Caesar was fascinated by their many rituals. When Cleopatra joined him, slipping her hand into his with a little smile, he was as conversant with the mystery of Osiris as any well-informed Egyptian.

Through the river valley formed by the rocky cliffs on either side of the Nile, they came at last to Thebes and its magnificent temples to the gods at Karnak and Luxor. Side by side they strolled between the massive columns of the Temple to Amen. Together they gasped at the grandeur of that other temple built by Queen Hatshepsut fifteen centuries before, and dedicated to the love goddess, Hathor, and to Anubis of the jackel head.

Here beneath these brooding red sandstone cliffs, they seemed to be one with eternity itself. Far away was the struggle for world power, far away the sons of Pompey and the threat of Pharnaces in Pontus. The air of timelessness drew them closer even than they had been.

So touched was Caesar that he gave a bag of golden coins to the slavegirl Athys and sent her back to Cleopatra. "Tell your mistress that, having known her, I no longer have a need for other women."

Cleopatra was pleased and told him so, but she understood that within a week, or perhaps two, the fires of Eros would burn again in Caesar's loins. She pondered over this, holding consultations with the priests of Hathor. Athys she sent back to Alexandria, since she was not with child, and cast about for some other way by which to keep Caesar entertained.

The days passed into weeks.

2.

Conon was getting drunk.

He swayed as he walked between the wooden tables and benches of the inn of the Silver Serpent, carrying a leather mug filled to overflowing with barley beer. There was a sullen anger in him that made him scowl darkly and push away anyone who came to share the bench where he ate his beans and bread and swallowed the cool flagons of beer. He knew a need for loneliness.

Every time he lifted a tankard to his lips he saw the face of Cleopatra floating inside it. Or was it the face of Ione? His eyes had become glazed with liquor, and it was hard at such times for him to differentiate between the two. He loved them both in his own way, but for different reasons.

Sometimes he would chuckle, staring down into his mug. "I love two women and I can't have either one of them. One's dead and the other might as well be, since she's a queen. Thea! Thea! We could have been so happy, you and I."

A woman came from the shadows to slip onto the bench beside him, putting a bare arm around his throat and letting him know the heaviness of her breasts through the thin tunic she wore over her nakedness. She smiled brightly when he stared at her.

"Come with me, Conon. You've been too long by yourself."

"I need no woman," he growled. "Go away."

"Every man needs a woman. Caesar needs Cleopatra, doesn't—"

His hand on her shoulder thrust her off the bench so that she landed on her buttocks in a puddle of spilled wine. She swore feelingly, struggling to her feet and pulling the cloth from her reddened rump.

"No need to lose your head," she snapped.

"Don't mention his name. Or hers!"

She leered at him. "Touched you on a raw spot, didn't I? You and your harlot queen!" His hand stabbed out, tangled its fingers in her loose black hair. Savagely he bent her head, banged it down on the wine-wet tabletop until she howled.

The onlookers applauded, encouraging Conon to do more than wipe her face on the table. When a big man who was blind in one eye got to his feet at the far end of the room, they began to pound the tables with their tankards. Osorkon had only one eye but he was the strongest man in the dockside tavern—excepting perhaps for Conon himself. They had never matched muscles, these two. Now the crowd saw a possibility for free entertainment.

Conon was rubbing the woman's face in the spilled wine when Osorkon came up to the table and growled at him. "Let her go, Conon. Ma'at is my woman."

The Guards captain showed his white teeth in a mirthless grin. His hand moved back and forth more slowly, dragging Ma'at's face this way and that across the wine puddles. It was a defiant gesture and it made the crowd bellow delightedly.

Osorkon lunged with both hands stretched out.

Conon was not there when his hands closed on empty air. Kicking free of the bench, he slipped to his feet and stood waiting. Osorkon slammed into the table, almost upsetting it.

His face red with embarrassment, he pushed himself to his feet.

He was a heavy man, this Osorkon, but his belly was distended from overmuch beer, and he was slow. Conon, who faced him with both palms held upward, was almost his size, but hard and solid as a sword.

"No need to fight over a woman, Osorkon," Conon said.

Ma'at wailed, rubbing her raw cheek. "He tried to kill me. He would have, if you hadn't interfered."

Osorkon growled, "Quiet, wench." He liked young Conon, who was a well-behaved lad. Usually he could hold his beer and the cheap Cretan wines he drank when he came to the Silver Serpent. There was something eating in him these days. If he didn't know better, he'd think he was in love. Osorkon scowled and scratched his shaven head.

"I guess the wench deserved it," he grumbled at last.

His fairness touched Conon, who put a hand to the purse hanging from his swordbelt. "No, I shouldn't have been so rough. Ma'at, take these silver pieces and excuse me."

Ma'at stared at the sesterces on his palm. Of a sudden her cheeks no longer burned. She licked her heavy mouth with a thick wet tongue. "I only wanted to cheer you up," she apologized. Those silver coins were a fortune in her eyes. For that much money Conon could do as he liked with her. Hesitantly she reached out and took them from his hand.

The crowd was disappointed. Here and there a few catcalls sounded but they stopped when Osorkon turned and laid his hard eyes across the room. "Conon is my friend," he said heavily.

"And mine," nodded Ma'at, biting into a coin.

Conon stumbled to the barrel counter and paid his reckoning to the fat man seated there on a stool. Nausea worked in his middle. He was sick to death of cheap beer and stinking taverns, of cheaper women who could be had for as little as a copper obol.

Life for Conon had lost its savor.

He moved at an erratic pace along the cobblestones of the Harbor quarter, staring heavily and with drunken gravity straight ahead. Twice wandering bands of sailors heard the jingle of his coin-sack but decided against attempting to take it from him after a look at his hard, cold eyes. Once a dockside harlot came up to him, catching his hand and pushing it under her dress before she caught his air of sullen savagery and backed away.

At last he came to the great stone mole that ran between

130

the great harbor and the sea. It was night and moonlight made a silver radiance on the waters. A vague sadness worked in Conon. He was young and healthy. It was madness to waste away his strength because the woman he loved was out of his reach. He ought to find a girl from his own class and marry her, maybe even open a *ludi,* a school for gladiators. With Cleopatra securely on the throne, business would be good in Alexandria. Rich men would make even more money and so give more gladitorial shows. There would be a need for men trained in the use of sword and shield, net and trident.

Moonlight flashed far out on the waters.

Conon blinked his eyes. Almost it seemed that—

There it was again. Brilliant moonlight and—no! The reflection of the moon and the water off metal. And a hundred candles lighted, gleaming in the darkness! As he held his breath he could hear the thump of oars in tholes, the hammer on the gong as a slave beat out the rhythm for the rowers. A galley, moving parallel with the eastern frontier road from Pelusium.

The royal galley! The Thalameyos.

His heart leaped high in his chest and his drunkenness fell away from him as if by some sorcerous incantation. His lips opened to bellow out his joy. Cleopatra was home again. What did it matter if she brought the Roman with her? He could feast his eyes on her again, drink her in with his every breath.

He would go to her now. This instant!

He hurled his cloak from him, slipped out of his leather cuirass, dropped his undertunic and loincloth on the cobbles, kicked free of his sandals. With a running dive, he went deep into the salt sea water, began swimming with strong, powerful strokes.

They heard his bull voice first on the slave benches. Then a slavegirl cried out at sight of his bobbing head between the choppy waves. Naked, he was lifted by strong arms and brought like that before Cleopatra who clapped her hands and laughed in sheer delight at sight of him.

"Now I know I'm home again," her voice called out to Caesar where he stood at the port rail, smiling faintly. "Conon has come to scold me."

Caesar considered the big ex-gladiator. Of an age with his young queen, he obviously adored her like a dumb beast. As long as he was satisfied to be only that, and not to know the stab of ambition, Caesar was content. Since he had to leave Cleopatra, he wanted her served loyally and without question.

A Guard captain had little authority, however.

Caesar frowned. He must arrange matters differently at the first opportunity. And soon. He had spent enough time—and yet, oddly, not nearly enough time!—on the river Nile at holiday with his little Egyptian queen. He had to go back to work, to mold the world in which he lived into something which he could hand over to his son, Caesarion, from his deathbed.

If indeed, Cleopatra bore him a son.

And if he could win the world.

3.

At the farewell feast to Caesar, Conon lay at table in the solid silver armor of a general of Royal Egypt. Where Achillas once had stood with relation to young Ptolemy, now he stood within the shadow of Cleopatra. His table was but one removed from that of the queen. Noblemen and their wives fawned on him, seeking small favors, begging his intercession with the queen. Lovely women hinted that they would not be averse to spending a few hours in his chambers once the feast was over.

With all this, Conon was uncomfortable.

He was a plain man, asking little out of life. The leather tankards of the dockside tavern tasted the same to his lips as did the golden goblets of the banquet hall. The food was richer here—peacock's tongue simmered in wine sauce, goose livers thick with mushrooms—but black bread and beans were just as palatable to the tongue. And probably a lot healthier! He grinned sourly into his wine goblet. Isis! He was becoming an old boar. Instead of being grateful to Caesar, he found himself resenting his promotion.

To his mind, it smacked of bribery.   .

Yes, this was what he resented most. The Roman thought he had to bribe him to take care of Cleopatra. Of Cleopatra and his child. Conon would have died for her. Oh, aye—and the child as well, since it was fruit of her flesh.

He needed no titles, no fortune in golden *aurei* which was the pay of a general of the army, to make him do his duty. The trouble with those Romans was, they thought everybody who wasn't a Roman citizen had a price. They couldn't understand that a man could do what was right because it

132

was expected of him. Loyalty they conceived to be exclusively a Roman virtue.

Conon grinned coldly. Some day he would like to teach them loyalty! With a sword in his hand and Cleopatra at his back. Gods, how he would fight for her. He wondered if the time would ever come for him to prove himself.

A slim white hand caught his golden goblet, drew it from his fingers. It was bent out of shape; only then was Conon conscious of the tight grip by which his muscular hand had held it. The slavegirl replaced the cup with another and filled it with rich Thasian.

Over the silver ewer, Conon stared at Caesar.

The Roman was studying him, so Conon sat up straighter, lifting his chin, conscious of a sense of defiance. There was a roaring in his ears, so violent was his resentment of this man.

Then Caesar was speaking loudly, calling the eyes of everyone at the feast to Conon in his new silver armor, "General Conon, you are angry. Or—can it be that you are worried?"

There was a cold amusement in the eyes that stared so directly at him, as though Caesar could read the thoughts swirling around in his mind. Conon heard the quick mutter of conversation up and down the tables and knew that the pampered Alexandrines expected to see him baited and discomfited.

"Neither, highness," he called back. "I only consider the gravity of my new position here at court."

"You are alarmed at your new duties, then?"

Conon laughed. "My duty is to protect Cleopatra from all her enemies, even from—Romans. Such a task will be my pleasure, not my problem."

Ah, that stirred them up. A dozen of his high-ranking officers made as if to rise from their couches, but lay back when Caesar gestured at them. He was smiling more broadly now, as if pleased at the way the talk was going.

"Don't you like Romans, Conon?"

"I am indifferent to them. If they are friendly to my queen, I am their friend. If they prove her enemies, then they are my enemies."

"A simple philosophy. Yet I find it acceptable. I sail with the morning tide, Conon. I can spare few soldiers and no officers to protect your queen. This becomes your task."

"I knew that when I let you name me general."

"I can as easily demote you to the rank of captain of guards."

"Demote me, then. You'll be doing me a favor. I won't have any duty then except to see that Cleopatra is safe." Conon rose to his feet, hand reaching for the silver phalerae and torques which denoted his high rank. With a sudden jerk he ripped them from his cuirass.

His hand threw them on the floor before Caesar. "Take back your promotion, Roman, if it worries you so much. I'm not your man, anyhow. I belong to Cleopatra."

Cleopatra applauded, squealing in ecstasy. Caesar looked momentarily annoyed, then laughed and began twisting a huge emerald ring off his finger.

Conon growled, "I want no bribe, either."

Caesar said coldly, "The ring is not for you but for your queen. She won a bet just now. She said you didn't care one iota about your new rank. I taunted you to see if you did. I believe her, gladiator." He gestured at the phalerae on the floor. "Take them up. Put them on. They come from Cleopatra, not from me."

Cleopatra nodded and said, "Put them on again, Conon. Don't you know I need a general, now that I am queen in truth?"

He flushed as a slavegirl ran to fetch the silver discs. He fidgeted as she pinned them back into place. She was a pretty little thing, all dusky reddish skin and black hair, a true Egyptian. He was very conscious of her perfumed nudity.

"Take the girl too, Conon," cried Cleopatra. "Her name is Athys."

He wanted no slave, but he muttered his thanks.

Caesar and his legions sailed with the morning tide. From a balcony of her bedchamber, Cleopatra watched as the triremes sank slowly into the distance. She wondered during those long, empty hours if she would ever see Caius Julius Caesar again.

He might meet his death in Pontus, fighting Pharnaces. Or the blade of an assassin, hired by the sons of Pompey, might find his back in an unguarded moment. So many things could happen! An illness—he was not a young man!—might put him on his bier. Fear thrust an icy chill into her middle where her child was stirring.

If Caesar should die—what would happen to his son?

Would the legions come to claim him as rightful ruler in Rome? Or would the legions come to slay him and his mother lest they prove annoying to some future dictator come to power in the city on the Tiber? Cleopatra shivered. If they came in strength against her, she must be ready to defend herself!

She would need an army and a navy.

Alliances too, she must make, with fellow rulers such as King Amyntas of Galatia and Lycaonia, Philadelphus, king of Paphlagonia, Saladus, king of Thrace and Mithradates, king of Commagene. If possible, she must form an iron ring around Egypt, hedged with swords and spears, through which no enemy could penetrate.

It was an almost impossible task.

Yet during the weeks before her child was born, she threw herself into this business of statecraft with an obsession that kept her on the throne long hours, speaking with ambassadors, granting privileges to wealthy merchants in return for which she accepted shares in their ventures, dispensing justice with an eye to her own personal needs.

When her labor pains began on a cold and cheerless morning, Cleopatra told herself that she had made a start toward strengthening the kingdom which her child would inherit. She had added substantially to the treasure she had brought with her to Alexandria when she had come to Caesar, from the coffers of the Roman, Rabirius Porthumus. She had allied the throne, not only to the kingdoms which were neighbor to her land of Egypt but to the energies of the merchant princes of Alexandria and Memphis, as well.

Olympus her physician was with her now, day and night, as were Iras and Charmion. Votive bowls offered incense to Min and to Hathor, to Isis and Osiris, for the grace of a fortunate birth. Everywhere in Alexandria men and women gathered in taverns and on street corners to listen for the bray of trumpets from the palace wallwalks that would signal the birth of an heir to the throne.

She was in labor three hours. For most of that time she was delirious, fancying that she was once again rolled up in a carpet and smothering, that it was too tight about her loins, squeezing them until they were on fire. She cried out to Apollodorus to loosen them, to free her of this burden, but he was deaf to her cries.

Sweat ran down her face, was wiped away by cool cloths.

She screamed many times, terrible cries that resounded from the walls and all across the Brucheion. Her little fists hammered the bedcovers and her legs lashed out as though she would flee from this awful agony that had come upon her flesh.

Conon heard her wailing and suffered with her. He would

135

have gone to her, to try in some way to ease her suffering, but Olympus had forbidden him. Nor was he a husband to override his vetoes. He must wait in silence and think of Caesar, blaming him for this that had happened to his Thea.

And then there were no more screams. The palace was silent, hushed. Conon waited, staring up at the window which was that of the royal bedchamber. Was she still alive? If so, why didn't she cry out? At least then he knew she was suffering the pangs of motherhood. This way he could not know whether the child had killed her or—

A white cloth waved in the window recess.

A son had been born to Cleopatra! Conon went weak and leaned against the marble railing where he stood. His heart slammed in his rib case with savage vigor. A boy! Caesarion. Everything was all right with Cleopatra. Right now she might be smiling, nursing her child.

It was time to send the news to Caesar.

NINE

Rome 46-44 B. C.

1.

At Zela in Pontus, Caesar fell upon Pharnaces and destroyed him. In his letters to the Roman Senate he wrote on wax, *Veni*, I came. *Vidi*, I saw. *Vici*, I conquered. It was a catch-phrase that was to please the Roman people and forge one more stone of the pedestal on which was to rise the image of Caesar as emperor, as a divine *augustus*. It was in his mind, certainly, the evening after the battle when his clerk made the impressions with his stylus according to his commands.

Outside the tent-walls could be heard the tramp of marching troops, the groans and cries of the wounded being carried back for treatment by the army physicians. Caesar paced the hardpacked dirt floor slowly, his mind alive, seeking words, questing for the proper method of saying what must be said to the people, to Antony his cavalry general—a madcap who was always getting into some sort of trouble, one way or another—to the Senate, to young Horace, whose brilliant prose could make or break a reputation.

Caesar was tired. His hands touched his forehead, stroking slowly. He should sleep but there was so much to do, so much. If it had not been for that holiday trip down the Nile—he smiled whenever he thought back on it—he would not have been so filled with energy for this latest campaign here in Asia Minor.

In his letters to the Senate he stated that he fought this war with the son of Mithradates, Pharnaces, because Pharnaces endangered the eastern borders of the Roman world. A proud man, Pharnaces believed that what his great father had won, then lost, he himself could win—and keep.

Within five days after entering Pontus, Caesar and his legions came up with Pharnaces. The battle lasted four hours. When it was over, the son of Mirthradates lay dead of wounds on the battlefield. His army was broken, his kingdom was no more.

The truth of the matter was simply that Caesar was eliminating a possible menace to Cleopatra and her child. Asia Minor was closer to Egypt than it was to Rome. If Pharnaces had grown in power he might have looked across the wilderness of Shur at Egypt and coveted its wealth for himself.

Now he was free to travel to Africa, where Metullus Scipio and King Juba of Numidia held together what was left of the Pompeian party. Destroy them—and after them the sons of Pompey—and he would have won the world. The great energy that had burned him throughout his life was in ebb, now. He could not do the things he had done ten years earlier. Like a miser, he must conserve his strength and use it only when needed.

The main thing he must do is stand alone in Rome without a rival. Smash Scipio and Juba, smash Pompey's sons in Spain, and he would be ready to consider the title of emperor. Time was of the essence. He must ship his troops to the shores of Africa at once. There must be no delay.

Not even his tiredness, his fatigue and aching head must stop him. He continued pacing, dictating steadily. The scratching of the stylus echoed his every word. The sounds of the camp after the victory gradually faded out. . . .

Caesar was gone when the ship bearing news of the birth of Caesarion arrived in Pontus. There was nothing left to do but weigh anchor for Africa; the messenger dared not return to Alexandria with the report of failure. He consoled himself with the thought that he might buy a pretty slavegirl in the great marketplace of Zela. He would while away the hours until the ship beached at Leptis Minor, which was Caesar's base in Africa, by teaching her a few of the vices to which he was particularly addicted.

The African sun was hot. Underfoot the sands were like red coals, burning, sheer torture in the march. Caesar soon discovered that the enemy would not stand and fight as Pharnaces had done in his arrogance. It was a case of Britain all over again, running his quarry to earth like fleeing hares, moving cavalry units like draughts pieces on a board, trying to pin down Scipio and Juba where he could hit them with his veterans.

Caesar walked with his troops, encouraging them by his actions. It was like the old man, they thought, to show them he was as good a trooper as any of them. It was one of the things they admired most about him. Tepid water and stale food, hot sun and blazing sands, he accepted them as his lot because they were their own.

The days drifted slowly into weeks.

Caesar became impatient. He lay encamped at Thapsus and gave orders that his men were not to offer battle to the enemy but were to disengage and run wherever two patrols might meet. In this way he hoped that Scipio or Juba might believe his men afraid, worn out by this constant attack and withdrawal, diffident to the point of despair.

Scipio would have none of it, knowing Caesar too well.

"He is a fox, that man," he told King Juba in their war tent late one afternoon. "He is always thinking, always planning just a step and a jump ahead of you."

Juba was inclined to disbelief, even to the point of contempt. No Roman, he boasted an arrogance almost as great as that of Pharnaces. His own father, Juba the Elder, had been king before him, here in Numidia. His father had failed—like Mithradates—to overcome the Roman legions. Pharnaces had been unable to make good his boast to do what his father could not; he, Juba the Younger, would not fail.

"We will attack," he said heavily to Scipio. Huge and muscular, with a chest covered by thick reddish hair, he was a bull of a man. In fur kaunake and broad leather belt from which hung two swords and a dagger, he adopted the trappings of a barbarian prince, having long since discovered that as a barbarian he might be excused for boorishness which in a sophisticated Roman would be unpardonable.

"But Caesar—"

"Caesar is one man. Brave he may be, but he is over fifty years of age. His soldiers will do his fighting, and his soldiers have no stomach for it. My hot African sun has cooked the guts out of them."

His thick laughter rose into the tent, stirring echoes.

"I don't like it," the Roman protested. "I tell you—"

Juba hurled his winecup across the tent, face flushed angrily. "My troops advance at dawn. Will yours support them?" They locked eyes, these men whose backgrounds and whose training were so very different. Metullus Scipio would have stalked from the tent but he was well aware that a divided army is a beaten army. If Juba was so intent on fighting—

"I'll support you. But against my better judgment."

Juba only laughed and shook his head. These cold Romans. If they spent half the time fighting that they spend thinking about fighting, they would—

He scowled. They would own the world? They owned it now, except for a few places like his Numidia or like Parthia in western Asia. Juba shrugged and bawled for a slave to come bring him another goblet and wine to go in it.

The armies met on a level strip of coastal plain not far from Thapsus. At first onset, so savage was the attack of the Numidian cavalry wings of Juba, the Aludae and the other legions gave ground. The onslaught was fierce, bitter. Horses reared, kicking into the helmeted faces of the legionaries with their hoofs even as the dreaded short swords stabbed upward into their bellies. Lances drove down at shields ornamented with the thunderbolt design. Men screamed and fell, to be replaced by others in the ranks.

Blood flowed freely where steel bit into their flesh. Where hooves drove into faces and heads, there were only sodden sounds and the slow, wet gurgle of dripping blood. The legion shields bent and moved inward, but they held.

In the instant of their holding, when Juba's cavalry was engaged all along its front, Caesar moved his own horsemen, fierce savages out of the forests of Gaul and serving under the eagles for Roman gold. They drove onto Juba's flank, enveloped his main cavalry body and pinned them to the *gladii* of the foot soldiers.

Juba raged until his mouth foamed.

A cavalry unit must be mobile. It loses its effectiveness if contained in one spot. Without his wild riders to back up and help out his infantry, he was lost. There was no soldier in the world so effective as the Roman legionary and the men who fought with Julius Caesar were veterans of a hundred battles. Slowly the shields and the stabbing swords filled in the curve of their first bending and inched forward.

African sunlight on their short blades and on the points of their pilums danced and winked all across the plain. Reinforced with Thracian bowmen and a corps of slingers from the Balearic islands, they surged to the offensive. Scipio—raging in despair because this is what he could have predicted, had Juba been less hotheaded—was fully involved by now.

The savage struggle went on.

A trumpet blared the Roman charge.

All along the line, Juba and Scipio were pulling back. More than half their army was gone, lying dead and motionless in the desert dust, beginning already to be cooked by the awful heat. It was time now for Caesar to hit them with the reserve and with those units of the advance forces still able to attack. Arrows and pilums flew through the air. The legionaries roared and ran forward.

Less than half the men under Juba remained to brace against this final thrust. The rest simply threw away their shields and weapons and ran. To his right, Scipio drew his own command closer about him, determined to sell himself as dearly as possible.

Juba tried to escape on a fast Numidian mare. A cavalry unit overtook him, and a husky rider dove through the air from the back of his own mount, wrapping muscular arms about the Numidian king. Juba crashed into the dust and bounced. Half conscious, he was still struggling when manacles were brought and his thick, hairy wrists were clamped into them.

In chains, he was dragged before Caesar.

He stood panting, great chest lifting and falling inside his fur kaunake. His black eyes were brilliant, fearless. The wind fluttered his long red hair, caught in a caul of golden wires.

"Kill me," he demanded of Caesar.

The Roman only smiled and shook his head, saying, "I have something else in mind for you Juba. Something you will hate worse than death."

Scipio, they cut to pieces amid his own soldiers.

It was here, while Caesar watched the captured thousands marched off to the blacksmiths who would put them in iron chains, that the messenger from Cleopatra caught up with him. Going down on a knee, he held out a thin ivory cylinder which held the papyrus scroll written by the queen of Egypt in her own hand.

Caesar shouted at sight of those words.

A son had been born to him! Cleopatra had been right.

Caesarion! Or more properly, Caesar Ptolemais.

He was too dignified a man, especially surrounded by his officers, to do the little dance his happiness urged. He contented himself with light laughter and a pleased smile, but from time to time his aides could hear him humming under his breath.

Before the last captive was in camp, he was dictating a letter to his secretary to be carried by Cleopatra's messenger back to Alexandria. In it he invited the queen of Egypt to come to Rome with the son Caesar had not yet seen.

2.

Cleopatra made a floating temple of the royal trireme which would carry her to Rome, and in its large main cabin she placed a lifesize statue of herself as Isis, carved by Diomedes of Rhodes on Caesar's request. It glistened redly in the reflection of half a hundred candles. Before it burned a dozen bowls of natron, filling the air with a sickly sweet scent. It was flanked by an ebony and ivory depiction of Astarte and a painted alabaster masterpiece of Aphrodite, looted from an Athens temple two centuries before.

In this pantheon she held court as Cleopatra-Isis.

A highbacked chair was set up before the states so that it seemed the living Cleopatra was one with the statued goddesses. She wore few clothes. The statues, being of love goddesses, were nude except for the jewels that glittered from their throats and arms and ankles. Moreover, the temperature in the room was oppressive; besides, as a goddess of the carnal pleasures, she had no secrets from her worshippers.

No common man went near her, of course. Only the captain of the vessel, Hathotep, who had been an admiral under Achillas and had wisely switched allegiance before Caesar had struck down the Alexandrine army—and two handsome young slaveboys—were permitted into her godlike presence. As gifts for Caesar's high officers, she brought along ten of the most beautiful slavegirls she could find, each of them an expert in the Venerian arts.

Caesarion was in a cradle in her sleeping cabin.

From the captain she received reports as to their progress across the Inland Sea twice daily, in the morning and then before the evening meal. It was the summer of the year, an excellent time for sea travel since the Etesian and the *ponento* winds were at their best behavior. Usually it took at least nine days to travel from Alexandria to Rome, but at her urging Hathotep had crowded on sail until it seemed his trireme would be overborne by their sheer weight. He also ordered the oarsmen to stroke on through the night, letting them sleep by day.

Seven days, she had said; in seven days she must set foot on Roman soil. Privately, Hathotep did not believe any ship ever built could make such a swift journey, but as the winds held and the oars moved steadily, he began to wonder. Perhaps the incense burning before the love goddesses in the pantheon might have something to do with their luck. They were making fantastic strides over this sea the Romans called Mare Internum, and its waters boiled merrily in their wake.

After the captain had left, the heavy doors were barred against the intrusion of any male other than the two slaveboys. It had been over a year, including the time of her pregnancy, since Cleopatra had participated in any fleshly pleasures. Her loins burned for attention.

She knew well enough that Caesar, being an older man, would never be able to attend her with enough passion to satisfy her fevers. His energies too, would be depleted by his recent military campaigns. And so this sea voyage must be another kind of trip for her, a venture into the world of erotic pleasure, without rest, without inhibition.

On her high throne, she commanded the youths to please her. In her ceremonial jewels she bade them kneel and caress her with hands and lips until the blood in her veins was lava and her ripe ivory hips twisted and writhed in uncontrollable spasms. Her soft cries of delight became screams. Sometimes her voice was audible on deck, but only barely; the wind blew too steadily for sustained hearing. To the oarsmen and the officers and soldiers of her guard, it seemed that sirens were calling from distant lands, putting thoughts in their heads of the carnal pleasures waiting when they dropped anchor.

In the pantheon, Cleopatra permitted herself to be teased and tormented until there was an actual pain in her flesh. Only then, sweating and crying out in fevered passion, would she allow the slaveboys to take her, pinning her down on the thick carpets covering the floor, making them come at her like maddened beasts hungry for relief.

She fed them drugs that had been old when Sumer was young, that they might be giants in their potency. At her order, the pretty slavegirls kept the youths in an almost perpetual state of lust, yet were forbidden to gratify them. This was the task Cleopatra set herself, that she might be gentle and understanding with Caesar if he failed to meet her sensual demands.

Day by day and night by night, she held her carnal court before the statues of herself, of Astarte and Aphrodite. There were occasions when she dispensed with her jewels and came with hair undone like a Corybante to the worship of Cybele, stark naked and without shame, to the caresses of her slave-boys and the worship of the goddesses. At such moments she locked out even Iras and Charmion, wanting no witnesses to the degradations to which she submitted, not to the animal actions that governed her body, that convulsed her flesh and brought erotic cries to her twisted lips.

Every abnormal pursuit of which the ancient writers had treated in the forbidden scrolls in the Alexandrine library—which she had read and memorized in the years before Caesar had burned it down—she practiced. On her back, on her front, on her knees, on her hands, she accepted homage to her beauty. Standing, sitting, kneeling, she was adored. There was no part of her body which was not known and enjoyed a dozen times over while the sails filled with wind and the oars rocked back and forth in their tholes.

On the final night of their journey, the seventh since leaving the great harbor of Alexandria, she closeted herself with the youths until dawn. Then while they slept she ordered their throats to be slit and their lifeless bodies dumped overboard. She bathed in cool fresh water, her body was perfumed and decorated in the finest linens and the more ornate of her jewels.

She was ready now to show herself to Rome.

And to Caius Julius Caesar.

To every Roman general after a successful military campaign, the city of Rome extended a triumph. In a parade of captured standards, of wealth in the form of gold and jewels taken during the campaign, of conquered kings and queens in chains, the *imperator* would be honored.

From the Campus Martius the triumph would move through the main streets of the city, flanked always by the howling mob who looked upon the Triumph as an occasion when its own drunkenness and sexual antics would be condoned. Scarves and ribbons fluttered in the air, voices called out praise and invitations to drink and assignations. The soldiers marched along with military precision, but the centurions and the legates were often deaf and blind to their voices or to the fact that a girl or woman might run alongside his troops, or that coins might be caught in midair by his men.

Trumpets blared in the warm air. Senators who might be friends of the general would march proudly, bowing and smiling; often it was their votes, their financial support of the campaign which entitled them to such a privilege. After them would come more troops and then the flat wagons on which scale models of conquered cities and territories would be displayed, as well as any strange animals which normally inhabited them, in cages if they were dangerous or lead along by strap and bridle if domesticated. Statues of the gods of the conquered lands, human victims to be sacrificed in thanksgiving to the gods, great bulls with golden horns, and thousands of prisoners taken in battle to be sold in the slave markets, followed after them.

Cleopatra stood between Iras and Charmion on a little balcony overlooking the cobbled street up which this most magnificent of all Triumphs was marching. The famous Triumph by which Pompey had celebrated his victory over Spain, Spartacus, and the pirates of the Mare Internum was dwarfed in ostentation by this parade of Julius Caesar. Caesar had three victories to celebrate, over Egypt, over Pharnaces, over Juba and Scipio. Models of Alexandria, of Zela and the Numidian capital gleamed where the sunlight caught their toy towers and temples. Dusky Egyptians marched before black Numidians, followed closely by the rattle of chains as swarthy warriors from Pontus walked in their wake.

Suddenly Cleopatra hissed. Her hand came up, pointing.

Her slim wrists held by manacles, staggering from shame and from the jeers and insults poured in her ears by the populace, came her sister Arsinoe. To add to her degradation, she had been stripped naked. Her long black hair fell down about her shoulders, her young breasts shook and jumped as she struggled against the chains that dragged her sandalled feet along the cobblestones. She was weeping softly. The crowd screamed its delight at sight of her. In their eyes, she might be her sister Cleopatra, and Cleopatra was not popular with the Roman masses.

The chariot passed below the balcony. Cleopatra leaned on the rail and watched her sister jerked along behind it, aware of a strange sensation in her mind. This woman was flesh and blood with her; yet, she had been an enemy. In a sense, she was sorry to see Arsinoe like that, reviled by the mob; after all, she was a Ptolemy.

Yet she would rather have her where she was than free to make trouble in Egypt. Cleopatra sighed. She might seem heartless to the multitude, if they could read her thoughts, but that was only because none of them had ever been a ruler whose main concern always must be the safety of the throne on which he sits. No, though she felt pity, she understood that Arsinoe was too dangerous to be anywhere but where she was.

The crowd was screaming again.

Another naked woman, a fullblown beauty with ebony hair and pallid white skin, was being yanked along behind a war chariot. This was the wife of Pharnaces, captured with her children in Trapezus. A proud, beautiful woman, this was the absolute nadir of shame to her, being exposed so boldly to this screaming riff-raff. Unlike Arsinoe, Heracate had known what it meant to be a queen, a sovereign ruler over millions of people.

Now the lowest of the low could see what only a king had seen in the royal bedchamber in the past. But Pharnaces was dead, his kingdom was now a Roman province, and for lovely Heracate there was only a private sale ahead, where she would be turned over to some rich man who would enjoy the bodily pleasures of a former queen.

Cleopatra shuddered, staring down at her.

She would never come to this. She vowed it, hand clenched and hammering slowly up and down on the marble balcony rail. No Roman mob should ever jeer at her, see her privacies bared to the four winds.

Ah, and—even worse!

Chained to a chariot behind his mother was the young son of Pharnaces, also naked, crying out in rage and vituperation, his tears blinding him. His mother walked ahead of him— what were his thoughts when he was forced to see her nude like this, mocked by all?—the target for shameful jeers and insults. Filth covered the boy, thrown from the gutters.

Caesarion, at the age of twelve?

No! By all the gods there were—no!

Fear made a tight ball in her middle as her wide eyes found themselves hypnotized by young Mithradates. A handsome lad, he too was accustomed to being obeyed instantly under pain of death. Now to be shown to the people of his conqueror, later to be sold into slavery where he would be at the whims of a master or a mistress or both, was utterly intolerable. And yet, unless he killed himself, the boy would end by being a slave.

Caesarion, this shall never be you!

145

On my life I swear it!

Behind the boy came his sisters, girls fifteen and sixteen yet with bodies fully developed in Oriental adolescence. They too were naked and though they tried to shrink and turn away from the eyes that devoured them, there was nowhere to turn. Virgins, both of them. They would be virgins only a little longer; a private sale of such appetizing morsels would fetch rare prices.

Cleopatra felt tears in her eyes.

The roar of the crowd grew more sullen. Juba was coming, clad in his fur kaunake, with his sword and dagger at his side, as if to mock him. The cruelty of the Roman was exquisite. The women they bared lewdly, the men they gave their arms, as if to taunt them while they displayed their own power.

Juba bellowed with rage and hate and agony, baring his teeth. Behind him came his own wife, stripped as had been Arsinoe and Heracate, unable to protect her body from the eyes or her ears from the voices of the onlookers. Juba heard the voices, too, and bellowed in insane fury, which added to the delight of the crowd.

There was a little boy chained behind his mother.

Cleopatra shook her head and turned aside. "Come, Charmion. Iras. I—I can watch no more. There is a voice inside me that says—I too may wind up like this, naked and alone behind the chariot of a Roman warlord."

Iras closed the shutters but they could still hear the mob.

3.

Candles gleamed in the chamber as the man and woman on the huge couch stirred, moving away from one another. Sweat dampened the black hairs at her temples as Cleopatra lifted a hand to brush away those strands. She lay on her back, content. Her worry had been for nothing. His wars seemed only to invigorate Caius Julius Caesar. He had been making love to her for the past three hours.

He also lay on his back, staring upward.

"I shall be emperor in Rome," he announced suddenly. "You shall be my empress. Our son Caesarion shall be emperor after me."

She laughed softly and rolled over so that her breasts rested on his chest. With her fingertips she caressed his ears, smoothed down the few greying hairs on his head.

"When, lover? When?"

146

"Within the next two years."

"Two years?"

She came upward and rolled to the edge of the couch, sitting there and staring at him. In two years, he might be dead. His good fortune might turn. At this moment in the early morning hours of a Roman day, two years seemed a lifetime.

He said gently, "There are many things that must be done. Pompey's sons are in Spain. They must be smashed. There are groups of Senators who must be educated to the idea of an emperor, brought over to my side with money or by influence."

Caesar hesitated then turned his head to her with a faint smile. "The people I can always control. The rabble is an unthinking beast led by the nose of its hungers. Feed them, give them something at which to marvel or jeer, first excite and then gratify their animal natures, and you will be adored.

"When word came of my victory over Scipio and Juba, the Senate declared a forty day period of thanksgiving. A statue of me was placed opposite that of Jupiter Rex on the capitol. I'm to be dictator for the next ten years. They're afraid of me—all of them.

"One by one, my enemies have died. Scipio. Cato. Lentulus. Afranius. Cicero is thinking of retiring to Naples." His hand lifted and his fingers slowly closed, making a fist. "The world is an oyster waiting for me to devour it."

"And you will? For me? For Caesarion?"

"I will, for you both. Nothing can stop me."

She kissed him, caressed him. "Empress of the world shall be my title," she whispered. "Cleopatra Thea Philopater, *mundi imperatrix*. It has a good sound."

"Only the sons of Pompey remain. Destroy them and I can act without fear of opposition anywhere."

"I don't want you to leave me," she pouted.

"It will be only for a little while, I promise."

The great Triumph of Caesar lasted four days. A massive feast was held during which over twenty thousand Roman citizens were fed. It was a time for bacchanal and Saturnalia. Wine flowed faster than men could drink it, and sheep and cows and all manner of fowl were butchered until the arms of the slayers pained with weariness.

Cleopatra walked beside Caesar in his public appearances, radiant in her Egyptian finery. The legions cheered her because they knew it would please Caesar. The mob bellowed her name because she caused money to be thrown to them. Caesarion remained hidden away in the park apartments on the right hand side of the Tiber which belonged to Caesar. The time was not yet when he could be shown to the Roman people and acknowledged to be the heir to the world which his parents soon would rule.

In early Autumn, Caesar sailed for Spain.

This was the final move in the long game of power politics which he played with the city of his birth. Gnaius Pompeius, oldest son of dead Pompey, had been joined by the officers who had served under Metullus Scipio in the African campaign. Men like Sextus Varus, Scapula and Labienus were offering their services in this last stand against the Dictator.

Originally Caesar had hoped that he could conduct the war from Rome, that his lieutenants might handle the legions in his name, but too much was at stake to risk failure. He himself must be on hand with advice, to be an example to his troops.

After a month of maneuvers, of minor conflicts, the two armies met at Munda. The Caesarians occupied a slight hill, the Pompeians the whole of a great plain. The latter charged with drawn swords, straight up that slope, shouting defiance. They were met and halted by the calm veterans of the Tenth, stopped in their tracks by their upraised shields and flying swords. The battle joined in hot blood and cold steel.

These were not Numidians nor yet the horsemen of Pontus that faced Caesar, but young Roman legionaries, trained by veteran centurions. They too bore the pilum and the gladius, and were braced with a discipline that was almost a physical force. For long hours the battle was a raging maelstrom of long lines of men stabbing, cutting, seeking without success to cut a hole in the opposite shield wall.

Once Caesar went on foot among his veterans, asking them if they would deliver him over into the hands of two boys like the sons of Pompey? His men bellowed coarse defiance of the enemy, but words alone were not enough to win a victory. Their opponents were refugees from Africa, men who had fought against them on those hot sands under the golden eagles of Metellus Scipio; they conceived that they had a score to settle and they knew well enough that they would be given no quarter if defeated. They fought as men fight who know that anything but overwhelming victory meant their death.

The battle was decided by an error of judgment.

Toward sunset, seeing that certain Moorish allies of Caesar

were attacking the command post where Gnaius Pompeius was entrenched, Labienus ordered a withdrawal of his troops to hurl them against the Moors. His disengagement was interpreted as a retreat, both by Caesar's legions and his own. Encouraged, the Tenth fell upon their enemies; discouraged, the young recruits who had fought so well and so valiantly all day, began to give ground.

The command post was taken and its defenders killed by swordstab or pilum thrust. Making a great pile of dead bodies, Caesar fought behind it, surrounding the Spanish town of Munda in which the remainder of the Pompeians had taken refuge. After that, it was only a matter of time.

News of the victory came to Rome in a little over a month. Caesar was victor. The civil war that had raged in Rome and in its provinces was over. The people began using a strange word about this time, strange when applied to a Roman citizen. The word was *rex,* or king.

Caesar *rex.* Or, royalty added to godhood.

It was thought to be a prophecy.

4.

Caesar returned to Rome as Liberator, wearing the red shoes that were a special attribute of the kings of Alba, from one of whom Caesar claimed descent. The golden laurel wreath—first given for victory, then for royalty—adorned his head. His toga was of purple trimmed with gold. The Senate stated that his name was to be prefixed by the term Imperator. Originally this word designated a victorious general; from now on it was to be given the same understanding that all other nations affixed to emperor.

Honors fell on him like raindrops in a storm.

And yet—

There was a hard core of old opponents who had been members of, or at the very least, sympathetic to the party of Pompey, still free in Rome. Cicero, Brutus, Cassius. They had no power to stand in war against Caesar as Metellus Scipio and the Pompey boys had done. Perhaps because of this they were the more dangerous.

They waited, watching. . . .

During the fading months of 46 B.C., Cleopatra shared in the triumphs and the privileges of her lover. There were those who called her Cleopatra Regina, giving her almost equal importance with Caesar Rex. It was common gossip that Caesar was to put aside his wife, Calpurnia, as he had done already with a former spouse, Pompeia. After this, it was said, he would wed Cleopatra and would announce that he and she would rule the world.

For the first time, Caesarion was shown to the Roman populace, carried aloft in a small litter made of solid gold and carried by a dozen brawny Nubians. The people looked at the little boy silently, but they were thinking that the boy was only half a Roman, that the other part of his blood was Grecian, and that he was heir to a throne in Egypt.

Their days together were occupied with statecraft. Caesar was more than thirty years the senior of the young queen, and he thought it imperative that she learn the reins of government so that, as queen-mother, she might reign for Caesarion when Caesar died.

They visited Cicero at his villa in Puteoli, where they were entertained by the old Senator in an almost audible acknowledgement of their right to rule in Rome. They made of their travels from Rome to Naples, from Naples back to Rome, something in the nature of a parade. The mob loved Caesar. They shouted for him to assume the laurel diadem which would make him truly king in Rome, but when first Licinius and then Cassius and finally Antony put the crown upon his head, Caesar wrenched it off and tossed it aside. To rule in Rome, he needed the support of the Senate, and though the people wanted Caesar to be king, the nobles did not.

It is a tribute to the power of the people and their fear of it, that noblemen like Brutus and Cassius now plotted to strike at Caesar in the only way still open to them. Jealous, petty, vindictive, each man had once served Pompey and had been pardoned by Caesar for his part in the opposition party. Resentful of what they considered a slight to their honor, fearful of what might happen if Caesar became king in Rome as he was king in name and fact in the provinces, they spoke with one another of assassination.

The day chosen was the fifteenth of March, 44 B.C.

Calpurnia had nightmares during the early days of March. The soothsayer Spurinna warned of dread portents and auguries. It were better for Caesar to leave Rome with Cleopatra and Caesarion at his side, than to remain.

Caesar laughed at the prophecies. Cleopatra wept with him, clawing down her thick black hair, saying that she too had had visions of a great lake of blood with Caesar floating in it white as death. Flee now, while there was yet time. Flee to

Alexandria and the East. He wanted to wage a war with Parthia, which had defeated Crassus years before, to wipe out that blotch against the Roman name with the blood of fifty thousand Parthians? Wage that war from Egypt!

Presently, presently, he replied.

And so he went to the Senate house carried in a litter, there to meet daggers in the hands of men like Brutus, Cassius, Casca, Cimber, Decimus and Trebonius. He fell to the floor with his flesh bleeding from twenty-three wounds. He died almost instantly.

And Rome exploded into a hotbed of political factions. The strong hand that had held Romans together was gone. The city on the Tiber belonged once again to the man who was strong enough to take it.

For Cleopatra, a dream had died.

No longer would she be queen in Rome, mistress of her world. Instead her own life was in danger, for there were many who hated her for her influence on Caesar. The assassins' daggers which had drawn the life of the Dictator might now be turned against her own.

It was the Roman mob which saved her. For the people had loved Caius Julius Caesar. His every victory had been the signal for a feast and a holiday for them. He gave them something to enjoy, wine and loose women and long nights of merriment. These daggers had robbed them of such delights. The mob turned sullen, and bared its teeth to the men who had killed its idol.

Most of the men involved fled overseas. A few remained in Rome, in hiding. Others were afraid to set foot on the streets for the people might well tear them to pieces. As a result Cleopatra was able to make plans to flee Rome herself and take Caesarion with her.

She left on a moonless spring night, by longboat along the Tiber to Ostia, where a trireme waited for the rising tide to carry her to Egypt. She did not weep; the time for tears was over; she had torn her breasts and wailed to prevent Caesar from going to the Senate. He had gone and now lay dead. She had more important things to concern her.

Cleopatra was still queen in Egypt. But—

For how long?

After Caesar would come chaos, and from chaos would rise his successor. Would it be Brutus? Cassius? Desperately, she hoped not. They hated her for she had been favored by the man they murdered. Octavian, the nephew of Caesar, whom Caesar had adopted before Caesarion was born?

An equally impossible choice, according to her views. Octavian was cold, remote, a man of reason rather than of passion. Caesar had been a happy blend of both.

But Caesar was dead. And there was no one else.

Cleopatra shivered in a fear that made her sweat.

TEN

The Harbor of Tarsus in Cilicia, 41 B. C.

1.

The barge slipped slowly through the harbor waters of the city of Tarsus in Cilicia. Perfume wafted with it over the rippling surface amid a sensual throbbing of harp strings and dulcimers. The red sun, low on the horizon beyond the stone Mole, caught its golden bulk in its rays and made it seem on fire. The many thousands who lined the shore stared in utter awe, for to their credulous minds, it seemed that a goddess had come to earth.

Cleopatra reclined on a couch formed of lapis lazuli coated with pearl in the shape of a gigantic seashell. Her bower was placed on the raised deck, covered over with an awning made of cloth-of-gold and held by solid silver spears so as to shade her from the setting sun. Handsome boys and girls crouched at her feet like cupids, flooding the air about her with music. Her female attendants stood behind her, softly singing.

She wore a transparent tunic through which her body might be seen, belted by jeweled ovals. Bracelets on her arms and rings on her fingers, together with a diadem in her black hair, added to her barbaric beauty. The soles of her feet were tinted red with henna, and the brilliance of her long-lashed eyes was heightened by a delicate shading of green malachite. A fan held by a small black boy dipped and lifted, bathing her with a cooling breeze, for it was late summer and the air was thick and sultry.

She seemed completely at her ease.

And yet—

Worry held her quick mind. She had come to Tarsus on the invitation of Mark Antony, a former cavalry commander under Julius Caesar, a very Hercules of a man, thickly thewed and muscular, with a reputation for liking strong wines and loose women.

For the past three and a half years, Cleopatra had ruled Egypt from the Lochias palace in Alexandria. The terror which had gripped her on her return from Rome had proved to be no more than swampfire which withers with the rising sun. She had kept to herself in Alexandria, ministering with a natural ability and the quick wits she had showed to Caesar again and again.

From the ashes of the Alexandrine war, she had formed the phoenix of a new, a vital Egypt. Conon had built her a powerful army, Hathotep had gathered a fleet that might menace that of Rome itself. But it was not enough. In the East she was supreme; no neighbor dared attack her; yet she remembered the lessons of her childhood and young womanhood, remembered Berenice bowing to the axe and Arsinoe naked in chains behind a Roman chariot.

For complete security, for the safety in which to build a kingdom for her son Caesarion, she would need the help of Rome. Of this she had no doubt. With the priests in the Temple of Isis on the Tiber she had kept in close touch; nothing of a political nature happened in the Forum or the Senate but that a swift ship was despatched to Alexandria with the news.

Brutus and Cassius were no more. They had been pinned down on the plains of Thrace a few miles from the city of Philippi by Mark Antony and Octavian Caesar, and there destroyed. Cassius had been beheaded by his own servant at his command when he feared the battle was running against him. Brutus, struggling on for another two days, finally ended his life by falling on his sword.

Julius Caesar had been avenged.

The satisfaction that had come to her at the news of Philippi was tempered by her concern over the future. Brutus and Cassius were dead, no longer threats. But what of Octavian? And Antony? Both would now rule Rome. Cleopatra was too astute a statesman to believe this condition would last. Caesar had sought to make himself emperor, and failed. Octavian might aspire to the laurel now, and so might Antony.

One of them would win, but which one?

She had to side with one or the other. There would be no middle course permitted her; Egypt with its corn granaries was too important to be allowed to indulge in any waiting game. Egypt must declare for one man or the other and the choice was hers alone.

Now Antony had sent for her.

She dared not antagonize him. There was no open rift as yet between Octavian and his adoptive father's cavalry general. If she had refused to come to Tarsus, Antony might have made an incident out of it, decided he had an excuse to invade Egypt and take over its rich corn exports, giving them to Rome as a gesture. Octavian would have kept them for himself. It was a proof of the fundamental difference between the two men.

Since she could not avoid traveling to Tarsus, she would do so in the manner best calculated to win over Antony to her side. She would come as a love goddess, as Venus to his Bacchus, as Aphrodite to his Dionysus.

For Antony had been staging a triumphal parade through the East, through Thessaly from Philippi, to Athens where he gave himself over to a month of sports—at which he excelled —and drinking. Stories were told that he roamed the streets of Athens as once he roamed the streets of Rome with a few chosen companions. When they found a pretty housewife or maidservant, they beat off her escorts and carried her into a nearby tavern to amuse themselves with her body for the evening.

Cleopatra smiled grimly, remembering Caesar.

He enjoyed the pleasures which a woman could bring a man, none more; yet he was discreet about it. He indulged in no public brawls, no kidnapping of decent women. Moreover, Caesar had a fine mind and employed it. She wondered about Antony. From what she had heard of him, he was only an animal with an ability to win military victories.

It might not be enough to win the world, which usually demanded something more of those who sought to conquer it. Ah, well. Perhaps she could furnish the brains while Antony furnished the legions.

Her smile broadened in mockery at herself. Already she was planning how best to work with Antony, and they had not even met. Perhaps she was too confident of herself as a queen, as a woman. Ah, no. Never that! Her feminine instincts, her beauty of face and form had won her Julius Caesar. After him, what man could resist her?

She stirred lazily, feeling her nipples come to rigid life on the swollen mounds of her breasts. Her loins tingled and there was a sultry heaviness in her thighs. She was always a woman, first and foremost. If anyone could conquer Antony, it was she. Somehow, and in some manner, she would bring him to his knees.

A messenger from Antony was standing at the great stone quay to which her sailors were making fast the royal barge, with word that Antony waited for her in the Forum. Would she come at once? There were many matters to be discussed between them.

Cleopatra sent back word that she expected the future master of the world to visit her. Let him come and be entertained, as Dionysus might visit Aphrodite. While she watched the staring thousands crowding the streets, trying to seek entry onto the stone wharf itself, she told herself that Antony must be deserted, back at the Forum. Even his own officers were here, gawking at this woman who had so captivated godlike Caesar. Her sharp eyes could make out the phalerae decorating their armor which marked them as veterans of Philippi, of Zela, of the Gallic and the Spanish and the African campaigns.

Cleopatra turned, clapping her hands.

It was growing dark. Candles must be brought up from below—where the oarsmen were already being shepherded so that they might not make a jarring note in this aura of godlike luxury—and lighted against the night. When Antony came, he must stand dazzled both by her wealth and by her beauty.

Within the hour he was stepping from the quay to the deck, a big man with powerful arms, lean belly and thick shoulders. He wore a purple toga and golden sandals. His black hair, only faintly touched with grey, for he was in his early forties, curled like the wool of Astrakhan lambs. He was a handsome man, Cleopatra admitted as she sat up straighter on her seashell couch, apparently filled with the energy of a stallion. It would be pleasant to conquer such a god or man or animal, or whatever Antony was in his most secret heart.

He adanced upon her with the rolling gait of the horseman. His eyes darted to the towering candles which made daytime out of darkness, arranged in geometrical patterns here and there on the deck, and to the women those candles revealed in their nudity or in the scant attire which Cleopatra had permitted some of them. His eyes widened as they took in the sleek thighs, full hips and rounded rumps of these females, most of whom were noblewomen in Alexandria who had come along to Tarsus in holiday spirit.

Antony was a Roman, above all else.

He was not used to the sybaritic qualities of the East and its oriental overtones. The matrons of Rome would not, in their sober senses, give their bared breasts to the sight of an entire city or the secrets of their loins to any who cared to look. Yet these women, all highborn, stood straight and proud as he walked past, and smiled invitingly into his eyes that raked their nakedness.

And the woman who commanded these other women,

156

Cleopatra! How sure of her loveliness she must be, to display these beauties before him! Almost he stumbled in his anxiety to see her.

She was not exactly a stranger. Antony had seen her in Rome from time to time, but Rome was west and its excesses were bawdy, not subtle. In Rome she had been Caesar's future wife, the coming mistress of the world, if he had understood the gossip correctly. Here she was—

The breath caught in his throat.

He came to a standstill. This was Anadyomene rising from the seashell, goddess of the waves. Aphrodite Callipygos. Venus Volivaga. Naked under tissue so fine it was like a film across the eyes, she was rising from the couch, extending her white arms and smiling up at him.

Candlelight touched her jewels and baubles, as if to blind him. Almost instinctively he lifted a hand to his eyes, to shade them. The ripple of applause on the tongues of the Alexandrine women made him realize they mistook his gesture as a supreme compliment to their queen. Antony was quick of wit; he played up to their mistake.

"Your beauty dazzles me, Cleopatra," he said hoarsely.

Indeed, he merely spoke the truth, he realized. She was not a tall woman, this Egyptian queen, but her body was absolutely perfect. Round breasts pressed large nipples almost through the thin linen of her *mafortes* even as her hips revealed their intimate curvature below. Her navel was a dimple in a gently mounded belly. Her thighs were ripe, full, soft, and her legs were very handsome. Jealousy of dead Caesar bit into Antony.

To hold this loveliness in his arms! To take her as he was wont to take women far less lovely, to hear her moans and plaints of love! If Catullus had seen her so, how much more masterly would be his love poems!

He caught her extended hands, kissed them, found the skin smooth and warm and faintly scented. Was all her body this kissable? She was shaven, as were all highborn Egyptian women; he had seen that much through her byssus tunic. A sense of anticipation grew in Marcus Antoninus.

"Welcome to Dionysus," she whispered.

"To Aphrodite, *ave!*" he answered.

Her hand turned him so that she might walk toward an ebony and gold chair carved like the throne of the Etruscans, early ancestors of the Romans, representations of which Cleopatra had seen in Rome. She contrived to touch his upper arm with the tip of a breast as she did so, gently scraping the

157

nipple across his flesh. Antony quivered, alive with her desirability.

"As Tarquin once sat on such a chair as this, sit you also," she smiled. Antony could not take his eyes from her; he fumbled with a hand for the ebony seat and sank into it, still with his gaze locked with her brilliant eyes.

He had sent for Cleopatra to discuss finances with her. The war with Brutus and Cassius had cost him a fortune. He was desperately in need of gold with which to wage his struggle for Rome against Octavian. Yet all this was forgotten in this larger, greater need which obsessed him.

When she turned to move toward her seashell couch, his eyes dropped to her gently moving buttocks and to the slim and shapely legs below them. His tongue touched his lips. He found it hard to breathe. He could not remember when the mere sight of a woman had so affected him.

As if a discussion of the mundane might remove the spell of her nearness, he sought to draw her attention to the state of his finances, pointing out that by a military allegiance with him, she might widen her own borders and increase the extent of her trade connections.

Cleopatra listened for a little while but she soon turned to a contemplation of her slim white leg—somehow it was out of her tunic and being moved this way and that before his eyes—and by so doing, distracted Antony from his thoughts. When he would have resumed the discussion, after her transparent tunic had been drawn over her smooth thigh, an Alexandrine noblewoman thrust a golden goblet of chilled white Oethalian under his nose.

Antony drank gratefully, vaguely aware that the young musicians had begun a lazy, sensual rhythm and that from the shadows were coming a group of Gadean dancers. The women of Gades in Spain possessed the reputation of being the most lewd dancers in the known world. Antony had watched them in the waterfront taverns while his pulses pounded to the erotic arts of their bodies. These girls before him were no dockside harlots but young beauties, however; he wondered, as they began to shimmy their shoulders so that their unbound breasts leaped and shook, where Cleopatra had found them.

Then as they began to intertwine in the more voluptuous poses of the dance, he forgot to ask questions, forgot to do anything but stare and breathe and swallow the cold wine the women of Alexandria kept pouring into his cup. Each one of these dancing girls was inviting him to have her. There could be no mistake about it.

158

Then they were gone and steaming sea food was being placed on the table to his right, with leeks and onions flavored with sauces, and the popular flesh of peacocks. The noble-women were switching to a new wine, a strong red Falernian which better suited his Roman palate than the more delicate Oethalian. Antony hitched his throne-chair closer to the seashell.

Casually his hand went out to Cleopatra, resting on her knee. He stroked her smooth flesh, not sensing the fact that she had stiffened slightly at his touch. He began to tell her of a story current among his troops of a legionary and a Thracian farmer's wife.

After that first instinctive firming of her muscles, Cleopatra let herself relax. *How unlike Caesar he is, telling me jokes like this in public and fondling my thigh. Caesar would have died before committing such a public display of his sensuality.* It came to Cleopatra suddenly that Caesar and Antony were two entirely different men; the tactics which enthralled the one might bore the other to distraction.

"Now Thrace, as you know, is noted for the quality of its stallions," he was saying, leaning closer so that he might peer into the low bodice of her tunic.

Cleopatra abetted the journey of his eyes by leaning forward as if fascinated with the story he was telling. She was aware that her women were smiling at one another behind his back, but she had no thoughts to spare for those jaded Alexandrine belles. Her only concern was Rome, and here in the East, Marcus Antonius was Rome.

She laughed with him, then bent forward even more to tell him a story about a gladiator and the noble lady. Antony roared at its punch line. Cleopatra watched him, gauging his nature. He would be easy to lead, this one, for a clever woman. There was no subtlety in him. Spies had brought her the tale of how Lucillus, seeking to save the life of Brutus after Philippi, rode to the camp of Antony rather than of Octavian, knowing that in the latter he would meet absolutely no mercy. And Antony had embraced Lucillus, crying out that it were better to have such a one as friend than as enemy. How like the man who sat here exchanging jokes with her! Simple, generous, good natured for the most part, hearty and bluff, with a thick vein of sensuality in his makeup that made him seem almost like an overgrown child.

Her eyes touched his thickly muscled arms. They would crush a woman to his barrel chest as easily as the African rock python crushed anything around which it wrapped its coils.

159

Ah, but it might be a pleasant hurt. If the hair on his broad chest, black and thickly matted, were any indication of his virility, if the stories she'd heard of his wenchings were in any measure true, it might be very pleasant indeed.

Cleopatra reached for a fig to munch.

Antony was beginning another story.

Not until dawn did the festivities aboard the barge come to an end. The dancing girls and acrobats lay sleeping in exhaustion, and the heads of the noblewomen of Alexandria nodded heavily. The candles burned low. Beyond the harbor waters the city itself was dark, silhouetted against the eastern sky where a faint touch of red was making itself seen.

Cleopatra stifled a yawn, marveling at the vigor of this man who had swallowed almost two gallons of wine this night, with assorted foods, who belched his appreciation of each drink, each new course, with unfeigned enjoyment. His big hands had clapped applause for her Gadean girls, for her jugglers and acrobats. Himself accustomed to the finest entertainment—his Metrodorus was world renowned as a dancer, Xuthus as a singer—he sat enthralled by her offerings.

She wondered if he pretended his enjoyment as a compliment.

But no. She credited him with too much subtlety. Caesar might have done so, while inwardly laughing; not Antony.

He was standing now, grinning down at her. "Walk with me, highness. At least as far as the quay. We've had a lot of fun tonight, but we haven't talked any business." He chuckled. "That's why I wanted to see you. I need money."

She held out a hand, letting him seize it and draw her upward from the seashell couch. He used his grip to bring her against his hard body, folding a corner of the toga about her so that she was hidden from all eyes.

This close, she could see the blue stubble on his jaws, the sensual curve to his wide mouth, the curling black hair on his head. He was a handsome man, and her womanhood responded to his animal appeal. The arm at her back was an iron bar locking her softness against him.

He bent his head suddenly and his open mouth dove for her lips. The arm behind her lifted her off her feet. She felt her mouth crushed by his, knew the sliding thrust of his tongue, and her insides suddenly boiled as if with fever.

Moaning, she lifted her arms and wrapped them about his thick neck. She clung to him, letting his hand move where it willed across her fulsome breasts and down over the curve of her haunches to her thigh. She had been many months without

160

physical pleasure. That may have been a mistake, she thought wryly as her flesh came alive to his touch. A wanting woman is a foolish woman.

She was not quite so foolish, however, as to let him take her standing on the deck of her own royal barge, like any Suburran harlot in Rome. His hands were raising her tunic to bare her hips when she threw back her head and laughed.

"Like this, Dionysus? Like two human beings?" she taunted him.

"Then what?" he asked, nonplussed.

There was only directness in Mark Antony. He must be schooled in eroticism, gentled by a firm and understanding palm. Cleopatra lifted her hands and trailed long fingernails down his throat, feeling him shiver. His eyes were pools of lust in his heavily tanned face. He reminded her of a hunting hound quivering with the need to be about its business.

"Like gods we are, you and I," she whispered. "Bacchus and Venus. In an appropriate setting, not like dogs on an alley's cobblestones."

His arm loosed and fell away. Though he was breathing heavily, he nodded down at her—he was remembering that she was queen of Egypt, no *scorta erratica,* she thought with amusement—and stepped back.

"You're right," he growled. "As gods. But when?"

"Soon," she whispered, cupping his stubbled jaw in gentle palms.

"Tomorrow—no, this night you shall come to my palace off the Forum," he said. "Let me entertain you."

"I shall come," she nodded.

He gathered his toga about his body, tossing one end over a shoulder, and moved across the deck and gangplank up onto the dock. Cleopatra stared after him, marveling that after so much wine he could walk so straight. "Maybe his blood is half wine from the amount he's drunk all his life," she said and giggled.

She hiccuped suddenly, and laughed aloud.

"I am no female Antony, for sure. The ship reels about me. A few more goblets and I'd have given in to him." She had a strong feeling that to yield too soon to Marcus Antoninus would be to lose his respect.

Cleopatra slept late next morning. In the afternoon she ordered the royal barge rowed out beyond the Rhegma to the clear green waters of the sea where she swam about for over an hour. She found her brain stimulated by the cold water. Here amid fish and floating bits of driftwood, she could compose her mind as how best to win Antony to her side.

First, she must not become drunk this night at his banquet. Well, she could take care of that easily enough, by sipping a raw egg before leaving the barge. As for the other matter, that of subduing Antony with her body, it must be more carefully planned.

It was while her women were drying her glowing body that the answer came to her. If she posed as Venus, then as Venus she must win him.

Carried by litter through the streets of Tarsus to the old palace which had been built, according to legend, to house Alexander the Great when he suffered from fever during his Persian wars, Cleopatra found herself the target for the eyes of the populace. They lined the streets, staring at this queen who was a fable in her own lifetime. An ancient town founded by Sardanapalus of Assyria close by the river Cydnus which bisected its streets and buildings, Tarsus had prospered under Roman rule; its great road over the Taurus mountains, its mighty harbor, afforded its merchants access to trade centers by land and by sea. Yet its people considered that they lived in a backwater town compared to sophisticated Alexandria and mighty Rome.

They flocked to see this renowned beauty. They gaped and gawked like shepherds on a hillside. Perhaps they sensed the destiny which she might make before her visit here was done, Cleopatra thought. In any event, it was good to be admired, to be whispered about with awe as though she were in truth a deity.

She forgot her godhood at the banquet Antony had prepared, mainly because she realized he expected it of her. She exchanged broad jests with his officers, she stared breathlessly at the sight of a bull fighting a black panther to the death in a great cage, she drank cup after cup with him throughout the evening. Midway in the banquet she came at his call to his couch where she suffered him to caress her flesh through the slits she had cunningly designed in her sheer tunic.

For entertainment, Antony had arranged a broad farce about a townsman, his wife and daughter and two Roman soldiers stationed in their house during the occupation of their city. There was much carryings-on between the wife and the two soldiers, then between the daughter and the two soldiers, and finally by an error in judgment, between the townsman and his daughter. There was nothing left unsaid, nothing left unseen. Accustomed to the shameless presentations on the Alexandrine stage, Cleopatra was not shocked. She laughed when she was supposed to laugh and applauded as did the Romans.

Her only complaint was the crudeness of the play. Its appeal was to the animal emotions alone. *Caesar would have been amused, not aroused as was Antony, at the vigorous couplings of the players. But—I must stop comparing them. They are two completely different men.* She could feel his delight in the portrayal of the several adulteries. *He is a big man, far larger than—no! No more comparisons. Accept him as he is. If this is the sort of thing he likes, give it to him.* Above all else, she must not prove a spoilsport.

She left the palace with the feeling that she had been despoiled, though no final intimacy had taken place between them. That was to be reserved for the morrow, on the royal barge.

2.

Antony came to the barge as he had come before, at sundown.

From the quay he could see its entire deck surface covered with the red petals of roses so that the scent was sweet and cloying. At his elbows were his officers, a handful in all, gaping just as he gaped. Covered objects lined the rails, very large and all the more mysterious for the white sheets which hid them from the eyes. Drawn up before the gangplank in twin rows, at dress position, were the Egyptian guards. Beyond them were the Alexandrine noblewomen, their hair wrapped in golden cauls, their throats hung with strings of pearls, their bodies white and depilated.

"Jupiter rex," whispered a legate.

The boat had become a garden. There were trees and shrubs here and there, and marble benches, even a fountain splashing wine. No oarsmen could be seen, a temporary flooring having been built above their heads. Statues of Priapus and of Venus Volgivaga sat in the bow and in the stern. Everywhere there was music, soft and sensual.

Antony drew a deep breath. "What a woman. She can perform miracles. She has brought us to Elysium, the abode of the blessed." He broke into a run in his hurry to go aboard. Behind him his men followed close, their eyes on the waiting noblewomen.

163

A gong sounded belowdecks. The oars lifted, churning into the harbor waters. Antony, who was walking past the Alexandrine women, felt the barge begin to move. "Where do we go?" he asked.

"Out of sight of the world," he was answered.

From the open sea came a cooling wind that seemed almost to swirl about the ship, joining its scents and musical rhythms together. Eagerly he stared about him, hunting for the queen. Behind him he could hear his officers and the laughing, teasing Alexandrine noblewomen. Ah, but where was Cleopatra? Surely she should have made her appearance by now.

Over by the fountain, goblets were being dipped deep into the chilled Setinian splashing so merrily in the deep bowl. Antony grinned. He was Dionysus, god of wine, according to Cleopatra. Why should he not also drink of the nectar sacred to his name?

His hand caught up a golden cup, plunged it deep.

Then with the rim at his lips, he paused. Idiot that he was. Fool! The answer was so simple. If he was Dionysus, she would be Venus. Not Venus victrix nor Venus genetrix but Venus volgivaga, sacred to harlots.

At one end of the boat was Priapus, wrought in marble.

At the other end, at the bow—

He whirled, feeling wine slosh over his hand and wrist. Venus sat unmoving, her thighs parted as if to call attention to her womanhood. Of white marble from Caria—ah, but was it marble?—she sat waiting for her worshippers. Antony drew a deep breath.

No statue, this! Instead—a living woman!

Cleopatra!

He drank the wine, not taking his eyes from her body. He tossed aside the goblet, walked over the scattered rose petals to the little dais that held the goddess. This close, he could see that it was not marble but white powder, thickly applied, covering her flesh.

His heart slammed like a mad thing in his ribcage as his eyes assessed the nakedness of this woman who meant so much to him. He bent and kissed a knee. His hands clasped her ankles, moved them apart. He began to stroke her legs with his palms.

"Venus volgivaga," he whispered. "Come and be a woman for the night. Forget your godhood!"

She quivered to his caresses, unable to control herself. When he bent his head to kiss her flesh, her breasts lifted firmly, hard and eager. Those palms that stroked her so avidly were building a flame deep inside her body.

She sobbed suddenly, writhing to his tongue.

Antony shouted, caught her up in his arms, dragging her from the marble chair. "Dionysus commands, this night. As does Venus!" Light-headed from his nearness to her nudity, he was falling completely under her spell. Never had there been such a woman!

Before he could do more than kiss her, the noblewomen and his officers were all around them. To his surprise, his men were out of armor, every one of them naked. Half drunk, they began removing his purple toga, aided by the women whose hands darted here and there as if to abet the purposes of Venus. Someone pushed a goblet into his hand. He drank eagerly, for his mouth was dry. He felt like a desert long baked by the sun. Not since he had taken his first woman had he known this almost uncontrollable excitement.

Tarsus was fading astern. The moon and the stars were overhead, the sea restless and surging underkeel. To his fevered senses, with Cleopatra naked in his arms, it seemed indeed to Antony that he was entering a strange world, a universe of elemental ocean, of male and female in an Elysium of their own making.

Bacchantes came running with platters of steaming food. Corybantes with their long hair flying in the wind brought spiced wine, heated and flavored with the aphrodisiacal thorn apple and the equally potent shredded bark of the Yohimbe tree.

Cleopatra drank with both hands on her goblet, eyes gleaming at Antony above its golden rim. There was devilment in her stare, and erotic challenge, but when he reached for her she twisted aside so that all he got was a rubbing of white powder on his fingertips.

Laughing and shrieking, she ran to the first of the covered objects beside the rail. With a cry of "*Io, Io!*" she yanked it down.

Antony bellowed in delight as he saw the living statues above him, joined in a form of lovemaking favored among the ancient Egyptians, in which the woman served as rider and the man as horse. The others who had paused at his cry now came clustering around to admire and comment on the loveliness of the powdered, painted woman, the powerful body of the man.

Antony ran his hand down the haunch of the motionless woman. She stirred. He shouted and clapped her rump, forcing

165

her forward and down. She gave a sudden scream and collapsed on the man who now felt free to wrap his arms about her and hold her to him.

The others realized suddenly that there were more statues to be unveiled. Willing hands went to the shrouding robes and tore them loose. The garden now became a grove truly sacred to the carnal arts. Everywhere the eyes went they could see a living representation of the art so enamored of the god Priapus and the goddess Venus, in all its many phases.

"We shall play this game of living statues ourselves," Antony shouted, and lifted Cleopatra high above his head, carrying her around the fountain.

Music and laughter was everywhere. Underfoot were the thick, soft petals of the roses. Flesh clung to flesh, and mouth sought mouth, as hands stroked and fondled, as men panted and women cried out softly in their passions. The living statues were pulled from their pedestals and made to perform with the men and women who desecrated them. Here a man displayed himself and challenged all women to exhaust him. There a woman screamed thickly, drunk with wine and maddened by aphrodisiacs, shaking her breasts and twisting her loins in invitation. The wine flowed on, bubbling in its fountain, while Dionysus and Aphrodite leered and laughed in some wild bacchanal of their own.

Cleopatra exhausted Antony, over and over again.

With her flesh she fashioned a chain about his body, catching up his will and his manhood in faery nets against which he could no longer struggle. It was a victory greater than any which might be won on on a battlefield. She hoped that with him, she was also conquering Rome.

For three weeks Cleopatra remained in Tarsus.

During that time Antony gave up his residence at the old palace and openly took up quarters with the Egyptian queen. Couriers crossed a gangplank now to place scrolls in his hands which told of the news from Rome, and every message Antony read he gave to Cleopatra for her comment.

Octavian, who had been ill to death, was now recovering and busying himself with the internal affairs of Italy. Antony chuckled when he read how unpopular this adopted son of Caesar was proving. The soldiers of his legions who were to have been given land as a reward for their long service, found there was no land to be had, and were in rebellion. Sextus Pompeius, last living son of Pompey the Great, and a famous sailor, was raiding the corn-ships from Egypt, burning them and selling their crews into slavery so that the people of Rome hungered. Unreasoning as was every mob, the Roman people blamed Octavian and not the son of Pompey for their empty bellies.

"The people may save me the trouble and depose Octavian themselves," he confided to Cleopatra as they partook of a typical Roman breakfast of dry bread and honey, with olives and cheese.

"Especially if Fulvia can goad them to action."

Antony glanced at his companion, wondering if she were jealous of his wife. His marriage with Fulvia, twice a widow—her husbands Clodius, and then Curio, had been killed in battle—was a matter of political convenience. She was wealthy, but above all, greedy for power. Privately, Antony thought she should have been a man. She had married him because she thought that one day, with Caesar dead, he would be master of the world. Accordingly, she did all in her power to strengthen his cause against that of Octavian.

Cleopatra caught his look and smiled. "I'm not concerned about Fulvia, other than how well she looks after your interests."

"She does that, all right," he grumbled. It was like having a part of yourself there to oversee affairs. She left him free to roam the world, to enjoy himself as he would. Fulvia was interested in power, not prurience.

"Perhaps the time is ripe to push her aside, to take the reins yourself."

"That would mean fighting Octavian," he protested.

Her plucked eyebrows arched. "Well? Won't you fight him sooner or later?"

"I suppose so."

She leaned toward him, making a fist of her little hand, hitting it against the arm of the curule chair where he sat. "Then strike now, Antony. Octavian is hated in Rome. All his old veterans are in arms against him, plundering the land they were supposed to have been given. Sextus Pompeius holds the seas. He'll make terms with you when you whip Octavian."

Antony brooded, his lower lip pushed out. Caesar would have seen the obvious long ago, Cleopatra thought, and hated herself for making the comparison. Antony was essentially a lazy man, able to stir to fevered action when the cause was thrust upon him, but too indolent and good-natured to go seeking trouble on his own. It was a fault that might be fatal, she decided, loosing her fingers and leaning back on her couch.

She had to be his brains, must do his thinking for him, be spur to his moods, be whip when the need for action demanded it. Yet he could not be led as was the bull with the ring in its nose. With a honeyed tongue she must cajole him.

He balked at her arguments like an unruly colt. "In my own good time," he promised.

"If you want Egyptian gold—"

"If you want Caesarion to rule according to his inheritance—"

They paused and stared at one another, their heated blood swiftly cooling. Ah, here it was. The truth which each had avoided since their first meeting on the royal barge. Raise Caesarion, son of the beloved Caesar, with the eagles. Declare him a contestant for the throne which had eluded his father. Backed by gold and corn, by the legions and Antony's military genius, he might win out.

"I do, I do," she breathed. "Caesarion, emperor of the world. It's all I dream about!"

"I too," he nodded. His big hairy hand waved in the air. "Oh, I know my limitations. I'm no Caesar. I'm not even Octavian. I like a good time too much to care about ruling a world. But for another, for this son of yours—why didn't you bring him with you, by the way?—I could do a lot. I could put him on a throne and keep him there."

She studied him, instinctively understanding he meant what he said. A follower, a man who was at his best when obeying orders, he could do for another what he might not do for himself. He lacked the driving need for power that had possessed Caesar, that now possessed Fulvia. And Octavian. Cleopatra frowned. Lacking this basic need, he might be too poor a weapon for her hand.

Still, he would have no personal axe to grind.

He might be a weapon made especially for her hand. And he was a Roman, with authority over the legions. She stirred and said, "Come to Alexandria, Antony. You can meet Caesarion there."

"I'd planned on visiting Antioch, then Palestine," he muttered thoughtfully. "Egypt isn't so far away."

"I'll be making arrangements for your entertainment," she said.

His eyes lit up, like those of a child promised a special treat. It was one way of consolidating her hold on him, through his senses. Not a good way, for she had seen other

Romans affected by the sybaritic vices of the East, yet she had no choice.

By any means at all, she must win this man.

So that Caesarion might be king in Rome.

ELEVEN

The Fleshpots of Alexandria, Winter, 41 B. C.

1.

"And you? What of your ambitions?"

Conon spoke quietly but there was an edge to his voice. He stood before the great bronze astrolabe that decorated a corner of her chambers as Cleopatra lay stretched out for the ministrations of her masseuse. The astrolabe had been a gift from Archelaus, king of Cappadocia; it had been designed and created by Milo of Ephesus. Men said it was the most perfect of its kind in the known world. But Conon, as his hand slapped against its finial, was thinking of nothing but the woman who had been absent from Alexandria for the past two months.

"Antony!" he snarled angrily. "A cavalry captain, no more. He made his reputation under Caesar, following orders from a man with a brain."

"I thought you hated Caesar."

He turned and stared, his eyes bright and hard. In the six years since Caesar had been in Alexandria he had been more than a right hand to Cleopatra; when she left for Rome, he remained behind to govern in her place. Hard and as muscular as ever, for he attended the gladitorial *ludi* to exercise his swordarm every day for at least an hour, he looked fit enough to enter the arena. His hair had thinned a little at his temples, but it was still brown and wavy.

"I did," he grated. "I hated him because he was a Roman and a danger to you. At the same time I admired him for his brain. They did a bad thing when they killed that man. With him alive, there would have been no Philippi, no division of power between—"

He bit off his words, hammering at the astrolabe.

"And I would be queen in Rome," Cleopatra said sweetly. "Safe and secure as you want me to be. Oh, Conon! We've been over this so many times."

"Always you turn aside my advice."

She rolled over obediently in response to the hands of her masseuse. For an instant he eyed her heavy white breasts with her dark, pulpy nipples before she covered them with the sheet. Conon sighed. Maybe he needed a woman. He lived an unnatural life, attending always to the affairs of the throne, to its army and the navy, to the duties which Cleopatra pushed off on him more and more often of late.

"You advise me always to seek out Octavian, to make a bargain with him," she stated lazily. "With my corn carried to Rome in Egyptian ships, protected by my navy, and my gold at his back—in exchange for eternal friendship, for an alliance with Rome that would put legions here under my command—Octavian would come to power."

"It's good advice. Octavian would snap at an offer like that. He's no bumbling lecher whose thirst is—"

"*Conon!*"

She was up on an elbow, face flushed with fury. Their glances touched; his fell away as he swung toward the window. Cleopatra closed her eyes slowly. "Conon, Conon," she whispered softly. "Why am I always at dagger's point with you? We both want the same thing, really."

"Your happiness," he said, pushing his words into a pause.

"Yes, my happiness. Only what you consider will bring me happiness and what I know will make me happy, are two entirely different things."

"Make it part of your bargain with Octavian that he adopt Caesarion as his son, just as Caesar adopted him. He would do it. Oh, how fast he'd do it. What does he care about what happens after he's dead? He'll overthrow Antony, come to sole power in Rome—which is the world—and when he goes to his ancestors, Caesarion will ascend his throne."

"You make it sound so easy," she said.

"Has Octavian a child?"

"A daughter, Julia."

"He will need to adopt a son to succeed him, then."

"I'll think about it," she murmured weakly.

"This Antony has bewitched you."

With her hand she slapped the table on which she reclined. "Go away, Conon. Go away and don't come back until you've learned to hold your tongue. Do you understand?"

She sat up and the linen fell away but she was too furious to care for modesty. "I dreaded coming back to Alexandria because I knew it would mean facing you and that tongue of yours. Go away from me."

Conon stood white-faced, his back rigid as she lashed out at him. He waited her out; when she was done, he made a little bow. "You are still queen in Egypt, Thea. For how long this will continue, now you've plotted this mad course with Antony, I don't—"

"*Get out!*"

The masseuse looked stricken. Slaves who overheard words not intended for their ears were often summarily disposed of, that their tongues might not babble secrets. Cleopatra was red with fury, sitting up on the table with her linens almost off her entirely and screaming like a dockside fishwife, slapping her hand on the table for emphasis. Conon in his silver armor and scarlet cloak was rigid, chin held high. His eyes were on her, the slave thought, in an agony of reproach.

When she was done and sobbing, head bent and shoulders shaking, the man stirred beside the astrolabe. With a weary motion he passed a hand before his eyes. Suddenly he looked older than his years. Hoarsely he said, "If you've done, Thea, may I take my leave?"

"Go! Just go!"

There was a silence after the general of the armies was gone. His last footfall had echoed and re-echoed when Cleopatra raised her head. The slavewoman was surprised to see tears streaking her cheeks. She had never before seen Cleopatra weep.

"He called me Thea. After all I said, he called me Thea." She glanced up at the masseuse and her face turned ugly. "Keep a still tongue in your head about this, do you understand? You have clever fingers but you don't need a tongue to do your work. And you don't know how to write."

The slavewoman was shaking. "Highness, I am deaf!"

"That might not be a bad idea," Cleopatra said harshly and turned over on her belly. "Finish me."

She lay under the soothing hands, chin propped on her forearms. She should not quarrel with Conon. He was the one true friend she had in all the world. It was like fighting with herself. Well, she had done that too, in her time. The trouble was, Conon did not think as did a woman.

Conon could not understand—or would not understand— that she had only her body for a weapon. With Octavian, her body was next to useless. He was cold. Cold! His brain was

171

everything. Sometimes, from the rumors she heard, all his blood was good for was feeding his brain. With such a man a woman was a mere plaything, a toy to relieve tensions. No more.

Ah, but Antony! There was a human bull for you. A sexual giant, capable of erotic feats that surpassed belief. Her full mouth quirked into a languid smile as she remembered those weeks in Tarsus. He had brought more pleasure to her flesh than she had ever known. Caesar had been a man long past his prime when she came to know him. True, he had been potent still but he was no satyr as was Mark Antony.

She felt the molten heat touch her loins. Almost imperceptibly her hips moved gently. To have him here with her in the Lochias! This would be Nirvana. And he was coming. Yes, he would arrive in Alexandria for the winter. The fun they would have! She must begin her planning now for their mutual enjoyment.

The masseuse was done. She stepped back and waited until Cleopatra made a little gesture with her hand. Then she turned and left the apodyterium. When she had gone, Cleopatra turned over and lay on her back with her legs bent, soles flat on the tabletop, staring at the high ceiling.

Isis! What she wouldn't give to call in a young slave. Just thinking about Antony had fired the fevers that always lay just under her skin. The Ptolemaic disease, the wits of Alexandria called this hunger for the erotic which was a heritage of her blood. Ah, let them. She put her hands on her swollen breasts and squeezed them.

She would not. No longer would she permit herself such easy assuagement of the senses. She would wait for Antony in an enforced celibacy that would make their meeting so much the more exciting. Gods! She would be almost a virgin by the time he got here.

Hurry to me, cried her flesh.

Hurry, screamed her blood.

Hurry! Hurry! Hurry!

2.

Conon flung his military cloak into the far corner of the bedchamber as he stamped across its tiled surface. His fingers wrenched at the straps of his armor; in his impatience he ripped off buckles and tore leather from metal studs. Hurling the silver cuirass from him, he struck by accident a small statue of the goddess Aphrodite given him by Cleopatra. With a clatter, the red sandstone image fell from its pedestal and rolled across the floor.

It came to a stop at his feet.

Conon stared down at it, fingers opening and closing. "Bitch goddess," he breathed. "You—Isis—Venus—all of you think with your bellies, rather than your heads."

His foot went back, kicked the sandstone image across the room. It hit the wall and bounced. Women! Because a man gave them a good time on a bed, they thought the world revolved about him. It was as if a veil were drawn over their eyes. Isis damn them all.

His fury was growing almost to hysteria.

Her Ptolemaic blood was dooming Egypt, as the blood of all her ancestors had doomed it, beginning with Ptolemy himself, three centuries before. Little by little Egypt had grown weak where it should have grown strong, had the Ptolemies been able statesmen.

And Cleopatra, who had the ability to be the greatest of them all, selling her birthright for a phallus hung on the loins of a living man. Conon groaned. Behind him there was a sound, the scrape of a sandal on tile.

He whirled. His Greek majordomo stood shivering, head bent. Just beyond him was Athys, the slavegirl who had been Cleopatra's gift to him on the last night Julius Caesar spent in Alexandria. His eyes narrowed. These two had served him well and faithfully these past five years. Together they ran his household better than he could have done.

Danaeus was an old man.

Athys was a pretty woman. Conon scowled. In the five years she had been a member of his household, he had not laid a hand on her. There were times when she looked at him oddly as if she suspected he might favor boys—he smiled grimly at that thought—but she made no complaint to him. Women were not usually so reticent. Women! His grim smile became hard and cold.

"Leave us, Danaeus," he growled.

The old man made a little bow and almost ran into the shadows. Athys stood waiting, eyes never leaving his flushed face. She wore her black hair high in back in the latest Roman fashion, and her thin white stolla was belted by silver links. Long ago, Conon had told her that he wanted her to conduct herself as might a free woman who had taken service with him; he insisted she dress as did the wife of any Egyptian citizen. At the time he had told her, "Having you

173

here will keep these Alexandrine noblewomen away from me." Athys had been sure then that he meant to make her his concubine.

There was something in his eyes that made her know fear in his house for the first time, a kind of madness glinting there as he studied her.

"Master, have I offended you?"

"Yes—by being a woman."

Oh! Sudden understanding came to Athys. He had quarreled with Cleopatra, whom he loved. In the past there had been other flareups, always caused by word-battles between them. Never before had he been quite this wild, however; she wondered what the queen might have said to make him so bitter.

He moved toward her, slapped her across the belly.

"This is where you think, every last one of you. With those parts sacred to Isis."

"Master, I—"

"*Isn't it so?*"

Pride touched her. It had been so long since she had been a slave in truth as well as name, that she had forgotten the habit of subservience. Her head went up despite the fact that her flesh still stung where his hand had landed. "Not all women are like that. There are some of us who are decent and use our heads and our hearts."

"Your hearts," he sneered. His hand went out so swiftly she could not turn aside, to fasten in the bodice of her stolla and rip it down. His quick tug brought her off her feet and up against him.

Their faces inches apart, he stared down into her bright eyes. "Whore," he whispered. "You have no heart. Show it to me, if you can."

He pushed her back. The stolla hung in shreds from her shoulders. Down the front it hung wide open, baring her firm breasts. Conon put his hand between them, felt the steady thumping beneath her skin.

"You feel my heart now," she whispered.

"A pulsebeat, nothing more, carrying your false blood throughout your body. It knows nothing of such things as loyalty, truth, decency."

Her cheeks were flaming with embarrassment but she held her arms by her sides. No man had looked upon her breasts since the trip down the Nile years before, when Caesar himself—

"You lie," she said softly but clearly.

For those words her owner was entitled to kill her in any manner he saw fit. With any other man but Conon, angry and desperate as he was, she might not have dared to say them. He had been kind to her, thoughtful and considerate; so much so that she no longer thought of herself as a slave but only as a respected servant.

He laughed at her mockingly. "Do I? We'll see."

His hands came up to cup her breasts, lifting them gently while his thumb moved back and forth across the stiffened nipples. She opened her mouth to protest but the surging flow of pleasure burgeoning in her veins made her close her eyes and let her head fall back. Mother Isis! Not even Caesar had given her such delight. Sometimes at night when she could not sleep, Athys wished Conon would come to her bed and take her. His restraint had puzzled her at first, then pleased her. Another owner—

His lips touched her throat and she gasped.

She wanted to fling her arms about him, to hold and cherish him, to remove the torment and the loneliness from his mind and body. But she must not! In his mood he would only taunt her, laugh at her. And this she could not stand. Not when she—not when she loved him. Yes! She had been blind, these past five years. She did love him, with all her heart.

Conon caressed her breasts, shoved the stolla down off her shoulders until it clung to her only by the silver links at her middle. His palms went all over her, hungrily, while he stared at the flesh he was stroking. It had been so long since he had been with a woman! There was a fire in his loins burning so fiercely that he trembled.

Glancing up, he saw tears on her cheeks.

He stepped back, stunned. "Am I so distasteful to you? Must you weep when I touch you as a man touches a woman he loves?"

"I'm no whore," she breathed.

"Every woman is a whore."

She slapped him in pallid fury, the sound of her palm against his cheek ringing in their ears. He stared at her dumbly, putting fingertips to his face. There was indecision and amazement on his features which flooded out the anger and the mockery.

A moment he stood staring at her, then turned and moved across the chamber to the bed. He sat down on its edge and put his head in his hands. He breathed harshly, heavily.

"Master," Athys whispered.

"Go away. Leave me," he told her.

175

He was sick at heart. If the queen were a harlot, it did not make her female subjects whores. This was the reasoning of a madman. Just now, for a little time, he had been insane. Oh, he had reason to be concerned. Cleopatra was betraying Egypt, selling it into the hands of Rome. Not now, not tomorrow or next year, but eventually. Antony was not a man to win the world.

A sound made him glance up. Athys was lifting a slim white leg, stepping out of her torn stolla. Naked but for the belt of silver links about her middle and her sandals, she dropped the stolla in a pool of crumpled linen. His breath caught in his throat at sight of her nudity. She turned and smiled at him, her full red mouth curving as if to secret thoughts.

Her hands went to her carefully coiffed hair, pulled pins and combs from its piled perfection. "You've been a misogynist too long," she told him gently. "You love Cleopatra and you love Egypt and your love is being twisted like a kudo's horns as a result."

The black hair came tumbling down about her smooth body. She let her head drop back as her fingers pushed it about, freeing its last snarls. "I should have realized this long ago, and come to you when you would not come to me. You had so much on your mind, ruling her kingdom while she was in Rome and in Tarsus, you had no time to think of yourself."

She walked toward him, breasts gently nodding. With gentle hands she pushed him backward so that he lay stretched out below her. She knelt above him and began undoing the straps of the leather jerkin which he had worn under the silver cuirass. When he lay naked she bent and kissed him.

"You have been hurt, so hurt you must lash out at anyone. You chose me. Then punish me, master. But punish me in a way which will most please you. With your body. You named me whore. Treat me as one."

"No," he gasped, fighting against the pleasure her nudity was giving him as she lay down on top of him.

"Yes," she cried and laughed.

He could fight no longer. Too long had he deprived himself of these joys. He shook and cried out at what she did. Then he was reaching for her, putting his hands on her skin and caressing and kissing it, making her moan in pleasure. Bury himself in delight, cover himself with enjoyment, lose himself in her flesh, in her love.

What was he, after all, but a man. No statesman. No

royal governor come to his appointment by birth in a noble family. He was only a gladiator, a man with a strong back and thick muscles. Use those muscles to crush this panting woman to his chest. Use them to rid himself of all the worry, the frustration, the ceaseless vigilance against danger.

Hours later he rolled free of her body. He lay in the dark staring up at emptiness, aware only that he was drained of everything, all the trouble, all the problems. He had been a fool to have refused this pleasure over the years. Athys had taught him common sense, this night.

When he felt her move to leave the bed, he put out his hand to detain her, gripping her wrist and bringing her down beside him. He put her head to his chest and his arm about her shoulders.

"I'm going to set you free. This very night I'll sign the manumission tablet."

"I don't want to be free," she breathed.

"Can I ask a slave to marry me?"

She caught her breath and would have come up on an elbow to stare at him but his arm kept her prisoned where she lay. "Marry you?"

"Well?" he growled. "Do you mean to say you won't?"

Her fingertips touched his lips, stilling them. He became aware that she was weeping softly, then that her head was nodding agreement on his chest. The thought came to him that she loved him, that she had loved him for a very long time.

Conon chuckled wryly.

He was even more of a fool than he had thought.

3.

Antony came to Alexandria without his legions.

He was not calling as a statesman or a general, only as a man. A handful of officers would suffice, just enough to give him a little dignity. With his legions he left behind his armor, adopting a Greek himation and white leather sandals as his garb.

There was a holiday atmosphere all over Alexandria. Spirits were gay and carefree. When Antony went fishing, a diver brought fish to his hook and made certain they were caught before he swam away. If he should ride abroad in a chariot, runners preceded him, to be sure that only the loveliest women could be seen, that no sight should greet his eyes but what was planned for him to see. Cooks labored night and day in the palace kitchens in order that any meal might be called for at any hour of the day or night.

It was a time for laughter and for mirth.

Io paean!

The palace gardens were alive at every hour of the night, until the dawn. The feasting that went on was worthy of the god, Comus. Rare spices were used to flavor the meats and fish. Unusual table delicacies were brought from Pontus, from Cilicia, up the Nile and across the desert sands to decorate the straining tables. Girls and women came to the Lochias to dance and remained to grow wealthy by prostituting their bodies.

The games of living statues was played again, this time— so said gossip in the streets of Alexandria—with the men gilded like those images of the Roman god Liber on whom virgins sacrificed their maidenhood and the women—here the sophisticated Alexandrines howled with glee—playing the part of virgins. Cleopatra was Europa and Antony with a bull-mask on his head, became her kidnapper. Antony was Pan at times, playing on a syrinx; Cleopatra was a dryad. If the Roman pretended to be Adonis, then the queen was Venus.

Slowly but with an inexorability that denied freedom, Cleopatra made Antony her own, binding him by invisible chains stronger than the hardest metal. Every pleasure that man might imagine, she made sure he should enjoy. In the broad *mimi* and *pantomimi* staged in the palace, he took active parts while the queen, delighted, always led in the applause. When he became temporarily sated with the flesh and joined in the philosophical discussions in the Museion, she made certain that his own arguments always should prevail. Where he walked, slaves scattered flower petals.

It was like living in a fabled paradise.

And Mark Antony was its god.

The wealthy Alexandrines formed a club, calling themselves the Inimitables. Each member would entertain the others, seeking always for the outré, the unusual, the bizarre. If one dreamed up the idea of a slave mart, where all the women were auctioned off to the men—only the cream of Egyptian society took part in these games—another would devise an erotic torture chamber in which each member must serve a certain length of time at the mercy of the others. There was no limit, either of reason or of strength, to which they would not go.

The days and the nights were perfumed.

And then—

Fulvia struck in Rome. Cleopatra had the news first through her spies in the Temple of Isis. Fulvia had incited a civil war against Octavian. She had fled with Antony's mother to Athens, where she was making an alliance with Sextus Pompeius, Octavian's deadly enemy. Antony's brother Lucius had been besieged at Perugia by Octavian.

This was disaster. The *pax Romana* no longer existed.

Antony must leave Alexandria, rejoin his legions. He had to march at once. True, Octavian had sent messengers, laying the blame for all that had happened on Fulvia. It was not his brother-in-arms, Marcus Antoninus, who had renewed the civil fighting but the she-wolf, Fulvia!

Though he cursed his wife, Antony was adamant. He had no other choice but to go. Cleopatra might entreat and plead; his mind was made up. There was such a thing as duty. Yes, yes, he told her, he would be back at the earliest opportunity.

If the circumstances proved Octavian correct, he would divorce Fulvia. His word on that, as a nobleman of Rome. Then he would come back and they would be wedded, he and Cleopatra. After that, perhaps they would make their own kingdom here in the East.

Cleopatra had to be satisfied with his promise.

As evidence of his good intentions, Antony ordered the assassination of her sister Arsinoe, exiled to Miletus after her part in the Triumph of Julius Caesar. Moreover, when a pretender to the throne—Cleopatra would not see him to judge the truth of his statements—appeared and called himself the lost Ptolemy who had perished at the battle of the Nile by drowning in his armor, Antony dispatched stranglers to remove him as a threat to the throne of Egypt.

Cleopatra vowed to keep in touch with him.

Their last night together they spent alone, the Inimitables forgotten, in her private apartments in the Lochias. The slaves later swore that they made love all night long, that only when his officers came to escort him to his ship did Cleopatra permit Antony to leave her side.

She wept when he left and would not watch his going. Antony had already agreed to keep in touch with her by letter. It was not much, but it had to satisfy her.

For the next four years, there were few intimate letters between them however; Antony was too busy fighting to think of love-notes. On his way to Athens to meet Fulvia, he had been dismayed to learn that the Parthians were erupting out of their old boundaries and were even now besieging Tyre in Syria. At the very gates of a Roman province!

He must turn aside to raise the eagles, to stop the Parthians at Mylasa and Stratonica. While there, he had other news which, because of the hazards of winter voyages on the Mare Internum, had to come overland by horseman. His brother Lucius was in exile. He had been permitted to leave his unsuccessful defence of Perugia alive and unharmed, although Octavian had made sacrifice of nearly four hundred senators and officers who had thrown in their lot with him.

Octavian was imitating Antony with orgies at which he and his friends and their wives ate up food which should have been sent on to Rome, which was in a state of famine. He had become less the misanthrope and more the miscreant of late, had the adopted son of Caesar. He ate little and drank even less, since wine often made him ill, but he flung his body into those bodily lusts which until now had been almost the exclusive prerogative of Antony. The people called him Apollo, lord of death, and clamored for Antony to come home.

Octavian was making overtures to Sextus Pompeius about this time, but the son of Pompey the Great chose rather to unite with Antony and made an offer of alliance and friendship to him. In Alexandria, Cleopatra burned incense to Isis to make Antony accept this offer. Together, they could sweep Octavian into oblivion.

Antony felt it would be an irreparable breach between himself and his fellow Triumvir should he consent to join forces with Pompeius however, though in Gaul Octavian was arrogantly taking command of legions sworn to Antony. When in early autumn Antony sailed to Brindisi to make this seaport city his base, Octavian sent troops to drive him away. Antony routed his forces and made ready for actual war.

An interruption came from an unexpected source.

Fulvia died at Sicyon, no one knew why.

Instantly Octavian extended the olive branch of peace. Fulvia was the entire cause of their squabble, he stated. Since she was out of the way, no cause for annoyance between them existed. He excused himself for what he had done, pleading the cause of Rome; Antony hastened to reply in the same vein, begging forgiveness for the acts of his late wife, adding that she had done what she did without his knowledge and most certainly without his consent.

The two strongest men in the world met at Brindisi in an atmosphere of rejoicing by their soldiers, of celebration for the peace which each brought with him. There was to be no more civil war. Octavian and Antony were friends, not enemies.

They divided the world between them. Octavian took as his own Italy, Gaul, Spain and Dalmatia. Antony was to have Greece, Macedonia, Thrace, all Asia Minor, Cyria and even Cyrenaica in northern Africa. Neither side would again make friendly gestures toward Sextus Pompeius.

Most important of all, Antony would take as wife the sister of Octavian, the widow Octavia. She was a beautiful woman, but even more important, she was a good woman whose home was her all. Octavia would be no Fulvia, to call him back from the erotic delights of Cleopatra and Alexandria, Antony knew. Marry her, perhaps give her a child to bear—she already was the mother of two, with a third on the way—and he would be free to roam the world as he wanted.

4.

In Alexandria, Cleopatra was in labor.

The fruits of the long winter assignations with her godlike Antony were ripening to maturity, now. As once she had borne Caesarion, now she was giving birth to twins, a man-child and a girl-child. Alexander Helios would be his name, Cleopatra Selene that of the girl. Once again Conon paced the palace walks, his bride Athys momentarily forgotten, and rejoiced when two waving scarves floated at the upper window to signify all was well.

He and Cleopatra had made their own peace soon after Antony sailed for Asia Minor. Conon had come upon her sobbing one afternoon on a marble bench in the gardens while he was seeing to the changing of the guard. She had thrown herself into his arms, kissing him, begging him to forgive her, telling him she had been out of her mind to quarrel with him. It had been her loneliness speaking, Conon realized, but he had been content. It was enough for him that matters were as they had always been between them.

When Cleopatra heard he had married Athys, she reproached him and insisted on a state wedding, replete with priceless gifts from the Inimitables and in absent Antony's name, a villa on the Nile a few miles above Abydos. Athys had never told Conon that her body had been enjoyed, long years before, by Julius Caesar. On her knees and with tears in her eyes, she begged that Cleopatra also keep silence.

Conon had lost one woman to the great Roman. The knowledge that his wife had been Caesar's plaything might prove too much for him. Cleopatra had laughed, kissed her and wiped the tears from her eyes, swearing secrecy on the name of Hathor. Athys wondered how much the promise of the queen was worth. Royalty had a way of forgetting promises when they stood in the way of gain.

Cleopatra insisted that they leave right after their state wedding to their new Nile villa. Egypt was at peace; it had never been so prosperous; she had Caesarion to keep her company. This was the time for Conon and Athys to be alone.

Nor was Conon slow to obey the royal whim. Caesarion was living proof that Cleopatra had given herself to one Roman. Her giving birth to Antony's child was something he could not stomach. He had no love for Antony.

Yet he insisted that riders gallop between Alexandria and Abydos with the latest information on the relations of Octavian and Antony, and Cleopatra indulged him. Thus he learned that things went well with Mark Antony in Rome. The famed singer Mycenas composed ballads in honor of his new wife. Coins designating Antony as the sun-god, Sol, were struck. Octavian was naming himself the son of god following the official deification of his adoptive father, Julius Caesar. It seemed that Antony and Octavian were settling down to a mutual sharing of their world.

Sextus Pompeius still held the sea lanes and was called *Rex Oceanus* by the hungry mobs of Rome who stormed the streets bellowing imprecations against Octavian. That young man did what he could, attempting to levy taxes, to build a navy with which to sail against Pompeius but the people tore down his tax posters and would have killed him except that Antony himself appeared with troops and saved his brother-in-law's life.

"The idiot," Conon said to Athys as they ate figs and cheese for breakfast in a villa summerhouse overlooking the Nile. "He had a chance to take power by standing still—and he couldn't even do that!"

"Why do you hate him so?"

"The man's a fool. Strong? Yes! Brave? Yes! But intelligent? No. Do you think Caesar would have stormed out with a couple of cavalry units to save the life of a man he'd have to fight some day? Not on your life."

She toyed with a pleat of her byssus tunic, head bent so he would not see her face. Is he still in love with Cleopatra? she wondered. Is that why he's so furious? Caesar he hated once, but Caesar is dead, now. Antony is alive and so he rails against him. She was jealous of her queen, but only in a somewhat vague way, for she knew well enough that Conon had never enjoyed the embraces that went instead to the Romans.

"How will this friendship of Octavian and Antony affect Egypt?" she asked aloud.

Conon brooded. "I think it would be good for Egypt, especially since Egypt is in the East, which belongs to Antony. The longer war holds off between those two, the less chance there is of it. It would have been far better for Egypt, though, if Antony had let the mob kill Octavian. The stupid fool!"

Cleopatra was calling Antony worse names than fool.

In sheer amazement she had learned that he was married to the sister of his enemy. Once Fulvia died, she had been positive he would drop everything and come back to Alexandria for her—wed her in the Temple of Isis—then sail for Rome to try conclusions with Octavian. Or at least set her up in Rome as a royal goddess and his wife. So strongly had she believed he would do this that she had ships waiting, loaded with her goods and baggage, ready to weigh anchor as soon as word came that Antony was sighted. How bitter had her mood been when she was forced to give the signal to disembark those loaded coffers and bags!

Cleopatra now considered herself betrayed.

"If he loved me," she whispered to her tear-wet bed, "he would have come for me like Mercury, with the wind."

Instead, he had remained in Rome to bed another woman. It was this fact and her female jealousy that ate most bitterly inside Cleopatra. She could have forgiven his saving the life of Octavian, though it was admittedly foolish, almost stupid —but how typically Antonean! This matter of Octavia was something else again.

The palace could hear her scream with rage when she read the words of the priest of Isis who related the wedding. She tore her tunic and hurled her jeweled diadem across the audience chamber. With her body all but naked she stormed from the throne room to her bedchamber where she lay weeping for hours.

Even now, days after the event, she would fly into a paroxysm of fury at the slightest cause. Slaves walked on tiptoe in her presence. Her servants effaced themselves from her eyes as soon as possible. She was like a caged panther newly caught and starving.

If Conon had been in Alexandria, he might have calmed her. Almost, she was on the verge of sending for him, to discuss this new twist in her political fortunes; always she desisted, reasoning with her female love of romance that he must not be disturbed with his bride.

One night as she lay sleepless, she remembered Hardedef and went seeking him in the slave quarters with a lantern in her hand. Fat Hardedef stumbled to his feet, eyes bulging.

"Highness, what—?"

"Have you any handsome male slaves?" she asked crisply.

"Of course, highness." He was too frightened to leer. "Very many. A young Cilician, a Parthian, even a few Egyptian lads sold for debt."

"Send them to my bedchamber," she ordered. *"All* of them."

She chose half a dozen and dismissed the others. For two days and three nights she remained closeted with them in her rooms. The palace staff could hear her cries of enjoyment, her obscene language, and guessed at the foul actions she compelled them to practise with her.

For Cleopatra it was a purge of the flesh.

She dismissed the slaveboys, ordering them not to be killed but to be kept healthy and happy, that they might be always at her call. Now she could turn to the needs of queenhood with untroubled visions of Antony and Octavia. In her own way, she had answered his insult.

To Antony she sent a mage, a man learned in magic and the allied arts, with instructions not only to spy on the Triumvir but to influence him as much as possible against Octavian. Cleverly, Cleopatra understood there was no need to fight Octavia the wife. Antony himself would do that, remembering his Alexandrine winter with Cleopatra, once he broke with Octavian.

Conon returned to Alexandria just as news came that Octavian too had married. His first wife, Clodia, he had sent home to her parents untouched. His second wife, Scribonia, had been with child when he met Livia Drusilla, wife of Tiberius Claudius Nero; Livia also was pregnant at the time.

"They have a taste for swollen bellies, those Romans," Cleopatra told Conon when he stood before her at last. "Octavia was pregnant when her brother espoused her to Antony, Scribonia when Octavian divorced her, and now Livia. What is it that makes them so seductive?"

Conon said nothing, knowing Cleopatra spoke only the idle musings of her mind. She was sitting in a straightbacked chair placed on the wallwalk looking out over the harbor. It was summer and the heat was stifling.

"Is it too late?" she asked suddenly.

He understood her at once and shrugged. "Who knows? Antony is in Athens with Octavia, behaving like a proper married man. I doubt that Octavian would want to stir up trouble now. After all, he did give his sister—whom he loves very much—to Antony as a pledge of peace between them. Why, he's even made friends of sorts with Sextus Pompeius, handing over the three islands of Sicily, Corsica and Sardinia to be his little province.

"No, the time for alliance with Octavian has passed. Who can say whether it will ever come again?" He eyed her closely before asking, "What of your fine friend Antony? I thought—"

The face she turned up to him was so twisted with fury that he stepped back a pace. "That traitor? That—that thing who spurned me—me, Cleopatra Thea Philopater!—for that wishy-washy matron, Octavia! Isis, how I hate them both."

Conon understood that she still loved Antony. Her diatribe was merely the outcry of a woman scorned. He let her rage for several minutes, knowing it would ease her injured pride. By then she was weeping softly into her cupped hands.

"What shall I do, Conon? I—I feel so abandoned."

"Watch. And wait."

They watched together, this queen and this man who loved her so deeply, while across the sea Octavian went into Gaul to join his general, Agrippa, in putting down a number of tribal rebellions. He was named Imperator and given a Triumph, hoping thereby to instill an image of himself as a military conqueror in the minds of the people.

Antony remained in Athens and despatched his general, Ventidius, to conduct his war against the Parthians. Ventidius won an overwhelming victory, avenged the defeat of Crassus, and cutting off the head of the Parthian king's son, displayed it in the frontier cities as proof that the Parthian power had been broken. It was Ventidius, not Antony, who went back to Rome to enjoy the Triumph accorded a victorious general.

Cleopatra and Conon waited until the following spring.

Then Antony sent Fonteius Capito to Alexandria.

Capito extended an invitation to the Egyptian queen to meet Mark Antony in Antioch. The general was heading into the East with several legions to take up the Parthian war once again and so secure forever the far eastern boundaries of his kingdom. He had sent Octavia back to Rome, saying publicly that a war campaign was no place for her; besides, she was pregnant with his child. She would be safer in Rome under the doting eyes of her fond brother than here in the East where Antony must be free to wage the war that would give him the Triumph which had gone to Ventidius.

Antony would be free also to renew relations with Cleopatra.

"Do you intend going?" asked Conon in surprise.

"I do," she answered from the marble bench in the gardens where they watched the twins at play. At a thought she lifted her head and laughed. "You think me wanton, don't you? I have my reasons."

"What can they be?" he pretended to ponder.

She gestured with her hands. "You see them before you, tossing that leather ball. Alexander Helios. Cleopatra Selene. Ceasarion, of course is at the Gymasiarch watching the wrestlers. My three children—all of them bastards."

Her smile was not pretty to see. "I'll legalize their births by marrying Antony. That's why I'm going to join him."

"A Roman can have only one wife."

"A Ptolemy can have two. I shall make a Ptolemy out of Antony. It will be that simple."

Conon hoped so, but not out loud.

TWELVE

The Parthian Campaign, 36 B. C.

1.

Mark Antony was angry. He was also worried.

During the past two years he had remembered so many things about this woman who strolled beside him past the red pillars of his private rooms in this Antiochean palace. She had been like the stormy *khamsin* of her own Egypt, hot and restless, given to many moods. His hands recalled the feel of her breasts and buttocks, his loins remembered the fervid clasp of her own. He had pretended to himself that Octavia was Cleopatra, but the Roman woman was no oriental seductress.

But now Antony was finding Cleopatra cool, almost cold.

To his hints and sly remarks that they bed together as they had done three years before, she seemed utterly deaf. It was as though she were another woman. Yet she wore the thin *mafortes*, as if to taunt him with the loveliness of her body, completely visible under its transparency. She still laughed at his jokes and willingly joined him over a dozen goblets of Rhodian wine.

At last he came to begging. "What's the matter? Why are you so distant with me? What have I done?"

Cleopatra could not believe her ears. Her tongue trembled to answer him as might a fishwife her wandering spouse; she controlled herself; she played at more than intercourse between them.

"I thought you loved Octavia," she said slowly.

Antony hooted, vastly relieved. She was only jealous! Well, he had dealt with jealous women before. He caught her with his arms in the shadows of the red pillars and kissed her hungrily. Cleopatra was no shy virgin. She kissed him just as eagerly, permitted the play of his palms upon her hips. Let them build a fire in his loins! No man can think when his blood is bubbling! She gurgled laughter as she pressed into him.

"Are you saying you don't love her?" she breathed.

"Compared with you she's a cow. Could I love a cow?"

"Ah, but you married her."

"To keep peace, to keep peace."

She smiled up at him. "You've seen Alexander? Cleopatra Selene?"

"Wonderful children, both of them. The girl takes after me."

"It's a pity she can't acknowledge you as her father."

Antony flushed. "If I divorce Octavia—"

"Oh, there's no need to do that," she said casually.

He was in a mood to snatch at any reed by which to make his peace with her, to get her to ease the torment in his loins. And so he listened carefully while Cleopatra explained that in the East—this same East of which he was the acknowledged overlord—a Ptolemy might take two wives. Many of her ancestors had done so. One even had married a mother and a daughter. All that was needed was for Antony to add a name to his own and become Marcus

Antoninus Ptolemy. For a man who was a god on earth, this was an easy matter.

His laughter boomed out, his simple nature pleased by such a resolution of his problem. If this would please her, then let it be done. At once, without delay. But for now, surely she must guess how desperately he needed her? She would no longer hold herself from his embrace? He lifted her easily into the air, threw her up and caught her, grinning as she squealed.

When he let her go she caught her tunic in both hands and yanked it open so that her heavy breasts tumbled out before his eyes. Antony shouted with glee. Ah, this was better. This was his old Cleopatra, the only woman he had ever really loved—he actually believed it when he said it, she told herself wryly—and his wife to be. His hands reached for her.

She twisted away from him and ran.

Antony pounded after her, seeing her slip off a bracelet and toss it aside, watched breathlessly as her fine *mafortes* slid from her shoulders to the middle of her bared back. Now her hands were pushing it down beyond her hips—how her plump buttocks shook to her running!—and about her slim legs.

She stumbled before she could rid herself of the tunic, and this was when he caught her. Naked, she was swung up into his arms, kissed everywhere that his lips could reach.

"The bedchamber," she breathed harshly.

"No, no. Here! This instant!"

He let her slide downward and she gasped.

Some days later, Marcus Antoninus Ptolemy married Cleopatra Thea Philopater. Publicly, Antony recognized Alexander and the little Cleopatra as his children. Upon his new bride he lavished rich gifts: Coele Syria, Nabataian Arabia, Chalcis in Lebanon and other cities, portions of Cilicia and Crete and the Roman province of Cyrene.

Among her many new possessions were parts of Lebanon, rich in timber for a strong Egyptian navy. Octavian—at odds once more with Sextus Pompeius—was ship-building on the Tiber. Antony did not want to be penned always to the land. The sea victories of Sextus Pompeius, the ease with which he prevented Egyptian corn ships from docking at Ostia and Puteoli, Rome's seaports, were fresh in his mind. If he could control the flow of corn and wheat to Rome, he might bring

Octavian to his knees—if it came to an open rupture between them—in a bloodless manner.

Cleopatra agreed to build the ships with her gold. A strong navy would make her own land strong. These triremes would bear the insignia of the lotus and the papyrus, not the Roman eagle. Her crewmen would be Egyptians, sworn to obey only her commands.

She could scarcely lose in such an agreement.

For Cleopatra no longer trusted Antony. She was committed to him by their past, by their mutual natures, by their concern about Octavian, but the confidence of a woman in love had been shattered when he married Octavia. In her mind, Antony had assumed the characteristics of a weather-vane that swung to every shifting wind.

Too, it was expedient for Antony to win Egypt to his following, and so he was taking a new name and a new wife. Should it be as necessary to shed her, she had no doubt that he would do just that. It was bitter knowledge for her as a proud woman, but necessary knowledge to her as a sovereign.

Although their political life together was limited by her realization of his unsteadiness, their romantic life was under no such restraint. He was once again the devoted lover, not averse when the mood suited him to drawing her against him and disarranging their garments so that he might take her as he would a common slavegirl. As a woman, she gloried in his ardent worship. It made no difference to either of them that they might be surrounded by slaves or servants. It was the heat of their bodies that was of paramount importance, the need each had to bring pleasure to the other.

They spent a few months in Antioch together while the legions gathered to march with Antony into Parthia. There were celebrations and entertainments at all hours, processions and parades, exotic feasts and parties. It was a continuation of their winter idyll in Alexandria those years ago. Almost it seemed that they had never parted.

Antony paraded his military might before his wife, one hundred thousand disciplined Roman legionaries in full battle equipment. They would be leaving soon for Zeugma; he was sending them on ahead so that he himself might enjoy a few more days with her. He intended marching his men by an overland route into Parthia rather than strike it by marching east; this had been a master plan conceived by Julius Caesar; Antony meant to adopt it for his own use.

The days fled too swiftly for both of them.

At the end, Cleopatra could not bear to be parted from

189

him and traveled with his guard as far as Zeugma. Here she swung back toward Alexandria, for she was carrying his child and was determined not to risk a miscarriage through some misadventure on the road.

Antony went with the legions into Parthia.

2.

Conon stood at a map of brightly colored tiles inset into the wall of a small chamber hung with heavy drapes to keep out of the misty wind from the sea. It was late autumn of the year and the squally *euroclydon* was raging up and down the coastal waters. Candles had been lighted against an early darkness.

Cleopatra sat at ease before a small table, from time to time sipping chilled wine. She was frowning in puzzlement at the moment.

"I understand," she said slowly, "that Antony took over a hundred thousand men into Parthia. He was joined in Media by his allies, King Polemo of Laodicea and King Artavasdes of Armenia. Artavasdes was especially important to him because of his many thousands of cavalry who fight in the manner of the Parthians, with bows on horseback. Yet now I hear that Antony," the words scratched her throat, "—that Antony has made some sort of bargain with the Parthian king to be allowed to retreat unmolested." ·

Conon nodded. "According to three different accounts of what happened, Antony entered Parthia over the Araxes river and attacked the city of Phraaspa." Conon made a wry face. "His siege train he left behind at Gaza. King Phraates of Parthia ignored Antony to attack and destroy that siege train with its engines and baggage, food, armor, equipment—everything he had except what his men wore.

"He burned a furtune in a few hours, leaving Antony destitute in a foreign land." Conon lost his cold tones and lashed out with a snarl in his throat. "I told you the man was a fool. To move fifty miles from his supply wagons in enemy country! Is this the great Antony who calls himself Autocrator—supreme ruler—these days?"

Cleopatra made no answer where once she would have flared at him. Conon dropped his eyes and shuffled his feet. "I'm sorry," he muttered.

"No," she said clearly, "I'm the one who's sorry, Conon. Sorry I didn't take your advice those years back when you

190

told me to offer Egypt and its corn to Octavian and not Antony. Instead—I was so young then!—I invited Antony to Alexandria and cast my lot with him."

Her little fist hit the tabletop. "I should have gone to Octavian, if I went to anyone at all. You were right! You were right! Now I'm chained to Antony, with nowhere else to turn."

Conon cleared his throat. He said, "It may not be as bad as the news says. Still, when Antony tried to come at grips with Phraates by laying siege to the city of Phraaspa, he was beseiged in turn by the horsemen of King Phraates. His men are now forced to depend on the countryside for food and every foraging party has to fight a battle to keep what it can steal. Our latest news says that Artavasdes of Armenia has quarreled with Antony and has left camp and taken his cavalry units with him. If so, this is really bad. Those Armenian mounted bowmen were the one check Antony had against the Parthian method of fighting."

"There is nothing newer than that?"

"Only a bit of gossip picked up by a courier at a wayside tavern. It seems Antony tried to make a treaty with Phraates who told him his terms were for Antony to leave Parthia as fast as possible. Otherwise his men would be cut to ribbons."

Cleopatra bowed her head. There were no tears in her eyes; she had wept enough over Mark Antony. But there was a savage, frightened desperation in her veins. She was fighting with all her strength for the throne which was to be Caesarion's inheritance. Antony was her husband. For him to meet defeat so soon after their marriage—

The people of her world were superstitious. They might think her unlucky. Or conceive Antony to be unlucky, which was just as bad. The baby in her womb kicked out and made her smile tiredly. She wondered what it was like to have your child with its father close at hand? It was an experience she had never known.

"We will talk tomorrow, Conon," she murmured, shaking her head.

He helped her from the chair and guided her steps along the corridor. It seemed to Conon that she leaned more heavily on him than she had ever done.

They had the whole story by springtime.

An armistice declared with King Phraates, Antony had marched back toward Syria. Afraid of treachery on the part of the Parthians, he met with treachery. The dreaded bowmen of Parthia in their scaled armor hit him again and again. Dur-

191

ing the twenty-seven days of his retreat, his men had to fight eighteen times. No food, poisoned waters, even a rebellion of his own troops: all these were a part of the bitter potion Antony had to swallow.

Cleopatra was sorry for him, yet oddly glad at the same time. She said to Conon, "Suppose he had won a great victory over Parthia, what would he have done?"

"Gone to Rome, I suppose, for a Triumph."

"And been reunited with Octavia, the recent mother of his child." Her laughter rang out shrilly. "He sows children as a farmer scatters oats, does Antony." Her own baby, the infant Ptolemy, was not quite a year old. "Yes, gone to bed with Octavia, made friends with her brother—and left me and Caesarion to rot! But with defeat," and now her eyes gleamed, "with defeat he will have to turn to me!

"He won't go back to Rome and let the story of his debacle be made public knowledge. He'll stay here in the East until he gets a chance to redeem himself."

Her cause was not yet lost. Let her hasten to meet Antony with food and supplies, with weapons, armor and ships, and together they might salvage something on which to build anew.

They came together on the beach below Sidon, Antony standing up to his knees in the surf, his hands under Cleopatra's armpits swinging her out of a longboat into his arms. He waded ashore, carrying her high on his chest, covering her lips with kisses, calling her his Bona Dea. There was no need for exotic entertainment in either of them any longer. Matters were too grim, too serious for that.

Side by side, they ate a cold supper in his battle tent, then planned their future moves. The King of Media, another Artavasdes, had recently quarreled with the king of Parthia. Now he turned to Antony, seeking to make an alliance with him, inviting him to attack Parthia once more, this time with the help of his own mounted bowmen. This Artavasdes would be no traitor such as was the Armenian Artavasdes! With the prospect of a mounted archer corps to flank his veterans, Antony was exuberant.

"I'll march east within the week," he told Cleopatra.

She laughed at him. "You'll travel west, my dear stallion of a husband—to Alexandria. I've missed you. I'm tired of goodbyes."

Antony shook his head. "Parthia," he grinned.

Her eyebrows arched. "And if I take back my cloaks, my clothes, my food, my weapons, all the gold I brought you in

192

those little teakwood coffers? Where will you be then, Antony?

"You wouldn't! Why—you Egyptian bitch!"

"You Roman boar! Your brains are located below your navel. A child might have seen the trap into which you let yourself fall in Parthia. To be so far from your supply base. Is this what you learned from Caesar?"

"Damn Caesar! It was the treachery of Artavasdes of Armenia that did me in."

"A poor carpenter blames only his adze."

He might have hit her, so awful was his fury, but this was a different Antony than the man who had marched out of Antioch those months ago. His brain still remembered the terrible Parthian horsemen and the nightmare of the twenty-seven day retreat where death came flying on wings of long arrowshafts. It put a curb over his temper.

Yet they fought. He finally cuffed her, not in playfulness as once he might have done but in cold anger. She clawed his face, running furrows down his cheeks with her nails. His hand tore her thin tunic and with her buttocks bared, he spanked her. She howled and cursed like a cavalryman and bit his thigh until the blood ran.

She threw a lighted oil lamp at him that splashed and set fire to the tent. His men came running with water to douse it while they stood and cursed one another so everyone could hear. They were bitter and angry and curiously aware of one another.

When the fire was out and she led the way inside the tent, he looked at her tear-stained face and felt the bite of regret. He put his thick arm around her and when she would have struggled free, held her motionless so he could kiss away her tears and tell her how sorry he was. Nor did he neglect to slide his hand into her torn tunic so as to add prurience to his plea. When she shivered under his touch, he knew she was his to take.

They made their peace on his camp cot.

Two days later, a rider dropped from the saddle before the scorched tent and extended a scroll from Octavia. His wife was in Greece with supplies and reinforcements for a new Parthian campaign. She longed to see him, to show him their child.

With her letter was a note from Octavian.

Antony swore when he read it. In it, Octavian sympathized with his old friend and fellow Triumvir on his recent crushing defeat in Parthia. It was so worded, as if with tongue in cheek, that even Antony could imagine the intense delight with which Octavian had dictated it. Octavian was sending, he added, two thousand soldiers with his sister to show his good intentions.

"Good intentions," rasped Antony. "He'd like nothing so much as to see me wreck myself and all my hopes in Parthia, just as Crassus did." Then Antony turned to her, with worry on his face and in his eyes.

"What shall I do?" he asked.

Cleopatra closed her eyes in triumph. At last, at last! Finally he was turning to her in his need. No longer was he the fiery animal, the trampling bull, the trumpeting stallion, proud of and dependent solely on his own strength. There was a weakness in Antony but she was here for him to lean on.

All the worry and the frenzied hours of the past few years were forgotten. So long alone herself, so afraid of Rome and its legions, forced by circumstance to play the harlot first to Caesar and then to this big, heavyset man, she could see now the final culmination of all her work. Caesar would never have asked her advice, except in amusement. Antony not only asked her advice, he was in desperate need of it.

"Write to Octavia, telling her to remain in Athens," she said gently. "The Parthian campaign on which you plan to embark is no place for her."

"It's what I told her last time."

"Now that you know the tribulations you met in Parthia, your reasoning is doubly sound." He nodded at that, thoughtfully, then brightened. Cleopatra went on, "You're still tired from that campaign. Come with me to Alexandria, to rest. It is autumn and will be winter, soon. Let your officers spend these months gathering supplies and equipment, recruiting men."

"Any competent tribune could do it," he rumbled.

She rose to her feet, pressed herself against him and felt his arm slip about her middle to hold her closer. There was a new communion between them, she realized. *The man loves me at last! Not only for my body but for my gaiety, my companionship, my laughter.* In his way, Antony had come to realize that what he wanted, Cleopatra wanted. Their fates were linked together by bonds which he no longer sought to break.

"If you pardon the men who served with Sextus Pompeius they might join your standards," she suggested.

During the past year while Antony had been in Parthia,

Octavian had chased the last living son of Pompey into Phrygia. While Pompey the Younger lived, Octavian would know no peace. The seas were not safe and Rome had come to depend on the seas for its food. Pompeius was a lesser enemy than Antony.

And so Octavian gave command of the seas—and many big warships—to his friend and general, Agrippa. Octavian had a talent for getting others to do what he could not. Agrippa cornered Sextus Pompeius at Mylae near Sicily and beat him. Pompey the Younger escaped that debacle to fight again at Naulochus, some miles away. Again Pompeius met defeat, though managing to disengage many of his vessels and flee with them to Asia Minor where once Hannibal himself had fled after Zama. Agrippa was an extremely competent general. He went after his enemy as fast as wind and oars could take him, but he never quite caught up with him.

Sextus Pompeius had landed in Phyrgia and attempted to fight his way overland into Parthia. Antony himself had sent a general, Marcus Titius, to stop him. In the brief battle that followed, the son of Pompey the Great was killed.

His men however, still remained prisoners in Pontus. "Free them," Cleopatra urged. "Offer clemency and forgetfulness in return for their promise to serve you in Parthia."

Antony grinned. His personal charm was such that he had no doubt of the outcome. As Octavian had walked into the camp of Lepidus and seduced the allegiance of his soldiers, so he would do with those hardened pirates who had served Pompeius. Lepidus' power was broken; Octavian was taking over his African provinces and sending Lepidus into exile. For the past half year or so, there had been only two Triumvirs in Rome, Octavian and Antony.

Soon there would be only one, Antony told himself.

He hugged Cleopatra and kissed her. "And with my letter to Octavia, shall I ask that her supplies and soldiers be sent on to me?"

"Why not? You won't sleep with them."

Antony roared with laughter. It was the sort of jest he appreciated. "Only with you, pet, from now on! Come, help me compose those letters." He reached for her hand and walked with her from the scorched tent toward the little writing tables where clerks waited with waxed tablets and styluses.

Her heart told her that this was a new Antony, one dependent on her wits and brain and beauty. Her colder reason assured her that Mark Antony would never change, that he was a boy at heart, with boyish enthusiasms, boyish impulses.

Let Octavia do some minor thing that might catch his eye or heart, and he might very well be off to her, abandoning her once more. Her mind said that if she could cement Antony to her solidly—by something more drastic even than their marriage—then for him there would be no turning away, ever again. Her heart added that she must bend every ounce of energy to accomplish this, for it was a prospect that pleased her very much.

3.

Alexandria welcomed Antony with a wildly thudding heart.

He came into it not as a Roman conqueror but as an Oriental king, resting on a gilded litter borne aloft by slaves. He wore not the toga but the Egyptian tunic and on his head was placed the royal pshent. Behind him came the litter of his queen, Cleopatra, and the steady tramping of marching feet was not that of Roman legionaries but of Egyptian soldiers following after them.

Jugglers and acrobats performed here and there in the cortege. Flat wagons held large leather sacks of coins and slaves who distributed them by the handful all along the Canopic Way to the cheers and shouts of the people. The statues of Isis and of Hathor were carried aloft, surrounded by priests and temple dancing girls. Little boys threw flower petals here and there.

Conon rode a white horse at the head of his troops. His cuirass was of silver, decorated with golden phalerae. He was not a happy man. To his way of thinking, Cleopatra had emasculated Antony.

"All her life she's fought to ally herself with Rome," he complained to Athys later that night after the feasting at the Lochias. "Now she has the chance, she throws it away."

"In what manner?"

"Antony is no longer a Roman. Doesn't she understand that? He's changing into what she wants him to be. She's so afraid of losing him to Octavia—did I say once that all women were whores?—that she's bringing him under her power. She is Egypt, unable to stand without help from Rome. Yet she kicks the props out from under her because she's afraid of going to bed alone."

"Antony's a Roman," protested Athys.

"Not any more he isn't!"

The winter was a quiet one. Antony and Cleopatra were

not so much lovers as they were married folk. The palace re-sounded to the shrill cries and happy screams of their three children. Antony busied himself with the problems of his vast Eastern lands; Cleopatra with her government of Egypt and its provinces. While Antony was preparing for his coming campaign against Parthia, despatching couriers, reading accounts of his officers, planning military strategy, Cleopatra was the loving mother, surrounded by her children.

They were happy together, so happy that sometimes doubts came to both of them about the coming war with Parthia. Antony was a man of fifty, Cleopatra a woman of thirty-five. Each was well past the first flush of youth and its lordly ambitions. They held power in their hands and neither wished to give it up.

"For what?" Cleopatra asked one night as she was prepar-ing for bed. She wore only a thin himation that came to her hips; in summertime she would wear nothing at all. She turned her head, glanced over her shoulder at him where he sat on a Greek solia and studied a scroll from his legate in Syria.

Antony glanced up. "Eh? What was that?"

"For what? Why do you fight Parthia? What can you hope to gain?"

"A victory. The return of the captured Roman eagles taken when Crassus was defeated. The return of any prison-ers still alive."

"And for this you risk everything?" Her hand made a little gesture taking in their world. She made a pretty picture to the eyes in the soft glow of candlelight, Antony thought. The thin himation did more to make her appealing than would complete nudity.

He grinned at her and tossed aside the scroll. She saw his sudden interest at sight of her shapely legs bared all the way to her upper thighs. "Now, Antony. I'm tired."

His grin became a laugh. "Of course, my dear. I am my-self. But never that tired. Come here."

She sighed in mock exasperation, but she was very pleased. She put down the silver mirror in which she had been study-ing her face for possible coarsening of her skin—in which case she would have applied an ointment made of cucumber juice and olive oil—and came to sit on his lap.

"I mean it, Antony. About Parthia." She let him nuzzle her throat while she spoke. "You're risking everything you've built up. And I ask again—for what? For some old Roman standards and men who've probably long since been put to death or sold into slavery throughout Asia as far away as the land of Serica."

"But—"

"Suppose you don't get the promised help from Media? Or from Artavasdes of Armenia, who is so eager to help now that he sees which way the wind blows?"

Antony stopped kissing her neck. "Artavasdes! That treacherous bastard!"

"Exactly. Can you trust him again? Dare you put any trust in the man who ran away once, taking the cavalry you so desperately needed? Parthia is no land for foot soldiers alone. You need mounted bowmen. Artavasdes deprived you of them."

"I owe Artavasdes something for that."

Cleopatra nodded, eyes brightly shining. If she were only able to stir his rancour against Armenia enough, she might dissuade him entirely from crossing into Parthia. Roman standards? Roman prisoners? As well say, Roman pride. It was no more than this which was taking him into that distant Asiatic land. Certainly Phraates of Parthia would not dare to invade Roman provinces, having already been taught a lesson by Ventidius. He was content to stay at home in peace, if permitted to do so.

Antony wanted a Triumph. In his generosity, he had insisted that Ventidius Bassus go alone to be welcomed for his victory; but there was still a bit of jealousy in Antony. Boyishly, he wanted a Triumph of his own.

Armenia would be an easier opponent than Parthia.

She bit his earlobe. "Do you think Artavasdes is laughing at you?" she wondered idly. His head jerked, but not from the bite of her sharp teeth.

"Laughing at me? At me?"

She spread her hands, looking innocent. "He left you in Parthia. He ran away. Because he did, you were defeated. I can just imagine him telling his court, 'Antony is afraid of me and my bowmen. Does he attack me? No! He suffers my desertion in silence because he can do nothing else.' "

"By Mars," Antony growled.

Cleopatra was a wise woman. She was content to plant a seed and seek no promises. Antony swore by Mars. Soon he would swear by Eros. She slid a hand along his thigh and fondled him. Torn between pride and prurience, he yielded to those stroking fingers.

His hands slipped under the thin himation to her breasts, then down to cup her buttocks. Under his muscles, the

198

himation ripped and her nakedness was exposed to him. She laughed and tried to cover herself with her hands but he held her wrists and drawing her upward between his thighs, began to kiss her hungrily.

Cleopatra shrieked with pleasure.

But later when they lay apart on the vast bed, Antony went back in his mind to their earlier discussion. "If I should wage war against Artavasdes, it would bring ruin on Armenia. I wouldn't want to despoil a land that would belong to us, then."

"Certainly not! Your quarrel is with Artavasdes alone. Make him your prisoner. Once he's taken, his land will fall into your hand."

"Now how may I do that?"

Antony did not notice it, but Cleopatra did; she was doing his thinking for him. She said slowly, "Offer him Alexander Helios as his son-in-law, to be wedded to his daughter."

"What?" he shouted, coming up on an elbow.

She restrained her gesture of impatience. "Reflect a moment. When this offer is conveyed to him, what will he think?"

"He'll believe I'm afraid of him!"

"Of course he will, and that you take this means to repair the breach between you. He will come to meet you, not suspecting what we mean to do."

Antony grinned wolfishly. "By Mars! I'd hate to have you for an enemy," he exclaimed honestly.

Caesar had once said almost the same thing.

But Artavasdes declined this signal honor which Antony and Cleopatra would bestow on him. He would wed his daughter as he saw fit, he told them. It was the excuse Antony wanted.

He marched his legions into Armenia, straight to the great capitol of Artaxata. The army that Artavasdes sent against him was brushed aside, for Antony had made alliance with Media, and reinforced by those mounted bowmen, had little to fear from the cavalrymen of Armenia. Against foot soldiers, the Roman legion was supreme.

Desperate, Artavasdes came to Antony under a flag of truce. Antony put him in chains—as a mark of respect for his kingship, they were of solid silver—and sent him back to Alexandria. Then he turned his attention to those Armenians who raised up Artaxes, the son of Artavasdes, as their ruler in place of his father. These too he crushed in battle, and Artaxes fled into Parthia.

For a few weeks, Antony permitted his troops to loot and

pillage the conquered country, always under supervision of their officers, however, so that they should not grow too wealthy at the expense of their own commander. Messengers were sent to Artavasdes, king of Media, a permanent alliance being proposed between them by way of a marriage between Alexander Helios and Iotapa, daughter of the Median king. Armenia should be a province of Media, which in turn should be a province of Rome, under Antony.

It was a cunning move. The Artavasdes who ruled Media wanted no Roman legions in his land. The tribute he should have to pay would not be too great a burden; an outright war would cost him far more. He agreed to these terms and to the marriage contract.

Almost bloodlessly, Antony Autocrator had broadened his kingdom.

Now he could have his Triumph.

4.

In Rome, Octavian bided his time.

His own armies were engaged in a war with his eastern provinces, Illyria and Pannonia. He was too clever a man to wage a war of his own making on two widely separated battle fronts, so he contented himself with propaganda.

He permitted a Triumph to Marcus Titius, conqueror of Pompey the Younger, at which he ordered the attendance of Octavia and the children of the absent Antony. He pointed out to the Roman people that Mark Antony was nowhere at hand, that he had as good as abandoned his Roman wife and Roman children for the Egyptian harlot, Cleopatra.

According to Octavian, Antony scorned his Roman citizenship. Rome was no longer. good enough for him. He preferred the sybaritic luxuries and vices of Alexandria, his Egyptian children to his Roman offspring.

The people of Rome began to growl.

THIRTEEN

Actium, 31 B. C.

1.

Four tiny crowns glinted in the Alexandrine sunlight.

They rested on a dais before two mighty thrones erected in the great stadium, guarded by a detachment of the Macedonian Guards. The stadium was empty at this hour; the people who would later fill it to the last seat and then stand watching, were now lining the streets between the Stadium and the Lochias Palace.

They were waiting for the Triumph. Antony had returned from Armenia with captives and with loot. These would be displayed before the eyes of the Alexandrines today as other captives and other wealth had once been shown to the people of Rome. Alexandria had never seen a Triumph; it was a Roman custom and never took place anywhere but in the city on the Tiber.

Today would make history.

Trumpets blared. The great bronze gates of the palace clanged wide. Out of them at the march came the Royal Household Guards, equipped as had been the Macedonians of Alexander the Great, in high-crested Grecian helmets and cuirasses, carrying the round shields, swords clanking at their sides, spearbutts thumping the pavements. Behind them came the Roman legionaries, those of them selected to parade here this day.

Mounted Gauls, Balearic slingers on foot, Median horsemen, Roman cavalry, all made the procession a panoply of color and a symbol of military might. Trumpets and cymbal clashers, pretty girls playing on small lyres, came after them. Behind these were the flower girls, tossing rose petals to form a red carpet over which came Antony.

He stood upright in his war chariot, in full armor. A famous charioteer handled his reins, a slave held his helmet. At sight of him, all Alexandria roared. This was Marcus

Antoninus Ptolemy Autocrator, the man who would make Alexandria the rival of Rome. The greatest soldier on earth, the husband of their queen, he was a god come down among his people.

Close behind him, upright on a golden throne encased by the four golden pillars of a mighty litter, so heavy it must roll along on wheels, came the queen herself, lovely Cleopatra. She would share these military honors of her husband, for she ruled half the world with him.

The people bellowed their delight.

Small boys ran alongside these warriors who brought wealth and honor to their city. Pretty girls called invitations to assignations later, at the city taverns. The more sober citizens, merchants and their wives, saw in these marching men a promise of good times to come. With new markets added by their conquests, with their shields and swords to defend them against all enemies, peace would come to Egypt and in peacetime, all trades flourished.

Then Artavasdes was before them, chained to a chariot by silver links. The little boys shouted, the girls squealed, even the merchants cried out in pleasure. This was the enemy, he who had flouted their king and queen. See him now, flushed with shame, brought to his knees in subjection. After him one could see his family, his wife and children, permitted by the clemency of Cleopatra—whose memory of Arsinoe naked and dragged along like a slavegirl through the streets of Rome was always fresh—to wear their best garments and to ride inside the chariots.

Here was living proof of the might of Egyptian—oh, and Roman as well—arms and men. More soldiers were coming, moving with their martial step. The crowd was torn between two choices. Remain and see the rest of the soldiers, or go on to the Stadium where Antony and Cleopatra would ascend their thrones and make gifts to all their people. The small boys and the amorous girls remained. The merchants and their families departed.

And when the Stadium was filled, a herald appeared.

He recited the lists of Antony's conquests, of the possessions of the Autocrator and of his wife, the deity Cleopatra. The list was long but the names rolled trippingly off the tongue. Coele Syria. Cilicia. Pontus. Armenia. Media. Lycaonia. Caria. Pamphylia. Galatia. Cappadocia. The list went on and on. Wealth, people, riches and land beyond imagination. Surely as far away as Rome, Octavian must hear the echo of these vast possessions and be afraid!

The four little crowns were lifted, one by one.

The first was placed on the head of Caesarion, son of Julius Caesar and heir to all this pomp, this might. He was named King of Kings, joint ruler with his mother Cleopatra of Egypt and Libya, of Cypris and Syria and the lesser lands which made up mighty Egypt. Caesarion stood proudly, aware that he was coming into his birthright.

The second crown was placed on the head of Alexander Helios, prince of Media and Armenia, later to be known as their king. Cleopatra Selene was named future queen of Cyrene and of the island of Crete. The final crown, the tiniest of all, was put on the head of the baby, Ptolemy Philadelphos, king of northern Syria and Cilicia.

So much for the children.

Cleopatra now came forward, robed as Isis, mother goddess, her black hair crowned by the hawk headdress, the pshent, and the golden crown of Macedonia. She was breathtakingly lovely in a sheer byssus *mafortes* girdled with emeralds and rubies set in golden wires. She was crowned Queen of Kings and the Mother of Kings. It was an impressive hour. Antony Autocrator sat upon his throne and conferred titles and lands as might a god. Indeed, for this occasion he was clad as Dionysus.

Dionysus and Isis. A good omen, said the people.

Even better were the heavy sacks of newly minted coins now brought forward, to be passed among the people that each might snatch a handful. These were souvenirs that Armenia had been conquered, tangible proof that Antony and Cleopatra ruled their world; they named Cleopatra as the living Isis, Antony as world conqueror. Before sunrise many of them would be spent in the taverns by men and women drinking the health of their king and queen and crying down damnation on all their enemies.

For Cleopatra, this was her finest hour.

The Ptolemaic empire was at its greatest spate. Its boundaries extended for thousands of miles. It was an empire that compared favorably with the territories of mighty Egypt when Thutmos III and Rameses II had been Pharaohs. Certainly no Ptolemy had ever ruled over so many lands and so multitudinous a people.

All this, Mark Antony had given her.

Conon had ridden with his troops during the Triumph, having been accorded a place of honor at their head by Antony. During the ceremonies he stood erect in his war chariot, head bared to the warm sun. With an almost de-

203

tached interest he watched as each new honor was heaped on Cleopatra and her sons. From time to time he saw Cleopatra glance at him and smile.

As the festivities were ending, she summoned him to her golden throne with an imperious movement of her hand. "Well, Conon?" she asked lightly. "Have you seen everything that happened this day? Did you hear my titles and those of my children? You know who made it possible?"

"Antony Autocrator, highness."

She smiled impishly and raised her plucked brows. "And no word of reproof from you? No biting analysis or dark forecast of future gloom to remove the happiness in my heart?"

He smiled grimly, and bowed.

"None, queen of kings. As always, my only wish is for your happiness. May you always be as you are this day."

Her eyes darkened. "Tell me the truth, Conon! Compliments and good wishes I can get from the meanest of my slaves."

He sighed and shrugged. He would have been more at ease if the documents with which Antony distributed his gifts were countersigned by Octavian, but a man cannot ask for everything in this world. Enough for now that Cleopatra was happy. Too long had she been lonely and frightened.

"The truth is obvious, Isis incarnate. You rule the East."

She inclined her head, saying graciously, "We shall not forget our friends in our own hour of triumph, Conon. You too shall be rewarded. Come to the palace for the feasting tonight, you and Athys."

He murmured his thanks and excused himself from the royal presences so that he might rejoin his men. Athys was in the crowd in the Stadium boxes, watching and applauding each new honor to the royal family. Later, he must ask her opinion of what the day was worth.

In the end, of course, he merely told her his own impressions. "Aye, Cleopatra rules the East today. But for how long? What of tomorrow and all the tomorrows after it? She holds her glories today through the generosity of Mark Antony. Will Octavian be as gracious?"

Cleopatra had no thought of Octavian. She threw herself into her role of Isis-Cleopatra just as Antony did into his own pose of Dionysus-Osiris. Construction of a temple to him was begun at Alexandria, and to while away the hours until it was completed, and to celebrate their mingled godhoods, feasts and costly celebrations became almost commonplace.

Octavian, however, had thoughts of Cleopatra. His military campaigns in Illyria and Pannonia were over now, the Iapudes and Dacians at last subdued. Antony, if he had troubled to look at a map, might have understood that with these conquests Octavian was closing off the land routes by which Antony might march down into Italy, and extending Roman rule to the northern boundaries of Thrace and Macedonia.

From his border wars, Octavian turned to internal affairs. Always it rankled in his heart that Antony was so popular, himself so unpopular. This public conception he labored to overthrow by building the Porticus Octavia in which to display the captured standards of the many peoples he had overthrown and brought under the Roman yoke. He repaired the old aqueducts bringing water into Rome and built new ones all in marble, fixed the cobblestoned streets and erected larger and always finer temples.

It was a period of breathless waiting, of calm before a storm. All the world knew the struggle was coming. It was as inevitable as the sunrise on the morrow. The authority of the Triumvirs would end under law in early winter the following year. Octavian would scarcely give up his powers without a hard struggle. Nor would Antony.

News traveled slowly, by trireme or horseman, but it came to Rome that Antony was making alliances, and gathering in Pontus, Syria and Media a mighty land army, the greatest ever seen. Nineteen Roman legions alone called him *dux*. Add to this a navy being built by Egyptian gold, add coffers bulging with money with which to buy food and hire mercenaries, and the worry that made Octavian sleepless of night could be readily understood.

His own army regarded Antony as their real general. The people of Rome, no matter what he did for them, took Antony as their hero. Octavian fumed and raged in private, though he always put on a good face in public. Antony! Antony! Antony! The man was a hobgoblin out of nightmare, always mocking him no matter where he turned!

And then—Cleopatra blundered.

It was an excusable mistake she made. She appeared with Antony everywhere he went, even in his military camps. They were very much in love and she could not stand to be parted from him. Had she been less the sweetheart and more the statesman, she might have remembered the cold, remorseless brain of Octavian Caesar.

As Conon once said, she was thinking with her heart.

Octavian took advantage of her mistakes. He came out with the information that Cleopatra was arming for war with Rome, that Cleopatra went about the provinces, seducing good Romans with Egyptian gold. Cleverly, he made it seem that by necromancy she had dulled the wits of Marcus Antoninus and had in some supernatural way, reduced him to the status of an automaton. How else might Rome explain the defection of its favorite son, its great hero?

This was no longer a quarrel between Octavian and Antony.

If war must come, Octavian said piously while sacrificing to the gods to prevent it, then it would be no civil war. It was Cleopatra and Egypt who threatened Rome. Antony was demoted to the rank of scapegoat. He was enchanted by the Egyptian Circe, bereft of his wits. Perhaps he walked in golden chains for all the Eastern world to see, a captive.

It would be an act of mercy to rescue Mark Antony.

Not from himself, but from Cleopatra. Cleopatra! The name became a kind of incantation, conjured up to frighten children. The witchwoman of the Nile. The harlot of Egypt. She would turn all Rome into a vast bonfire when her thousand warships landed at Ostia. She would overthrow the gods and raise up Isis and Hathor and herself above all, to be worshipped. The people would be ruled no longer by honest Romans but by sybaritic foreigners.

Octavian had no equal as a politician who used propaganda as another might an army. He put cold fear in the heads of his people and since fear breeds hate, he saw to it that their eyes saw only Cleopatra when they looked at Antony. The woman was their enemy, not the man. The woman, Cleopatra.

2.

"The odds are in our favor! We cannot lose."

Her voice rang in the little room of the Lochias where she was closeted with Conon. All about them was the slapping feet of running slaves and servants, preparing for the sea voyage which would carry Cleopatra north across the Aegean Sea to the island of Samos.

She was radiant with loveliness as she paced the floor tiles. Never, decided Conon gloomily, had she looked so beautiful. And why not? She was on her way to her marriage —this time, by Roman law—to Mark Antony.

His divorce decree dissolving his marriage with Octavia, had already been received in Rome. Octavia and her children had moved from his palace. He was no longer wedded to her and the way was clear for Cleopatra to don the yellow *tunica recta* and its knot of Hercules of the bride, as decreed by the Roman wedding rites.

Joy and happiness flushed her cheeks as Cleopatra reflected on this approaching ceremony. At long last, after all these years—some of them so bitter and so lonely!—she would be united with the most powerful Roman in the world. The crown which Caesar planned to place on her head had been denied her by assassins' daggers. Nothing could stop Antony from putting it on her thick black hair.

Only defeat by Octavian could do it, and that was impossible. As she had stated in her ringing voice, the odds were all in their favor.

"One hundred and fifty thousand troops. Over eight hundred ships of war. This is our strength, Conon. Against this, Octavian has less than eighty thousand men and only two hundred odd triremes."

"Then come back to Egypt when you're married," he said bluntly. "Let Antony conduct this war. You stay out of it."

"What? And miss the thrill of seeing the battle that will make me queen of the world? Oh, no! I'll be there."

He shook his head in slow anger. "Will you never understand that when you are with him Antony is never really himself? Half his mind is on you. And against Octavian who is cold and deadly as a snake, no man can wrest a victory with half his head."

She caroled laughter, clapping her hands. "Conon, I adore you. Always you sing the same song to me. Beware! Stop! Don't! Watch out! Gloomy, gloomy. For once—smile! For once—share my happiness."

"I share it. It's only because I want you to keep it that I become gloomy. I see things with eyes unshadowed by love, by anticipation of a marriage. I know, I know. This is the culmination of everything you've ever wanted. Join Rome to Egypt and rule the world! It's a simple slogan. Popular here in Alexandria, but hated in Rome itself."

"Pooh for Rome. Antony is Rome."

"No longer."

She stamped her little foot. "Conon, honestly! You caw like a wounded crow. Tell me, does Octavian have the men, the ships, to defeat Antony?"

"No."

She flung her hands apart. "Well then?"

"Octavian will have his wits about him, be sure of that. Antony won't, with you looking on."

"Should I turn over my navy to him, my troops, without remaining to command them in person?"

"Yes. Let him be the general. I say this though he is a Roman, though I think him but a lusting animal. I'm honest, at least. He has a flair for military tactics. He's a hero and a hero can inspire men where nothing else can. If Antony is alone when he meets Octavian—and lets himself be seen by Octavian's troops—who knows? Many may desert to him, as troops deserted to him before Philippi. The man has an air about him."

"I want to watch. I want to see Octavian humiliated."

Conon shrugged his helplessness. He managed to smile and say, "Perhaps you're right. I may be afraid only of shadows. Let me be the first to say that I hope it is no more than shadows before my eyes. Go to Antony. I'll stay on in Alexandria and guard your interests here."

From Samos, Antony and Cleopatra went to Athens.

In Athens they played the part of world rulers which already they were in their own minds. Defeat was unthinkable. Impossible! The ancient Greek city fell in love with Cleopatra as did every city she visited. Her air of vitality, her love of life and all it held, were so strong that they encompassed the people all around her.

Her delight in games and performances, in the outward trappings of her coming sovereignty were so great that Antony could not deny them to her. His veteran officers urged him to hit Octavian now, before he was entirely ready to wage war. Sail for Ostia. March on Rome, itself—not as conqueror but as liberator. Above all, leave Cleopatra behind, for while the Roman mobs loved Antony, they hated Cleopatra.

Overcome Octavian as Antony. Once power was in his hand, then there would be time to set Cleopatra on the throne beside him.

It was good advice. Instinctively, Antony knew it; but when he broached the subject to the woman he loved, she went into a tantrum. If he thought she should be content to go back to Egypt, to sit like an abandoned housewife—like Octavia, now divorced?—he must think a second time. His mighty army and navy was born of her gold. Her sailors manned over half his ships. She had some rights and she meant to enforce them.

Conon might have made her change her mind, but Conon was in Alexandria. She trusted Conon. She trusted no one else, not even Antony, for she remembered how Antony in those earlier years had thrown her over to marry Octavia. Of course she had a vague remembrance of some such advice

208

just before leaving for Samos; but she had been about to sail for her wedding, and what bride can think deep thoughts before the ceremony? Cleopatra insisted on her privilege, as donor of gold and ships and men, to be on hand to see their use.

The chance to strike slipped from Antony's fingers, for he dared not march on Rome and bring Cleopatra with him. This in truth would make it seem it was Egypt that warred with Rome. He waited in Athens, instead, and let Octavian come to him. It may be he did not realize that the initiative thus passed from his hands into that of his enemy.

As a result, he was lured into a seafight.

The promontory of Actium juts out into the gulf of Ambracia. It was here that Octavian marched his army to take up positions on its high land. Antony came north to meet him, thrusting with cavalry to pin him down until his massive army could come to grips with him. Meanwhile Octavian's navy—under that clever soldier who was both general and admiral, Agrippa—moved in to blockade the great naval force which Antony and Cleopatra conceived to be unbeatable.

The situation was a stalemate. Neither Octavian nor Antony cared to take the offensive. During an entire spring and summer, both men waited. Octavian always had spies to serve him, and the sprawling monstrosity which was the Antonean camp, filled with all manner of races and peoples, was as easy to slip men in and out of as were the neighboring farm fields and meadows.

Octavian learned that Cleopatra and Antony were quarreling more and more, that Antony daily drank himself into drunken stupors, blaming Cleopatra for his plight because she would not go home to Egypt when he wanted to march on Rome. In turn, Cleopatra no longer trusted Antony, even accusing him of wanting to be reunited with Octavia. As a result, Octavian was overjoyed. His enemies were fighting among themselves.

All Octavian need do now, his advisers said, was to sit quietly and the gigantic Oriental edifice which Cleopatra and Antony had reared about themselves would collapse of its own weight. Cleopatra wanted to go back to Alexandria; she was disgusted with Antony, said the spies, aware at long last of the fact that she was universally hated.

When strategy was discussed, Octavian was informed, the queen of Egypt screamed like any fishwife that Antony must fight on the waves, not on land. Octavian could understand her concern whereas Antony, because he was in love with her, could not. By sea she could escape to Egypt if anything went wrong. On land she could be penned in and captured.

Cleopatra had a horror of being taken in chains to Rome and being exhibited as had her sister Arsinoe. Or beheaded, as she had seen Berenice beheaded. It was this fear that affected all her thinking.

Octavian said to Agrippa, "The woman will win her argument. Antony will give in to her. She is his blind spot."

Agrippa was delighted. "I can smash Antony on water. We might not, on land. His legions are foot soldiers, not sailors."

Octavian was too smart to quarrel with this man who had twice defeated Sextus Pompeius in naval battles. He himself would do little or no fighting. It mattered not to him how he won.

"Do what you will," he told Agrippa.

Agrippa built lean fast ships called laburnians and with them threw up a blockade so that no food could come to Antony by sea. His vast army began to starve. Desertions now infected his troops like a plague. The kings who had gathered about his standards fled to Octavian. Soon they were joined by Roman officers, tired of the disputes between themselves and the Egyptian queen who thought not of how to beat Octavian but how best to serve herself.

The inexorable tides of Time itself wore away the vast army which Antony had collected. Half starved, given no orders to attack, men became disspirited and lost their fighting edge. A counsel of war was held. Antony must fight now or not at all.

Cleopatra argued loudest and longest. The navy must smash the blockade, move out onto open water and hit Octavian. As she conceived the plan of battle, so it was carried out. What with all the desertions, land troops were needed to fill the ships' complements of fighting men. The extra vessels for which neither oarsmen nor soldiers could be found, were burned. Cleopatra supervised the storing of the treasure chests on her own Egyptian ships.

Antony moved his hundred and eighty ships out of the harbor on the second day of September. The Egyptian fleet —sixty triremes in all—were to take up a position directly behind the point of the wedge, to be ready in time of need.

Antony waited, but Agrippa refused the bait. He made Antony come out to him, onto open water where his fast little liburnians could harass the taller, heavier triremes in much the same way that cavalry harassed the flanks of a legion. The battle joined in a shower of catapulted rocks and fire-arrows, and for two hours the ships battled back and forth, with victory still to him who fought the hardest.

From the decks of her flagship, the *Antonias,* Cleopatra watched the struggle in a frenzy of indecision. The past half-year had been like a nightmare to her. Driven by her intense desire to put Caesarion on a world throne, afraid of being caught and chained in a Roman triumph, loving Antony but unable to stop quarreling with him because of her conflicting interests, she had held firm to her own welfare at all costs.

Slowly now, she began to understand that her own interests would best have been served if she had gone off to Alexandria and left the war entirely in Antony's hands. He was the general, the accomplished militarist. She was a queen, a mother battling for her children. An individual man she might conquer with her beauty, her personality, but not an entire army.

She watched great stones thudding into masts and deck-planks, splintering wood as though it were paper. She saw men cut in half by flying javelins, or falling overside to drown in their heavy armor. There was confusion everywhere she looked. She could not tell friend from foe, and terror gripped her. Must she remain here and be caught like a rat on a sinking ship? No, no. It were better to push through those lines of struggling ships and flee straight south to Egypt.

Her captains were aghast at her orders.

Leave Antony now? When a determined sortie might push the tide of victory to their side? For all his clever naval strategy, Agrippa was outnumbered. Antony was holding his own. One push—an attack by the mighty Egyptian navy—would tip the scales in Antony's favor.

Attack! Attack Octavian and Agrippa!

Carry victory on her flagship. Be Minerva, goddess of war, as she was already goddess of love. Say the word, stand back and let her captains carry on the struggle.

She could not say the word. It was as if her mind were paralyzed. The indecisiveness which had held Antony in its spell this past year was contagious. She wept and stormed.

"Get me out of here. I won't stay to be captured."

Her officers stared at one another helplessly. What she asked was tantamount to a surrender to Octavian Caesar. She merely delayed the inevitable. They tried a little longer to argue but when she struck out at them with the sceptre she carried always with her—a length of ivory, it contained a golden eagle at its tip—they yielded.

She went belowdecks and lay on her cabin bed while

her fleet weighed anchor and its sails bellied outward, filling with wind. Majestically and in formation, the Egyptian vessels slid through an opening between the battling ships.

Antony saw them go. At first he thought they were moving to aid him but when they did not turn, when their prows pointed steadily southward, horrified understanding came to him. Cleopatra was abandoning him to his fate. She was turning her back, carrying away the body he loved, the woman he worshipped. He could stand anything but not seeing her.

His eyes returned to the fight. It was not yet lost. Had he his old vigor he would have bellowed to his men, dared them to move on to victory. But he was tired, tired! The wines he had drunk, the countless hours when he had spent himself on the loins of the Egyptian queen, had taken their toll. He could no longer even think clearly.

All he could see was Cleopatra leaving him.

"No," he screamed for his men to hear. "Don't leave me. Wait for me. Wait! Wait!"

He ran to the rail and dove into the water. He would swim to her. Surely she would not let him drown! Cleopatra would order the *Antonias* to slow and turn, to pluck him from the cold sea waters. He screamed to her.

His voice sounded like the wail of a lost soul.

3.

Conon stood on the quay of the Lochias palace and watched as Cleopatra was rowed across the harbor waters. She sat crouched on a thwart, her robe drawn up to cover her face as though she feared to see the light. Beside her, wrapped in a blanket and shivering like an old man with fever, was Mark Antony.

He had no need to ask their news. One look at them was enough. Egypt was lost. Octavian had been the victor. Conon wanted to yank out his sword and fall on it.

How bad had it been? Beyond the Pharos lighthouse he could count sixty great ships riding at their anchors. They seemed untouched by battle. Absolutely unmarked! His spirits lifted. Surely if Antony had been defeated he would not return with so much sea power. He and Cleopatra would have been in a single ship, scarred and pitted by battle.

He went down to meet his queen with outstretched hand.

Her eyes were dark, swollen with weeping as she glanced at him. In her pitiful stare, he glimpsed something of the

212

truth. Not until later, when he and Cleopatra were closeted alone, did the full impact of what had happened strike him.

"You ran away?" he asked incredulously. "*Ran away?* When everything for which you've fought all your life was ready for the taking? All you had to do was send your ships into battle! I don't believe it."

She sat huddled in a cloak, broken in spirit. "It was my fault. I should have listened to you. Had I come back home after my wedding with Antony on Samos, all would have been well. Today I'd be queen of the world." Her laughter rose upward, harsh and discordant. "I couldn't realize there was a chance of defeat."

Her fist pounded her thigh. "All through the spring and the summer I felt we would win. I thought defeat impossible, either by land or by sea. Antony was a great general. Octavian was a—a nothing." Her breath sobbed in her throat as she breathed, "I wouldn't let him be a general. I was too much the bride. I kept seeing him only as a husband."

Later, he got the story from her captains.

Even they did not understand the full tragedy. Abandoned by their Antony, his ships had disengaged and had drawn back into the harbor. His army was still at full strength. The naval engagement had been indecisive, even in the eyes of Octavian and Agrippa.

Had Antony only remained on his flagship! What a different story might have been written. Deserted by Cleopatra, he might have found his lost manhood in the company of his officers. Always at his best in adversity, he would still have had the chance to smash Octavian on land.

The man who should have remained at Actium, to stand or fall with his troops, had wept shameful tears on the foredeck of the *Antonias* all the way across the Mare Internum instead. His head and face covered by a cloak, he had· sobbed out every last vestige of his manhood.

When he was assisted onto the Lochias quay, he was an old man. During the voyage from Actium, his hair had turned white.

"What will you do?" Conon asked gently.

He no longer mentioned Mark Antony, who sat like an insane man in the little pleasure house, the Timoneum, that Cleopatra had built for him, staring straight ahead, saying no word to anyone, eating little, sleeping much. It was as if he were already dead.

Cleopatra stirred restlessly. She was haggard with sleeplessness. The mother in her now took precedence over everything else. She must save her children at all costs. The shadow of Octavian lay over Alexandria and it brought terror and fear where it touched.

"He will kill Caesarion, because he need fear only Caesarion," Cleopatra whispered. "He must not be allowed to do so! No matter what else happens, Caesarion must go on living. Conon! Promise me this. Guard him with your life."

"With my life," he agreed.

Cleopatra sank back into that same state of mindlessness which so afflicted Antony. She could not rouse herself from this disinterest, this acceptance of calamity. She sat hunched over and her fingers toyed with the hem of her tunic.

"We can still fight," Conon reminded her. "Octavian is at Samos, levying fines on everybody who can pay him money. He's forgiven Antony's troops, naturally enough. They're Romans like himself. Besides, by not taking vengeance, he will be popular in Rome. But the Senators, the high-ranking men who defected to Antony when it seemed he—"

She raised her head and stared at him, and he bit down on his tongue. Not yet had he said one word of reproach to her, though he understood well enough that it had been Cleopatra who was responsible for the debacle. She was suffering enough. Words could not undo what was now history.

Conon sighed and accepted her sorrow as his own. He would wait, as did the rest of the world, for Octavian to strike.

Octavian took his time. Six months after Actium it became clear to him that he no longer need fear Antony or Cleopatra. Their power was forever broken. It was more important that he consolidate his gain, strengthen his grip on Rome and the East, which was already acknowledging him as its sole ruler.

Most of all, he needed money.

And Cleopatra, despite the vast sums she had expended to build an army and a navy for Antony, was still the richest person in the world. Her wealth, as nothing else might have done, sealed her doom.

Octavian made his move at last.

He marched his legions by way of Syria into Egypt. There was nothing to stand in his way. Antony had lost his great army. The legions he had stationed in Egypt to prevent a surprise attack by Octavian before the defeat at Actium, now went over to his rival. The Egyptian army by itself would be no match for the legions.

Antony tried to fall on his sword in despair, but was prevented from doing so. Even his old friend, King Herod of Jerusalem, also paid homage to Octavian. One by one, then by twos and threes, the old allies were falling away like snow-flakes before the sun of mighty Octavian.

Cleopatra kept up appearances. She held court as always, robed and jeweled as she had been at the height of her powers. Frantically she sought a way to escape from the coils slowly tightening around her. Antony was no longer any help.

"I can count only on you, Conon," she told him.

He might have reminded her that it was too late even for that. She had ignored the military brilliance of her husband. He could fight and die for her, but he was only one man. Instead, he offered her the only way out of her difficulties.

"Run away," he said bluntly. "As you ran from Actium. Take your children and your wealth and flee to India. Under an assumed name, perhaps even posing as my wife, you can live out your days in peace."

She smiled wryly. "What of Athys?"

It was a question he had long dreaded, because he had long known what his answer must be. "She shall remain here in Alexandria, as a blind. No one would imagine that I would leave her behind me." He shuddered when he thought of how Octavian might avenge himself on her body, but for the woman who once had been his Thea, he would have sacrificed anything.

They laid their plans well. Small ships were dragged overland to the Red Sea, there to wait the coming of Cleopatra and her children. Two days before they were ready to make a run for it, word came that the ships had been attacked and burned by bandits out of the rock city of Petra.

Cleopatra wept when the news was told her, not for herself but for her children. Octavian could not be eluded. Even the fates were working with him.

"There is nothing left to do," growled Conon.

"I can always die!" she replied.

Ever since she had seen Berenice beheaded—and most particularly since she had watched Arsinoe dragged naked in chains—Cleopatra had vowed to die by her own hand before suffering such degradation. Now she bent her talents into studying ways and means of cheating Octavian, to find a method of denying him what he most hungered for.

Never would Cleopatra be yanked along the cobblestones of Rome to the glory of her conqueror. No common eyes should see the body that had belonged first to Caesar, then to Antony. She shuddered and her skin perspired at the mere thought of it.

All her talk was tinged with the purple hue of death. How

215

was it easiest to leave this world for the next? By poison or the sharp stab of a dagger blade? Might a trusted slave or servant possess the ability to use a sword so that its keen edge brought not pain but only quick lifelessness? Conon would not do so; him she trusted fully, but he refused.

"Ask me to kill myself, and I will. Ask me to do the same to you and I would be frozen with horror."

Secretly, she never thought she would be forced to such straits. Her harbor held fast ships. On one of them, with the royal treasure, she might run to Spain or to that barbarian island, Britain, which her lover Caesar had conquered over twenty years ago. Suicide was merely a philosophical problem to be discussed and laughed over while at dinner.

For Antony was beginning to stir himself at last. A man can know despair for only so long; then he must yield to it or bypass it. Antony had attempted suicide but had been restrained. Partly in disgust at what he had done, partly because he wanted to prove himself once more to the woman he loved, he threw himself into a furor of military activity.

There were legions in Syria and Asia Minor willing to fight for whatever man paid them money. Antony borrowed more gold from Cleopatra and sent it overland in wooden coffers, as an inducement for the troops to march to Egypt. He was like a child with a new toy.

Cleopatra understood this, and made her own plans.

She began to fill her tomb with the treasures of a lifetime. Years before, when she had been emulating the pharaohs, she had caused a mighty stone edifice to be built in the Brucheion, which was to be her last resting place. In some secret corner of her heart, she thought that now, at long last, she would be using it.

And then she sent for Conon.

FOURTEEN

By the Red Sea Shore, 30 B. C.

1.

A dozen chariots rattled at the gallop over the gravelly flats which formed the westernmost boundary of that vast wasteland known as the wilderness of Shur. To the south lay the expanse of the Red Sea. Behind them was Egypt, the delta mouth of the Nile and beyond that, the coastal city of Alexandria.

And the Roman legions, marching with measured tread, shields and helmets polished as if on parade. Octavian commanded those legions, with his great general, Agrippa. Opposing them were Antony and Cleopatra.

As the chariot bounced under his feet, Conon wondered whether those two armies had met in battle. If Cleopatra were alive or dead. Or captured, which would be worse, from her viewpoint. Even Conon shuddered when he thought of Cleopatra alive and in chains behind Octavian's chariot. Caesar's mistress! Antony's wife! She who had enthralled the beloved Antoninus of the Roman people in an evil spell, according to their way of thinking!

She would be naked, of course, for them to feast their eyes on the body which only their heroes had seen, and weeping in bitter frustration, in an agony of despair at this most degrading of all ends. The Roman populace would not spare her. Had she not been used as a bogie to frighten their children? Had she not brought war upon them, with her hunger to rule the world? Charm them, the way she charmed Caesar and Antony, they would howl. And laugh. And throw filth and rotten fruit and ordure.

Conon drew a deep breath.

Cleopatra would know all this. It had been all she spoke of during the last few days when Conon had been in Alexandria, making plans to bring Caesarion with him out of Egypt.

He glanced at the boy, tall and straight, handsome with features inherited from his mother, clever with the braininess that had been Caesar's. Caesarion would have made a good ruler, if he had had the chance. It was too bad, in a way, that Caesar had not lived just a little longer, until he had been made emperor of Rome. Ah, what a different life this boy would have led, then! Or if Antony or Cleopatra had been a little less in love with one another; or, being in love, if only they had taken sensible advice.

Octavian would not be in Egypt now, battering at the gates of Alexandria. Caesarion would be in Rome, learning to rule an empire.

Were these tears for the might-have-been, stinging his eyes? No, he had not wept in years. The wind off the gravelly plain was cold and biting, that was all. He tightened his hands on the reins and snapped them along the backs of the big black stallions. Behind him came the picked Macedonian Guards who had volunteered to go with him and Caesarion into exile.

He swung south toward the shores of the Red Sea.

2.

In Alexandria, Cleopatra stared down at the almost lifeless body of Mark Antony. Less than an hour ago he had stabbed himself in his apartments. Though her physician had gone at once to him, there was little hope that the Roman might survive. His aim with his dagger had been too true. There was internal bleeding, and against this Olympus could do nothing.

From the man, her eyes lifted to the cold marble walls of this building which was to be her mausoleum. Her tomb! In what high hopes had she ordered it built! It was intended to be a monument to the first woman who had ever ruled the entire world; actually, it was a grave which would hold the clay of a man and woman who had loved one another beyond the bounds of reason.

She might have wept when she thought on this most bitter of ends to such ambitions. If her army had only fought for Antony, those short days ago when he went out to meet Octavian; but her sailors and then her soldiers, Egyptians and Roman alike, had turned and run at sight of the pilums and stabbing swords of Octavian's legionaries.

After that—

There was no hope. Only death.

Well, Antony was almost dead now, at her feet, where she had commanded them to place him. She herself would soon join him. From a little table that held a bowl of fruit and a silver ewer of water, she lifted a slim dagger.

One quick stab between her breasts and—

There was a sound of metal scraping stone. Cleopatra turned toward the window through which Antony had been lifted. A Roman officer stood there, resplendent in polished helmet with its red crest in burnished cuirass, a red military cloak billowing from his shoulders. He cried out at sight of her.

Too late, so stunned were her senses at the realization that the Romans under Octavian had made their way into the palace compound, she tried to use the dagger on herself. Her skin felt the touch of the point but then a hard hand was at her wrist and the steel was being jerked aside so swiftly that the inner globe of her left breast was slashed in a thin red line.

"Highness," said the Roman, "Octavian would have you live."

"I would rather die," she told him, but lifelessly, making no effort to prevent him from twisting the dagger from her fingers.

A little to her surprise, she was brought before Octavian in all her finery. He was seated in a curule chair, examining a number of the golden coins which she and Antony had caused to be minted at the time of the Triumph in Alexandria. He will melt them down and stamp his own face on them, she thought dully. There was no life left in her. She kept seeing Berenice dragged naked around the arena sands, Arsinoe dragged naked over Roman cobblestones. It was the turn of Cleopatra, now.

Octavian rose at her entrance. He was polite. He expressed regret that Antony had seen fit to kill himself, and congratulated her on her wisdom in not yielding to emotional impulse.

"And the boy, Caesarion? Is he well?"

She inclined her head. Octavian turned his attention to a gold coin, holding it to the light, moving it this way and that. After a moment he spoke again. "We have the other children, you know. Alexander Helios, Cleopatra Selene, Ptolemy Philadelphos. Even Antony's son by Fulvia. No harm shall come to them, I promise."

His eyes were cold and hard, without emotion of any kind. "The only one who is missing is Caesarion. The most important one, your child by Caesar."

Her mother instinct made her lift her chin. "Thank Isis, he is safe from you. You can do what you want with me. But my boy will live—always you will dread his return—the havoc he may bring when it is known that he is the son of Caesar the god! I—"

"You!" he snarled, slapping the arm of his chair. "You shall go naked behind a chariot through the streets of Rome. Close your eyes if you want. Aye, bite your lip! This shall be your fate. Can you hear what my fellow countrymen will call out at you? They will see the body not even I have seen, all naked."

He went on at some lengths to paint her degradation. Cleopatra listened as if some instinct for self punishment held her every sense alive to his words. Her eyes were closed; on their lids her mind made pictures until she was nauseous.

"Everything I have said will occur, unless—"

Her eyes opened and she stared at him. "Unless what?"

"Unless you tell me where I can lay hands on Caesarion." Octavian was smiling graciously. "I have nothing to fear from you, Cleopatra. It's the boy who worries me, as Antony might have worried me had he not killed himself. The people despise me, for some reason. They would take Antony back to their hearts, believing him to have been enthralled by you with magic. The boy Caesarion, since he is Caesar's son, would be adored. And so he has to die."

"No!" she cried. "No—I beg—"

He laughed at her and gestured with a hand. Cleopatra let her eyes slide toward a curtained doorway. A Roman centurion was entering with a richly clad woman in a thin *mafortes* belted by carnelians.

"Athys," said Cleopatra numbly.

The former slavegirl looked at her with hate in her dark eyes. "You told Conon I had belonged to Caesar. I asked you not to tell him. He hated Caesar as he hated Antony. All because he loved you—his Thea! Gods, how I abhor the name! you must have known how it would hurt him. And perhaps how it would hurt me."

Octavian was chuckling, "She must bring everything down about her ears in her own ruin, must our Cleopatra."

Cleopatra shook her head, eyes veiled with tears. It was not the way they thought, at all. She had only told Conon about Athys because he wanted to take her with him to the Red Sea when it was necessary for her to remain behind so the Romans would not suspect Conon had fled with Caesarion. She was a mother fighting for her firstborn! Couldn't they understand that?

Octavian asked with apparent concern, "You say this Conon has left the city? Your husband has run away? The general of Egypt's armies?"

Athys pointed at Cleopatra. "She made him go to save her son. My husband knew her when they were children. Ever since, he's been heels over head in love with her. Conon has taken your precious Caesarion with him. My guess is, they've gone to the Red Sea to find an Egyptian trade ship to carry them to India."

Octavian slapped her chair arm. "My thanks, noble lady. In return for your information, we'll spare your husband's life—if we can."

He looked at Cleopatra, then gestured his soldiers to take her away with them. There was no pity in his eyes, as there had been hate in the eyes of Athys. Cleopatra shivered, remembering Arsinoe. To drag a living, naked Cleopatra in the wake of his chariot would make the Triumph of Octavian Caesar something mankind would never forget!

She was imprisoned in her own apartments, which had been searched for anything with which she might cut or hang herself. Every metal instrument, every tasseled cord or rope, was removed. A guard was set at her doorway. She was permitted only one woman attendant at a time, lest more strangle her at her command.

Toward midnight she asked that a little fruit be brought to her. Charmion carried it past the officer and guards at her doorway who only glanced at it perfunctorily. There was no harm in any fruit, especially since they knew it had been selected by Roman hands to avoid the possibility of poison.

There was an asp hidden in the bowl, however.

Cleopatra reached for it, felt its moist scaliness and closed her eyes in a sudden revulsion of spirit. *I cannot do it. I have not the courage. And yet I dare not live to walk in shame and misery behind a Roman chariot.* Her fingers tightened and lifted the snake. She had no other choice.

She nestled the asp between the breasts where she had clasped her lovers. Tears came into her eyes as she felt its bite, like a wild mad stinging in her flesh. Then she hurled the asp away and sat proudly, waiting.

Strange that she should see Conon now, as he had been those years ago, young and vital. She heard him whisper her name. Thea.

Cleopatra smiled.

She was still smiling in death, rigid, when the Romans came. At the very end, in her own way, she had triumphed over them. They might have her wealth, her gold and silver and all her jewels, even her beloved Egypt. But Cleopatra they could not have.

3.

Conon stood on the sandy shore of the Red Sea and stared north and westward where approaching chariots made a yellow haze in the sunlight. Shading his eyes with his hands, he saw the Roman helmets, the Roman armor. His heart thudded crazily.

Instinctively he knew Thea was dead. Otherwise no Roman would have found him. Well, she had avoided the Triumph, at any rate. She had lost the world, so why not her life? Then he saw Athys, muffled in a white cloak, waving to him. Sympathy moved in him.

All his life, the women he loved had belonged to the Romans. Thea. Athys. Ah, but not Ione. She alone had been a virgin, and he had been the only man she had ever known. He wondered, when he died, if he would find her in the underworld of the Egyptian gods.

The chariots came to a sliding halt. An officer—a high-ranking tribune, by his decorations—leaped to the ground and saluted him. Conon returned the gesture.

"Greetings from Octavian, noble Conon. We have come for Caesarion. Octavian wishes to do him honor, to name him co-ruler of the world. As Caesar's son—"

"Is Cleopatra dead?" he asked harshly.

"By her own hand, of the bite of an asp."

He bent his head and sighed. His intuition had been correct. His way of life was at an end. His hand itched for his swordhilt, so that he might die under Roman steel. There was a little whisper of flurried sand; Athys was running toward him; she flung herself into his arms.

Her eyes were wet.

"Let them take him, Conon. Octavian wishes only to do him honor," she begged. "He would have honored Cleopatra, if she had waited."

She was lying. They were all lying to him. They wanted the boy, Caesarion. They would have to kill him to get him. The Romans were ringing him around, now, not drawing their weapons, just waiting, watching him silently. It was up to him whether there was to be war or peace between them.

"Who is it, Conon?" cried an imperious voice.

Caesarion came from the tent where he had been sleeping. The Romans turned their eyes from Conon to stare at him. Did they see Caesar in his height, in his obvious intelligence? Or were they looking only at a boy they had orders to kill?

Before Conon could speak, the tribune made a gesture and his soldiers went to one knee. "Noble Caesarion, Octavian sends greetings to his co-ruler of the world. He—"

The boy broke in excitedly, "Conon, did you hear that? Octavian named me co-ruler with him."

"He wants only to get you in his power," Conon said wearily. The Romans were smart. They knew Conon would fight to save the boy, so they went over his head and appealed to Caesarion himself.

Caesarion stamped his foot. "You lie. Mother always told me how you opposed her, how you advised her against everything she wanted to do."

Conon smiled grimly. "She followed her own advice, did your mother. And now she's dead by her own hand. As you'll be dead if you refuse to listen to me."

Caesarion took a step forward. His hand cracked against Conon's face. Almost instantly he shrank back fearfully. Never before had he struck anyone but a slave.

"You were her general," he shrilled. "You are not mine. I shall select my own generals!"

The Romans were looking at him with hard smiles. They knew the whims and follies of rulers. A wild anger surged up in Conon. The boy was a fool. He was going to his death. It was up to him to protect him for the sake of his dead mother. For Thea.

His sword flashed out. Athys screamed and leaped at him, catching him off balance, holding his swordarm. Her face was convulsed with fear, inches below his own.

"They will kill you," she panted. "All they want is an excuse. Let him go. He isn't worth your life!"

Caesarion moved away from him toward the Romans; Conon stopped trying to free his arm. Athys leaned her head against his chest and stood there, sobbing.

Caesarion said, "I will go with my friends, Conon. To remain longer by your side would be to do myself an injustice." He turned his back and moved toward one of the waiting chariots.

Mockingly the tribune saluted Conon.

Athys shivered, waiting until the chariots were turning and moving away before speaking. Then she said, "You can kill me now. I told Octavian where he could find Caesarion."

He looked down at her in surprise. "Caesarion? Who cares about Caesarion? He is a Roman, like those others. Let them kill off one another as much as they like, for all I care. I only protected him out of a duty to Cleopatra."

She stared at him in dumb amazement. "Aren't you angry with me for coming here? I—she told you that she gave me to Caesar and I thought—"

Her voice broke. She covered her face with her hands and wept. Conon put an arm about her shoulders and drew her in against him. "I've had a lot of time to think since I've been here with Caesarion, waiting for a trading ship to pick us up.

"It came to me that every man Cleopatra touched—died! In one way or another, at her orders like her handsome slaveboys or by the daggers of assassins like Caesar, or at his own hand like Antony. I meant to have the Romans kill me. I would have been one more dead man sacrificed in her name."

She stared up at him wonderingly, "And?" she asked.

"Suddenly I remembered my father. He used to collect garbage in Alexandria when I was a boy. A garbage collector! I myself was a gladiator. What right had I to lift my eyes to princes and royalty? I'm only a common man. Caesar made me a general. When Caesar died, I should have resigned and opened my *ludi*, as I wanted. Instead I stayed on at the palace and let their poisons of greed for power and lust for flesh infect me."

He tilted her chin up and kissed her. "Caesar owned you for a while. In another way, Cleopatra owned me. Both of them are dead. Why should their spirits affect our lives?"

She breathed deeply and pressed against him.

"We have gold, more than we can ever use," he said thoughtfully. "We'll take ship for India, just the two of us. We can begin a new life there."

They walked side by side toward the little tent.

FIFTEEN

Epilogue

Octavian caused Caesarion to be killed, once he was in Alexandria. At the same time he ordered the death of Antyllus, Antony's son by Fulvia. The other children he spared, bringing them to Rome to be raised by his sister Octavia. One of them, Cleopatra Selene, he wedded to young King Juba of Numidia, son of that Juba who had been in the Triumph of Julius Caesar. He had nothing to fear from this Cleopatra; the only one he had ever feared was dead.